Contemporary American Crime Fiction

Hans Bertens
Professor of Comparative Literature
Utrecht University

and

Theo D'haen
Professor of English and American Literature
Leiden University

palgrave

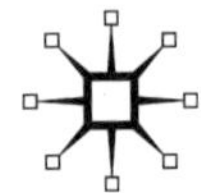

First published 2001 by
PALGRAVE
Houndmills, Basingstoke, Hampshire RG21 6XS and
175 Fifth Avenue, New York, N. Y. 10010
Companies and representatives throughout the world

PALGRAVE is the new global academic imprint of St. Martin's Press LLC Scholarly and Reference Division and Palgrave Publishers Ltd (formerly Macmillan Press Ltd).

ISBN 0–333–67455–3 hardback
ISBN 0–333–68465–6 paperback

This book is printed on paper suitable for recycling and made from fully managed and sustained forest sources.

A catalogue record for this book is available from the British Library.

Library of Congress Cataloging-in-Publication Data
Bertens, Johannes Willem.
Contemporary American crime fiction / Hans Bertens and Theo D'haen.
p. cm. — (Crime files series)
Includes bibliographical references and index.
ISBN 0–333–67455–3 (cloth)
1. Detective and mystery stories, American—History and criticism. 2. American fiction—20th century—History and criticism. 3. Criminals in literature. 4. Crime in literature. I. haen, Theo D'. II. Title. III. Series.
PS374.D4 B47 2001
813'.08720905—dc21

2001024590

10 9 8 7 6 5 4 3 2 1
10 09 08 07 06 05 04 03 02 01

Printed and bound in Great Britain by
Antony Rowe Ltd, Chippenham, Wiltshire

Contents

List of Writers and Detectives

Writers and detectives discussed in some detail – in order of appearance:

Marcia Muller	Sharon McCone
Sue Grafton	Kinsey Millhone
Sara Paretsky	V.I. Warshawski
Stuart Kaminsky	Porfiry Rostnikov
Robert B. Parker	Spenser
Lawrence Block	Matt Scudder
Nancy Pickard	Jenny Cain
Margaret Maron	Deborah Knott
Sharyn McCrumb	the tiny police force of Hamelin, Tennessee
Katherine V. Forrest	Kate Delafield
Nevada Barr	Anna Pigeon
Lynn S. Hightower	Sonora Blair
James Ellroy	generations of LAPD detectives
Michael Connelly	Harry Bosch
Robert Crais	Elvis Cole
George P. Pelecanos	Nick Stefanos
Harlan Coben	Myron Bolitar
Janet Evanovich	Stephanie Plum
Martha Grimes	Melrose Plant and Richard Jury
Elizabeth George	Thomas Lynley and Barbara Havers
Steven Saylor	Gordianus the Finder
Maan Meyers	Pieter Tonneman and descendants
Margaret Lawrence	Hannah Trevor
Caleb Carr	John Schuyler Moore
Mary Willis Walker	Molly Cates
Patricia Cornwell	Kay Scarpetta
Walter Mosley	Easy Rawlins
Dale Furutani	Ken Tanaka
Michael Nava	Henry Rios
Barbara Neely	Blanche White
Terris McMahan Grimes	Theresa Galloway
Nikki Baker	Ginny Kelly
Valerie Wilson Wesley	Tamara Hayle
S.J. Rozan	Lydia Chin and Bill Smith

Preface

Contemporary American Crime Fiction intends to trace the major developments in American crime writing of the past fifteen years, with a focus on the 1990s. Although we will occasionally – as in our introductory chapter – refer to the history of crime writing and to the various theoretical approaches of the genre, we will primarily offer discussions of the work of writers who in our view have made a difference because they have reoriented established codes and conventions and explored new directions. This is not to say that our discussion will not be informed by historical knowledge or by theoretical considerations, but history and theory are not our primary concern.

Most of the writers we have selected for detailed discussion have published a substantial body of work, usually a series of novels with a recurring cast: the protagonist and his or her human entourage. They also have received substantial recognition on the part of fellow crime writers or of crime readers, a recognition concretized in awards – or nominations for awards, such as the Edgar Allan Poe Award, the Hammett Award, and the Anthony Award. If occasionally we discuss an author who does not satisfy these criteria, we do so because her or his work nevertheless can serve well to illustrate a particular point we want to make.

As we will see, the 1990s have consolidated fascinating trends visible since the mid-1980s. Most conspicuous, of course, is the veritable explosion of women's crime writing. We will return to the phenomenal success of crime writing by women in the second part of the introductory chapter. Another success story is that of the emergence and subsequent popularity of the ethnic detective. Then, there is the sudden proliferation of crime fiction with a historical setting. But white male crime fiction, too, is still going strong and has developed significantly in terms of plot, protagonists, themes and settings. But let us save this for the chapters that follow. Of these thirteen chapters, Theo D'haen has written Chapters 1 (first section), 3, 6, 7, 9, and 11, while Hans Bertens has contributed the second section of Chapter 1 and Chapters 2, 4, 5, 8, 10, 12, and 13.

[illegible]
logical
processes

1
Introduction

Crime writing, in the sense of 'writing about crime', predates the rise of the detective story. We already find it in the sixteenth and seventeenth centuries in the numerous pamphlets and broadsheets detailing the heinous deeds of murderers, robbers, and highwaymen. In the eighteenth century, Daniel Defoe, next to his many other writings, not only turned out numerous 'true crime' stories; he also turned them into literature, for instance *Moll Flanders* (1721). In the nineteenth century, crime fuels the plot of some of the best known works of Honoré de Balzac, Edward Bulwer-Lytton, Charles Dickens, and the great Russian writers, first and foremost Fyodor Dostoevsky.

It is also to the nineteenth century that we can trace the origins of the two main streams in detective fiction. In Edgar Allan Poe's 'tales of ratiocination' and Arthur Conan Doyle's Sherlock Holmes stories, we encounter the gifted amateur detective. He is the forerunner of the heroes of Agatha Christie, Dorothy Sayers, Margery Allingham, and numerous other practitioners of the genre in the period that is now commonly referred to as the 'Golden Age' of British detective writing – a period that begins after the First World War and ends with the outbreak of the Second World War. In the same period the amateur detective develops into the American 'hard-boiled' private investigator, the 'private eye' who detects for a living. The nineteenth century also announced what would eventually become the police procedural in novels by Charles Dickens and Wilkie Collins (*The Moonstone* (1869)), and, on the European Continent, in the work of French writers such as Emile Gaboriau. These precursors would seem to have been inspired by the actual activities of the then newly created police forces or detective departments.

The British Golden Age mystery typically features a closed setting (a country manor, a university college, a library, a train, a cruise ship, a country village), a middle to upper class milieu (from the modest means of Agatha Christie's Miss Marple to the nobility of Dorothy Sayers's Lord Peter Wimsey and the near-royalty of Margery Allingham's Albert Campion), and a usually eccentric detective. The detective's task is to repair an individual violation of a social order that embodies a collective and unchanging ideal of 'Britain' (or perhaps even only 'England', as few Golden Age mysteries seem to bother with what is felt or thought beyond the home counties). In the 1990s, a number of American crime writers, particularly Martha Grimes and Elizabeth George, have shown remarkable skill updating this essentially British interbellum mystery mode. In a different vein Peter J. Heck has his American mysteries – featuring Mark Twain – echo Agatha Christie.

In contrast to the classic English 'whodunit', the setting and form of the American private investigator novel are open. The setting is urban. Even where some scenes are set in the country, as in Chandler's *The Lady in the Lake* (1945), the story starts and ends in the big city with emphasis placed on the continual movement of the protagonist, especially by car. The private investigators of Dashiell Hammett, Raymond Chandler, and Ross Macdonald stand for a certain idea of decency, honor, comradeship, in short, for what it means to be 'an American', particularly a male American. The world that Sam Spade, Philip Marlowe, and Lew Archer operate in, though, is rotten at the core. The private eye has to break or bend the law himself in order to reassert an ideal 'America' founded on equality, justice, and the right to life, liberty, and the pursuit of happiness. However, that reassertion always remains both incidental and temporary. The private eye remains incapable of structurally righting his world. The British-style Golden Age detective guarantees a reassuring return to a well ordered and closed universe. The American-style hard-boiled private eye, on the contrary, leaves us with a sprawling urban jungle pressing in on us, and no guarantees whatsoever – or, to put it another way, with many questions but no answers.

The alienation that results from the fundamental incompatibility between the private eye's moral ideal and the unruly reality of the world he lives in only deepens as the twentieth century wears on. Raymond Chandler's *The Big Sleep* (1939) indicts the ecological, social, and moral waste occasioned by the oil industry. Ross Macdonald's *The Moving Target* (1949) denounces the exploitation of Mexican illegal immigrant labor in California's postwar agricultural industry. To take an example from the 1990s, James Crumley's *Bordersnakes* (1996) focuses on the absolute and arbitrary use of power by Texan ranchers along the Mexican border, and on the morally corrupting army background of the wealthiest of these. In novels featuring ethnic private eyes, such as Walter Mosley's 'Easy' Rawlins series, the exploitative nature of white-dominated America with regard to its non-white citizens is simply a given.

Though the private eye is still going strong – if not without some modifications to the original formula – it may well be that the police procedural is much better suited to our age than private eye fiction. As Peter Messent puts it in *Criminal Proceedings*,

> the police procedural ... seems to be supplanting the private-eye novel as 'realistic' crime fiction ... while the latter relies on a model of rule-bending individualism, the former puts its emphasis precisely on procedure and *collective agency* ... a fantasy of extra-systemic freedom and authenticity gives way to a more problematic vision of individual detectives operating through systemic procedures. (Messent, 1997, 12)

As such the police procedural more accurately reflects the increasingly complex and organized nature of present day society. The private investigator, then, has to move over. In fact, in much 1990s crime fiction the protagonist, if male, no longer is a professional private investigator, but rather someone who drifts into 'detecting' almost by accident, and often against the grain. Such an investigator of sorts often is, or at least starts out as, a marginal down-but-not-quite-out – a former lawyer or newspaperman who has fallen on hard times. John Lescroart's Dismas Hardy, Steven Womack's Harry James Denton, Doug J. Swanson's Jack Flippo, and John Morgan Wilson's Benjamin Justice fit this category. Eventually, such characters may apply for a legitimate private eye license. For instance, Lescroart's hero, when we first meet him in *Dead Irish* (1989), is an ex-marine, ex-cop, ex-lawyer, ex-husband, who now works as a bartender in San Francisco. The other novels in the Dismas Hardy series, *The Vig* (1990), *Hard Evidence* (1993), *The 13th Juror* (1994), and *The Mercy Rule* (1998), see Hardy mount the social ladder again. He rejoins the DA's office, then sets up as a defense lawyer. These later books more and more turn into courtroom dramas or legal thrillers.

Female private eyes of the 1990s, in contrast, more often have a past within the police force and usually immediately set up as private eyes after leaving the force, though in true hard-boiled fashion they, too, have to struggle to make ends meet: Valerie Wilson Wesley's Tamara Hayle, Grace F. Edwards's Mali Anderson, and Kathy Hogan Trocheck's Callahan Garrity all fit this bill.

Some recent private eyes, such as George P. Pelecanos's Nick Stefanos, verge on the grotesque. Others combine the roles of private eye and heroine of a screwball comedy, as, for instance, Janet Evanovich's Stephanie Plum. Or they completely cross over into zany humor, as in the case of Groucho Marx look-alike (and talk-alike) Kinky Friedman. Those that remain on the serious side, like Dennis Lehane's Kenzie and Gennaro, and Harlan Coben's Myron Bolitar, often end up openly despairing at the final ineffectualness of the present day private eye. Rare indeed seems to be the private investigator who comes across as absolutely credible and simultaneously conveys a reasonably optimistic message. In the last fifteen years, only Robert Crais's Elvis Cole fits this category, even though Crais only succeeds by ironizing his classic hard-boiled predecessors.

However effectual private investigators may be, in the final analysis they always remain outsiders to the social, economic, and political bodies whose corruption and decay they expose. The police procedural allows for detailing such corruption and decay from *within* the very institutions that theoretically should safeguard America's ideal order. In the 1990s, especially James Ellroy and Michael Connelly have fully exploited the possibilities of this subgenre in linking the themes of individual, institutional, and social corruption. James Ellroy focuses on the moral decay of political, big crime, economic, and media America in *L.A. Confidential* (1990) and *American Tabloid* (1996). In Michael Connelly's Harry Bosch novels, society's official guardians themselves turn into criminals often as the result of injustices or humiliations they suffered at the hands of that same society. *The Black Ice* (1993) explicitly traces the turning into a drug baron of an LA detective, and the resulting string of brutal murders, to the exploitation of Mexican and Asian immigrant labor along the US–Mexican border during the early part of the twentieth century. In the same writer's debut, *The Black Echo* (1992), a high-ranking FBI official, who was once on the staff of the US embassy in Saigon, turns into the leader of a gang of bank robbers composed of Vietnam veterans. More in general, even when the criminals in recent police procedurals are psychopathic monsters, they have been made that way by society, witness the serial murderers of James Ellroy's *Blood on the Moon* (1984) and *The Black Dahlia* (1987), Thomas Harris's *Silence of the Lambs*

(1988), or Caleb Carr's *The Alienist* (1994).

Not surprisingly, given the 1990s climate of political correctness, racism, ethnicity, and gender feature prominently on the agenda of much present day crime writing. However, outspoken critique largely remains the province of ethnic and female detective writing. The mainstream white male detective – both the private investigator and the police detective – has largely moved into the realm of the personal and psychological – see for instance Lawrence Block's Matthew Scudder and Connelly's Harry Bosch – or of the grotesque and the horrible, as in Harris's *Silence of the Lambs*, and much of Ellroy's fiction. This is not to say that the latter works do not reflect on society. It is rather that in these novels that social dimension is to be inferred from the situations, actions, and characters they present us with. In fact, the result can politically be very powerful, as in Ellroy's *American Tabloid*, or T. Jefferson Parker's *The Triggerman's Dance* (1996), where the protagonist is pressured by the FBI into infiltrating a rightwing outfit financed by a wealthy businessman intent on keeping America white. Another rightwing conspiracy drives the plot of James Lee Burke's *Dixie City Jam* (1994), in which Lousiana Cajun detective Dave Robicheaux is up against a band of neo-Nazis that threaten not only the life of his wife, but also the fabric of American society.

The rise of multiculturalism in the 1980s and 1990s has led to a veritable explosion of 'ethnic minority' crime writing. Of course, even well before the advent of multiculturalism, non-white protagonists were not unfamiliar in American detective fiction. From the 1920s on at least, African American detectives have held a place in American crime writing, and Chester Himes's Coffin Ed Johnson and Grave Digger Jones played a prominent role in 1950s and 1960s crime fiction. In the 1920s and 1930s, the ethnically Chinese Honolulu Police detective Charlie Chan featured in a popular series of novels by Earl Derr Biggers, and subsequently in a long string of even more popular movies. The early 1970s saw the introduction of a native American detective in the figure of Tony Hillerman's Lieutenant Joe Leaphorn of the Navajo Tribal Police, who in the course of the 1980s was seconded by Sergeant Jim Chee who later went on to replace him. Hillerman gained both early and lasting recognition for this series, winning the Edgar Award for *Dance Hall of the Dead* (1973), an Anthony Award for *Skinwalkers* (1986), and a Macavity for *A Thief of Time* (1988). In 1991 The Mystery Writers of America named Hillerman Grand Master. However, although their protagonists are non-caucasian, Biggers and Hillerman themselves were, or are, definitely Anglo. Until recently only African American authors seem to have featured detectives representative of their own ethnic minority.

In the 1990s, however, there has been a very definite change, as we can gather from the increasing recognition on the part of award-granting bodies of writers with non-caucasian backgrounds. In 1994 Chinese-Korean American Laura Joh Rowland's *Shinjū* (1994) was nominated for a Hammett Award. With *Death in Little Tokyo* (1996), starring a Japanese-American computer executive who turns into an amateur detective, Dale Furutani was co-winner of an Anthony for Best First Novel. The novel also won a Macavity for Best First Mystery, and was nominated for an Agatha for Best First Mystery Novel. If we look at African American authors we see that Walter Mosley won a Shamus for Best First Novel with *Devil in a Blue Dress* (1990), and a Hammett Award nomination with *White Butterfly* (1992), while Barbara Neely's 1992 *Blanche on the Lam* won Anthony, Macavity, and Agatha awards for Best First Novel of the year – a feat almost repeated by Terris McMahan Grimes's *Somebody Else's Child* (1996).

Regardless of ethnic or gender background, we find that social issues dominating public discussion at the time of writing increasingly filter into crime writing. This is very clear in Sara Paretsky's Vic Warshawski mysteries. *Tunnel Vision* (1994), for instance, addresses incest, single parent families, the housing conditions of the poor, and their attendant health problems. Pornography, snuff movies, and the sexual exploitation of youth set the themes of Lawrence Block's *A Dance at the Slaughterhouse* (1992). In different ways, some of these same issues also inform Grace F. Edwards' *If I Should Die* (1997), Valerie Wilson Wesley's *When Death Comes Stalking* (1994), Dennis Lehane's *Gone, Baby, Gone* (1998), and Michael Nava's *The Burning Plain* (1999) – a motley crew comprising two African American women writers, one white male, and one gay Chicano. It is worth noting that these 1990s crime writers sometimes cast doubt on the socially and legally correct solution to the issue they raise in a particular novel. Lehane's *Gone, Baby, Gone,* for instance, which seems at least partly inspired by the dismal string of child abductions and murders that came to light with the arrest of Marc Dutroux in the summer of 1997 in Belgium, takes an unexpected turn when the four-year old whom the PI duo of Kenzie and Gennaro are eventually able to return home, might really have been better off with her kidnappers, who actually were trying to rescue her from her irresponsible mother.

New, also, is that the social issues just mentioned heavily impinge on the private life of 1990s detectives. The fact that detectives have a private life is of course in itself already a major departure from the hard-boiled tradition. Since the 1980s, and especially in the 1990s, characters increasingly develop over the series in which they feature. Personal and family relationships may influence the progress of the detective's case. Lehane's Patrick Kenzie and Angela Gennaro novels, the first of which, *A Drink Before the War* (1994), won a Shamus Award in 1995, are set in Dorchester, a south Boston Irish-Italian, and increasingly also African American, working-class suburb where both PIs also grew up. Kenzie and Gennaro's familiarity with the neighborhood, its people, its cops, its smalltime hoods as well as local mafia bosses, is vital to their ability to solve the cases they get involved in. At the same time, these cases also have a strange way of taking them back to their own youth or childhood.

An author who gleefully exposes his private investigator's very personal life, and does so in an inimitably idiosyncratic way, is Kinky Friedman, whose series features a New York-based 'Texas Jew boy' named after his author. The Friedman novels offer pungent social commentary, but unlike for instance Lehane's Kenzie and Gennaro novels, they do not do so by way of their plot, but rather in the form of acerbic asides to the reader. In fact, in a 1990 interview in *Clues* Friedman (the author) stated in the tongue-in-cheek tone typical of his work that 'plots are cemeteries ... if you get a plot in a Kinky book, you can consider it gravy ... basically, they evolve ... I deal in loops more than in plots' (Friedman, 1990, 5). To say that the Kinky Friedman novels have no plot at all is perhaps an exaggeration. What plot there is, though, is usually quirky, and driven by verbal pyrotechnics rather than what one would call narrative logic. Here, for instance, is part of a telephone conversation between the 'Kinkster' and a prospective client in *God Bless John Wayne* (1995) – Friedman's cat has just knocked his 'large, Texas-shaped ashtray' upside down onto his crotch:

> 'Get off the goddamn desk', I said to the cat in a stage whisper.
> 'I beg your pardon?'
> 'Nothing,' I said. 'Domestic problem.'
> 'There will, of course', she continued, 'be a very handsome retainer.'
> 'My teeth are fine', I said. 'God's my orthodontist.'
> There was a fairly long silence on the line. The woman, obviously, was not amused. I looked up at the cat and saw that the cat, obviously, was not amused either. If you always spent your time trying to entertain women and cats, I reflected, life could be a hard room to work.
>
> (*Wayne*, 2–3)

Still, while the series in question is undoubtedly interesting in its own right, and a welcome addition to the varied landscape of 1990s American crime writing, Friedman's handling of the conventions of the detective genre is so idiosyncratic that it is difficult to see how anyone else could build on his particular achievement.

A number of stock attributes of the hard-boiled private eye – the weather, drinking, smoking, music, cars, clothes, literary quotations and references – continue to play a role in 1990s crime writing, though often they are used tongue-in-cheek to playfully reflect on the genre itself. For instance, in Hammett's *The Maltese Falcon* (1930) it rains heavily throughout most of the action; Joe Lansdale's *The Two-Bear Mambo* (1995) takes this device to its logical limit when constant rain brings about a flood with grotesque consequences for the plot of the novel. In Vicky Hendricks's *Miami Purity* (1995) the sweltering heat that weighs down the characters is only one of many pointers to James M. Cain's *The Postman Always Rings Twice* of 1934 (with the novel's title recalling the popular 1980s television series *Miami Vice*).

The 'thick' description of details of dress, food, drink, and cars typical for crime writing undoubtedly has something to do with the reality effect that crime fiction typically strives for. Beyond this, though, and particularly in 1990s crime fiction, description also serves to signal certain qualities about the characters and their world. The only car that will work for Evanovich's Stephanie Plum, for instance, is a 1950s Buick. In *Bordersnakes,* James Crumley's Milo Milodragovitch drives a superb Cadillac El Dorado, whereas the Mexican drugs dealers go around in Japanese jeeps. Michael Ventura, in *The Death of Frank Sinatra* (1996), has his private eye Mike Rose enjoy the Las Vegas air in a fabulous white 1972 Cadillac convertible. In general, good guys drive American makes, bad guys Japanese cars (even if built in the United States) or (less frequently) expensive foreign imports. Connelly's Harry Bosch drives a Ford Caprice (police issue), just as he drinks domestic brand beers, and smokes domestic brand cigarettes. Rock music from the 1970s and 1980s draws the line between between 'us' and 'them' for Pelecanos's Nick Stefanos, while jazz serves that function for Connelly's Bosch and for Grace F. Edwards' Mali Anderson in *If I Should Die*.

Particularly noteworthy in the crime fiction of the the late 1980s and the 1990s is the fascination with serial killers – undoubtedly sparked off by a number of notorious real-life instances. Probably the best known novel in question remains Thomas Harris's *The Silence of the Lambs* (1988), not least because of the highly successful movie version. Beyond this, though, certain plots and themes regarding serial killers seem to take on a life of their own in this period, and particularly so in white male crime writing. In Ellroy's *Blood on the Moon* (1984), the killer sends the woman he eventually intends to be his final victim a red rose after each murder. To taunt the detective investigating the case the killer each time sends a poem. In Parker's *Crimson Joy* (1988), a serial murderer leaves a red rose at the scene of each crime. The killer in Philip Margolin's *Gone, But Not Forgotten* (1993) leaves a (black) rose at each murder scene, and writes poems to the detectives on the case, as does the killer in Connelly's *The Concrete Blonde* (1994).

In what follows it is our aim to survey the work of some of the groundbreaking crime writers of the 1990s. Before we start on our tour, it is necessary that we first say something about what has probably been the most remarkable development of all, namely the astonishingly prominent role of women writers on the contemporary American crime fiction scene.

Given the prominence of women writers on the American popular fiction scene of the second half of the nineteenth century, it is not surprising that American women writers were among the first to explore the possibilities offered by the then still brand-new genre of detective fiction. Anna Katherine Green, for instance, published her first mystery in 1878, thus preceding Arthur Conan Doyle by ten years, and remained active well into the 1920s. Moreover, some of these early female mystery writers achieved massive popularity. Mary Roberts Rinehart, who can rightfully be seen as Green's literary heiress, and who published books from 1908 until the early 1950s, was at one point in her career the highest paid author in the United States.

However, while in the 1920s and 1930s British women authors succeeded in establishing themselves as major contributors to the mystery, their American counterparts, for all their success in terms of sales, were slow in finding similar recognition. When in 1930 the doyen of British mystery writers, Arthur Conan Doyle, died, a whole range of female successors had either already made a name for themselves (Agatha Christie, Dorothy Sayers, Patricia Wentworth), had just started doing so (Margery Allingham, Josephine Tey), or was waiting in the wings (Ngaio Marsh, who was born and bred in New Zealand, but would firmly situate herself in the British tradition). By the time the Second World War broke out the great names in British detective writing were female rather than male. In the United States critical success was almost exclusively reserved for men. Rinehart may have been the biggest seller, but for the critics the pace was set by her much younger male colleagues. As a matter of fact, in the crime fiction canon of the American interbellum women are still virtually invisible.

In retrospect, we can see that the (male) American crime writers who started their careers in the second half of the 1920s and the early 1930s were, in some cases perhaps unwittingly, engaged in masculinizing a genre that in the USA maintained up until that point strong links with the 'women's novel' of the second half of the nineteenth century; the novel whose widespread popularity had so aggravated not exactly bestselling contemporary writers like Nathaniel Hawthorne. Although the romance-cum-suspense mysteries of Rinehart, who at the time easily outsold all of her young male colleagues, are of course not a straight continuation of the 'women's novel', their setting, manipulation of gothic themes, and 'romance' character, have strong affinities with the genre. The masculinization of American crime writing took several forms. From the mid-1920s on, S.S. Van Dine and, a little later, Ellery Queen and John Dickson Carr (who in spite of his utterly British detectives, Dr Fell and Sir Henry Merrivale must be unconditionally claimed for the United States) took their cue from Conan Doyle and intellectualized the genre, presenting ingenious puzzles, often involving arcane information, and what seemed to be rigorous exercises in logic on the part of a superior mind. In 1933 Erle Stanley Gardner published the first of his countless Perry Mason books, bringing the macho clash of personalities and wits of the American courtroom into the genre. The following year James M. Cain's *The Postman Always Rings Twice* brought a new, and what at the time seemed a stark and unsentimental realism to crime writing. Cain held a seedy world of sorry and almost accidental criminals up for anxious but spell-bound examination. Last but not least, between 1929 and 1934 Dashiell Hammett published the five novels that for all practical purposes established the field of private eye fiction, a field whose tough-guy masculinity seemed almost designed to keep out female writers, let alone female protagonists. Even if the private eye preferred a strictly regulated and sedentary life style to the usual fast and unpredictable action, as did Rex Stout's beer-swilling Nero Wolfe who made his first appearance in the 1934 *Fer-de-Lance*, his masculinity and, in this particular case, hostility to women, was strongly emphasized.

This masculinization of American crime writing (or detective and mystery fiction as most of it was until recently called) marginalized its female practitioners. It was not until the 1950s, thirty years after their

British colleagues, that American women began to be a real force on the American scene. Dorothy B. Hughes, Margaret Millar, Charlotte Armstrong (who all had started publishing in the early 1940s) and Patricia Highsmith (whose first novel appeared in 1950) won the respect of their peers that had been denied to their predecessors. In 1956 the Edgar Award was won by Margaret Millar's *Beast in View*, while Patricia Highsmith's *The Talented Mr Ripley* featured on the shortlist, and the next year the Edgar went to Charlotte Armstrong, for her *A Dram of Poison*. A few years before, Dorothy Salisbury Davis's *A Gentle Murder* (1951) had already won her a reputation as a highly skilful writer of suspense tales, a status that was confirmed by the Edgar nomination for her 1959 *A Gentleman Called*. Still, if one looks at the history of the Mystery Writers of America's Grand Master Award – surely the most prestigious and coveted award in the field of crime writing – it is hard to avoid the conclusion that critical recognition of the achievement of the older generations of female American crime writers has been rather slow in coming. While the first ever Grand Master Award went to Agatha Christie, in 1955, in was not until 1971 that the honor was conferred upon the first American woman, Mignon Eberhart. Interestingly, Eberhart's election as a Grand Master may be interpreted as a sort of breakthrough. Eberhart, who had produced a steady stream of novels since her debut in 1929 – coincidentally also the year of Queen's and Hammett's first novels – owed a good deal to Mary Roberts Rinehart and borrowed liberally from the gothic romance whose influence her male contemporaries had sought to remove from the crime writing scene. With hindsight, then, Eberhart's election to crime writing's Hall of Fame may be construed as a belated re-evaluation of one particular strand of crime fiction that had earlier been ignored because of its links with women's fiction. And perhaps we may see John Dickson Carr's flirtation with the gothic in the later part of his career in the same light.

Still, Eberhart's election was something of a fluke. It took seven years until the next woman, Dorothy B. Hughes, was similarly honored. Hughes, however, had to share the honor with Daphne du Maurier and Ngaio Marsh in what seems a transparent attempt to right a historical wrong. This triple election was in any case rather insulting: 1978 is the only year in which three Grand Masters were created in one single swoop, so that for once the honor conferred was unpleasantly diluted. It is only since the early 1980s that the female contribution to American crime writing has been more adequately recognized. Between 1983 and 1990 Margaret Millar, Dorothy Salisbury Davis,

Phyllis A. Whitney (another writer heavily indebted to the romance and gothic traditions) and Helen McCloy (who had started her career as early as 1938) were added to the roster of Grand Masters.

It is tempting to think that this belated reappraisal is related to similar reappraisals of female achievement that have taken place under the pressure of feminist scholarship in a whole range of artistic and semi-artistic disciplines. Another reason may well be that the vitality and strength of recent female crime writing have contributed to the substantially increased visibility of the work of earlier generations of women writers. The female boom of the last two decades – see Walton and Jones for detailed figures and charts (1999, 27–30 and 41–3) – is of course part of the more general revitalization of crime writing that we have witnessed since the early 1970s (and for which Patricia Highsmith and her British colleagues P.D. James and Ruth Rendell had helped to pave the way).

Tony Hillerman published his first Joe Leaphorn book, *The Blessing Way*, in 1970; two years later George V. Higgins started his series of talkative crime novels with *The Friends of Eddie Coyle;* Robert B. Parker introduced Spenser, heir apparent to Philip Marlowe and Lew Archer, in the 1973 *The Godwulf Manuscript*; Elmore Leonard abandoned the Western for taut, ironical, and streetwise crime stories; Lawrence Block's Matt Scudder made a first, tentative, appearance in three mid-1970s paperbacks; Martin Cruz Smith was flexing his muscles (meanwhile making a living as Nick Carter and Simon Quinn) for the smash hit *Gorky Park* (1981), and so on and so forth. But even if we take that general renaissance, in which women crime writers begin to fully participate in the early 1980s, into account, we must still conclude that in the second Golden Age of crime writing that we are still witnessing, female crime writing stands out because of its power, its breadth, its innovation, and even its irreverence, no matter if that irreverence at times takes the form of a somewhat childish mischievousness (but Thomas Harris's unpleasant Hannibal Lecter stuff did deserve the awful parody in the title of Jill Churchill's *Silence of the Hams* (1996)).

Women writers are prominent in every subgenre crime writing has produced and have in fact recently added some. Patricia Cornwell has pioneered the forensic medicine novel, her debut *Postmortem* (1990) winning the Edgar, Anthony, Macavity, and John Creasey awards for Best First Novel plus the *Prix de Roman d'Aventure* in an unprecedented triumphal march that points both to the novel's groundbreaking qualities and the fact that women writers are now fully visible to award-granting juries and committees. Furthermore, since the publication of *Postmortem,* multiple awards have also gone to Nancy Pickard's *I.O.U.* (1991), Barbara Neely's *Blanche on the Lam* (1992), Margaret Maron's *Bootlegger's Daughter* (1992), Nevada Barr's *Track of the Cat* (1993), Sharyn McCrumb's *She Walks These Hills* (1994), Mary Willis Walker's *Under the Beetle's Cellar* (1995), and Terris McMahan Grimes's *Somebody Else's Child* (1996), to mention only those books that will be discussed in the following chapters. Nevada Barr, whose fascinating first novel *Track of the Cat* has just been mentioned, Judith Van Gieson, Karin McQuillan and others have developed what one might call ecological mysteries, with Barr specializing in National Parks, Van Gieson in endangered species, and McQuillan in Africa's wildlife.

We may add to this the meteoric rise of crime fiction with a lesbian protagonist. Initially limited to small specialized presses (Seal, Naiad), lesbian detectives have since the early 1990s found mainstream publishers in what must be seen as a major emancipatory breakthrough, even if the stance of their creators (Sandra Scoppettone, Ellen Hart, Katherine V. Forrest) is middle-of-the-road rather than radical. And then there is of course that most visible of all female subgenres: the private eye novel featuring a female investigator. Female private investigators were not absolutely unheard of before the early 1980s, when the current female PI boom took off. However, they were very rare and very hard to take seriously. Erle Stanley Gardner's Bertha Cool and G.G. Fickling's Honey West are equally implausible, even if they could not be more different. Unfortunately, the male hand of their creators is all too obvious (since 'G.G. Fickling' presented the combined creative efforts of Gloria and Forrest E. Fickling the hand is only half male in the case of Honey West). It is the new wave of women writers that began publishing in the late 1970s and early 1980s that gave us the credible and intelligent female private eye that now seems to have been around forever.

The late arrival of what are now the most visible subgenres within female crime writing – the police procedural (with its variations such as Cornwell's series featuring a medical examiner and Barr's series featuring a park ranger), and the PI novel – of course finds it explanation in social circumstances. Until well into the 1960s, the world of professional investigators, either salaried by a law enforcement agency or self-employed, was practically off-limits to women. They were employed to type up reports and to bring around coffee, but were only rarely allowed to do detective work. Moreover, the few women who were admitted to the sacred halls of actual investigation met with stubborn resistance. The career of Dorothy Uhnak, whose Christie Opara, police officer in New York City, is a very early female professional (her Edgar-winning first novel *The Bait* was published in 1968), illustrates the odds that female professionals faced even after their admission to the force. Having joined the New York City Transit Police Department in 1953, she became a detective in 1955, but left in disillusionment twelve years later: '" ... I wasn't allowed to take the examination for promotion, so that after fourteen years, I left the department and returned to college ..."' (Budd, 1986, 116). (See also Uhnak's account of such routinely discriminatory practices in her *Policewoman: A Young Woman's Initiation into the Realities of Justice*, 1964.) As a result, female crime writers who wanted to work with a realistically embedded female protagonist had to opt for the amateur formula. It is only in the last twenty-odd years that female professional investigators have been accepted by their superiors and colleagues, and often with great reluctance, so that fiction featuring a professional female detective could claim that it indeed reflected an emerging social reality.

Implicit in this is that certainly during the 1970s and 1980s crime fiction featuring a female professional almost inevitably possessed emancipatory qualities. With regard to the police procedural this emancipatory dimension consisted first of all in the simple, but very important, fact that women were shown as serious participants in law enforcement and in the bringing to justice of criminal offenders. But the police procedural was also prefectly equipped to show how one of society's most important institutions resisted such integration because of its masculinist nature. Bringing women into police departments almost invariably made the institution show its true, thoroughly masculinist colors and thereby undermined its supposed neutrality. If one does not see the female police procedural as a form of betrayal – with women defecting from their group and identifying with the masculinist State – then the genre quietly empowers its protagonists in their efforts to hold their own in a sometimes inimical and often condescending environment.

This empowerment is far more outspoken in the case of the female private investigator, especially if she is modeled after the classic male PI with his masculinist language and behavior but retains her own identifiably female perspective. (It is of course even more outspoken if the female investigator also adopts the classic PI's masculinist outlook. However, since a major aim of female empowerment is to detach power and gender from each other, adopting a masculinist stance that implicitly confirms the identification of power with masculinity is counterproductive. We will look at some examples of that counterproductiveness later in this book.) The female PI, then, is most effective if she simultaneously affirms and undermines the tradition because both strategies are means of self-empowerment. That empowerment begins with her self-employment and its corollary: her economic independence. Female PI's often emphasize that their independence is hard-won and difficult to maintain, which of course only adds to its symbolic value. A second, extremely important means of self-empowerment is the characteristic PI voice, wisecracking, ironic, self-mocking, sometimes conspirational (in the sense that the reader is made to feel an insider who is granted the privilege of sharing the PI's thoughts) and always irreverent and resolutely anti-hierarchical. Since the male PI already uses the style to empower himself, with female PI's the classic voice has a double impact: it signals that they are aware of one important source of power and that they are willing and able to cross gender lines in order to make it available to themselves. Female PI's can deploy this masculinist idiom and the accompanying attitude very effectively because its socially leveling thrust is in their case hooked up with the undermining of traditional gender roles, in particular if it is used against powerful males. (They must of course be on their guard against genuinely adopting the wilfully unemotional and detached stance that so often comes with the PI voice.) Moreover, the female PI novel, with its first-person female narrator, breaks with the format in which we have men looking at women (subjecting them to the power of the 'gaze', as modern literary theory would call it). Instead, we have women looking at men, or, even better, narrators who are aware of their narratorial power and subject it to scrutiny.

I should immediately add that very few female PI writers get around to such theoretical subtleties. The feminism of crime writing by women is almost invariably liberal rather than radical, so that the acts of resistance of their detectives get a personal rather than a political coloring. In other words, they often do not seem to be up against an impersonal, systemic form of discrimination, but against incidental and personal slights. Except in a number of novels featuring lesbian investigators we do not find the sort of theoretical awareness or politics that characterizes much contemporary academic feminism. Female investigators give no indication of having read Derrida or Lacan or of seeing the true phallocentric nature of things. However, even if its social origins remain obscure, there is no denying that they are aware of the inequality and the unequal power-sharing that confronts them wherever they go, or that they work consistently to resist and change the roles that Western society has traditionally reserved for women.

Dedicated readers of crime fiction know that female investigators do so consistently because they have been able to follow many of them through a whole series of novels. Since a series offers writers much more scope for developing a character or a group of characters than single novels which invariably lead to closure (especially in crime fiction), our focus will be on series and series protagonists. In discussing these series characters we will largely forgo theoretical exposition. This is not to deny the importance of theory, but it would be silly to pretend that crime writing is undertheorized and needs another book with a heavily theoretical approach. Anyone interested in theoretical perspectives can easily find them. Among such publications, we can especially recommend Sally Munt's *Murder by the Book? Feminism and the Crime Novel* (1994), some of the essays (including his own) in Peter Messent's collection *Criminal Proceedings: The Contemporary American Crime Novel* (1997), and Priscilla L. Walton and Manina Jones's *Detective Agency: Women Rewriting the Hard-Boiled Tradition* (1999). We will primarily, and from an openly evaluative point of view, look at the novels themselves.

2
The Old Guard in the mid-1990s: Muller, Grafton, and Paretsky

Like the next chapter, which will do the same with regard to male crime writing, this first chapter on female crime writers will link the not-so-distant past with the present. While the other chapters will examine truly contemporary crime writing, that is, crime writing of the 1990s, these first two chapters will make a modest attempt to chart the passage from the great renaissance of crime writing of the 1970s and 1980s to where we are now. The attempt will be modest because instead of the larger picture, which we hope will emerge from the discussions of the new developments in crime writing that will follow in the later chapters, we will offer discussions of a small number of writing careers. Needless to say that such a strategy runs the risk of resulting in a one-sided and unrepresentative picture. Much, then, will depend on the writers which will come under scrutiny. For that reason it seems a good bet to go with writers of an undisputed status, writers who by both readers and by their crime writing colleagues are seen as absolutely major figures, and as having made seminal contributions to the genre.

In the field of female crime writing, Marcia Muller (1944), Sue Grafton (1940), and Sara Paretsky (1947), who between the three of them created the contemporary female private investigator, belong indisputably to the grand old ladies. Muller is generally credited with creating the new-style female series PI – a view that I will qualify in a moment – in her 1977 *Edwin of the Iron Shoes*, which introduced San Francisco private investigator Sharon McCone. Grafton and Paretsky, who both published their first female PI novel in 1982, when Muller published her second McCone book, consolidated the new format while substantially expanding its range and potential. Grafton's *'A' Is for Alibi* presented private investigator Kinsey Millhone who, in apparent homage to Ross Macdonald, operates in the fictitious southern California town of Santa Teresa, and Paretsky's *Indemnity Only* – whose title, in an equally low-keyed manner, signals her familiarity with the classics of crime fiction – gave us V.I. Warshawski, who 'specializes in fraud, arson, and commercial misbehavior' in Chicago (*Tunnel Vision*, 2).

The procedure of this chapter is to look in considerable detail at McCone, Millhone, and Warshawski at the beginning of their respective careers, in 1977 and 1982, and then to focus on the way Muller, Grafton, and Paretsky present their investigators in the mid-1990s. The implicit question here is: where have the most prominent female crime writers of their generation taken their protagonists over a period of fifteen years? Given their undisputed status in the field, such a comparison should tell us interesting things about the development of female crime writing in general, or at least about the way the most influential female private investigators have been handled by their creators.

I: Marcia Muller and Sharon McCone

> *'I always wanted to be James Bond.'*
> 'Oh, hell, Bennis.' I knew what he meant. I felt that way myself.
> Police Officer Suze Figueroa (height: five feet two) in Barbara D'Amato's *Killer. app* (1996)

Edwin of the Iron Shoes launched the highly successful Sharon McCone series, built around a San Francisco private investigator whose rather diluted Shoshone blood has unaccountably given her an undiluted Amerindian appearance, which, although frequently mentioned, plays no role of significance in the novels. McCone and *Edwin of the Iron Shoes* are of more than common interest because of the widespread notion that with McCone Muller also launched the tough female private eye of so many contemporary crime novels. However, if we compare McCone in her debut novel with the heroines of Grafton and, in particular, Paretsky, she looks too tame to qualify as a tough investigator. This is not to criticize Muller, who has never claimed to have invented the new female PI, but it is only fair to say that McCone does not develop into a truly contemporary PI until Grafton and Paretsky have set the standard.

McCone works as the only investigator for All Souls, a co-operative law firm that aims 'to provide quality legal service at reasonable prices for its member clients' (*Edwin*, 10) and that in its idealistic spirit even adjusts its fees to its clients' incomes. Since All Souls' clients are 'a nonviolent bunch' McCone does mostly simple, routine work. Not surprisingly, she never describes herself as a private eye. She may qualify as a PI because she is an investigator and does not, in any capacity, represent the law, but she is on All Souls' payroll and gets her assignments from the co-operative, so that she lacks the independence and autonomy traditionally associated with private investigating. This is not to say that Muller does not try to give her heroine the necessary requisites. In good PI fashion McCone is, for all practical purposes, without family (members from her estranged family do appear in later novels, in line with a more general development in 1980s and 1990s PI fiction). She has been fired from an earlier job with a detective agency for what amounts to moral independence, and she has rejected becoming a cop because when she was younger (she is almost thirty by the time of the *Edwin* case) '[l]ady cops were confined to typing, taking shorthand and juvenile division' (*Edwin*, 187). Refusing such gendered roles and the dependent inferiority implicit in them, she does not only see herself as equal to her male fellow citizens, but even as equal to the more dominant among them: 'Greg Marcus was a headstrong, domineering man, and I was an equally self-willed woman' (184). This assertive self-image – elsewhere she tells us that she has always made her own choices and has refused to be held back – is supported by her boss at All Souls who speaks of her 'strength and independence', but is unfortunately more or less given the lie by the novel itself. McCone shows courage and intelligence, but falls for a sensitive, well-dressed, art-loving, yet thoroughly masculine, no-nonsense detective who is twelve or thirteen years her senior and has the patronizing and more generally offensive habit of calling her 'papoose'.

In *Games to Keep the Dark Away*, the fourth McCone novel published seven years later – after her debut, McCone was kept on ice until 1982 – Muller is a good deal surer of her touch. The occasional awkwardness of *Edwin* has disappeared, and the rather implausible relationship with the art-loving but overbearing cop is in the course of the novel replaced by a much more convincingly created relationship with a radio broadcaster. Curiously, when she has McCone think about her ex-lover, Muller again falls back on cliches and fails to convince: 'our stormy natures had turned our affair into a battleground', McCone muses rather pompously. Still, McCone has clearly grown in the intervening years: 'what woman could remain in love with a man who called her by such a ridiculous nickname?' she asks herself, finally realizing that 'papoose' is totally unacceptable, even if she still does not see that such terms of 'endearment' are part of a power game. McCone shows a convincing blend of determination, personal courage, and undemonstrative self-confidence. Surely not accidentally, she now refers to her years as a 'private detective' (14), whereas in *Edwin* she never was more than an 'investigator'.

McCone's increased self-confidence has of course everything to do with how Muller handles her protagonist. A good and convincing touch is the playfulness with which Muller approaches her. McCone is taken seriously but not overly so, as is demonstrated by the scene in which McCone is caught snooping by the owner of a yacht:

> ... he lifted me and stepped over to the rail.
> 'Don't say I didn't warn you,' he said.
> In seconds, I was flying through the air, and then hit the water. I started to yell but closed my mouth just in time before I went under. When I bobbed to the top, my hair was plastered to my face, and I had to part it to look up at the boat. Keller leaned on the rail, laughing uproariously.
>
> (*Games*, 141)

Contrary to our expectations, the man is not punished for this disrespectful and indecorous treatment of the heroine. Although he is at this point still a suspect he turns out to be innocent, moreover, McCone never gets around to the personal revenge she promises herself when swimming to the dock after her involuntary plunge.

There is more of this refreshing attitude towards the protagonist. Running after an escaping murderess, McCone slips and falls 'ungloriously on [her] rear' (202). But there is also something else, something that with hindsight may be interpreted as an early manifestation of the far more sensational stuff that we find in Muller's recent McCone books. The murderess flees from McCone, rather stupidly, down a stairway leading to a beach that is already under water, with the tide still rising. She swims to a reef some thirty yards away from shore. All McCone has to do is get somebody to call the police and keep an eye on the stairway. Instead, she swims out to persuade the woman to come with her and give herself up. Predictably, the desperate woman tries to kill her, too, and almost succeeds. The scene, in which the murderess finally drowns, borders on the gratuitous, but is saved by the fact that, with some effort, we can imagine the blind panic that can lead a person to entrap herself and accept McCone's attempt to save her.

Unfortunately, by the time of *Till the Butchers Cut Him Down* (1994) the playfulness of *Games* has completely disappeared, and so has much of the plausibility of the early novels. Remarkably, that diminished plausibility did not unfavorably impress reviewers while the novel that preceded *Butchers*, *Wolf in the Shadows* (1993), even got an Edgar nomination.

Butchers opens with a sort of prelude – curiously, it is 4 July – that initially suggests that McCone confronts a momentous, life-or-death decision: 'Make the right choice and it's golden; make the wrong one – I didn't want to think about that' (*Butchers*, 1). The solution to what seems a heart-rending dilemma comes to her when a wild mustang (she has come to California's White Mountains for some mustang-watching) runs away from her, 'tail and mane streaming proudly – a shining, free creature' (2). And so we find that the decision that will either be golden or will lead to things too awful to contemplate simply involves staying with All Souls, or striking out for herself: McCone Investigations. And as the freedom of the mustang and the fact that it is the Fourth of July have already signaled to us, Sharon McCone opts for freedom and independence.

The wholly artificial suspense and excitement of the preamble characterize the whole novel, which is set up like some sprawling saga, with four parts that all have their own headings indicating place and time ('Lost Hope, Nevada; September,' and so on). Early on McCone suggests that she should have heeded the instinct that warned her to walk away from her prospective client 'Suits' Gordon. The suggestion of impending doom, however, turns out to be groundless – just a trick to jack up the reader's expectations. In fact, the Gordon case nets McCone a fantastic profit, including half of a substantial piece of choice real estate on the California coast.

With every single character Muller strains for maximum effect. 'Suits' Gordon, a so-called 'turnaround pro' who saves business enterprises from seeming inevitable disaster, is a weird genius who started Harvard aged 14 and left three years later with an MBA. McCone's lover Hy Ripinsky, who is 'tall, lanky, and handsome in a hawk-nosed, shaggy way', has 'a wonderful off-the-wall sense of humor,' is fluent in French, Russian, and Spanish, and fluent in bed to boot (103). McCone's over-eager nephew Mick, who to the reader is mostly a pain in the neck, and who would seem to develop into yet another substitute child to an aging and still childless female PI, will turn out (mostly in the next McCone novel, *A Wild and Lonely Place*) to be 'a computer genius [who has] a natural talent for investigation' (*Place*, 38). Finally,

McCone's credibility almost collapses under the combined weight of her own sense of self-importance and the role that Muller burdens her with. We see her easily holding her own in a confrontation with the largest illegal gun dealer in the Bay Area, go without proper sleep or rest for four nights running, and generally act in a way more readily associated with James Bond and other wildly idealized males than with the contemporary private investigator.

A Wild and Lonely Place (1995), which earned Muller a Macavity nomination, continues and even intensifies this pattern, with McCone rescuing a kidnapped child from a privately owned Caribbean island that is controlled by an international criminal and his gang. What is more, she is able to do so because she can swim for what must be at least one mile, carrying the exhausted child on her back. Later, she demonstrates her accomplishments as a pilot, fighting to save the plane that carries her, the child, and the unconscious Ripinsky, from the treacherous winds above the Tehachapi Mountains, while again a little later she must cope with an engine failure that necessitates an emergency landing in Bakersfield. Piling it on, Muller has the plane come to a stop only a few yards from the end of the runway. The scene in which McCone fights to regain control of the plane is, in fact, the scene with which the novel opens. Again we have a prelude designed to grab our attention, and send chills up and down our spine. (This is not an unfair deduction since the flight does in reality not take place until we are far past the halfway mark, at which point the scene is literally repeated.) And again, after the hair-raising opener, we get a saga-like structure ('Part One'; 'Northern California; May 18–22' and so on).

McCone's sense of self-importance is also carried over from the previous novel, and more than occasionally borders on unintentioned parody. We learn that Adah Joslyn, a 'fifteen-year veteran of the SFPD', has involved McCone in the case of the Diplo-bomber, a maniac who over the past five or six years has bombed buildings, cars, and people connected with certain embassies and consulates, most recently the 'Azadi' consulate in San Francisco. In violation of PD policy, Joslyn has made the complete dossier available to McCone. 'Together', McCone tells us, 'we'd brainstormed till both our heads ached' (15) – which is remarkable since there is nothing to go on and is mainly indicative of the way McCone has come to see herself. We are not surprised to learn a little later that it is McCone's input that 'had often helped to make Joslyn make her collars' (46) or that the 'departmental brass' is fully aware of her unsalaried contributions. Wholly in line with this idea of her own importance is her conviction that she is getting close to the bomber's mind: 'I was beginning to understand him in a way that reading a dry psychological profile couldn't duplicate. If I could get farther inside his mentality, until I was almost in sync with it, I might be able to figure out what he wanted as his ultimate payoff' (215). We are of course not reminded of this passage when McCone fails to discover the bomber's identity until just before the novel ends. As a matter of fact, McCone's increasing infallibity creates a serious novelistic problem: since these novels derive much of their suspense from our, and McCone's, ignorance concerning the criminal's identity, McCone must in spite of her infallibility in some plausible way be kept from finding out about it.

With *A Wild and Lonely Place* Muller leaves her less gullible readers far behind. In *Games that Keep the Dark Away* we have a convincing missing persons investigation – convincing in the sense that the case is a typical PI case but also in the way that Muller handles it. Here, in *A Wild and Lonely Place*,we have a typical FBI case involving a fanatical, deluded bomber who has attacked targets in a number of major American cities and who is presumably modeled upon the UNA-bomber. McCone's involvement is totally implausible, as are her rescue mission, her plane trouble, the bomber's selection of her as his contact, and so on. In her pursuit of ever higher levels of excitement and suspense, Muller has turned her private investigator into a sort of international crusader and one-woman rescue team. Having abandoned the serious, yet playful attitude towards McCone that characterized the early novels she has uncritically fallen in love with a superwoman of her own creation. The McCone series has of course never been at the heart of the PI tradition. Although McCone values her independence in true PI fashion, there is very little of the admittedly rather unfocused social concern and the compassion with the downtrodden that we find in Marlowe, Archer, and their countless successors and that also characterizes the great majority of female PI's. But even if McCone was always off-center as a PI, in the earlier novels she still qualified for the guild. By the mid-1990s, however, she has developed a self-aggrandizing streak and has become involved in a line of work that has very little to do with time-honored private investigation. Unfortunately, investigative megalomania no longer is an exclusively male vice, as we will also see in a later chapter.

Sue Grafton and Kinsey Millhone

Sue Grafton's *'A' Is for Alibi* (1982) drew immediate and enthusiastic attention, even though the awards, as if to make up for an oversight, only began to flow with its sequel, *'B' Is for Burglary*, which in 1986 won both the Shamus and Anthony awards for best novel. Since then, Grafton has been a regular at award ceremonies. *'C' Is for Corpse* and *'G' Is for Gumshoe* again won her Anthony awards (1987 and 1991) while *'K' Is for Killer* gave her a second Shamus in 1995. This could mean an enviable continuity in quality or else a special knack for meeting mainstream criteria. In fact, both are true, although not equally. The quality of Grafton's novels varies more than their mainstream outlook. In spite of its award, for instance, *'G' Is for Gumshoe* suffers from a highly implausible plot in which Grafton's private investigator Kinsey Millhone solves a forty-year-old murder – and with it a number of subsequent ones – while in a totally unrelated plot line she herself is the target of a sadistic killer with a contract who, more or less in passing, takes care of the now septuagenarian murderer. In spite of such lapses, however, the novels have tended to get more self-assured and better over time, with Kinsey more than once acting more like a catalyst whose sleuthing, or even mere presence, sets things in motion, than as a detective who tries to reconstruct a crime after the fact. After establishing the PI format that Grafton creates in her first Millhone book, I will look in more detail at her 1996 *'M' Is for Malice* which is one of the high points of the series.

Kinsey Millhone, who in *'A' Is for Alibi* is 32 years old, is close kin to the classic private eye. She is without family, having been orphaned at five, does not have pets or house plants, and lives by herself after two childless marriages (and divorces). She once qualified for the police academy and has worked for two years in the Santa Teresa Police Department – Santa Teresa being located somewhere northwest of LA, between the Sierra Madre and the Pacific – before quitting and setting up herself as a private eye for a familiar reason. As a police lieutenant with whom she entertains the equally familiar strained relationship puts it, she did not like working 'with a leash around [her] neck.' Apart from this desire for a sort of independence that a police job cannot give her, her dissatisfaction with the gendered attention of her male colleagues has played a role in her decision to quit: 'back then, policewomen were viewed with a mixture of curiosity and scorn. I didn't want to spend my days defending myself against "good-natured" insults, or having to prove how tough I was again and again'

(*'B' Is for Burglar*, 1). While Kinsey's sensitivity to gender – intermittently present in all the novels – is new to the PI genre, the standard battered car she drives, her broken nose and the fact that she can just make ends meet are not.

In line with this traditional image, she at various times emphasizes her toughness and independence. We hear that she is 'a real hard-ass when it comes to men' (*'A' Is for Alibi*, 49), that she is 'hard on people' (176) and that she has 'never been good at taking shit, especially from men' (174). In spite of her two marriages, and the occasional affair, she professes not to know what love is, and does 'not believe in it anyway' (183). Her essential privacy is expressed in her preference for driving at night. Private investigation is her whole life, she tells us, and solitariness is more or less what she expects from life, as the very last line of the novel makes clear: 'in the end all you have left is yourself' (215).

But there is a certain wistfulness in the way this is phrased and if we look somewhat closer much of the hard-boiled image evaporates. Under close scrutiny Kinsey Millhone turns out to be a rather sensitive and vulnerable young woman. She is as scared of things – angry geese, for instance – as the rest of us, she feels tears form in her own eyes when the mother of a murder victim starts crying, she develops all sorts of stress-related minor ailments when under pressure, and in a brilliant inversion of that mysogynistic classic pattern – honorable male PI brought into temptation by seductive murderess – even starts a passionate relationship with a man who turns out to be the killer. Even though she ultimately kills him in self-defense, which leads to a bad case of self-recrimination and guilt, this is a far cry from the ideal of detached professionalism that for instance determines Sam Spade's attitude vis-à-vis Brigid O'Shaughnessy in Hammett's *Maltese Falcon* (we are reminded of Hammett because Grafton pokes a little fun at him by way of a dog called Dashiell). It is, by the way, in the earlier novels of the series not quite clear whether Grafton wants us to take Kinsey's claim to hard-boiled toughness for granted and to ignore the evidence to the contrary. In other words, it is hard to determine whether she shares her protagonist's illusions about herself or is busy directing our attention towards their illusionary nature. In any case, by the time of *'M' Is for Malice* this sort of ambiguity is clearly resolved.

As we have seen with regard to her decision to quit the force, Grafton's private eye is presented as sensitive to the role of gender within social structures. Moreover, with the sort of vulnerability that has just been described, she is firmly gendered herself. While in the new millennium Kinsey's open vulnerability and sensitivity are no longer the prerogative of female PI's, in 1982 such character traits were still exclusively associated with femininity (at least in the world of private investigation). Apart from this, Grafton has her heroine display knowledge that even now is still gendered. Although Kinsey herself tells us that she is strictly a blue jeans and blazer person (to the point that she owns only one single dress), she exhibits a gendered knowledge that reminds us of Miss Marple: 'She was wearing . . . a pale mauve sweater, which she must have knit herself since it was a masterpiece of cable stitches, wheat ears, twisted ribes, popcorn stitches, and picot appliqué' (23). Finishing off this image of woman-disguised-as-PI Grafton has Kinsey occasionally shave her legs, an act we do not immediately associate with Spade or Marlowe, let alone Mike Hammer. Much more clearly than Muller, Grafton undermines the traditionally masculine, gendered nature of the PI and replaces it with an ambiguous identity that emits contradictory gender signals. This low-key liberal feminism finds support in a plot in which utterly selfish, predatory males destroy a number of (relatively) innocent women. More in general, although Grafton is clearly not a radical feminist and is not much concerned with larger social structures, what may be called the evils of patriarchy, and more in particular the patriarchal abuses within the family, constitute recurring themes in her work.

Finally, although Kinsey is without family – at least until *'J' Is for Judgment* (1993), in which she discovers that there actually are family members she has never been aware of living not too far from Santa Teresa – she is not without a stable social network, central in which are her 81-year old landlord and the also none-too-young owner of the restaurant where she often has her meals. As several commentators have pointed out, the arrangement suggests another departure from the classic format in that Kinsey would seem to have found substitute parents. Like Sara Paretski's V.I. Warshawski she has built an immediate social environment that serves to give her the necessary emotional support. In the wake of Grafton and Paretski a good many female PI writers have created such small private communities for their protagonists, until in the course of the 1990s female PI writers deviated even further from the traditional format and began to make the PI's immediate family, more in particular her mother, part of her world. While in 1994 Sally Munt could still claim that an extensive search did not yield any PI's with immediate family (Munt, 167), now we have Sandra West Prowell's Phoebe Siegel, Sandra Scoppettone's Lauren Laurano, S.J. Rozan's Lydia Chin, Martha C. Lawrence's Elizabeth Chase, and a whole lot of other female PIs whose mother is a force to reckon with.

By the time of *'M' Is for Malice*, fourteen years onward, Kinsey has not really changed. She is only 35 now (which situates the novel in 1985), still lives in the same converted garage (renovated after a bomb attack), but now has $25 000 in a savings account. As those savings already make clear, she has drifted even further away from the standard PI format into middle-class security. Grafton, who now gives the impression that she knows exactly where she is taking her heroine, has her own up to her conservative leanings with just a shade of self-mockery:

> At heart, I'm a law-and-order type. I believe in my country, the flag, paying taxes and parking tickets, returning library books on time, and crossing the street with the light. Also, I'm inclined to get tears in my eyes every time I hear the National Anthem sung by somebody who really knows how to belt it out. (*'M'*, 243)

Compared with her early self, the mid-nineties Kinsey is far more open, has more insight into her deeper motivations and is a good deal more self-confident. Perhaps the novel's central statement is the one Kinsey makes to her one-time lover Dietz (their relationship begins in *'G' Is for Gumshoe* (1990)) who turns up out of the blue and whose presence spells no good for her equanimity: 'People have rejected me all my life. Sometimes it's death or desertion. Infidelity, betrayal. You name it. I've experienced every form of emotional treachery there is' (*'M'*, 96–7). A little later she asks herself a question to the same painful effect: 'Why does everyone end up leaving me? What did I ever do to them?' (111). Kinsey is aware that as a result of this deep sense of rejection she is 'into caution and control' (56) and has 'developed a neat trick for shutting off [her] feelings' (109).

The private eye's independence is shown to be the product of emotional trauma, and is not the self-willed autonomy that must guarantee distance and objectivity. This insight has been building ever since Kinsey's discovery, in *'J' Is for Judgment*, that she is not completely without family. Thinking about her newly found relatives, she has there 'felt a sudden shift in perspective' that enabled her to 'see ... what a strange pleasure I'd taken in being related to no one. I'd actually managed to feel superior about my isolation' (*'J'*, 142). In fact, the private eye has as much 'need for love' as the rest of us, and if Kinsey does not immediately embrace love – as here with Dietz or in her reluctance to engage with her newfound family – it is only because 'the instinct for survival and the need for love [are] at war' (*'M'*, 137).

It is this sense of rejection that feeds Kinsey's recurring identification with the rejected and downtrodden: 'Amazing how quickly someone else's problems become yours' (152), which of course confirms the long-held suspicion that the classic PI's involuntary empathy with society's losers has a similar basis. In what Kinsey again somewhat ironically describes as 'battling against evil in the struggle for law and order' (2) her personal needs thus come together: the detached involvement of a private eye working on a case allows her to identify with one or more victims of negligence or crime while she can still keep up her defenses.

'M' Is for Malice strips these defenses away. Hired to find a missing person, one of four brothers who disappeared almost twenty years ago and is now wanted in connection with an inheritance, Kinsey must afterwards face up to the fact that in finding and taking him home she has consigned him to his death. She has, as a matter of fact, been manipulated into doing so: the murderer has destroyed the will that disinherited him and under the older will he shares in the inheritance and must be found. As the murderer tells Kinsey in the final scene: 'You did all the work for me. I appreciate that' (368). What is even harder to accept is that his murder is the result of an awful mistake: the murderer acts in the mistaken assumption that before his disappearance the long-missing brother has ruined the life of her sister and, indirectly, her own life too. The fact that her grievances are so real – *'M' Is for Malice* is another Grafton book in which the social structures that privilege males are indirectly put in the dock – and that the real culprit, one of the surviving brothers, is an egocentric coward, is an extra twist in this tale of tragic ironies.

In the brief time that she has known him, the murdered brother, a man of rare gentleness, has made an unforgettable impression on Kinsey. His goodness, simplicity, and trusting attitude have easily penetrated her defenses. His death is a deep loss which first triggers what are either brushes with the supernatural or else very powerful emotional states – 'I struggled to make a sound. I would have sworn there was a presence, someone or something that hovered and then passed' (236) – and then leads to a catharsis in which she comes to terms with every loss she has ever suffered:

> The tears I wept for him then were the same tears I'd wept for everyone I'd ever loved. My parents, my aunt. I had never said good-bye to them, either, but it was time to take care of it. I said a prayer for the dead, opening the door so all the ghosts could move

on. I gathered them up like the petals of a flower and released them to the wind.' (372)

Grafton's sense of tragic irony turns *'M' Is for Malice* into a deeply serious crime novel in which for her heroine the personal and the professional become inextricably interwoven. In a sense, the murdered man's loss is Kinsey's gain: his death, and perhaps also her instrumentality in his fate, allows her to accept the past and the losses she herself has suffered. His death, and the subsequent death or suicide of his killer, also drive home a somber message. The heartless and the worthless survive, with an increased share of the loot, while the good and the victimized, who are not accidentally female or female-identified, go under. If Kinsey has made a difference, it is a difference for the worse. We are far removed from the mind-boggling exploits of Sharon McCone and her massive self-preoccupation. But we are in a place that makes us stop and think.

Sara Paretsky and V.I. Warshawski

Sara Paretsky's private investigator V.I. Warshawski has right from her debut in *Indemnity Only* (1982) been an exceptional case. Tougher, acutely sensitive to (especially male) slights, and a good deal more short-tempered than either McCone or Millhone, she represents the classic urban spirit of the private investigator that is almost wholly lacking in McCone's early adventures – except for the physical attacks, *Edwin of the Iron Shoes* is almost 'cozy' in atmosphere and tone – and that only occasionally animates Millhone. Although Warshawski's urban attitude is in one sense wholly in accordance with the novels' setting, the city of Chicago, it also conflicts radically with Chicago's 'mythic masculine image' (Willett, 107). Warshawski is a woman who is in the business of laying claim to an exclusively masculine role in masculinist territory. As a result, the resistance she encounters is of another and much fiercer sort than that faced by her California sisters.

Warshawski, who resolutely refuses to divulge her first names because she hates to be condescended to, especially by men, is a lawyer who once was 'with the Public Defender', but who has given up the job because, as she tells us, '[t]he setup is pretty corrupt – you're never arguing for justice, always on points of law' (*Indemnity Only*, 156). Wanting to do 'something that would make me feel that I was working on my concept of justice, not legal point-scoring' (156), she has drifted into detective work by doing a favor for her friend Lotty Herschel. In a later novel she tells us that as a public defender she used to feel as if she had 'just helped worsen the situation' while as a private investigator, provided that the truth in a case has been established, she can actually 'feel as though [she has] made some contribution' (*Killing Orders*, 77). Like the classic private eye of the Marlowe–Archer tradition, Warshawski is motivated by the urge to establish truths and by a deep commitment to the socially disenfranchised: the poor and the powerless. Since Warshawski operates within a forcefully articulated liberal feminist framework special significance is given to the powerlessness, even if they do not qualify as poor, of women.

Such a classic moral mission requires an equally classic independence. In *Indemnity Only* Paretsky, far more radically than either Muller or Grafton, immediately sets out to establish a fiercely guarded independence for her heroine. Warshawski's attitude leads to a characteristically tense atmosphere in her very first interview with the client whose decision to hire her will ultimately be his undoing, to the first of many clashes with the police, to a dangerously tough attitude vis-à-vis a mob boss (for which, after upping the ante by kicking him in the crotch, she is severely punished), to the habitual deployment of one-liners and wisecracks that either keep people at a distance or put them in their place, and so on and so forth. In the classic PI mode, Warshawski antagonizes the three major players in the private eye's world: client, police, and criminal element. In fact, her 'I seemed to be alienating everyone whose path I crossed' (62) pretty well sums up her relationship with the outside world. Warshawski's habitually prickly attitude takes on more of an edge with every novel until in *Guardian Angel* (1992) she stops ironizing herself and reaches the point where any sort of opposition leads to savage anger, to a complete loss of control of a temper that at the best of times has a pretty short fuse. (In *Tunnel Vision*, the novel that followed *Guardian Angel*, Paretsky keeps her heroine on a tighter rein, apparently aware that Warshawski's tantrums – 'I was still shaking with fury, pounding my right fist against my thigh' [*Angel*, 322]; 'Fury had me so in its grip, I could barely see' [431], and so on – had begun to undermine her credibility.

Since an independent attitude is only genuinely admirable if it involves some sort of sacrifice, Paretsky repeatedly emphasizes Warshawski's chronic lack of funds and, that other standard feature of the classic PI novel, the shabbiness of her office, which comes cheap because the Wabash El virtually runs over her desk. More importantly, in every single novel Warshawski is punished for her independence. If some thug does not try to kill her she is at the very least severely abused, so that visits to the hospital become part of the standard repertoire. Like so many PIs, she suffers for our sins.

Paretsky thus takes care to place her heroine squarely in the mainstream of PI fiction, although clearly at its white collar end: Warshawski has a degree in law from the University of Chicago and is an opera buff (as if the interest in opera is a bit too much it is compensated for by something more down-to-earth: an alleged fascination with the exploits of the Chicago Cubs which, however, fades away in the course of the series). More interesting than the echoes of the classic PI tradition however, is the way in which *Indemnity Only* explores new territory. Apart from the controlling factor that we are dealing with a female protagonist whose outspoken feminism never allows us to forget it, there is, first of all, Warshawski's preoccupation with her long dead Italian mother. That preoccupation, coupled with her references to her also deceased Polish father, establishes the sort of family background that the classic PI novel avoids, in order to present the investigator as a free-floating moral force. The importance of family is underscored in Paretsky's second novel, *Deadlock* (1984), in which the case develops out of Warshawski's investigation of the apparently accidental drowning of a cousin, and in the third one, *Killing Orders* (1986), which has Warshawski start an investigation at the behest of an aunt. Perhaps we should not take this too seriously. As Stephen Knight has pointed out, this 'personalising of the case ... is a recurrent motif in private eye stories' because it 'prevents the hero acting as a mere agent, a tool whose labour is divided from his own interests, and so this pattern rejects the normal relations between employer and employed to realise ... a notionally self-controlled personality' (Knight, 1980, 160).

Still, family members keep popping up (a long-lost aunt is added to the roster in *Burn Marks,* 1990), and it is not implausible to see Warshawski's vivid memories of her long-dead mother and father and these admittedly sketchy family relations as an early manifestation of the vastly increased interest in family in recent crime writing by women. In fact, one may legitimately see Warshawski's friendship with Lotty Herschel and her later relationship with her septuagenarian neighbor in family terms (see Vanacker for an insightful discussion of both Millhone's and Warshawski's relations with older men, and women). In any case, Warshawski's friendship with Lotty goes deeper and is more sustaining than any of her erotic involvements. Needless to say that in her sexual life Warshawski displays the same sense of independence that governs her investigative career, effectively claiming another male prerogative for herself.

What from the beginning of her career has truly distinguished Paretsky from the classic PI tradition – and, incidentally, also from the many newer female PI writers who, in for instance the matter of embedding the PI in a family situation, have taken things further than she has – is her sheer ambition. In novel after novel Paretsky convincingly takes on the sort of crime that is seldom fully worked out in PI fiction. The criminals are often familiar enough: union bosses, shipping moguls, bankers, corrupt police officers, but also, and less familiar, prominent members of the medical profession and exalted representatives of the Catholic Church, whose involvement with the Banco Ambrosiano is at the center of *Killing Orders*. A Warshawski case may build from something as seemingly trivial as the unexplained withdrawal of a loan approval by a local bank (*Tunnel Vision*), will then take us past assault and murder, and will eventually always arrive at white-collar crime and its insidious, tentacular character.

Not content to simply expose the union bosses, corporate officials, and so on, at the top of the criminal chains of command that Warshawski brings to light, Paretsky shows us in detail how each particular fraud is worked. Judging by the novels, she seriously researches her subjects (which is perhaps what one should expect from someone with a Ph.D. in history) and in any case succeeds in integrating complex professional information into the PI structure. In so doing she has created a variation upon the genre that preserves its action-driven format while it transcends the limitations imposed by the generically restricted field of operation of the traditional PI. Paretsky is one the few writers in any of crime writing's diverse traditions who consistently confronts the organizational crime – corporate, union, professional, or otherwise – that hides behind the glittering façade of the contemporary urban agglomeration. According to Paretsky herself, it is this ambition that has made her opt for a series character: 'I find that [Warshawski] gives me the opportunity to look in depth, and over time, at issues of law, society and justice. I wouldn't be able to explore these as effectively in a stand-alone thriller' (Paretsky 1992, 60).

Still, the fact that in Warshawski's Chicago this sort of crime, and the corruption that it breeds, are endemic does not mean that Paretsky is much given to analyzing its origins. As a consequence, the Warshawski series does not add up to the social indictment that one might expect, at least not in this particular sense. True enough, again and again bankers, captains of industry, politicians and other prominent members of today's ruling classes are exposed as suave, well-educated, and ruthless thugs. But although Warshawski clearly has left liberal leanings – a point I will elaborate below – we do not find the sort of analysis of corporate capitalism that could conceivably follow from that perspective. For Paretsky, white-collar crime would seem to have no social roots, or if it does, then only in a paradoxical way: crime would seem to be the way in which those who in terms of assets and influence already belong to the happy few seek to increase or, as the case may be, maintain their status. Time and again, Paretsky's high-placed criminals turn out to have been motivated by greed and considerations of social prestige. Although it would not be too hard to connect this sort of motivation with the competitive individualism that is at the heart of the capitalist economic dispensation, Paretsky gives no sign of seeing things this way. Every now and then Warshawski seems to come close to an indictment of capitalism's executives as a class: 'Corporate egos are a much more disagreeable feature of the job than the occasional thug' (*Guardian Angel*, 396). However, such judgments have an esthetic rather than a moral base, witness the term 'disagreeable'. Warshawski primarily objects to the elitism and macho arrogance that derives from an unfortunately well-founded sense of power, but not to the system that has created that power in the first place. What we have in the Warshawski series is what George Grella has memorably called 'a quasi-Marxist distrust of the wealthy' (Grella, 111), a distrust that is of course one of the hallmarks of the classic PI. To say this is to emphasize the extent to which Paretsky continues the tradition. As we will see, she is very much aware of this.

Twelve years after her debut Paretsky published her eighth V.I. Warshawski novel, *Tunnel Vision* (1994). Warshawski is very recognizably herself and Chicago has not changed all that much either, especially not in the corruption department. At the same time, however, *Tunnel Vision* is in many ways superior to Warshawski's first adventures.

This has to do with the fact that Paretsky is both less and more ambitious with regard to her heroine: less ambitious in the sense that Warshawski is weaker and more vulnerable than she used to be, more ambitious in her attempts to come to grips with the social reality through which Warshawski moves.

In the early novels Warshawski is fearless – witness the kick in the crotch of the mafia boss in *Indemnity Only* – and virtually indestructible. Although Paretsky is careful not to overemphasize Warshawski's prowess and in so doing makes her at least superficially credible, not all of her heroine's exploits can bear much scrutiny. Neither can some of the crimes that Paretsky serves up. In the 1984 *Deadlock*, for instance, a fifty-million-dollar ship is blown up in order to block the only lock between Lake Superior and the lower lakes that can handle thousand-foot freighters, affecting shipping for at least a year. All of this so that a shipping magnate who has neglected to invest in thousand-footers can win back his share of the market and thereby recoup his fortunes. (Paretsky's acceptance of capitalism as a natural fact is illustrated by the fact that the shipowner who uses the law of scale to get an edge on the competition is such a sympathetic character that he gets the highest endorsement of all: after initial suspicion Warshawski sleeps with him.)

In *Tunnel Vision* both Warshawski and the crimes she stumbles upon in the course of her investigation have gained in credibility and thus in seriousness. What is more, Warshawski, although never a free-floating moral intelligence, now operates within a far denser social context than in her first investigations. As a result, her feminism, which in the early novels primarily takes the form of an attitude and of off-hand references to matters that to earlier female writers were unmentionable (the way she keeps track of her period, for instance), is now much more in the foreground as an integral part of her life. We see her sitting on the board of a battered woman's shelter – 'what energy I have for volunteer work goes to women's programs' (*Tunnel Vision*, 12); are reminded that she worked for an abortion underground in her undergraduate days; follow her in her attempts to keep a homeless woman from being separated from her children, and hear her say 'It's what they get for not believing women's stories' (390) after the police have acutely embarrassed themselves. Furthermore, in involving Warshawski with an all-female contracting firm, with an old law school acquaintance who turns out to be an abusive husband, and with the stiff and overly formal Officer Neely who turns out to be a former incest victim, *Tunnel Vision* constantly brings in issues with a strong feminist slant. Apart from this, the novel directs our attention to such widely different political issues as the exploitation of illegal aliens, the violation of the embargo against Iraq (which is the crime that hides behind other crimes here), and, through Warshawski's affair with a black police officer, the problematic nature of interracial relations. As a result, *Tunnel Vision* is the most overtly political of Paretsky's novels.

In other ways too, *Tunnel Vision* is more ambitious than its predecessors. For one thing, it acknowledges Warshawski's limitations as a self-employed private eye. The agribusiness giant whose violation of the Iraq embargo is the source of most of the mischief in the novel goes unpunished thanks to the influence of its US senator–owner. The abusive husband, who also turns out to be guilty of incest, also gets off virtually scot-free. What is perhaps even more difficult to accept is that he has completely repressed all memory of the rape he has committed, so that he is able to feel genuinely wronged by Warshawski's accusations. Paretsky has no illusions about the effectiveness of the PI, male or female, in a corrupt metropolitan environment: 'The books make it clear that after the curtain falls these guys are going to be let off with fines or slaps on the hand or even nothing at all and that those systems will stay in place' (quoted in Walton and Jones, 211). Warshawski too, has to accept the world's imperfections and her own very limited effectiveness: 'When I thought about all the men beating on women, beating on their daughters, beating on each other, I couldn't imagine my own efforts to intervene as anything but futile' (356).

Still, in spite of her limitations, Warshawski undeniably makes a difference: in the course of the novel she saves at least six people from drowning or from being shot. It must be admitted that Paretsky's down-scaling of her heroine has not yet really extended to the latter's exploits. In fact, as this already suggests, her attempts to make Warshawski more plausible result in contradictions. In another instance of this paradoxical mixture of new weakness and old strength, Warshawski, who is now almost 40, has very recently become sensitive to her age and her vulnerable position as a self-employed, almost middle-aged, woman. We are led to believe that as a result her attitude to both long-standing and prospective clients has changed: 'I'm almost forty. I can't afford to get fired' (18). As she herself sums it up: 'Incipient middle age was making me risk-averse. I didn't like that in myself at all' (28). But although she certainly shows more fear and other symptoms of physical distress, such as fainting upon discovering a corpse, than in earlier novels, she is tougher than ever in the sense that she even less than before cares how intimidating the odds against her are.

This is not to say that Paretsky is merely having her cake and eating it too: disingeniously presenting a more realistic, more plausible Warshawski who, if one looks beyond the surface of things, is still the old supergirl. We are dealing with a more fundamental contradiction here, a contradiction that returns us to the mainstream of private eye fiction in which Paretsky's work, in spite of its innovative and even trailblazing character, lies firmly anchored.

Central to the classic private eye novel is the notion that, even if he will not be able to eradicate evil, society is ultimately better served by the morally perceptive and sensitive individual than by any sort of collective agent, such as the police, which, precisely because of its collective nature, is always morally suspect. In *Tunnel Vision*, Warshawski more than ever subscribes to this belief. Again and again, she finds herself in direct opposition to friends and even her lover, police officer Conrad Rawlings, over this issue. She regards everything that smacks of supra-individual, organized action with a fierce, largely inarticulate and unexplained suspicion. So, even if she is now fully persuaded of the limited reach of individual action, she cannot imagine any other course.

In the novel's opening chapters Warshawski, who has discovered that a homeless woman with three clearly undernourished children is hiding in the basement of the condemned building in which she has her office, must decide whether to inform the proper authorities. Even though her old friend Lotty – who cannot be accused of holding a too positive view of official interference – and the other women she discusses the case with remonstrate with her, she keeps resisting: 'The city will come in, send the children to three separate homes, where at least one will be sexually molested. The mother will lose her remaining grip on reality' (11). One of the women asks her, 'Don't you think you should give the system a chance?' But Warshawski, utterly convinced of its depravity or, at best, ineffectiveness, never gives 'the system' a chance. She does not trust the courts – 'How many people are in Joliet who never committed the crime they were convicted of? One? Five? Five hundred?' (167) – and she does not the trust the police: 'they rate themselves by how many people they arrest. The pressure to make an arrest means that age or situation doesn't count. Can't count. So inevitably you end up across a chasm from them: you for mercy, they for justice. You for justice, they for law' (167). Her trusted friend Lotty tells her that she should stop playing God, but Warshawski never shows an awareness of the admonition's implication: the fact that she sees herself as in a (moral) class all by herself. It is this that at the end of the novel forces a separation between Warshawski and her cop lover who, as he tells her, can no longer see her 'plunge ahead without regard for anything or anyone except your own private version of justice' (447).

As these quotations make clear, Paretsky is very much aware of the narrowness of Warshawski's single-minded suspicion of 'the system'. What is more, she offers, by way of Lotty, Conrad Rawlings, and other characters, the alternative view according to which only 'the system' itself can effectively address its own malfunctioning and according to which, in spite of its undeniable shortcomings, the system's rules are still the norm. We have, especially in the relationship between the private investigator Warshawski and the police officer Rawlings, a number of highly interesting exchanges on the traditional PIs' radically individualist habitus. Paretsky handles this very well. A high point is the discussion in which Rawlings lectures Warshawski on the 'illegal search and seizure' she has resorted to in the course of her investigation. Warshawski is stung, realizing that as a self-proclaimed 'progressive' she would never condone similar police procedures. The issue which is raised here, and of which she is obviously aware, is her double standard. She allows herself, as an individual, a modus operandi that is off-limits to the representatives of 'the system'.

It is not easy to determine Paretsky's position in all this. On the one hand, through Warshawski's friend Lotty, Rawlings, and others, she offers sharp criticism of Warshawski's position. As Rawlings tells Warshawski, 'Look, Vic, it's why we have laws and give jobs to people like me to enforce them – so everyone doesn't go buzzing through the streets defining justice however it suits them that morning' (250). On the other hand, Paretsky definitely tips the scales in Warshawski's favor by making her virtually infallible in spite of her self-doubt: almost every hunch, almost every judgment, turns out to be correct. Whatever Paretsky's position, rarely has a private eye writer so intelligently and articulately laid bare the generic restraints upon the private eye's ameliorating power and the pervasive, if not always articulated, melancholy that results from those restraints. Warshawski's almost paranoid suspicion of 'the system' rules out any sort of political solution to the various social problems she encounters in the course of her adventures. Politics is the cause of the problems, not their solution. The only form of collective social action – as distinguished from Warshawski's highly individual brand – that *Tunnel Vision* actually supports, is that taken by the novel's feminists: the women who run the shelter for battered women and the all-female contracting firm. But even here we find discord while, more importantly, Warshawski's feminist friends and acquaintances literally, even if unwittingly, side with the enemy in their attempts to discourage her from pursuing her investigation.

Warshawski will have to save the world all by herself. She may not be the only one around with a genuinely moral vision, but she is the only one who does not compromise. Her lover, Rawlings, accepts the higher authority of his bosses in the force, and Murray Ryerson, the reporter who once again pitches in, must tell Warshawski that his editor has in effect killed the story that would implicate the United States senator. Warshawski firmly stands in that long and essentially Protestant tradition of the American moral radical: alone, battered, but unflinching and absolutely sure of the moral order she defends.

It is not, however, that she is not aware of the futility of that defense or of the price she has to pay. After all, Conrad Rawlings, no longer willing to cope with her uncompromising pursuit of her private moral vision, tells her that their relationship has ended. But the futility of her efforts, paradoxically, does not really matter. In the last analysis, Warshawski is not really out to save the world. Even her 'I spent a month risking my life for some abstract concept of justice' (460), although closer to the truth, is misleading. Warshawski is in the business of living out and protecting her moral vision, and strange as it may seem her victories over evil, small and large, are by-products rather than the major aim of her efforts. In the course of the investigation described in *Tunnel Vision* she self-sacrificially punishes herself – total exhaustion, cracked ribs, losing her lover – in order to maintain her moral purity. No wonder that in spite of the impossibility of effectuating real change, the novel can end on a bittersweet note: 'What else can I say, except that ... champagne flowed like water, and we danced until the pale moon sank' (464). This is the wistful, self-mocking irony of a bone-tired winner. Justice has not been served exceptionally well, the moral cancer represented by the novel's criminal element has not been removed, but Warshawski has passed another moral test with flying colors.

It must be sheer coincidence that the careers of Muller, Grafton, and Paretsky exemplify three major trends in contemporary crime writing and that they exemplify them so well. Muller has taken McCone from her humble origins as a salaried employee to worlds of superhuman effort, of glamor, and of sensation. Grafton has definitely feminized her PI and has used the vicissitudes of investigation to make her PI face emotional traumas that until recently had no place in the PI's life. Paretsky uses her PI to convey a fairly radical, although still decidedly liberal, feminism and to reflect on the PI's role and its moral limitations. Much of this will return in the following chapters, but before we get around to the crime writers of the 1990s we will look first at three male crime writers who date from an earlier era.

3
The Old Guard Continued: Kaminsky, Parker, and Block

Within the field of male crime writing, too, a number of older and already well-established writers, including Elmore Leonard (1925), Ed McBain (1926), Joe Gores (1931), Robert B. Parker (1932), Donald Westlake (1933), Stuart Kaminsky (1934), Joseph Wambaugh (1937), and Lawrence Block (1938), continued to produce good and at times award-winning work throughout the 1990s. In this chapter we will pay particular attention to the work of Parker, Kaminsky, and Block, and specifically the series featuring Spenser (Parker), Rostnikov (Kaminsky), and Scudder (Block).

For various reasons we will not go into the recent work of Leonard, McBain, Westlake, Wambaugh, or Gores, or into the more playful and light-hearted work of Kaminsky and Block, the so-called 'capers'. With *Get Shorty* (1990), *Maximum Bob* (1991), *Rum Punch* (1992), *Pronto* (1993), *Riding the Rap* (1995), and *Out of Sight* (1996), Leonard has undoubtedly been one of the top crime writers of the 1990s. Moreover, the 1990s film versions of most of these novels, as well as of the earlier *Touch* (1988), were box office hits. On top of all this, Leonard received a Grand Master Award in 1992. Still, none of Leonard's 1990s novels is concerned with detection as such – they for the most part feature amiable rogues that walk a thin line between staying on the right and straying on the wrong side of the law. Leonard, moreover, seldom uses recurring characters. McBain, who won the 1998 Crime Writers Association of Great Britain Cartier Diamond Dagger for his 'outstanding contribution to the genre,' tirelessly continues in the 87th Precinct police procedural groove he already set in the 1960s and 1970s. Wambaugh equally persists with his comic inversions of the procedural. Westlake, who in the 1960s and 1970s, and under various aliases, wrote 'serious' crime fiction, in the 1990s has concentrated on 'capers' featuring John Dortmunder, a middle-aged no-nonsense New York burglar. Entertaining and well-written as many 'capers' may be, they so obviously rely on stock characters and situations (Kaminsky's inept Los Angeles private eye Toby Peters getting tangled up with a different movie star in each successive novel, Block's New York antique bookseller Bernie Rhodenbarr committing the most unlikely burglaries) that we will ignore them here. Rare indeed is the invention shown by Joe Gores in the playful resurrection of his 1970s 'DKA Files', a series that originally had a grim undercurrent to it. His 1992 *32 Cadillacs*, for instance, wittily revolves around a scam run by the king of the American gypsies, who fakes mortal illness to defraud an insurance company and at the same time earn himself a brand new pink Cadillac.

'Capers' often explicitly signpost their ironic relationship to crime writing by tongue-in-cheek references to classics and contemporaries in the genre. Typically also, long-running as these series may be, their characters hardly ever age or develop, and the series themselves remain stuck in a time-warp – the 1940s for the Toby Peters series, a timeless present in the Dortmunder and Rhodenbarr novels. In a conversation with Carolyn, the owner of a dog-wash shop who is afraid that Sue Grafton will exhaust the alphabet with her Kinsey Millhone series, Block's Rhodenbarr neatly sums it all up at the end of *The Burglar Who Traded Ted Williams* (1994):

> 'You'll be reading about Kinsey fifty years from now', I told her. *"AAA" Is for Motorists, "MMM" Is for Scotch Tape*. You'll never have to stop. You'll keep on washing dogs and Raffles [Bernie's cat, and another intra-generic intertextual reference] will keep on playing shortstop. And I'll keep on doing what I was born to do, selling books and breaking into people's houses.'
>
> 'And we'll live happily ever after, huh, Bern?'
>
> 'Happily ever *now*', I said, and reached to pet my cat.
>
> (*Williams*, 372)

Stuart Kaminsky and Porfiry Rostnikov

An older author who in the 1990s has significantly expanded his oeuvre is Stuart Kaminsky. The first of his Rostnikov novels, *Death of a Dissident*, appeared in 1981, while *A Cold Red Sunrise* (1988) won an Edgar. Until *Hard Currency* (1995), the series featured a line-up of characters chiefly consisting of Moscow police inspector Porfiry Petrovich Rostnikov himself, and investigators Emil Karpo and Sasha Tkach. In

Hard Currency, Elena Timofeyeva, a new, young investigator, joins the team. *Tarnished Icons* (1996), which was nominated for a 1998 Best Paperback Original Edgar Award, adds yet another team member: Iosef, Rostnikov's son.

Rostnikov is a barrel of a man, weighing 220 pounds. He is immensely strong, an amateur weightlifter, who suffers from a bad left leg, the result of a Second World War injury. Originally, he is a detective in the office of the procurator general of Moscow. However, his unorthodox methods, his disregard for rules and protocol, and especially the fact that he always seems to run foul of the KGB – meddling in what they term 'political' affairs – result in his relegation to the Office of Special Investigations, 'a dumping ground for cases no one wanted' (*Icons*, 16). Ironically, he succeeds in solving most of the seemingly hopeless cases he is assigned.

Emil Karpo is a devoted Communist, and remains so even in the novels set after the collapse of the Soviet Union. For him, 'it was not Communism that had failed ... it was humanity' (*Icons*, 33). Karpo has steeled himself to complete control over his body: he never blinks, needs hardly any sleep, and is impervious to heat or cold. He lives alone, in a one-room flat. His appearance is unusually forbidding: tall, gaunt, extremely pale, with thinning black hair combed straight back.

A constant feature of the Rostnikov series is its interest in Russia's Jewish minority. One of the reasons Rostnikov is distrusted by his superiors, and why he was demoted, is that his wife is Jewish. Early in the series, Rostnikov applies for an exit visa for himself and his family. The visa is denied, and his son is called to arms. In *A Cold Red Sunrise*, Iosef (here spelled 'Josef') winds up in Afghanistan, defending the Communist regime there, and Rostnikov's main worry is that he will receive bad news about his son.

In *Tarnished Icons*, the murder of four men, three of them Jews, is one of the three cases that Rostnikov and his team have to solve. The others concern a serial rapist, and a letter bomber. With its triple plot-line structure, and with the various issues thus addressed, the novel is typical of the Rostnikov series. As in *A Cold Red Sunrise*, in *Tarnished Icons* too the murder case has political implications, as the politically and economically volatile post-Communist Russia cannot afford even the semblance of overt anti-Semitism. The serial rape case touches upon the warped psychology of persons in authority. The third case provides a measure of comic relief, particularly in the collaboration between Karpo and Paulinin, an eccentric scientist working for Special Investigations, and an expert in everything from meticulously conducted autopsies to the most devilishly clever detonation devices, such as those used by the letter bomber.

The three cases come to a head on the same day. If the ironic denouements of the three plot strands of *A Cold Red Sunrise* constitute a scathing comment upon how in the old Soviet system everything was finally reduced to politics, the endings to the three cases detailed in *Tarnished Icons* deliver an equally damning verdict upon the emerging capitalist order of the new Russia. *Tarnished Icons* is the eleventh Rostnikov novel, and for a reader familiar with the earlier volumes most of this instalment's characters, its structures, and its plot lines are somewhat old hat. The way Rostnikov solves his multiple cases, the habit he has of showing up in unexpected places at unexpected times, his ability to forestall the criminals, even at times to guess their very thoughts, increasingly begin to smack of the supernatural. Invariably there is the stage-setting first chapter or section, with Rostnikov and his team off-stage. Then there is the scene with Rostnikov's superior detailing what is at stake in this case as well as in some others presently open. This scene already signals to the reader, who is implicitly made to share Rostnikov's point of view, the deviousness of all governments and their representatives. Next, the team is split up to deal with the various assignments, with regular get-togethers at which to share information. And so on to the various denouements.

By now, characters like Tkach, his wife Maya and mother Lydia, and especially Karpo, with all their little tics and in their often caricatural physical appearance, are overwhelmingly familiar to us. What keeps us reading and caring about these characters are the relationships among them and what happens in their private lives. It is here too that the final thematic unity of each of these novels truly surfaces. The title of *Tarnished Icons* refers to the statue of a wolf, gold and jewel-encrusted. It is the theft of this statue, together with the murder of the dowager baroness who had promised it to the Tzar's Hermitage collection, that led to the 1862 executions with which the novel opens. When in the course of the novel the statue is recovered, it is literally tarnished from having lain buried for more than a century. However, the title also, and rather more pointedly, refers to other 'icons' that have lost their lustre over the last century: Communism, the State, religion, ideologies in general, and authorities in particular.

In such circumstances, only caring relationships between people can offer solace. Throughout the series, this is obviously true for Rostnikov and his wife, and for Tkach and his wife and children. It is also the case with Elena and Iosef, who enter into a love affair, and perhaps something more lasting. Likewise, Tkach's mother and Elena's aunt find a measure of comfort and even guarded pleasure in each other's company, as do Karpo and the mad scientist Paulinin over cups of tea. Perhaps most illuminating, however, is a scene towards the end of the novel in which Karpo goes to meet a 30ish prostitute in a little rundown coffee shop in the center of Moscow.

Throughout *Tarnished Icons* Karpo is perceived by the other characters as verging on the suicidal in the apparent disregard with which he risks his life. The reason for this attitude is that Mathilde, a middle-aged prostitute that Karpo first got involved with on a purely professional basis, but with whom over the years he has developed a genuine relationship, has recently been killed in crossfire between two rival Moscow gangs. The younger prostitute now offers to take Mathilde's place. Partly, she is interested in the money. Partly, however, she does it out of piety to the memory of Mathilde. Karpo does not take up the offer right there and then. If he is interested, he tells her, he will meet her, same time, same place, one week later. When we hear that Karpo has pretty much made up his mind that he will keep the appointment, we know that after all there is a future for him.

As Karpo is easily the most stereotyped figure in the Rostnikov series, and therefore, also the most likely to finally become unbelievable, it is touches like these that keep him, literally, 'alive' to us. Such insights into the inner life of the main characters of the series save *Tarnished Icons* from being just another formula novel. These personal touches also allow us to appreciate how the later Rostnikov novels draw a compassionate panorama of a much-troubled period in a much-troubled Russia.

Robert B. Parker and Spenser

The two 'old' masters that between them have largely dominated the last quarter century of private eye writing featuring a male PI are Robert B. Parker and Lawrence Block. In 1973, Parker's *The Godwulf Manuscript* introduced Spenser, the hard-boiled hero of a series which has remained consistently popular into the 1990s. Almost halfway through the recent *Small Vices* (1997), Susan Silverman, Spenser's longtime companion, tells him:

> You are able to apply the impulse to violence in the service of compassion. Your profession allows you actually to exist at the

> point where vocation and avocation meet. Few people achieve that .... I would not have you change.
>
> (*Vices*, 162)

Opposites meeting in a happy union: this is what the Spenser novels of the 1990s are all about. Spenser himself is an ex-boxer and a gourmet cook, who wields his fists equally well whipping an opponent as the cream to top a dessert. Genderwise, the 220–pound male private eye Spenser, healthy eater and guzzler of brand beers, is offset by the delicate female psychologist Silverman, dainty nibbler and sipper of choice foods and wines. On the PI workfloor Hawk, Spenser's African American side-kick, doubles as a personification of Spenser's 'black' inner self kept in check by a deep-seated loyalty to the 'good white' Spenser.

The deeper similarities between Spenser and Hawk, as well as the role each of the main characters in the series plays in relation to the law, to human society, and to the human psyche, are clearly spelled out when in *Small Vices* Susan and Spenser discuss a man who has just warned Spenser off a case if the latter wants to stay alive:

> 'Do you know who this man is?'
> 'Not specifically', I said.
> 'But you know people like him', Susan said.
> 'Yeah.'
> Susan thought about that for a few moments.
> 'He's like Hawk', Susan said.
> 'Yeah, he is', I said.
> We were quiet. Susan stared off through the doorway where the charcoal gray man had exited. She was slowly turning her barely sipped drink in a small circle on the table top. Then quite suddenly she looked back at me.
> 'And he's like you', she said.
> 'Maybe some', I said.
>
> (*Vices*, 137)

Parker is obviously having his fun here with Freud's trio of id, ego, and super-ego – the latter position being filled by Susan. As Spenser puts it in *Small Vices*, after he has had the occasion to feast his eyes on the more-than-willing and quite gorgeously naked Glenda Baker: 'My id was locked in grim combat with my super ego, and was going to prevail if I didn't get out of there' (172).

There was a time, through *A Catskill Eagle* of 1985, when all these relations still needed to be worked out. In fact, this provided some of the tension and fun, not to say interest, of a Spenser novel. After all, the various cases Spenser tackles are not radically different from what is typical of the hard-boiled detective genre. In fact, they are largely interchangeable throughout: murder, blackmail, missing persons, drugs-dealing, and both left-and right-wing conspiracies.

Susan Silverman first appears in the second novel of the series, *God Save the Child*, from 1974. She gradually comes to play a more important role, as the relationship between her and Spenser deepens. It is her presence, for instance, that turns Spenser from the macho womanizer of *The Godwulf Manuscript* into the faithful lover who keeps saying no to the beautiful women that keep throwing themselves at him – in *Small Vices* there are three: a high-powered lawyer, a forward co-ed, and most particularly a 22–year old aerobics teacher who invites Spenser to her flat where she drops her ankle-length fur coat to reveal her fabulous body clad only in boots. Nevertheless, tension regularly flares up between Susan and Spenser over the question of her independence. Two particularly noteworthy novels in this respect are *A Catskill Eagle*, and *Crimson Joy* from 1988. At the same time, Spenser's increasing self-control necessitates the introduction, in *The Promised Land* (1976), the fourth novel in the series, of Spenser's black shadow, Hawk, who feels free to engage in the strong-arm stuff that Spenser himself, always keeping on the right side of the law in the later novels, can no longer do.

In *A Catskill Eagle* Susan, feeling unable to fully have a life of her own in Boston with Spenser around all the time, has moved to Mill River, a small town in California. In Mill River, she has become involved with a local potentate, Jerry Costigan, who had persuaded her to come out to California to begin with. However, Susan now feels as much crowded by Costigan as she did earlier by Spenser. When she thinks she may want to move again, Costigan blocks her. Susan, unwilling to appeal to Spenser, calls Hawk to her aid. Costigan is waiting for him with a couple of thugs. When Hawk takes care of the thugs, killing one of them, he is promptly arrested for murder. This is when Spenser gets a call, telling him that Hawk is in jail, and Susan in trouble. Spenser flies out to California. Hawk is freed, Susan is rescued. Mission accomplished, the two lovers re-unite in the following terms:

> 'I take it we are together again', I said.
> 'Yes.'
> 'Forever?' I said.
> 'Yes', Susan said. 'Forever.'
> 'Go run your bath', I said.
>
> (*Eagle*, 366)

and

> 'It's like us,' she said.
> 'The champagne?'
> 'You have to pour it so carefully. It's like our lovemaking. Careful, gentle, delicate, being careful not to spill over.'
> I nodded. 'It's sort of like the first time.'
> 'It is the first time', Susan said. 'These two people, the people we are now, have never made love before.'
> 'But will again', I said.
> Susan smiled. 'Practice makes perfect', she said.
> We drank.
> 'Or nearly perfect', I said.
> 'Hell', Susan said, 'we're that now.'
>
> (*Eagle*, 368)

This passage also concludes the novel. Obviously, a lot of this is tongue-in-cheek, and Parker's use of language, particularly the quick repartee, remains an attractive feature of the Spenser novels, as are the references to literary greats (T.S. Eliot and Melville, among others) and famous movies (*Casablanca*'s 'here's looking at you, kid' on pages 83 and 205 of *Eagle*).

At the same time, the serious undertone to the conversation just quoted cannot be denied. Susan obviously also means what she says, and Susan almost always has the last word in a later Spenser novel. If the conversation with which *A Catskill Eagle* ends smacks of smugness, this indeed is the impression subsequent Spenser novels make. Of course, as far as the business of detecting goes, or where physical prowess is concerned, there never was a match for Spenser – or Hawk. Now, however, Spenser and Susan are so confident in themselves and in each other that there is hardly any room left for surprises.

In *Crimson Joy* from 1988, Spenser is called in by the Boston police to investigate a number of murders, in each of which a black woman in her forties is bound, gagged, and then shot in the vagina, a red rose being left as the killer's signature. Because the investigating lieutenant has received a letter, supposedly from the killer, in which the latter claims to be a cop, Spenser is called in as a neutral agent. When a red rose is left in the hallway of Susan's house, it becomes clear that the killer is probably one of Susan's patients. For her own safety, Spenser wants Susan to reveal what she has learned from her patient. She refuses, bound by her professional oath of secrecy. Spenser then arranges for protection for Susan, which she only grudgingly accepts: 'To have my autonomy violated by the Red Rose business is nearly intolerable', she said. 'And to have you or Hawk here watching over me' – her face tightened as she said it – 'is very bitter' (*Joy*, 120). The murderer indeed is a patient of Susan's – a man warped by his mother's possessive love. In the final chapter – presented in italics, like some other short chapters in which the thoughts and actions of the killer are reported 'offstage' – the murderer commits suicide on his first night in jail. Before this, however, Susan and Spenser have made their peace:

> 'I always liked you and me', I said, 'but this time had such potential for us being a mutual pain in the ass that I especially admire us because we weren't' .... 'It was a charged situation', she said. 'You telling me what to do in my profession and me telling you what to do in yours. And both of us a little worried about our autonomy.'
> (*Joy*, 288)

By the mid-1990s, the time of *Small Vices*, all these worries have evaporated into thin air. When Spenser fears that the man who has contracted to kill him might also be a threat to Susan, she immediately accepts around-the-clock protection from Spenser, Hawk, and a couple of friendly police officers. Moreover, when Spenser is shot and barely escapes with his life, Susan moves herself, Spenser and Hawk to California for a ten-month period of revalidation for Spenser. Needless to say, he bounces back in greater shape than ever. Whatever tension there is between Spenser and Susan in *Small Vices* arises from a very different source. Susan wants to adopt a child, preferably a small baby. Spenser, to say the least, is not over enthusiastic about the prospect. The plot of the book proves him right.

Small Vices is all about the death, presumably murder, of Melissa Henderson, a wealthy young student at an exclusive girl's college near Boston. The man arrested and convicted for Melissa's murder is Ellis Alves, a young black rapist and ex-prisoner. Alves's lawyer hires Spenser to try and exonerate her client. Sure enough, Spenser soon finds evidence pointing away from Alves, while Alves himself definitely seems to have been framed. The prime suspect now becomes Melissa's former boyfriend, Clint Stapleton, a 'Taft University' graduate and soon-to-be tennis pro. This is when Spenser is warned off, first by a couple of thugs, whom he easily beats off, then by 'the gray man' we met in an earlier quotation from the novel, and who obviously is a hired killer.

Upon confronting Clint and his parents, a rich New York couple, Spenser feels something is wrong. This is confirmed when he is shot at by the gray man, who later succeeds in gravely wounding him. Almost a year later, when he has recovered, Spenser goes after his assailant and discovers that he had been hired by Clint's father. In a confrontation between the police, the Stapletons, and Spenser, Clint confesses that Melissa died accidentally during a sex game they were playing. His father bought off the investigating officer, and had Alves framed.

Although Parker, like almost everybody else in the writing business, over the last decade has unwaveringly adopted a politically correct stance, fortunately with him this is never over the top. In *Small Vices* Spenser upholds the law, including the equality of all Americans before the law, but this does not blind him to realities. He is, for instance, quite aware that Alves is a decidedly unpleasant and unsympathetic character. Maybe, it is insinuated, everyone would have been better off if Alves had stayed in jail, including Alves himself, who without a doubt is headed there again before long. There is even a good deal of moral discussion with regard to the plight of the Stapletons, and we are asked to consider whether what Stapleton senior has done might at least be understandable as the act of a concerned parent. To leave it at this, though, is to miss a major point.

Clint Stapleton in the end is glad that all has come out, not so much because now his own conscience is clear, but more importantly because it breaks his father's hold over him. Clint's resentment is rooted in his position as an African American adopted by wealthy white parents. The resolution to this particular family drama that Parker presents makes a powerful point on the level of society – particularly American society in the age of multiculturalism. Parker underscores this by making the relationship between Spenser and Alves remotely mirror the Stapleton family situation.

On the level of the plot of *Small Vices*, and of the relationship between Susan and Spenser, the message is equally clear. It is further underscored by the visit of a friend of Susan's, who brings along her nine-year-old daughter Erika. The least we can say is that the visit is not a success. Here, though, is also where we can see that Parker is stacking the deck in favor of Spenser. Erika is the kind of child no one would want to have visit, and to use her as an instrument of deterrence, making it a good deal more difficult for Susan to adopt a child, is simply not fair. This becomes even more blatant if we compare the 'bad' examples Clint, Erika, and to a certain extent Alves, to their good counterparts: Spenser's fosterson Paul Gioacomin – who makes a brief appearance in *Small Vices*, for no other apparent reason than precisely that of balancing Clint – and Susan's dog Pearl. If it seems farfetched to name all these in the same breath, this is precisely what Parker does in the final scene of the book. Spenser and Susan speculate on whether Spenser would hire someone to kill in order to save his son, or whether he would rather do the killing himself.

> I put my arm around her and she leaned her head against my shoulder. 'But since we don't have a son, and won't, I guess the question is moot.'
> 'We have Paul', she said softly.
> 'True.'
> 'You'd kill someone to save him.'
> 'Yes', I said.
> 'And we have Pearl.'
> 'A son and a daughter', I said. 'No need to adopt at all.'
> Susan laughed softly. Pearl looked up at the sound and wagged her tail. And we stood together like that as night fell and the river ran.
> (*Vices*, 326)

Susan does not get the last word here. She merely assents to Spenser's sketch of the ideal family, and that ideal family is precisely what they already have. The same thing goes for everything else in the Spenser novels of the 1990s. In the conversation from *Small Vices* we quoted initially, Susan asserted that she 'would not have [Spenser] change' (162). The last scene of this same novel, frozen in the night, frozen in time, shows that Spenser and his band have indeed become impervious to change.

Indeed, Spenser himself seems to have become arrested in time. In *The Godwulf Manuscript* he is 37 years old. In *Small Vices* he and Susan are supposed to have met some 20 years ago, which actually tallies with the real time elapsed between the publication of *God Save the Child*, in which Susan made her debut, and *Small Vices*. This would make Spenser at least 57 years old at the beginning of the latter novel, and 58 at its end. However well-preserved a male specimen Parker may be, the physical feats he accomplishes in *Small Vices* would be hard to credit even in the case of a much younger man. To a reader of the entire Spenser series, then, Spenser in the later novels becomes totally unbelievable or he must be accepted as an eternal 45 year old, which again adds to the impression of timeless stasis. Perhaps that is why Parker at the end of 1997 surprised with *Night Passage*, his first crime novel ever – except for the two unfinished Raymond Chandler manuscripts he completed – to have as its hero not Spenser (after 24 novels that do), but a new protagonist, Jesse Stone, and a new setting, Paradise, Massachusetts. In 1999, Parker ventured even further into new territory, introducing a female private eye – Sunny Randal – in *Family Honor.*

Lawrence Block and Matt Scudder

If in the late 1970s and throughout the 1980s it seemed as if Parker had succeeded Ross Macdonald as the preeminent writer of serial private eye novels, in the 1990s it looked as if he had been edged out by Lawrence Block. Whereas Parker won no major awards in that decade, in 1994 alone Block received two Edgars – Best Novel for *A Dance at the Slaughterhouse* (1992), and Best Short Story for 'Keller's Therapy' (1993), a Shamus – Best Novel for *The Devil Knows You're Dead* (1993), and the Mystery Writers of America Grand Master Award. Parker's Spenser was a run-away hit from the publication of the first novel in the series, *The Godwulf Manuscript*, in 1973. Lawrence Block's Matthew Scudder debuted almost simultaneously with Parker's Spenser, in 1976, in *In the Midst of Death*, and appeared in four more novels in the late 1970s and early 1980s, yet only gained popularity and critical recognition starting with *When the Sacred Ginmill Closes*, from 1987.

Perhaps it is fitting that Scudder only really fully came into his own in the 1990s. Spenser is obviously in possession of a hard-boiled self-confidence and power, both physical and verbal. At the same time, he has a conspicuous *savoir-vivre* in matters of food, interior decoration, and literature. His relationship with Susan is easy, yet also caring. He goes out of his way to not be patronizing to her. He is not reluctant to raise or discuss matters pertaining to the relationship between the sexes. Yet, through all this, Spenser continues in his ultimately always vindicated self-assurance. As such, he projects the optimism of an earlier age, one that – specifically in its male impersonations – still thought itself on top of things. Scudder in many ways is a much diminished Spenser, reflecting the uneasiness and uncertainty of a later age – again, particularly from the male point of view. This reduction shows in all those instances in which Spenser's and Scudder's circumstances are at first sight much alike.

Both Spenser and Scudder work as private investigators. Both men are ex-police officers. However, whereas Spenser is a legitimate investigator, Scudder does not hold a license and whereas Spenser's going private is a conscious decision inspired by his uneasiness with institutional hierarchy, Scudder resigns after accidentally killing a small Hispanic girl during a shootout, and then drifts into private investigation. Spenser works out of a well-appointed office, and lives in a well-appointed flat, in the center of Boston. He is a connoisseur of wines and foods. Scudder lives in a rather shabby room in a very modest hotel on New York's West Side. A heavy drinker even while still on the force, Scudder became an alcoholic after the fatal incident that led to his resignation. In *Eight Million Ways to Die* (1983), which won a Shamus Award, Scudder joins Alcoholics Anonymous, and becomes a teetotaller. Visits to AA meetings are a regular feature in all the later Scudder novels, as is the continuing lure of the bottle, and the struggle to fight it off. That is why Scudder prefers to meet his clients in a coffee shop. If he ever enters a bar or a saloon while on a job, it is not without heavy misgivings. For meals, he has something sent up from a neighborhood restaurant, or eats on the go.

Spenser has his Susan, Scudder has Elaine; both relationships for most of both series can be described as living-apart-together. Susan, though, is obviously Spenser's love-of-a-lifetime, as he is hers, regardless of any affairs either of them may have had previous to their teaming up. Elaine, on the contrary, is a call girl, who throughout most of the Scudder series, even while she is having a continuing relationship with Scudder, goes on seeing clients. Scudder knows this and accepts it, even if he is not happy about it. He himself abandoned his wife and two small children upon his resignation and has occasional pangs of guilt about this. Moreover, in *The Devil Knows You're Dead*, although he has no intention of leaving Elaine, and against his better judgment, he gets involved with the young widow whose husband's death he is investigating. In *A Long Line of Dead Men*, from 1994, he still occasionally goes to see this woman.

Spenser easily mixes with criminals, both high and low, organized and (so to speak) self-employed, but always keeps his moral distance, refuses to shake hands with them, and generally puts them down even while availing himself of the information they can offer him. He certainly never befriends them – with the one exception of Hawk. However, Hawk's devotedness to Spenser exonerates him and his actions, and certainly if these happen to be of service to Spenser. When occasionally a particularly worthwhile adversary presents himself, who by definition then has to be almost – but not quite – as good in all matters physical and intellectual as Spenser himself, the former is carefully demonized, as when the 'real self' of the hired 'gray' killer in *Small Vices* is said to be a 'Satanic energy' (*Vices*, 321).

Scudder also has his underworld contacts, most prominently Mick Ballou, 'the butcher', saloon owner, robber, and killer. Ballou takes his New York underworld nickname from his father's trade. When on a 'job', he always wears a butcher's apron and always carries a meat cleaver. He regularly attends Butchers' (early morning) mass, especially after a killing. Scudder is well aware of Ballou's way of life. Still, he will not pass moral judgment on Ballou. In fact he considers him to be a friend, and someone to discuss metaphysical – and particularly religious – problems with, pretty much on a par with Scudder's AA mentor Jim Faber. If anything, Scudder is aware not so much of what morally separates him from people like Mick Ballou but rather of what binds him to them.

In *A Dance at the Slaughterhouse* Scudder calls upon Ballou to accompany him to a meeting with Olga and Stetner, a couple of arms dealers and snuff movie producers. When a fight erupts, Ballou uses his meat cleaver to kill Stetner. Scudder himself shoots Olga, even though she is not putting up any resistance. She, however, was the driving force behind the snuff movies that got Scudder on the case to begin with, and he apparently feels that she impersonates an evil that deserves to die. At the same time, and however twisted and perhaps morally objectionable, this is also Scudder's way of assuming responsibility for whatever is wrong with a society that produces monsters like Olga and Stetner, and for acknowledging society's need for people like Mick Ballou, who live by a code of honor if not by that of a law that would not have been able to touch Stettner and Olga anyway.

Scudder has his African American sidekick too. Unlike Hawk, though, who has been present throughout most of the Spenser novels, TJ is a late addition to the Scudder novels. He makes his first appearance in *A Dance at the Slaughterhouse*, where he acts as informant from the black and teenage drugs and sex circuit, particularly around Times Square, and he fulfils the same function in subsequent books. TJ provides some comic relief in these later Scudder novels, particularly through his inventive use of language. Such relief is indeed welcome because, although the Scudder novels never become dull or heavy-handed, they are pretty serious, if not actually grim.

Like most contemporary crime novelists, Block not only offers suspense but also reflection on topical social issues. Next to arms deals and particularly pornography, *A Dance at the Slaughterhouse* for instance forcefully focuses upon the plight of young runaways, and upon their vulnerability to peddlers in drugs, sex and violence. *The Devil Knows You're Dead* raises the issues of incurable disease, suicide, and the role chance plays in one's life or death, or in the choice of one's partner. It also discusses the practices of certain United States government agencies, like the Internal Revenue Service, to use and reward inside informers on tax dodgers. *A Long Line of Dead Men* poses the question of who is considered useful in our society and who is not, and how these things are determined.

Of course, Parker's Spenser novels also address these and similarly topical issues. *Crimson Joy*, for instance, reflects upon the psychological scars left by the possessiveness of parents and their sexual abuse of their children, and *Small Vices* looks at interracial adoption, and the different treatment rich and poor can expect from the American judicial system. The difference between Spenser and Scudder lies in the degree of personal involvement Scudder feels with the various cases he engages in. Though Spenser and Susan in *Small Vices* discuss the possibility of adoption for themselves, the reality of this option remains remote, and is ultimately – and predictably – rejected. Scudder, on the contrary, is really personally affected by the cases he engages in. In fact, this personal involvement often threatens to wreck the precarious, and always provisional, stability he has struggled so hard to gain. At the very least, it forces him to face up to some ugly truths about himself.

In *A Long Line of Dead Men*, for instance, Scudder is investigating the mysterious deaths of a number of middle-aged members of an informal men's club, and comes to wonder what he himself, at 55, has to show for his life. This in turn leads him to worry about whether he should get an official private detective license, and a regular office, so as to earn more money. As Elaine points out, this is partly also brought on by the fact that in the previous novel, *The Devil Knows You're Dead*, Scudder and Elaine have decided to move into a new apartment together. This apartment is bought with Elaine's money. She has invested wisely what she earned as a call girl, and owns some real estate. Scudder, however, feels he is not pulling his weight in their relationship. Finally, in *A Dance at the Slaughterhouse* Scudder has to make some very hard decisions concerning his personal responsibilities for the life and death of others, and for the proper functioning of society. Block here comes close to privileging private over public morality, and to condoning taking the life of some morally corrupt, but legally untouchable, criminal in order to preserve a higher morality. This is also the novel in which Block comes closest to joining the trend in crime writing, ever increasing since the early 1980s, toward heady cocktails of voyeurism, sex, sadism, and serial murder.

The 1990s Scudder novel that most effortlessly links Scudder's personal, intimate self and the case he is working on is *The Devil Knows You're Dead*. The case in question is much less spectacular than that of *A Dance at the Slaughterhouse* or *A Long Line of Dead Men*. Glen Holtzmann, a 38 year old lawyer working at a smaller New York publishing house, is shot to death late one night at a public telephone a few blocks from his flat. A destitute Vietnam veteran, George, is arrested for the murder. Decisive proof in the eyes of the police is that the shells from the bullets that killed Glen are found in George's jacket. George himself, who ever since Vietnam has been rather confused, is uncertain as to his involvement. George's brother hires Scudder to look into the matter. Scudder soon finds out that it is highly unlikely that George actually killed Glen. When Scudder informs George's brother, however, it turns out that George has just been stabbed to death in the mental hospital he was taken to. The case seems to have reached its end.

Then, however, Glen's widow Lisa hires Scudder. She has found among her husband's possessions a shoebox with half a million dollars in it. All of a sudden numerous reasons for Glen's murder present themselves. Was he a drugs dealer or a blackmailer? Was he involved with male prostitution? After all, the telephone he was killed at is close to a small city park known as a place to get drugs and pick up transvestite hookers. All through the book Scudder keeps chasing possible leads. They all come to nothing, even if he does discover that Glen probably got his fortune by selling information on relatives and employers to the IRS and other such agencies and has caused the failure of various businesses. In the end, though, it turns out that Glen was killed because he had the misfortune to physically resemble a pimp that some other pimp wanted dead. The real interest of this novel is in the development the characters go through, first and foremost Scudder himself who embarks on an affair with Lisa Holtzmann.

At 32, Lisa is a younger self of Elaine, who is in her early 40s, but also of Janice Keane, the third woman in the novel, who is in her late 40s, and whom Scudder used to be involved with before his present relationship with Elaine. Part of the tension in the novel arises from the fact that throughout Scudder and Elaine seem to be edging ever closer to a permanent relationship, in the sense that Elaine retires from her business as a call girl, sells her flat, and buys another one in which she and Scudder will live together. At the end, Scudder even proposes marriage, a subject he and Elaine have been carefully feeling their way around for some time, and which Scudder already more or less casually mentioned to Jim Faber as what he was heading for in *A Dance at the Slaughterhouse.*

At the same time, Scudder keeps silent about his repeated visits to both Lisa and Janice. These visits are very different in nature. With Lisa, the immediate object is sex. Yet, as Scudder himself admits, sex with Elaine is better than with Lisa. For both Scudder and Lisa, then, the sex they engage in is primarily therapeutic. Lisa was sexually initiated by her father, except 'he would never put it in', as she tells Scudder in *A Long Line of Dead Men,* 'because he told me that would be a sin' (*Line*, 80). In *The Devil Knows You're Dead,* Lisa, with her husband dead, is obviously looking for a substitute father. Scudder is equally obviously looking for his own younger self in Lisa, and particularly for the self that was involved with Janice, who is a sculptor while Lisa is an illustrator of books. The need to do so is brought on by the fact that Janice is dying from pancreatic cancer. In fact, she has appealed to Scudder to procure her a gun, so that she can commit suicide when the pain becomes unbearable. Scudder himself is quite aware that by turning to Lisa now he is repeating an earlier stage in his life:

> I didn't need to develop any hidden powers. I had enough brain cells left to figure out what was going on.
>
> Jan Keane had come back into my life, even as she was nearing the end of her own. She and I had almost lived together, had indeed been groping in that direction, then the relationship had instead broken down, and we had lost each other.
>
> And now Elaine and I were in a similar situation, and at a similar stage.
>
> (*Devil*, 122)

Realizing what is going on, however, does not absolve him from the terrible guilt that wracks him – a guilt that extends beyond Jan, Elaine, and Lisa to his broken marriage, his abandoned wife and children, and that even takes on almost cosmic dimensions:

> Afraid things would fall apart, because they always do. Afraid it would all end badly, because it always does. And afraid, perhaps

> more than anything, that when all was said and done it would all turn out to have been my fault. Because, somewhere down inside, somewhere deep in the blood and bone, I believe it always is. (ibid, 123)

Ironically, when Elaine eventually finds out that Scudder has been seeing Jan, she at first is jealous, and then, after she learns of Jan's impending death, feels terribly guilty herself. Elaine never finds out about Lisa, though. Scudder still occasionally goes to see Lisa, and Elaine still has not found out when, at the end of *A Long Line of Dead Men*, Scudder and Elaine finally get married. Or maybe she has, and Scudder knows she does, and maybe they are signalling to one another this understanding in their final conversation in the book, when Elaine tells him to hang on to his old room across the street from where they are now living together:

> 'Nothing has to change', she said. 'Do you hear what I'm saying?'
> 'I think so.'
> 'Your private life is your business. Just don't stop loving me.'
> 'I never have', I said. 'I never will.'
> 'You're my bear and I love you', she said. 'And nothing has to change.' (335)

This passage at first sight may seem to closely resemble one of the conversations between Spenser and Susan in *Small Vices*. However, while in Parker's novel nothing has changed, least of all Spenser, in *A Long Line of Dead Men* Scudder has changed considerably. In particular, he has accepted a number of social responsibilities and commitments he consistently shied away from in the earlier novels in the series. Not only has he entered into a new marriage, he has also decided to apply for a legitimate PI license – though he does not intend to set up a complete office – and he has accepted membership in the 'Club of 31', which has hired him to investigate the murder of some of its members. He even introduces a club member to Alcoholics Anonymous. At the end of this novel, then, Scudder to a large extent has rehabilitated himself and has re-entered the society he withdrew from when he handed in his gold shield as a police officer 20 years earlier.

As far as the emotional depth of its characters is concerned, Block's Matthew Scudder series easily carries the prize when it comes to work produced in the 1990s by an acknowledged and long-established master of the genre. At the same time, the relative equilibrium Scudder has reached in *A Long Line of Dead Men* leaves us wondering about the continuation of the series. Perhaps this is why in the years immediately following its publication Block concentrated on Bernie Rhodenbarr novels. He also fashioned a number of stories about a professional killer named Keller into the book-length *Hitman* (1998). And in *Tanner On Ice* (1998) Block even revived one of his earliest heroes, adventurer and secret agent Evan Tanner, after 25 years 'on ice'.

With *Everybody Dies* (1998), though, Block returned to Scudder. In this novel, which really is one long panegyric on friendship, Scudder helps out Mick Ballou in a feud with some other underworld characters. At the end of the story, it looks as if Scudder might lose the PI license he has recently acquired, but then,

> 'You never needed it in the first place', Elaine assured me. 'What, so you can work for a few more lawyers? And they can bill a little higher for your services? The hell with that.'
>
> 'Exactly my point.'
>
> 'Besides', she said, 'we know the real reason you got the license. You wanted to be respectable. And it's like all those folks on the Yellow Brick Road, baby. You were respectable all along.'
>
> 'No', I said, 'I wasn't, and I'm still not. But the license didn't change anything.'
>
> (*Everybody Dies*, 319)

This suggests that Block is not about to make too many changes to a winning formula. But he has surprised us before. Scudder's often unheroic and self-doubting travels down the mean streets of 1990s New York City have enriched a genre that, particularly in its male version, could do with a little less self-confidence.

4

The Personal and the Regional: New Forms of Authenticity in Female Crime Writing

Private matters

Classic crime writing is notoriously unpersonal: the focus is on the investigation and the private life of the detective is largely or even wholly kept out of sight. The detective's personality and personal qualities of course constitute a factor of some significance. A reservoir of arcane and somewhat dubious knowledge may matter, as S.S. van Dine's Philo Vance and other overeducated gentleman-sleuths have repeatedly demonstrated, or the tenacity that the detective displays may be crucial in the ultimate victory of justice, as is the case with Freeman Wills Crofts's Inspector French. However, the detective's private life and private emotions are deliberately left off-scene. As a result, the classic protagonist as often as not appears as a free-floating intelligence, detached and seemingly objective: a center of thought (or action) that is somehow not bound by time and place. The one exception, at least from the 1930s on, to this strange neglect of the private side of the detective's life is the love that leads to marriage. Dorothy Sayers's Lord Peter Wimsey, Margery Allingham's Albert Campion, Ngaio Marsh's Roderick Alleyn, Nicholas Blake's Nigel Strangeways and a good many others all fall in love with a woman whom they meet in the course of an investigation and whom they eventually marry. Except in the case of Sayers's Peter Wimsey and Harriet Vane, however, these love affairs are decidedly low-key. More importantly, they do not cloud the detective's judgment or interfere with the desired objective stance. They keep the detective's rather inhuman superiority intact.

In the last decades, however, things have changed. As Patricia Craig and Mary Cadogan tell us with regard to police procedurals that feature female detectives, '[b]y the early 1960s ... the profession of policewomen was sufficiently ordinary to warrant moderately realistic treatment in fiction; instead of the comic female with the bullying manner we find a credible girl who suffers from menstrual cramps' (Craig and Cadogan, 228). By the mid-1990s this intrusion of the personal had become one of the major developments in recent crime writing. Initially, this private matter is more or less what we may expect: material that is supposed to give the detective's life a semblance of reality. If we look, for instance, at the debuts of the three most prominent female PI writers of the last 20 years, we see that Muller's Sharon McCone, Paretsky's V.I. Warshawski, and Grafton's Kinsey Millhone are given personal histories that to some extent historically situate them (with Warshawski the most explicitly and Millhone the most sketchily situated), are part of, admittedly small-scale, social networks (from which, as in the classic PI's case, family is still conspicuously absent), and enter into sexual relationships.

In this phase the personal is introduced to create a greater measure of realism. Clearly, crime writing in which the focus is exclusively on the investigation is no longer found adequate. There is, however, not all that much room for verisimilitude in crime writing. Paradoxically, it is especially the detective element in crime writing that does not lend itself all that well to realistic treatment. It is no secret that much of the actual legwork involved in crime solving is hardly inspiring and cannot easily be turned into exciting reading. In the days of Freeman Wills Crofts readers could still take pleasure in the way his Inspector French meticulously put a case together – even when the identity of the criminal was fully known from the beginning – but few contemporary readers are so much interested in the fine art of investigation that they want to have verbatim reports of every interrogation and minute descriptions of what the magnifying glass reveals.

The new realism, then, almost naturally focuses not on the professional but on the private lives of investigators, except in those cases where detailed descriptions of, say, sadistic violence (Lawrence Block) or autopsies (Patricia Cornwell) would seem to offer an interesting new departure (interesting at least to the author, that is). In the course of the 1980s and the 1990s the realm of the personal rapidly expands from private habits, preferences in dressing, culinary taste and love affairs to include family members, usually in the form of parents and/or children, although we also have the occasional brother or sister (the latter in Nevada Barr's Anna Pigeon series – see Chapter 5). Initially it is almost exclusively women detectives who are provided with family members, although there is the occasional male. As often as not, however, that male is a female creation. An early example is Chris Wiltz's Neal Rafferty, an otherwise fairly standard New Orleans PI, who in the very first scene of Wiltz's debut novel *The Killing Circle* (1981) runs over to his parents' house in the Irish Channel for breakfast and has an uneasy conversation with his father. Since then parents, and, more in particular, mothers, have become a regular part of the cast in crime fiction written by women. In 1994 Sally Munt could still declare that she had 'yet to come across a female investigator who actually *has* a mother (most die off in the operator's childhood)' (Munt, 167), but if so, things have surely changed. More than averagely interesting (or irritating) mothers are provided by Janet Evanovich – whose Stephanie Plum also comes with an outrageous grandmother – by Sandra Scoppettone, Martha C. Lawrence, J.J. Jance, Sandra West Prowell, S.J. Rozan, Terris McMahan Grimes, Elizabeth George, and so on (to be fair, not all of them are investigators in Munt's sense.) Fathers are largely absent and if they are around they are usually marginalized by a mother who takes up most of the available space. Lone fathers, like the old bootlegger dad of Margaret Maron's Deborah Kerr, are exceptional. The central place that the mother often occupies sharply distinguishes female crime fiction from its male counterpart in which the mother only rarely appears and is usually dead if she really is a presence (as in James Ellroy). If we did not know that Grafton's Millhone and Paretsky's Warshawski are the first full-fledged female PI's and follow the traditional format fairly closely, we would be able to tell by the fact that their mothers are dead.

Children were until recently unthinkable as part of the detective's entourage, and certainly of the private eye's. Although there is the occasional male detective with a child to take care of – James Lee Burke's Dave Robicheaux, for instance – the introduction of children into the world of the detective is overwhelmingly a female affair and surely reflects the emergence of the working single mother as a substantial social category. (The detective/mother is almost invariably single. If she was not the children would presumably be taken care of by her partner and would remain invisible.) The fact that Jack Early, who in *A Creative Kind of Killer* (1985) introduced a male detective who is trying to raise two teenagers, turned out to be a pseudonym for a female writer (Sandra Scoppettone) comes as no surprise. We find women who combine investigation – as a police officer, private eye, or amateur sleuth – with the raising of one or more children in every imaginable category of crime writing. In the field of the cozy mystery there is Joan Hess's Arkansas bookseller Claire Malloy with her wayward teenage daughter; in the somewhat less cozy amateur mysteries we find Terris McMahan Grimes's Sacramento-based Theresa Galloway and her two children. In the legal thriller we have Lisa Scottoline's Philadelphia lawyer Grace Rossi with her six-year-old Maddie (plus a father who after 30-odd years suddenly makes a reappearance), while in the private eye sphere Valerie Wilson Wesley's black Newark PI Tamara Hayle has a teenage son. Among the female cops we have J.J. Jance's Arizona-based sheriff Joan Brady with her young daughter, Barbara D'Amato's Chicago police officer Suze Figueroa with a young boy, Lynn Hightower's Cincinnati detective Sonora Blair with two children, and so on. In a remarkable development, a number of childless women detectives have more or less pledged themselves to look after a child's welfare, as if their life is not complete without this particular kind of responsibility: Linda Barnes's and Gloria White's private eyes Carlotta Carlyle and Ronnie Ventana are among those who are involved in this surrogate mothering.

All this can still be seen as part of the continuing effort to situate the contemporary detective more realistically, to provide settings, including family settings, that convince us that we are dealing with extensions of the real world. Family settings can, moreover, be quite functional within a crime novel: the domestic element tends to highlight the 'abnormality' of crime, more in particular of violent crime. Needless to say that the presence of children can be easily exploited by writers who go for the less subtle thrills. (Scottoline's Edgar Award-winning *Final Appeal* (1994) offers an hilarious version of this: the man who would seem to stalk her protagonist's young daughter and who is wrestled to the ground by a fearsome female librarian turns out to be the girl's grandfather.)

We can also see this, however, as a further development of the explicit empowerment of the female detective that characterizes the female crime writing of the last decades. We are indirectly told that it is possible for single mothers to hold a demanding job and to raise children simultaneously. These mothers all suffer of feelings of inadequacy and of guilt and often despair of what they have undertaken, but that only gives their empowerment more substance: they are all the more empowered because they overcome the sense of failure and the guilt that so often socially crippled women of earlier generations. Interestingly, a disproportionate number of these single mothers is not divorced but widowed (Jance's Brady, Hightower's Blair, and Hess's Malloy, for instance), as if to suggest that the situation they find themselves in is not of their own making. Less conservatively, other writers give additional status to their protagonist by telling us that they have thrown out a no good, often philandering, husband and take full responsibility for the consequences. The surrogate mothering that I have mentioned can also be seen as a form of empowerment. It is presented as a conscious social intervention and functions both as a recognition of the 'other' (the white, middle class detective takes personal responsibility for a lower class, ethnic child) and as a form of female solidarity (the child is a girl).

In a number of recent books, however, the personal and the professional – in which I include here the activities of amateur detectives – do not simply exist side by side, as is usually the case, but gradually become entangled with each other, leading to often fundamental confrontations and insights. The case becomes a catalyst for personal growth. This fictional strategy can lead to a degree of, or at least a semblance of, authenticity that until recently was impossible in crime writing. We see it for instance in Elizabeth George's *A Great Deliverance* (1988) and, to a lesser extent, in Sue Grafton's more recent *M is for Malice* (1996), both of which are discussed elsewhere in this book. But also in Sarah Andrews's *Mother Nature* (1997), in which geologist Em Hansen is almost drowned by a man who has his hands around her throat and forces her head under water. The experience enables her to relive a similar experience – being kept under water as a child by her bully of an older brother – which in turn makes it possible for her to face the facts about her (formerly) alcoholic mother and to accept the latter's attempts to rebuild their relationship. Andrews's novel in more ways exposes its protagonist to unsettling but liberating experiences. In the course of her investigation Em Hansen pays a visit to a group of women who form a 'drumming circle'. Caught up in the event, Hansen finds a drum and joins the ritual. Much to her surprise the drumming takes over completely:

> I followed it into a dream place where I could feel stronger and more whole. I wanted to cry over its warmth, and found, to my pleasure and relief, that I could. Hot tears rolled down my cheeks, washing away a hurt that had no name. ... Leaping up from the floor I began to scream. I screamed and screamed, and no one tried to stop me. They were all still drumming ...
>
> (*Mother Nature*, 283–3)

In Julie Smith's *New Orleans Beat* (1994), homicide detective Skip

Langdon has an equally cathartic experience when she participates in a witches' ceremony; we are a long way from the rationality of Sherlock Holmes and the cynicism of Sam Spade. In a number of novels featuring a lesbian protagonist – Barbara Wilson's *Murder in the Collective* (1984), for instance – the process of detecting is intertwined with the detective's discovery of her sexual orientation and with her eventual coming out. In Sarah Dreher's *Stoner McTavish* (1985) the detecting process doubles as the gradual falling in love of the engaging amateur sleuth of the same name with the newly wed woman she is supposed to protect from evil. The thriller-like climax of the novel marks an at that point still unspoken declaration, of reciprocal love.

Crime novels in which detectives unravel the mystery surrounding the untimely death of one, or even both, of their parents clearly offer great possibilities for exploring sensitive personal issues. That that potential is not always realized is illustrated, in spite of its Shamus nomination for best paperback original, by Gloria White's *Sunset and Santiago* (1997) in which White's series PI Ronnie Ventana, 20 years after the fact, uncovers the real circumstances of her parents' death in a car crash in San Francisco. White, whose 1995 *Charged with Guilt* was also nominated for a Shamus (plus an Edgar and an Anthony, all in the 'best paperback original' category), glamorizes Ventana's parents beyond belief. The father a high class gentleman-burglar, the mother a stunning and vivacious beauty, they are absolute top of the bill in San Francisco's high society until their tragic death in the mid-1970s. (Curiously, White's descriptions suggest the roaring 1920s rather than the not-so-fabulous mid-1970s.) '"Big, big hearts. ... this city'll never see the likes of their kind of style again",' an old reporter muses (*Sunset*, 192) and to Ronnie herself – who of course has hardly known them – her parents still are 'two brave and noble souls' (314). The accident of course has been premeditated murder and after 20 years Ronnie can still dig up enough facts to tie the killer to the 'accident'. Having nailed the man she is 'somehow oddly at peace for the first time in twenty years' (313) so that in the novel's climactic scene she can find enough forgiveness in herself to save his life when he tries to commit suicide. The dramatic potential of all this remains, however, largely unrealized. What White offers is melodrama and a sort of wistful sorrow.

That it is possible to have real drama and real emotion and to achieve a high degree of authenticity in crime fiction is illustrated by Nancy Pickard's multiple award-winning *I.O.U.* (1991), the eighth mystery featuring Pickard's amateur detective-cum-trust fund director

Jenny Cain. Pickard has claimed that one of Cain's functions is to 'let me use her to honor, but also to experiment with, the amateur sleuth mystery tradition', adding that her protagonist 'gets involved with social and family issues perhaps more often and more deeply than her predecessors' (Pederson, 843–3). In its use of family issues, *I.O.U.* indeed far transcends the traditional format.

By the time that we get to Jenny Cain's eighth case she and her family are familiar characters. She herself is the director of the Port Frederick Civic Foundation, which dispenses 'charitable funds to worthy causes' in Port Frederick, Massachusetts. She is one of two daughters of the town's disgrace, handsome and debonair Jimmy Cain who 20 years before *I.O.U.* opens has fled to Palm Springs with his then 22 year old second wife after bankrupting the once thriving family business. Since Cain Clams was easily the town's largest employer, Cain's standing in Port Frederick has never recovered, just like his deeply embarrassed daughters' appetite for clams ('we still couldn't eat clams without gagging' (14)). Jenny has strongly ambivalent feelings about her impossibly evasive and superficial father, whom she cannot really take seriously. Her feelings about her younger sister Sherry are even more ambivalent and tinged with actual detestation because of the latter's utterly conventional middle-class values and life style. Her mother, finally, has spent the last 25 years in a mental institution, drifting into and out of catatonia. In the Cains' case the nuclear family has rather spectacularly failed to deliver.

I.O.U. opens with Mrs Cain's funeral, which, as is so often the case with funerals, is also the occasion for a family reunion. In the throng after the service Jenny thinks she hears a voice saying 'It was an accident. Forgive me.' 'Forgive me' also turns up in the visitor's book while the florist card attached to one of the bouquets says 'April 10, 1971', a date that roughly coincides with the beginning of Mrs Cain's mental illness. Naturally, Jenny's curiosity is aroused. But the investigation that carries the novel is also motivated by something more fundamental. Her mother's death comes as a profound shock and initiates a process of identification rare in crime fiction. This begins when Jenny lies down on her mother's hospital bed, the day after she has died – 'I tried to feel her body, to melt into my memory of it' (6) – and finds a first climax in the scene in which she goes through her mother's wardrobe: 'Then I slipped out of my funeral dress, my slip, and heels and pulled on my mother's black wool slacks and her black turtleneck sweater. They were classic styles that would never go out of fashion and, what's more, they fit me perfectly' (29). With this identification comes the realization that the circumstances of her life have conspired to rob her mother of her identity. Her death has not put an end to this injustice and the local paper's obituary leads to an angry outburst on Jenny's part: '"... how dare you define her by her former husband, for God's sake. And her father and her grandfathers! And her daughters' husbands! ... Who cares about all of these other people? Where is my *mother*? Who was *she*? What about *her* life?"' (19) Realizing that she herself, too, has never really known her mother and encouraged by the psychiatrist friend who tries to talk her out of a fit of guilty despair, Jenny decides to investigate her mother's life. Moreover, since she is equally ignorant of the circumstances in which Cain Clams went under, she decides to probe its bankruptcy. *I.O.U.* thus becomes a mystery in which the detective investigates the most traumatic events of her own life and returns to her family's past to exorcize her personal demons.

In so doing it also becomes, in its own low-keyed way, one of the most powerful feminist statements the mystery scene has yet produced. This is not immediately apparent, although the novel's drift shows itself fairly early in a scene – which must be pretty unique in crime fiction – in which Jenny has herself examined by an elderly male gynecologist who 'is nearly always wrong about what hurt and what didn't' (73). The interrogation for which the consultation is a pretext leads to a disconcerting revelation: her mother's mental illness has followed immediately upon a hysterectomy that no one has ever told her about. Even more shocking is the discovery that her mother's two pregnancies both had severe after-effects. After Jenny's own birth her mother suffered postpartum psychosis, which led to an extended hospitalization, while after the birth of her sister her mother actually tried to harm the infant and was again hospitalized. In the meantime, Jenny has also found out that her father's mismanagement of Cain Clams was neatly helped along, if it was not actually orchestrated, by a whole network of local business people – his banker friend, for instance, and the owner of the local paper – who took advantage of his lack of business acumen and his naivety to drive him out of business and take over the family firm. Since Jenny has known them all her life and considers some of them to be her friends the world of Port Frederick begins to look increasingly unfamiliar.

In the more or less unbalanced state that results from these discoveries – and, incidentally, from an attempt on her life that she barely survives – she goes to visit her sister, who habitually refuses to hear anything that might be a threat to her peace of mind, and picks a fight that also deserves special mention in the crime fiction annals. Fights are standard fare but fights between two sisters must be rare:

> I broke loose from her and hauled back my right hand and hit her across the face as hard as I could. She gasped and fell again, crying, clutching her right cheek. And then she was on me, hitting my head and chest, kicking my legs, screaming wordlessly at me, and crying. And I was giving it back to her. We fought ... until our clothes were torn and our skin bloodied and bruised, and until we were merely clinging violently to each other and sobbing. (185)

The fight is a sort of turning point. Even though they will never like each other, it more or less clears the air between the two traumatized sisters and prepares the way for other confrontations. In its wake Jenny is able to talk to her father's second wife, whom she has always seen as a detestable gold digger, and discovers, much to her surprise, that the woman is fully aware of the role her father's business 'friends' have played and has married him as much for his sake, in order to protect him, as for her own sake. The most significant confrontation, however, takes place with her father, who perhaps for the first time ever lets down his guard, starts crying and admits his failure as a parent.

These are momentous developments. The most important one, which will lead to another attempt on Jenny's life, is yet to come, and will throw a completely new light on her mother's mental illness. In the Jenny Cain series, which more generally aims for a certain realism, coincidence plays an important role and Jenny is deliberately not molded in the traditional superior mode even if she is faster than most in spotting connections and arriving at conclusions. Through sheer coincidence she discovers that her mother must have been pregnant before her final descent into madness, and that the hysterectomy must have been performed to cover up a botched abortion. This discovery leads to what is easily the most moving, and quietly, but deeply feminist, passage of the novel:

> She was Catholic, raised to believe abortion was a mortal sin. But she couldn't have that baby, no way, not a woman who'd already been hospitalized for psychosis related to child-birth. What if she had the baby, and hurt it, as she had tried to hurt Sherry? What if she had it, and then tried to kill herself? Those must have been the horrible worries afflicting her and paralyzing her. And where could

> she turn for help and counsel – to male priests and a male god and male doctors and her philandering husband, to an entire universe of powerful, controlling men who couldn't possibly understand the anguish growing within her. (221)

As the passage makes clear, Jenny's quest ends in a profound understanding of her mother's predicament as the victim of patriarchal social conditioning. Her mother was a female stranger in a strange male land, as she puts it a little later. As a side effect, her exposure of what really happened to her mother allows her to feel that all her debts are paid and that she is finally free, liberated from an oppressive personal past. In a sense even her mother is now finally free, living on through a daughter who looks like her, and who, more importantly, is the kind of woman she wanted to be but could never be (234).

I.O.U. is a prime example of the successful integration of deeply personal issues into a genre that for a long time has been extraordinarily resistant to such material, at least with regard to the detective, who until recently was not much more than a purportedly neutral, but in reality disembodied, male voice that questioned, hypothesized, and solved. It is not accidental that especially female crime writers, who have led the postwar effort to make detective fiction more realistic, have availed themselves of the possibilities offered by the detective's private life.

Regionalism

In a related development, female crime writers have increasingly moved away from the urban setting of much classic American crime fiction and have started to make use of regional backdrops. In one way or another, all narratives that place their characters in a non-urban, or perhaps even non-metropolitan, setting might be called regional. Francine Mathews's Nantucket; R.D. Meredith's Texas Panhandle; Sandra West Prowell's Billings, Montana; Karen Kijewski's Sacramento; Margaret Coel's Wind River Reservation in Central Wyoming; Nancy Pickard's Port Frederic, Massachusetts; J.J. Jance's Bisbee, Arizona, and a hundred other settings for recent crime novels are all regional. What I have in mind, however, is settings that are more than a mere backdrop and that are introduced for their own sake, to the point where they have a claim on the reader's interest that is wholly independent from the plot that they support. In fact, in some cases the plot is decidedly secondary to its setting. Such novels do of course make specific demands upon the writer: she must have intimate knowledge of the region in question and she must be able to conjure up a convincing representation by means of judiciously selected atmospheric detail, regional idiom, and scenic description (although not all regions boast landscapes that could easily qualify as scenic). Most importantly, if the aim is a representation that will strike us as authentic, she must invest emotion in the picture that she conjures up.

This new regionalism – new for crime writing, that is – is part of the drive towards authenticity that has given us the raw, uncontrolled emotions of Elizabeth George's Barbara Havers (see Chapter 8), of Em Hansen, and the Cain sisters. It offers us authentic, that is, emotionally charged *couleur locale* rather than the sort of schematic background we usually find and that it is only there because crimes do not take place in a geographical and social vacuum. Judging by the critical praise that has been bestowed upon many of its exponents, this authenticity of place is a resounding success. It has indeed led to a good many engaging novels. But the term engaging – which no one would use for the relevations of *I.O.U.* – also points at its limitations. In what follows I will explore those limitations with regard to some examples of the new regionalism, from both the far north and the deep (and not-so-deep) south.

A striking example is *Murder on the Iditarod Trail*, Sue Henry's first novel which in 1992 won both the Anthony and Macavity Awards for Best First Novel. With its Alaskan setting *Trail* is obviously regional. As the work of Dana Stabenow, John Straley, and other crime writers who situate their fiction in Alaska illustrates, it would be difficult to write about a place that is so distinctive and not highlight its uniqueness. What is special about *Trail*, however, is that its setting is not simply Alaska, but a uniquely Alaskan event: the Iditarod, a 1049 mile sled-dog race along a trail of snow and ice that winds its way from Anchorage to Nome. Organized for the first time in 1973, when it took the winner 20 days to steer his dogs to Nome, the Iditarod in the course of the 1980s achieved the status that attracts major sponsors and is now a landmark on the Alaskan calendar. As a bonus for both author and reader, the Iditarod also brings a historical dimension into the novel: the Iditarod initially relived and commemorated one of the heroic events of Alaskan history.

Although formally *Trail* is a crime novel – three participants in the race, so-called mushers, die in engineered accidents and a detective is brought in to find the killer – most of the excitement is generated by the race itself and the extreme circumstances that the participants must face. *Trail* is a rather poor mystery, in fact, but it does not much matter, because there is so much else to capture our attention. The Alaskan winter, for instance, is depicted in all its ferocity:

> the sea freezes out from the shore each winter. As it freezes, the force of the tide, combined with driving wind, cracks and moves the ice, shoving up giant blocks and breaking it apart to expose open water, which then refreezes. Until it gains solidity deep into winter, the frozen sea is frightening, creaturelike, as it groans and barks in its own violent voice. Later, during the most intense cold, it creaks with the tide in deep vibration. (194)

The mushers' constant battle with this unpredictable, hostile force takes up much of the book. Here we have a female participant trying to find her way across a stretch of sea ice in a snowstorm that is so blinding that she has to walk ahead of her dogs:

> Slowly, walking ahead of her team, Jessie found each marker. It grew worse until she finally couldn't see the next one. Stopping the team, she moved forward until she located it, then went back for the dogs. She remembered reading Riddles's account of her perilous crossing in the same kind of weather. It encouraged her, as did the fact that, somewhere to the north, Schuller and Martinson also struggled through the maelstrom. (201)

The Riddles whose account the female musher remembers is Libby Riddles, the first woman to win the race, in 1985. Henry has done her homework: her heroine remembers Riddles because the latter, too, charged alone into an arctic storm on Norton Sound. The actual situation, however, suggests the 1991 race when winner Rick Swenson fought his way through a White Mountain snowstorm by walking in front of his dog team. Drawing on the history of the race and charged by Henry's descriptive powers, *The Iditarod Trail* is a perfect armchair introduction to the rigors of the Alaskan winter and the intrepidity of those who challenge it. With such a setting-cum-subject for her first novel, it is not surprising that Henry's later work lacks *Trail*'s excitement, even though the regional element remains very strong, as in *Death Takes Passage* (1997), which centers around a re-enactment (complete with period costumes) of an 1897 gold shipment down Alaska's Inside Passage to Seattle.

Since this sort of regional writing caught on, virtually every American region of any distinction has had its day of glory in crime fiction. However, of all the regions that have added value for the crime novelist, the south is easily the most popular. The prominence of southern regional writing is illustrated by a number of success stories: that of Sharyn McCrumb's Appalachian or 'Ballad' series, of Joan Hess's 'Maggody' books (situated in the fictitious Arkansas hamlet of Maggody), of Margaret Maron's Judge Deborah Knott novels, Julie Smith's New Orleans-based Skip Langdon series, and so on. Southern regional writing has done extremely well in the award sphere. *If Ever I Return, Pretty Peggy-O,* which opened the Appalachian series, won the Macavity Award in 1991. Its sequel, *The Hangman's Beautiful Daughter,* was nominated for an Agatha in 1993, while the third novel in the series, *She Walks These Hills,* virtually swept the field in 1995, winning the Agatha, Macavity, and Anthony Awards. Julie Smith's first Skip Langdon novel, *New Orleans Mourning,* won the Edgar in 1991. Joan Hess's *Mischief in Maggody, O Little Town of Maggody,* and *Miracles in Maggody* were nominated for the Agatha Award (1989, 1994 and 1996, respectively). Margaret Maron's Deborah Knott debut, *Bootlegger's Daughter* (1993), had a dream start, winning the Edgar, the Anthony, the Macavity, and the Agatha in one majestic sweep. From such heights the only way is down, but the fourth Judge Knott novel, *Up Jumps the Devil* (1996), again won the Agatha. In recent years Teri Holbrook's *A Far and Deadly Cry* has been an Agatha and Macavity nominee for best first novel (1996), while her second book, *The Grass Widow,* was an Agatha nominee for best novel in the following year. Southern crime writing by women is unique in its strength, and in its more daring forms draws on either of two southern traditions: that of the Gothic (as in some of McCrumb's Appalachian books) or that of the backwoods comedy that we find in Faulkner's Snopes novels (Hess's 'Maggody' series, for instance). Southern crime writing is also unique in its breadth, however, and I cannot try to do it justice here. I will restrict myself to a brief discussion of the regionalism of Sharyn McCrumb and Margaret Maron.

Maron's *Bootlegger's Daughter* (1993) introduced lawyer, later judge, Deborah Knott, her father (the former bootlegger in question), an impressive number of family members, and the rural North Carolina setting of Colleton County and the small town that serves as its county seat. Deborah Knott is a likable free spirit and *Bootlegger's Daughter* is an equally engaging novel, but certainly not engaging enough to warrant four awards, including the Edgar. Even more amazing is the

Agatha Award for the novel I will focus on here, *Up Jumps the Devil* (1996). *Devil* opens with the story of a murder which is almost immediately solved and in which Judge Knott plays a somewhat unheroic role. It then proceeds to present, at great leisure, another murder and the various efforts – Deborah's, the sheriff's, and so on – to unravel the mystery. Deborah finally happens to do so, although it is more a case of a murderer wholly unnecessarily giving himself away. The solution is certainly not the result of any sort of detecting. But there is also very little plot to the novel (to the point that we never really know why the second murder takes place). We hear a lot about land deals, about the history of Colleton county, and about the extended Knott family – from the *pater familias*, the old bootlegger (and not inconsiderable landowner), down to his greatgrandchildren. And what we hear mostly has great charm:

> ... there are plenty of us that didn't roll far from the tree and on Wednesday nights, after choir practice or prayer meeting, anybody in the mood for more music shows up at a barbecue house halfway between Cotton Grove and Makeley for a late supper and a little picking and singing with the owner, a second cousin once removed who plays a righteous fiddle. Counting spouses and kids, there're never more than fifteen or twenty of us at any one time, but we flat-out raise the roof when we all get going.
>
> (*Up Jumps the Devil*, 59)

The harmonizing implicit in choir practice and in these musical outings stands for a much larger social harmony to which the various murders that Deborah Knott gets involved in can not seem to do any damage. The secondary role that these murders play in the novel emphasizes this. As a matter of fact, we hear more about the court cases Deborah presides over – usually involving sheepish offenders rather than tough criminals – than about the far more serious crimes that are supposed to generate the necessary suspense. *Up Jumps the Devil* presents a pastoral, just like the quotes from *Informations Concerning the Province of North Carolina, Addressed to Emigrants from the Highlands and Western Isles of Scotland, by an Impartial Hand* that precede each chapter and that supposedly are taken from a 1773 pamphlet that extolled the virtues of the North Carolinian land of milk and honey. The novel is a nostalgic hymn to family values, to an old-fashioned way of life, and to a fast disappearing rural North Carolina.

The subplot of the novel, which involves land deals and development projects, has us asking how long this part of an older dispensation will be safe from the ravages of an ever encroaching modernity – as always helped by the greed of the short-sighted. Here Deborah's father, taking it patriarchally upon himself to act for the best of all, achieves a compromise solution that will at least for the time being keep the world of developers at bay and invisible. Undeniably, Margaret Maron has a strong sense of place, at least as far as North Carolina is concerned. The New York of her Sigrid Harald books never comes to life, just like their heroine, in fact, which suggests that her imaginative powers are tied up with the specific locale of the Deborah Knott series. It will be clear, however, that the deep affection with which she obviously regards North Carolina also has its drawbacks: Norman Rockwell's spirit hovers too close over the attractive *couleur locale* she offers.

With some qualifications the same can be said about what so far has been the high point, at least in terms of awards, of Sharyn McCrumb's Appalachian series. Its first instalment, *If I Ever Return, Pretty Peggy-O* (1990), is a relatively straightforward mystery, with McCrumb effectively manipulating diverse points of view, in which a former folksinger of some note becomes the prey of a stalker after settling in the remote East Tennessee town of Hamelin. *Peggy-O* is a gripping novel with a surprise ending and a strong regional flavor. Hamelin, which lies deep in a river valley right on the edge of a mountain wilderness comes convincingly alive. The emphasis, however, is on the mystery.

In *She Walks These Hills*, published four years later, the emphasis has shifted towards Appalachian Tennessee, its socio-economic structure – if the term is not too pretentious here – and its history. Like McCrumb's other novels, *She Walks* develops several narrative strands, each with its own protagonist, allowing her to bring in disparate perspectives and to create a broad panorama. Central to the plot and to McCrumb's themes is the escape of a murderer who after 30-odd years in prison is suffering from Korsakoff's syndrome and has completely lost his short-term memory. While the con slowly finds his way through the mountains to his home town of Hamelin, the only place he remembers, old Nora Bonesteel, who has the Sight, once again sees the young woman she has seen so often in her 70 years, always running along the same stretch of woodland trace: 'The woman had been running through the woods a long time. Blood crusted in the briar-cut on her cheek. Her matted hair, a thicket of dry leaves and tangles, hung about a gaunt face, lined with weariness and hunger.' (*Hills*, 11) At again another place, a young and aspiring historian prepares to hike along the mountain trail probably followed by a young woman who over 200 years ago had escaped from Indian captivity and managed to find her way home and who is, of course, the woman seen by Nora Bonesteel. In Hamelin itself, we follow the activities at the sheriff's office, seen through the eyes of the dispatcher, later deputy sheriff, who is convinced that the escaped con will make his way home and present a threat to his former wife. Finally, we witness how the host of a local radio show, who more or less turns the con into a folk hero, tries to uncover what really happened and why the unpremeditated murder of a man who according to many deserved to be killed resulted in a life sentence without parole.

This complicated, but neatly managed, set-up allows McCrumb to work out her themes at a fairly leisurely pace while never losing sight of the necessary suspense. Did the escaped convict get a fair trial, 30 years ago? Will he make it home and, if so, what will happen? How, for that matter, will the naive historian fare on his lone hike through the mountains? We are kept waiting until the final denouement. But by that time we no longer read primarily for that denouement but have been captivated by McCrumb's main theme: Appalachian Tennessee and its history. The hiker's trials and tribulations have reminded us that at least some parts of the Appalachians are still as wild and uninhabited as in the Indian times to which the story of the running woman takes us back. The convict turns out to be a member of a legendary outlaw family whose exploits are after almost a century still remembered – and repeated for our benefit. Behind the story of his own violent exploit lies a story of systematic dispossession, of land robbing by an insensitive government and its corrupt agents. The clever trick of a call-in radio show allows McCrumb to introduce more voices and more stories. A case that temporarily distracts Hamelin's tiny police force from its focus on the convict involves 'trailer trash' up in the mountains and exposes its frightening emotional immaturity, leading here to infanticide. We are constantly reminded that we are dealing with the wilder, or at least less repressed, emotions, and the more direct violence of the past. We are in a time warp and because of that the tone is apologetic – except with regard to city folks who live in the sterile present and who therefore have no excuse for doing what they do. McCrumb's Wake County is a magical world. As one old-timer puts it: '"hardly anybody wants to leave. These mountains are more than just a *place* for folks around here. They're part of what we are."'

(226) Because of this magic, attitudes that elsewhere would be classified as pathological are accepted (and described) with great serenity: 'Now, about twenty feet from the nearest door, the sheriff stopped to "hello the house", a custom necessary for the survival of trespassers in the South. You let the householders know you're coming, so they don't take potshots at you for trying to sneak up on them.' (112)

The term magic is not only metaphorical but should be taken quite literally. As we have seen, Nora Bonesteel has the Sight – the woman that she keeps seeing is not a private hallucination but belongs to historical reality. Apart from that, she maintains an older, magical relation with the world: she stops all the clocks in the house where a death has occurred, sets a cup of salt on the windowsill, puts away the jar of honey (so that nobody will eat honey on the day of the funeral), arranges a scarf across the mirror, and hangs on to other customs and beliefs that have been pushed aside by 'progress'. What makes the novel truly magical, however, and in fact makes it leap into magical realism, is that the woman whom Nora Bonesteel has been seeing intermittently all through her life, also appears to the runaway convict and to the hiker and the girl who has run into him and is taking him back to civilization. The woman, too, has the Sight (which in the case of the undead does not really surprise us), telling the convict not to go home, and she extricates the hiker and the girl from a potentially dangerous situation. With these encounters McCrumb purposefully transgresses an ontological boundary and makes Appalachian Tennessee part of the magical realist universe, turning it into a place that might resemble our world but that in unpredictable but essential ways transcends it. As a magical realist region it definitely becomes a place of the mind.

It would be inaccurate to say that *She Walks These Hills* romanticizes the past. McCrumb does not gloss over its terrible injustices and cruelty. However, the novel glorifies the past, presenting it as a time when things were starker, less bland – in a sense more real. The inevitable march of progress has brought affluence but has diminished our inner being, made us unreal, even to ourselves. Expressing this sense of loss in her decision, the convict's former wife leaves her insignificant second husband and their comfortable middle-class home for a permanent reunion with the untamed natural force that she has divorced when he was jailed for life.

The regionalism that in the course of the last 15 years has become an important presence in crime fiction is almost always conservative. It either wants to preserve a status quo that is threatened by current socio-economic developments or go back to an earlier status quo that has succumbed to the pressure of history. We see this even more clearly in those regional novels that feature native Americans, such as those of Dana Stabenow or Margaret Coel. The world of native Americans is under severe and constant pressure and the sympathy of these authors is very firmly on its side. If we look for a moment over the fence we see a similar conservatism in a number of male regionalist crime writers, with some of them taking up a rather nasty stance that is fortunately absent from the work of their female colleagues. Peter Bowen's series featuring the Eastern Montana High Plains country, for instance, invariably sides with the local population in its instinctual suspicion of intellectuals, environmentalists, liberals, and of all kinds of authority, and in its disregard for the finer points of law. In *Notches* (1997) Bowen's protagonist Gabriel du Pré, whose *Métis* heritage is relentlessly romanticized, even resorts to a drastic form of vigilante justice. (The real mystery of the novel is how he discovers the identity of the two serial killers since he does not do much more than tear up and down the country in an old police cruiser which he loves to push up to Formula One speed.) An honorable exception to the rule that this sort of regionalism goes hand in hand with conservative attitudes is the work of James Lee Burke, whose Louisiana bayou country setting (and occasional change of scene to mountain Montana) does not adversely affect the compassion and sense of complexity of his detective Dave Robicheaux.

The conservatism that we see in regionalist crime writing of course does not come as a surprise. Crime fiction has an inherently conservative bias. It should be noted, however, that this conservatism is different from that of, say, the private eye novel. Regional crime writing presents an organic view of society that is completely at odds with the urban anomie that we find in most private eye fiction. That anomie is the natural habitat of the private eye, who would scoff at the organic, and often harmonic, view implicit in regional writing and who would also scoff, at least until recently, at the close family ties through which that harmony finds symbolic expression. With Black female crime writers (see Chapter 12), southern crime writers as a group privilege the family and stress the importance of family ties.

Because of their organic view of society, regionalist novels by female crime writers are regularly classified as 'cozy', hence the preponderance of Agathas among the awards and nominations they have won. Since there is often not much that is cozy about them – as in the case of *She Walks These Hills*, for instance – the label seems strangely inappropriate. Perhaps we tend to overlook their violence for the same reasons that we overlook the violence in the fairy-tales that they resemble.

5
Three Pictures from the Institution: Forrest, Barr, and Hightower

Although it has by no means elbowed the private eye novel out of the privileged position that it has occupied in the field of female crime writing since the early 1980s – witness the fact that excellent PI writers keep on emerging – crime fiction in which the female protagonist works within, rather than outside, the perimeters of institutional law enforcement has for female crime writers become a viable alternative to the PI novel. That institutional environment is not necessarily a police department, although police departments certainly head the list in terms of popularity. Two of the three law enforcers that we will look at in this chapter are members of an urban police force. But the third one is a National Park ranger, while in a later chapter we will discuss Patricia Cornwell's Kay Scarpetta, who as a medical examiner is continuously involved with law enforcement.

Clearly the temper of the times has changed. While 20 years ago the female PI was an almost natural choice for a female writer at the beginning of her career, we now see women writers abandon the almost inevitably adversial outsider position of the private investigator for a (still usually ambivalent) position within an institution that to the first generation of female PI writers – Muller, Paretsky, Grafton – and their heroines was far too gendered and more generally too confining. The popularity of crime novels featuring female reporters would seem to be a related development. Mary Willis Walker's Molly Cates and Edna Buchanan's Britt Montero, although enjoying more leeway than their law enforcement colleagues, are also tied up with organizations that, because they depend on the market, usually do not take a radical view of things and tend to have an institutionalized status.

Much serious female crime writing of the 1990s interrogates the relations between institutional law enforcement, in its diverse manifestations, and its female employees. Those relations range from fairly straightforward identification with its aims and procedures, even if its character is experienced as conservative and homophobic (as in the work of Katherine V. Forrest, which I will discuss below), to a good deal of contempt (as in the case of Nevada Barr's Anna Pigeon, who will also make an appearance later on). In between we find guarded acceptance of the institution and loyalty to the institution itself combined with a constant war of attrition with its male minions, as in Scarpetta's case. Since the institution's rules must be respected the protagonist's freedom of action is inevitably limited. Although we find exceptions (such as Anna Pigeon), the restrictions that come with working within the institution are generally and rather unproblematically accepted. One reason surely is that the institution's rules, not to mention its power, also offer protection and security. A second reason for the apparent ease with which women have begun to feel at home within the institution probably has to do with the fact that what Peter Messent calls the 'fantasy of extra-systemic freedom and authenticity' (Messent, 13) has never been as alluring to female authors as to their male colleagues. The astonishing number of female PI's that are so familiar with the police that they either have, or once have had, a relationship with a male police officer – including McCone, Millhone, and Warshawski – would seem to support this. Even if the female protagonist does not want to work within the institution, her aversion apparently does not extend to its male employees.

In any case, a good many female crime writers of the 1990s have given up the extrainstitutional position of the private investigator and offer us protagonists who perhaps do not feel as comfortable as their male colleagues in their institutional role, but who feel at least comfortable enough to stay and work within an institutional setting. The contrast with all those earlier female investigators who started out on the inside but opted out can hardly be missed. Perhaps the institutional female investigator is less of an example of self-empowerment than the female PI, because she is not self-employed and works within limits set by an overwhelmingly male professional hierarchy. On the other hand, she shows us within a usually realistic framework that females can function more than adequately within such a hierarchy and thereby signals that the institution, and by implication all institutions, has become accessible to determined women. This chapter will follow the law enforcement fortunes of three such women: Katherine V. Forrest's Kate Delafield, Nevada Barr's Anna Pigeon, and Lynn S. Hightower's Sonora Blair.

Katherine V. Forrest's lesbian cop

Off all subgenres that have sprung up in the last two decades of the twentieth century, crime writing featuring a lesbian protagonist has easily had the most critical attention (see, among others, Carr 1989, Cranny-Francis 1990, Klein 1995, Munt 1994, Pykett 1990, Paulina Palmer 1991 and 1997, Reddy 1988), not in the least, one suspects, because lesbian crime writing gratifyingly flaunts that rather grim law formulated by Kathleen Gregory Klein: 'As a variation on the original rather than the primary model herself, the woman detective trails several steps behind her male counterpart. Novels featuring women as detectives in the various sub-genres appear on the market only after the fictional model with male protagonists had proved successful' (Klein 1995, 151–2). True enough, Klein could point to Joseph Hansen's gay detective Dave Brandstetter, who made his first appearance in 1970, but homosexual detectives are too few and far between to have paved the way for what has become such a generally recognized and successful subgenre, that even non-lesbian authors have now created lesbian detectives. (Rather ironically, Laurie R. King, a married mother of two children, has so far picked up the mainstream awards: her debut *A Grave Talent* (1993), featuring lesbian police officer Kate Martinelli, won an Edgar for Best First Novel and more recently *With Child* (1996), another Kate Martinelli case, was nominated for the 'real' Edgar.)

The critical attention devoted to lesbian crime fiction, however, has not been evenly divided over all possible candidates. Some authors, in particular Barbara Wilson, Sarah Schulman, Mary Wings, and, to a lesser extent, Sarah Dreher, have been privileged at the expense of others such as Ellen Hart or Sandra Scoppettone. The reasons are fairly obvious. Wilson, Schulman, and Wings are seen as 'progressive', as contributing to the forging of new lesbian identities, while for instance Scoppettone, whose PI Lauren Laurano wears a 'wedding ring' and thinks of her long-standing relationship with her partner Kip as 'our marriage' (*Everything You Have Is Mine*, 225) is seen as buying into conventional social and sexual relations and hierarchies even if her detective has a female and not a male 'husband'. This lack of interest in Scoppettone – Walton and Jones have very recently been the first to take her seriously (Walton and Jones, 135–42) – is all the more curious since under the name Jack Early she won a Shamus Award for Best First Novel with *A Creative Kind of Killer* (1985). It might be argued that her Lauren Laurano novels are not first rate but neither are Wilson's, whose Pam Nilsen novels suffer from didacticism and are a good deal less innovative than they are usually made out to be, while the adventures of Cassandra Reilly, Wilson's other heroine, are not much more than highly entertaining romps (with a detective who may be different but rather neatly fits the tradition of the lone outsider). In between the overrepresented Wilson and the underrepresented Scoppettone we find Katherine V. Forrest (1939), who has had some serious attention (see Munt 1994, 133–8), but has also been taken to task for rather unquestioningly accepting the 'system' through her protagonist Kate Delafield of the Los Angeles Police Department as well as for the butch position that Kate exemplifies. Admittedly, the LAPD is an unlikely environment for a lesbian, even for one who has served with the Marines. As more than one critic has pointed out, the classic private eye, with his base outside the institution and his traditionally adversarial attitude, offers a perfect role for those, such as lesbians, who are marginalized by the social structure. And even if the PI role is not officially adopted, the outsider position and the strained relations with authority that characterize the traditional PI are a natural fit for a lesbian protagonist, as for instance in Mary Wings's Emma Victor novels. This, however, makes Katherine Forrest's Los Angeles cop all the more interesting, at least potentially. And while Forrest's early novels do not really avail themselves of the possibilities that Kate Delafield's institutional position creates, in her more recent work she has done exciting things with it. I will focus here on *Apparition Alley* (1997), which is not only a very good mystery, but also brilliantly succeeds in weaving lesbian and homosexual themes and issues into its plot.

After having published the first four Delafield books with a relatively small feminist press, Forrest moved to a mainstream publisher with *Liberty Square* (1996). There is nothing incongruous about that move, given the essentially liberalist and reaffirmative character of her work. *Murder at the Nightwood Bar* (1987), for instance, ends with what must surely be one of the most patriotic scenes in all of American crime fiction (all the more curious, by the way, since Forrest was born and raised in Canada): a gay parade in which 'leather clad men on motorcycles bearing American flags flying high on flag poles decorated with colored streamers, c[o]me thundering past' (187). Fortunately, however, Forrest's move to the mainstream has not led her to soft-pedal the message that gays and lesbians have the same rights and are entitled to the same sort of respect as everybody else. As a matter of fact, her second mainstream book, *Apparition Alley* (1997), presents that message louder and clearer than ever before.

Apparition Alley is Forrest at her very best. The only false note is the cloying psychotherapist Kate Delafield has to see after having being wounded in the line of duty in the very first scene. The novel is taut and gripping and is steered by a highly ingenious plot involving a police officer who frames himself in the hope that the inevitable investigation of the shooting he has apparently been involved in will expose the incompetence and malice of his colleagues. The officer in question, Luke Taggart, is convinced that his gay partner – police partner, that is; Taggart is not gay himself – has been killed by two of their colleagues in order to prevent him from coming out and, what's worse, from publishing a list of gay and lesbian members of LAPD. Taggart's hope is that the internal investigation that his framing himself has set in motion will expand, leading to an investigation of the killing of his partner and to the conviction of his murderers.

Forrest ingeniously inserts Kate in this intrigue. In the novel's opening scene, Kate is accidentally hit by friendly fire during an arrest. (There is a certain irony in the fact that a woman who served with the Marine Corps during the Vietnam War – another indication of unlikely patriotism – is hit by friendly fire in Los Angeles.) Taggart and Kate have never met but having seen his partner's list he knows that she is a lesbian and suspects that the gunshot that she has taken in her shoulder was not accidental but had to do with her lesbianism – a suspicion that eventually will turn out to be unfounded. Much to her surprise, not to mention chagrin, for Taggart has a reputation as a 'rotten cop', he asks her to be his representative at his Board of Rights hearing, a request that she cannot very well turn down. Taggart needs a detective who will see through the whole set-up and Kate, as he tells her, is as good and incorruptible as they come in LA, but he also hopes that Kate's lesbianism will make her an ally – if she is not one already. Because her name topped his dead partner's list he, again wrongly, suspects her of having been the latter's main source of information. Kate does not relish being used, for whatever purpose, and Taggart's amiable deviousness in his relations with her drives her crazy. But she gradually comes to see him for the morally serious and stubbornly loyal character he is: he owes his unenviable reputation to his refusal to cover up for corrupt colleagues and he knows very well that his convoluted attempt to get at his partner's murderers through a frame-up will destroy his career.

Forrest uses Kate's involvement in Taggart's case to present some serious dilemmas. Although lesbianism has become more or less tolerated by the LAPD, Kate has no illusions about the Department's acceptance of homosexuality: 'A grudging, contemptuous suffering of lesbian police officers had become the order of the day, just as it had when women had first fought their way onto street patrols and into the detective ranks in the early seventies, but for gay male police officers, absolutely nothing had changed.' (*Alley*, 63) But even if she has no illusions about the Department, she still feels bound to it by a deep loyalty that expresses itself in dramatic terms right after she has been shot and finds herself surrounded by anxious colleagues: 'My God, my whole family is here, she thought, tears leaking from her eyes. My whole police family is here.' (5) Although towards the end of the novel she comes to see this family as more than a little dysfunctional, she never rejects it or stops seeing it in those terms. Interestingly, in this post-Rodney King and post-O.J. Simpson novel Forrest cannot quite ignore what the whole world has witnessed with regard to the LAPD, but she firmly plays it down: 'From [Kate's] observation, racism was no more present in LAPD than it was in the rest of America, and ... Mark Fuhrman at the O.J. Simpson trial had been the same sickening news to her, and to every police officer she knew, as it had been to the rest of the country'. (62) Katherine V. Forrest is not much of a radical and neither is her heroine.

As a result, Kate can sympathize with Taggart's goal – solving the murder of his partner – but not with his radical methods: '"You're no longer a cop of any kind, Taggart, you're an anarchist."' (212) Taggart's radicalism is alien to the conservatism that we always sense in Kate. This is fully demonstrated in the dramatic move with which the novel ends. Taggart is not only after the murderers of his partner, he is also engaged in a self-styled crusade to end LAPD's homophobia. Assuming that Kate has found the list of gay and lesbian LAPD officers that his partner had assembled, he tells Kate that by publishing the list she '"can still put a stop to all the homophobe cops waiting in the weeds for any police officer that dares to say they're gay"' (209). In a subtle move, Forrest lets Taggart be seconded by one of her readers' old acquaintances. (Forrest, by the way, usually has Kate's views challenged by other characters.) Maggie, the owner of the Nightwood Bar, also urges Kate to make the list public: '"Every time we say it's okay for someone to stay in the closet, we practice our own version of homophobia. We agree that there's something wrong with us, we agree with all the people who claim we're inferior, we agree with all their excuses to despise us and persecute us, we agree that we deserve to hide our true selves away from anybody who doesn't like us."' (219) Kate, however, cannot bring herself to force people to come out in this way and in the very last scene of the novel we see her deleting the list, unread, from the computer on which she has found it. In a classically liberalist act, the right of individuals to make their own choices is deemed more important than what is arguably a group interest. That right is so sacrosanct that Kate never even looks at the list. Her horizon is limited to individual choice: 'May all of us on that list manage to find our own way out to the sunlight' (248).

It is not clear whether Forrest shares this liberalist individualism with her heroine. She has, in any case, not made things easier for Kate. A perhaps not quite plausible but brilliant twist has forced us – and Taggart – to revise all our assumptions. Kate has not only seen through Taggart's ingenious little scheme – which is, after all, exactly what he wanted her to do – but she has also found the real murderers. Taggart's partner has been killed by two of his brothers who, after he had told them about his homosexuality and his intention to come out, decided to kill him to protect their deeply religious mother and the family name – or the other way around. This is the real shock of the novel and it makes the idea of an LAPD 'family' somewhat less implausible. What is important here, however, is that Taggart's partner would in all probability still be alive (albeit despised by his brothers) if his homosexuality would have been made public by somebody else. The murder is supposed to keep a lid on things, which in the course of things it fails to do. If Kate is aware of the fact that the murder is a strong argument against secrecy she does not show it.

In the final analysis opinions may vary on the question whether Kate, although clearly endowed with a strong feminist sensibility, is an effective feminist, that is, effective apart from the obvious role model she offers. This is not only due to her liberalist perspective, it is also the result of the fact that Forrest stays fairly close to a familiar format in the creation of her heroine (needless to say that there is an intimate relation between liberalism and that format). Kate exemplifies that familiar attitude of the American hero: antipolitical individualism. Forrest's choice of terms suggests that she supports her heroine in the latter's contempt for politics: 'Kate sighed. The police intrigue and pressure that Girardi had described were some of the reasons why Kate had not wanted to advance beyond detective-three' (88–9). Elsewhere we read that '[p]aperpushing and politics were not her idea of police work' (170) and find her referring to the 'political whirlpools of LAPD' (239). What Kate either cannot or does not want to see is that what she describes as politics is undoubtedly by far the fastest and easiest way of getting gays and lesbians accepted by the force. In the end, her individualism and her desire to see the LAPD unit in which she works as a family, that is, as something organic rather than accidental and constructed, leads her to adopt a traditional atttitude that is politically ineffective. So, paradoxically, while the institution, which in *Apparition Alley* is presented as interested in and capable of self-criticism, makes political action fully possible, Kate refuses to avail herself of the opportunities it offers. What should be stressed, however, is that Kate's distaste for politics is not necessarily connected with Forrest's mainstream leanings (if the mainstream was antipolitical there would be far fewer politicians). Kate's antipolitical stance is tied up with a certain kind of individualism, not with individualist liberalism *per se*. Let us hope that Forrest will allow her protagonist to see that politics can address certain issues more effectively than individual action and that structural change is a whole lot easier effectuated through political pressure.

Nevada Barr's Park Ranger

> '... the impetus to go solo derived less from John Wayne than from Greta Garbo: she wanted to be alone.'
>
> Nevada Barr, *Endangered Species*, 309

The individualism that characterizes Kate Delafield is of course central to crime writing and to American crime writing in particular (see Knight 1980 for a brilliant discussion). As often as not, and especially in the private eye mode as developed by Raymond Chandler, it has a strong romantic slant (as Knight also argued) that is not necessarily part of the individualistic tradition. The investigator, private or otherwise, has 'a limitless capacity for pity', as George Grella put it with regard to Ross Macdonald's Lew Archer (Grella, 107), is as sentimental as he is cynical, and is intensely loyal to everything and everyone that in his private universe is deserving of such loyalty. Many contemporary women investigators fit this originally male bill: Kate Delafield, but also Kinsey Millhone, V.I. Warshawski, Karen Kijewski's Kat Colorado, Linda Barnes's Carlotta Carlyle, Dana Stabenow's Kate Shugak, and so on.

A fascinating exception is Nevada Barr's Anna Pigeon, who made her debut in the multiple award winning *Track of the Cat* (1993), the first novel of a series that is superior to everything else in what one might call environmental crime writing, that is, crime writing in which the natural world and a determined minority's attempt to preserve it in its natural state plays a major role. This ecological concern would seem to be a typical 1990s theme. Judith van Gieson's first ecological novel, *Raptor*, situated in Montana and involving rare birds and their survival, was published in 1990 and so was Karin McQuillan's debut *Deadly Safari*, which focused on the destruction of Africa's wildlife. In 1991 Les Standiford's *Spill* featured a major ecological threat to Yellowstone National Park (plus a heroic park ranger) and Lee Wallingford's *Cold Tracks* introduced a National Forest security officer with his partner and the glories of an Oregon National Forest. By the mid-1990s conservationism and its potential for crime writers ('conservation threatened by ruthless business interests' in its myriad versions) had established itself as a serious option, leading to variations such as the geologist heroine in Sarah Andrews's Em Hansen novels. It is tempting to see this development as paralleling the emergence of regionalist crime writing. Both subgenres draw on a conservative impulse, an anti-urban and, more generally, anti-modern spirit that seeks to retreat from the contemporary world.

This desire to retreat is, in any case, what motivates Barr's Anna Pigeon, who is, however, by no means a simple conservative even if she would seem to share many conservative impulses. Anna, though, is much more of a loner and much more genuinely independent than the conservative individualist we find in much environmental crime writing and who, like Kate Delafield, can usually be situated in the tradition of romantic individualism. Whereas Kate does not question her role in the institution – the LAPD – and even feels intense loyalty towards her immediate colleagues, Anna Pigeon's only loyalties are towards her older sister, a New York City psychiatrist, and the natural world. The institution she works for – she is officially a 'Federally Commissioned Law Enforcement Officer', in actual practice a park ranger with a mandate to enforce – only commands her loyalty in so far as it tries to preserve that world. Some of her first adventures center on preservation. In *Track of the Cat*, set in Guadelupe Mountains National Park in southwest Texas, she saves the local mountain lion by discovering a criminal set-up that will soon lead to the animal's extinction, while in *Ill Wind* (1995) she puts an end to the illegal dumping of toxic waste in Colorado's Mesa Verde National Park. In the other novels the natural world, even if not in immediate danger – curiously enough, the 1997 *Endangered Species* does not live up to the promise of its title – is always overwhelmingly present. Anna's deep affinity with the world of nature invariably leads to breathtaking descriptions, even of nature's more lethal manifestations, such as the cold and wild waves of Lake Superior (*A Superior Death*, 1994) and a North California mountain firestorm (*Firestorm*, 1996). In Barr's work nature writing vies with crime writing for our attention. This is not to say that it is not adequate on the crime and mystery side. On the contrary, the mysteries are quite good, if not downright excellent in her more recent books, which avoid the implausibilities of the first ones. *Firestorm* and *Endangered Species* even offer clever variations of the isolated-country-house murder, *Firestorm* because the murderer must be one of a small group stuck on a mountain top, *Species* because the scene is set on a small and virtually uninhabited offshore island. If the suspense is fine, the novels' evocations of nature are simply breathtaking and all the more convincing because they are offered in a spirit of loving realism (Barr was and perhaps still is employed as a park ranger, depending on her sales), a deep-seated feeling of kinship mixed with ironic detachment. Anna Pigeon may at times be almost one with nature but she feels no urge to romanticize it: 'Evidently [the vultures] did not feed at night. Anna was grateful. Not withstanding her appreciation of the food chain, she wasn't sure she could've stood a night listening to its graphic demonstration' (*Track*, 18).

Barr's novels sharply contrast the unknowable, dangerous, but essentially pure and healing world of nature with the fallen world of man. Neither Barr herself nor her protagonist have much patience with that world's various shortcomings. We have the self-serving indifference that allows man to thoughtlessly destroy his natural environment; the self-centeredness and greed that lead to crime; the inefficiency, stupidity, and, at times, corruption of the system (the National Park service, in this case); and the powerful self-delusions that legimitate man's destructive domination of our planet. *Track of the Cat* presents such a major self-delusion in what is surely one of the most arresting openings crime writing has ever seen:

> There hadn't been a god for many years. Not the nightgown-clad patriarch of Sunday schools coloring books; not the sensitive young man with the inevitable auburn ringlets Anna had stared through in the stained-glass windows at Mass; not the many armed and many-faceted deities of the Bhagavad Gita that she'd worshipped ... in her college days. Even the short but gratifying parade of earth goddesses that had taken her to their ample bosoms in her early thirties had gone, though she remembered them with more kindness than the rest.

> God was dead. Let Him rest in peace. Now, finally, the earth was hers with no taint of Heaven.
>
> (*Track*, 1)

God's death, however, has in Anna's view not conferred his powers upon man. And that, too, is strangely liberating:

> In her twenties she'd trusted [her mind] to guide her, answer her questions, make the right choices. Somewhere in her thirties she'd lost faith. She saw her mind now as a moderately useful, if highly overrated organ, one susceptible to chemical storms, hormonal droughts, and the phases of the moon.
>
> (*Endangered Species*, 274)

Anna Pigeon's perspective, then, is deeply colored by a pervasive skepticism regarding man, his endeavors, and his institutions.

Given this view of life, she is not an avid socializer. In fact, part of the attraction of her job as a park ranger is that it takes her to remote corners of mainland USA (and in *Species* even to an offshore island) where fellow human beings are definitely thin on the ground or, even better, wholly absent: 'Backcountry patrol – days in the wilderness – those were the assignments Anna lived for, times it made her laugh aloud to think it was being called "work" and she was being paid to do it' (*Superior*, 63–4). Allergic to hypocrisy, Anna does not see herself as any better than her fellow humans so that her often acute dislike of them extends to herself. She has no illusions regarding herself and is fully aware of her lack of genuine kindness, of the impulse to share, her weakness with respect to alcohol, the fact that she is capable of committing crimes, even murder, under the right circumstances (in *Track* she indeed commits murder by omission). Her virtues are entirely related to the natural world: 'She'd never been cruel to an animal and she wouldn't litter' (*Track*, 121). This sober view of herself makes the job all the more attractive. In the wilderness or, as the case may be, in the nighttime ocean (*Species*) she can lose herself, can 'feel deliciously small, magnificently unimportant', and can cleanse herself, can try to create such a distance between herself and the social world that 'the toxins of humanity would finally work completely out of her system, leaving her mind new again' (*Track*, 130).

In *Track of the Cat* Anna's skepticism is more or less attributed to the death of her husband in a Manhattan traffic accident a dozen years before. Unable to get over this disaster she now, in her late 30s, still keeps the urn with his ashes around. Her all-encompassing sense of irony, however, has prevented her from completely turning the urn into a shrine. In *Ill Wind,* where she keeps it in a drawer among her underwear, we find her reflecting with a sort of loving irreverence that her husband was always happiest when he was in her pants. Still, when in *Endangered Species,* with Anna now in her early 40s, his ashes are flushed down the toilet by a seven-year old child who has accidentally spilled them on the floor and has no idea what they are, she feels a strong sense of relief. More in general, *Species* suggests that Anna, without really being aware of it, is ready to begin a new life. The material tie with her husband is finally gone, even if it takes the innocence of a child – the only character to be romanticized in the series – to effectuate the break; she has her hair cropped short for the first time in her life; and she tells the offbeat FBI agent in whom she has ever since *A Superior Death* had a mild emotional interest that she will not give up her lonely existence in order to join him in the city (which, by the way, is just as well, because he has in the meantime come under the spell of her sister).

As her decision with regard to this as far as she knows potential partner suggests, Anna Pigeon's solitariness is a way of life, as is her pervasive skepticism. It is not a pose or an affection, as is so often the case with the cynically sentimental private investigators that we are familiar with, and is so deep-seated that it can only have been reinforced, not caused, by her husband's death. The fact that Anna has never wanted children and that her sister shares her skeptical, if not cynical view of things points in the same direction ('"Woman to woman love? Politically correct. Low risk of disease. High chance of getting grant money for artistic endeavors"' (*Track,* 91)). Anna can occasionally appreciate company, but only up to a point and never for too long. Barr subtly works Anna's ambivalence towards human company and communication into the structure of her novels. Although Anna has a strong bond with her sister and regards her as the only person she can open up to, she only does so by phone. We never see them together. Similarly, after in *Ill Wind* it becomes clear to Anna and Stanton, her FBI man, that they feel attracted to each other, we never again see them together. In *Firestorm* he comes out to California when he hears that after a raging wild fire she is trapped on a freezing mountain top, but they never meet. They only communicate by radio and any consummation is resolutely kept offstage. Likewise, in *Endangered Species* there is only telephone contact between them. This set-up is all the more effective since in both *Firestorm* and *Species*

Stanton gets chapters of his own. The novels follow him and present his perspective and in so doing emphasize that the final meeting with Anna does not materialize.

Anna Pigeon is the most private and asocial of female detectives, a semi-recluse who has not only fled the social world but who even within her own organization, at the edges of the civilized world, avoids all competitiveness and seeks to be marginal. But her occasional desire for self-effacement *vis-à-vis* a natural world that she feels infinitely inferior to, does not extend to her confrontations with her peers: other humans. She is intensely independent and, as might be expected from one who has so little affinity with her fellows, intensely tough. In *Track* she leaves a killer to die from exposure and frames his accomplice who otherwise would get off scot-free, while in *Species* she herself attacks the man who has just tried to kill her and then watches approvingly how one of her colleagues takes him on: 'Rick was causing Schlessinger unnecessary pain. Police brutality. Anna was all for it' (366). But of course her independence can also take her the other way. In *Firestorm* she allows a far more sympathetic killer to disappear into the wilderness where she knows he will easily survive. As these examples make clear, Anna is only nominally a law enforcer. The law she enforces is her own. The institution, in her case the Park Service, is almost unnecessary. It serves to legitimize her actions, but is as much a liability as an asset. In *Tracks*, for instance, her superiors refuse to take her suspicions seriously and another Park Service employee turns out to be the killer. For all practical purposes, Anna functions as an independent investigator, in all senses of the word.

That independence is also a perfect vehicle for a gender awareness which is always close to the surface: 'Gender had robbed Anna of a childhood spent throwing and catching spherical objects' (*Species*, 358). This gender deprivation does not prevent Anna from sabotaging a murderer's getaway by removing the spark plugs wires from her boat (*Superior*) and from otherwise intruding in what the culture has decreed male territory, but it is never far from her mind. Barr clearly uses her protagonist to present a light-hearted and ironical but insistent and effective feminism. Seeing two men fight in *Firestorm*, like 'two moose in rutting season', Anna feels 'desperately tired' and wishes 'she had a cattle prod or a can of pepper spray' (286). Already in *Track*, she has rediscovered the joys of 'girl-talk':

> Much-maligned girl-talk: sweethearts and hair, new clothes and getting your colors done, movies and books and music and gossip.

> But not the backbiting and undercutting that stung like a canker through all levels of the Park Service. Real gossip; gossip about why people did the bizarre things they did, said the outrageous things they said, believed the improbable things they believed. Gossip to ferret out what people must be thinking, what made them tick. So much more satisfying than the mannish 'I told the so-and-so, I said by God' variety that had buffeted Anna's ears for so long.
>
> (*Track*, 112–13)

More in general, the company of women is the one redeeming feature the human world has to offer. Although Barr does not even come close to offering a schematic view of things in which crime is a male prerogative and suffering a female one, with only one or two exceptions her males tend to be more insensitive and at times also more brutal than her women. (Anna is one of the very few women who are not above a little brutality themselves.) This is, however, not so much the result of a conscious effort to tarnish the image of the American male, as of Barr's sympathetic treatment of her female characters, in particular the middle-aged ones: 'Anna laughed. Her face could fall, her hands gnarl, her hair acquire another streak of gray. The camaraderie of women on the wrong side of *Mademoiselle*'s hit list was a joy she'd never been taught to expect' (*Ill Wind*, 29). However, this sympathy also extends to the old and the young. In *Species*, for instance, we have a very convincing and very respectful presentation of two retired school teachers who may or may not have a lesbian relationship (Barr is no prude, but old-fashionedly discreet), while in *Ill Wind* we cannot help liking the young *belle* Jennifer: 'this hair-sprayed and lipsticked magnolia blossom had a penchant for heavy drinking, late nights and speaking up for herself. Anna found herself warming up to the woman.' (102)

From the beginning, we have found ourselves warming up to Anna. We appreciate her for her insecurity, her vulnerability, her independence, and, not least, for the unusual, arresting perspectives that she offers: 'Roadkill provided food for a lot of animals. Anna sometimes speculated as to whether or not scavengers looked upon highways as a sort of endless buffet catered by Chrysler.' (*Ill Wind*, 33) Her unorthodox view of things has to do with the fact that Anna Pigeon is the most genuinely detached of all investigators, not indifferent but always at an ironic remove of what she happens to be observing, even if the object in question is Anna herself. She is wholly unsentimental, not given to acts of kindness, and even not without predatory instincts

– 'The dark, the stealth, the knowledge that she was the hunter and not the hunted, gave her a sense of power and freedom.' (*Species*, 263) What is more, she is fully aware of these and other possible shortcomings. There are very few investigators, male or female, who are so completely without illusions regarding themselves of others. But such a total lack of illusions also has its drawbacks. Anna wants to withdraw from the world, not improve it. Although at one level Barr's novels make political statements with regard to conservation and gender, at another they seem to prefer passivity to active involvement, except in those cases where reaction, rather than action, is almost unavoidable. But we should not complain. Barr has given us one of the most interesting, if not exactly outgoing, female investigators who have ever felt personally offended by crime.

Lynn S. Hightower's single parent

With Lynn S. Hightower's *Flashpoint* (1995) we return to the police procedural. When she published her first police procedural featuring homicide detective Sonora Blair, Hightower was not quite new to the crime fiction scene. In 1992 she had published *Alien Blues*, which would turn out to be the first instalment of a series of science fiction mysteries (featuring the alien Elaki next to more familiar life forms such as human beings) and the following year crime fiction watchers had sat up and noticed her *Satan's Lambs* of 1993, which introduced private investigator Lena Padgett and went on to win a Shamus Award for best first private eye novel. Apparently not a writer to cash in on this sort of success, Hightower moved on to her third protagonist in four years, police woman Sonora Blair, and relocated from Lexington, Kentucky (the scene for *Satan's Lambs*), to Cincinnati. Although the reasons for this writerly restlessness are unclear, Hightower's last move is certainly in keeping with the emergence of the police procedural as a serious rival to the PI novel. Whatever Hightower's reasons, the quality of her work did not suffer. *Flashpoint* (1996) maintains the high standard set by *Satan's Lambs* and so does its sequel, *Eyeshot*. In the third Sonora Blair novel, *No Good Deed* (1998), we find her rather implausibly straining for maximum effect, but even so the novel is an exciting piece of crime fiction. After the first three novels, *The Debt Collector* of 1999 is a bit of a disappointment. Sonora is still a quite convincing creation, but Hightower relies too much on sensation in keeping the novel going. But let us look in more detail at Sonora Blair.

Situated in Cincinnati, *Flashpoint* takes us on a hunt for a female killer who has forced her victim, a male college student, to handcuff himself to the steering wheel of his car, has then doused him with gasoline and set him on fire. More in particular, we follow Specialist – apparently the local code for homicide detective – Sonora Blair, from whose perspective the novel is told in her attempts to identify and apprehend the murderess. Blair and her partner Sam Delarosa find that they are on the track of a psychopathic serial killer who has a habit of revenging herself on people by whom she feels rejected by setting fires that as often as not kill them and for whom watching men burn up in their cars – of which she takes polaroid pictures – means sexual delight. After a climactic scene on the bank of the Ohio, in which Blair somewhat implausibly manages to miss shooting the killer from what is virtually point-blank range (although we have been warned that she is a lousy shot), they both end up in the river. In a rather surprising move, Hightower has Delarosa drag the killer from the river unharmed and ends with the suggestion that she will spend the rest of her life in an institution for the criminally insane. This is sensationalist stuff. Hightower, however, manages to defuse much of the sensationalism through Sonora's voice, which is terse, laconic, and both self-confident and off-handedly self-mocking, and through her decision to treat the killer, in spite of her monstrous practices, as a human being, no matter how inscrutable she ultimately is.

Sonora Blair is a convincing creation. In her mid-30s, she is a widowed mother of two – seven and 14 years old – who with a certain measure of desperation tries to combine single parenting with a demanding job with irregular hours. As a further complication there is the fact that she is by no means past her sexual prime and, being small, blonde, and well-rounded, has no trouble attracting males who would like to show her that they are neither. As she puts it in *No Good Deed*, she 'is missing romance [but] lust even more.' (*Deed*, 13)

One of the best things about Sonora is her matter-of-fact, somewhat sardonic outlook on life and the verbal dexterity with which that outlook is expressed. Through her protagonist's often witty reflections and observations Hightower conveys the message that in Sonora we have a free spirit, who has no illusions about herself or others. A female televison personality wears 'a high waisted lycra skirt that could only be worn by a woman who was a stranger to childbirth and chocolate' (*Flashpoint*, 11); a colleague has 'New Jersey manners that offended some people and attracted young women' (53); wanting to put an end to the attentions of an ex-lover she has just broken with, she entertains the notion that she 'could make those calls and visits …

disappear with one message left on his machine – just tell him her period was late.' Instead of being embarrassed by the smudge of lipstick on her Cincinnati PD coffee mug, it gives her a secret satisfaction: 'the mark of a woman in a room full of men. Plus it kept people from borrowing her mug.' (138)

This self-critically confident attitude is based on self-knowledge and an acceptance of her personal shortcomings. In *Flashpoint*, Sonora makes the mistake of getting involved and of sleeping with a witness, the brother of one of the killer's victims. What makes it worse is that the killer, who has started calling her on a regular basis, has explicitly warned her not to do so because she wants the man for herself – if not for a can of gasoline. Infuriated by what she sees as a humiliation, and seeking to burden her with both grief and guilt, the woman sets the fire that kills Sonora's brother.

The killer is a woman of Sonora's age who even looks a lot like her, which probably is not supposed to mean all that much, but may explain why she tries to establish some sort of rapport with her pursuer by way of repeated telephone calls. This unexplained partiality leads to one of the more uncanny strands in *Flashpoint*: the woman's attempts to make Sonora actually like her. First, as a kind of personal favor because Sonora, as a cop, cannot very well do so, she kills Sonora's troublesome ex-lover. Then, after Sonora's sexual encounter with the man she herself has her eye on, she breaks into Sonora's house and takes photographs of her sleeping children. The next day she mails the pictures to Sonora to make clear what she might have done but decided to forgo. Finally, when Sonora tries to arrest her on the riverbank the woman can easily shoot her but again decides against doing harm. Not surprisingly, Sonora is left with paradoxical feelings. Fully aware of what the woman has done in a murderous career that spans at least two decades, including the murder of Sonora's own brother, she still feels that she owes her and insists on conducting the official interrogations because that is the way the woman wants it. The novel ends in mid-interrrogation in an undefinable stalemate:

> 'Why didn't you kill me that day in the park?'
> Selma looked up. This time there was no question, no mistake. Selma Yorke smiled, lips curving gently in a way that was eerie and sensuous.
> And Sonora wondered who had who. (344)

It is such deviations from the standard format that make *Flashpoint* interesting. We have a female police officer who is fallible – apart from sleeping with a witness she also finds herself ignoring protocol and without thinking almost shoots a redneck macho who harasses a young girl – who is sensitive to a grisly killer's twisted humanity, but who yet manages to hold her own in a male world. She has earned the respect of her male colleagues because she is a good cop – we see her drawing intelligent conclusions from the facts that come to light – and because she is willing to take unconventional risks in the course of duty. In *Eyeshot*, her second case (1996), she is convinced that an ace District Attorney is responsible for at least two murders. Finding that her colleague Molliter functions as the DA's mole in the homicide department, she at one point handcuffs him to a drain pipe in the men's room – which is in temporary disuse so that he will not be found for the next hour or so – to prevent him from warning the murderer that she has traced his hideout. Her confrontation with Molliter – who finally has been rescued by a plumber – after she has at the very last moment succeeded in preventing a third murder shows her strength. Refusing his apologies, and making sure that he knows what she thinks of him, she also tells him that as a colleague she will be loyal and will not drag her feet when he calls for backup or act unprofessionally in any other way.

If Sonora's somewhat off-centered, although by no means negligible, place within the Cincinnati Police Department does not remind us that she is female, her children will. We get a strong sense of the pressures that result from being a single mother who doubles as a homicide cop. The children are a constant worry. In the morning she feels unhappy until they are safe at school, in the afternoon she worries until they are safely home and has put in a call to check on them. Since homicide 'ha[s] no respect for weekends' she finds herself dropping them off at friends or relatives or even taking young Hester with her (as in *Eyeshot*). She worries about their growing up without a father and about her own failings as a mother: 'She realized ... what babies they were. And how much she expected of them. Too much, maybe' (*Eyeshot,* 338). As a working single mother she works two jobs simultaneously. Remembering that she is supposed to deliver 30 homemade cupcakes for Hester's primary school class the following morning, she drags herself into the kitchen past midnight after a gruelling day on the case. Moreover, the fact that she is a single parent makes her fiercely protective: '... he had not been particularly nice to her children, the cardinal sin, for a single mother. He had not realized what a privilege it was to be accepted into the fold.' (*Deed*, 46)

This undramatic but convincing portrait of a single mother is oddly reinforced by Sonora's uselessness with guns and by the unusual endings of the first two novels. In *Eyeshot* the murderous District Attorney, a man called Caplan, shows enormous relief at being arrested just before he has the chance to finish off his third victim, a business that strangely enough causes him so much grief that he has to cry: 'The expression on Caplan's face was radiant. "I'm so glad, I don't mean to be like this." "I know", Sonora said. She looked around for something he could use to wipe his tears.' (339) Sonora's matter-of-fact and simultaneously mothering reaction is perfectly in keeping with what we know of her and a far cry from the violence with which the hunt for deranged killers usually ends in crime fiction of the 1990s (see Chapter 10). In these police procedurals Hightower uses the thriller format without, however, adopting the thriller's dehumanization of the criminal. It is this refusal to dehumanize her killers that allows her to create endings that have all the suspense of thrillers without their standard violence.

Hightower effectively shows that self-empowerment is not dependent on infallibility, great physical prowess, or the dehumanization of the criminal 'other'. For Sonora Blair, self-empowerment is a direct consequence of having joined the institution: 'Sonora stopped to rest, thinking that her job had made her hard .... In some strange way, the awareness of her hard edges gave her a new perspective, an easier attitude, and ... the cloud of anger over minor annoyances was refusing to rise these days.' (*Deed*, 322) This does not mean that she has adopted a traditional masculinist stance. The just mentioned passage with Caplan contradicts such a conclusion and so does her immediate sympathy for a rather unprepossessing young girl that she meets in *No Good Deed* ('The smallest was ... cute in the way of kittens, but it was the elder girl that Sonora wanted to gather up and hug', 35). Sonora's job teaches her to slow down and temper the rush of deep-felt concern with a measure of detachment and so allows her find a new self-confidence. This is admittedly modest, as far as self-empowerment goes, but at least it is, fictionally, real.

6
Los Angeles Police Department: Ellroy's and Connelly's Police Procedurals

Historians of the genre date the history of the police procedural from Lawrence Treat's *V as in Victim* (1945) and the 1950s American television series *Dragnet*, via Ed McBain's immensely popular 87th Precinct series (1956 to the present day) to James Lee Burke's, James Ellroy's, and Michael Connelly's highly acclaimed novels of the 1980s and 1990s. Of these last three, it is undoubtedly Ellroy who has taken this particular genre furthest in the direction of social analysis. Burke and Connelly, on the contrary, seem to use the police procedural largely as a vehicle for contemporary incarnations of what 50 years ago undoubtedly would have been private investigators: Dave Robicheaux and Harry Bosch. Indeed, whereas Ellroy potentially revitalizes the entire crime genre by his innovative, and socially explosive, treatment of the police procedural, Connelly basically regrounds the same genre in the classical private eye tradition, and he does so largely by 'shadowing' Ellroy's work.

James Ellroy

Unlike many of the more successful crime writers of the last few decades who have tried to combine a lighter touch with dead-serious matter, Ellroy aims to be serious all the way. There is nothing funny or laid-back about his characters, most of whom show the same kind of assertiveness and tenseness Ellroy himself projects in his public appearances and in the photographs that his publicity agents distribute. Ellroy obviously has an axe to grind – which he admittedly grinds well – and it shows in the compulsiveness of his stories. In fact, Ellroy is so successful at what he does that in the UK he has been hailed not only as 'the outstanding crime-writer of his generation'

(*The Independent*) and 'the most original crime writer of our time' (*The Spectator*), but even as 'a Tinseltown Dostoyevski' (*Time Out*). He himself, of course, likes to refer to himself as the 'Demon Dog of American literature', in which he is probably much less ironical than he is often taken to be. Ellroy's American universe is evil to the core, and it surely is his ambition to portray his society, and the evil that inhabits it, not just as a crime writer but as an American writer *tout court*. In fact, Ellroy seems to say, crime writing is the only genre capable of correctly describing contemporary American society. With *American Tabloid* (1995) and *My Dark Places* (1996) he certainly has moved his writing, and crime writing in general, another step closer to mainstream American literature.

The evil at the core of Ellroy's universe, the determining event in his life, and the source of most of his later writing, is the murder, on 21 June 1958, of Geneva Hilliker Ellroy. James Ellroy's mother was strangled, and her body was dumped in some bushes near a Los Angeles school. Her murderer was never found. Then ten-year-old James Ellroy was told of his mother's death on 22 June, shortly after her body had been found. *Clandestine* (1982), Ellroy's second novel, set in 1951, gives a thinly disguised and fictionalized account of Geneva Hilliker's death. It was nominated for an Edgar. *My Dark Places* (1996) recounts how Ellroy himself, with the help of veteran detective Bill Stoner, more than 20 years after his mother's killing, reconstructed the events leading up to her death and the investigation of it afterwards. The book has been described as 'a hypnotic trip to America's underbelly and one man's tortured soul' (back cover of *My Dark Places*).

A perspective that could indeed be linked up with a 'tortured soul' certainly colors much of Ellroy's writing, where the parallels with what happened to his mother are legion, whether it be in the form of the 20-odd murders of women that are the subject of *Blood on the Moon* (1984), the first novel in the so-called Lloyd Hopkins trilogy (the others are *Because the Night*, 1984, and *Suicide Hill*, 1986), of the spectacular real-life case involving the brutal murder of a pretty young prostitute, Elizabeth Short, in 1947 that provides the plot of *The Black Dahlia* (1987), or of the killings of prostitutes that so obsess Wendell Bud White in *L.A. Confidential* (1990).

'America's underbelly' is just as prominently present in Ellroy's writing. His first novel, *Brown's Requiem* (1981), nominated for a Shamus Award for best private eye paperback novel of 1981, draws upon the author's own experiences as a professional golf caddy, a profession he had turned to in 1977 in order to escape the life of petty crime, alcohol and drugs he had led since the age of 13. However, what is also evident from that novel is Ellroy's knowledge of the American crime writing tradition, and particularly that of the private eye novel created by Hammett and Chandler. Aware of this influence, in a 1995 reissue of *Brown's Requiem* Ellroy stated that in the meantime Chandler to him had become 'an icon that he had come to dislike quite a bit', and that he had come to realize that 'imitating him was a dead-end street on Genre Hack Boulevard'. In the foreword to the 1997 reissue of his Lloyd Hopkins trilogy Ellroy claimed that Hopkins – a racist, sexist and violent police officer – was 'his antidote to the sensitive candy-assed philosophizing private eye'.

With the move from the private eye of *Brown's Requiem* to the police procedural of *Clandestine* and the Lloyd Hopkins trilogy (in 1997 republished in one volume as *L.A. Noir*), and subsequently to the historical detective series of the LA Quartet (set, respectively, in the late 1940s (*The Black Dahlia*), the early 1950s (*The Big Nowhere*, 1988), 1951–58 (*L.A. Confidential*), and 1958 (*White Jazz*, 1992)), Ellroy has consistently broadened the historical and social scope of his writings. With *American Tabloid* he extends his view to the political life of the nation, a course he also seems set upon maintaining in his future writing if we are to go by the interviews he has given and the statements he has made over the last few years. In a 1997 *Worldguide* interview, for instance, Ellroy labelled *American Tabloid*, a novel covering the years 1958–63 and detailing the intimate relationship between politics and organized crime in the period immediately leading up to J.F. Kennedy's assassination, as the first of his 'Underworld U.S.A.' trilogy, the next two volumes of which would cover the years 1963–68 and 1968–73 respectively. The first of these, *The Cold Six Thousand*, appeared in 2001. Interestingly, *American Tabloid* was undoubtedly partly inspired by Don DeLillo's fictional account of the Kennedy assassination in *Libra* (1988). Since Ellroy's announcement of his plan to bring out an 'Underworld' trilogy DeLillo has, probably by sheer coincidence, published a novel with the same title.

Whatever genre they precisely belong to, what all of Ellroy's novels continue to share is what William L. DeAndrea, in his *Encyclopedia Mysteriosa*, calls 'a nightmare vision of the second half of [our] century' (DeAndrea, 109). Initially, this vision extended only to Los Angeles, 'awash in chaos and corruption, city of lurid and violent anarchy ... where the heroes are heroes only in comparison to the villains, who are unspeakably evil', as William Malloy puts it in the entry on James Ellroy in *Crime and Mystery Writers* (Pederson, 339). With *American*

Tabloid, however, it is Ellroy's ambition 'to go beyond his home town, and to create a panorama of twentieth-century America through a sprawling series of epic crime novels ... [as Ellroy himself states:] "I want to recreate America to my *own* specifications – big, broad, sweeping, dense, dark, sick – Tolstoyan novels".' (340)

A marked feature of the crime writing of the late 1980s and the 1990s is the high incidence of serial killers. Often, these killers are portrayed as loners and as crazed and obsessed individuals, as in Thomas Harris's *Red Dragon* (1981) and *Silence of the Lambs* (1988), Philip Margolin's *Gone, But Not Forgotten* (1993), and Michael Connelly's *The Concrete Blonde* (1994). In Ellroy's early fiction, the motives for the serial killings often have to do with white supremacism, fed by serious psychological problems. From the *L.A. Quartet* on, right-wing politics in general takes over as the agent responsible for the crimes committed.

Though at first sight the two protagonists of *Blood on the Moon*, Lloyd Hopkins and Teddy Verplanck, seem poles apart, in reality they are two of a kind – at least at heart. It is their opposite reactions to similar experiences – or perhaps it is the different way in which society rewards or punishes their parallel reactions to similar experiences – that makes the difference. Both characters are raped at an early age. The novel actually starts with a graphic description of Verplanck's violation by two of his high school classmates because they resent his intellectual aloofness and apparently unassailable arrogance. It is this experience as much as any innate urge that turns Verplanck into both a repressed homosexual and a serial killer.

Lloyd Hopkins, the homicide detective sergeant who is the central character of *Blood on the Moon* as well as of the other two novels in the trilogy named after him, was raped at the age of eight by an old derelict whom Hopkins until then had always considered his friend. Hopkins's mother kills the rapist, while Hopkins himself represses the event. His only ostensible scar is his absolute inability to tolerate music, as for the full two days in which he was sodomized, his torturer constantly played loud music. Like Verplanck, Hopkins is constantly after new women – not to kill them, however, but to have sex with them. Just like Verplanck, Hopkins is living down a terrible past. Again like Verplanck, he kills to appease his own doubts and fears. However, while what Verplanck does is rightly labelled a crime, Hopkins can kill within a legal framework.

Ellroy stresses the basic identity of the two protagonists of *Blood on the Moon* by having them both 'love' the same woman and by calling

Verplanck Hopkins's 'blood brother' at the very moment the two are locked in mortal combat. Actually, Hopkins only survives thanks to a massive blood transfusion from the dying Verplanck. He even has to be cured of his belief – a trauma he has incurred from the fight – that the latter is *not* his real brother. In the end, Hopkins can only get on with things – that is, keep himself and his bloodthirsty urges in check – when he is permitted to stay on as a policeman, the clear implication being that otherwise he would spin out of control as another Verplanck.

In comparison with *Brown's Requiem*, with which it shares some characteristics, but even more so in comparison with Ellroy's later fiction, starting with the *L.A. Quartet, Blood on the Moon* (and the entire Lloyd Hopkins trilogy) is definitely overwritten. The novel shows all of Ellroy's early stock-in-trade, present from *Brown's Requiem* on, of German opera staging, down to the use of words such as *walpurgisnacht* to retrospectively refer to Hopkins's battle with Verplanck, and the thematic use of music. On top of all this, in this novel the horror is overly cinematic, humor is conspicuously lacking, and the symbolism is heavy-handed. A good instance of these three elements coming together is when Verplanck sews together the main female character's eyes to make her 'see' the reality of her relationship to himself and to Hopkins. In general, the psychological justification for both Verplanck's and Hopkins's deeds is put on with a very heavy brush.

Though the crimes Ellroy depicts in the four novels that constitute the *L.A. Quartet*, and the characters that feature in these novels, are certainly not less dark or evil than is the case in the *L.A. Noir* or Lloyd Hopkins novels, the wider social context of the later novels more easily accommodates the kind of high-octane staccato writing, the wrenching metaphors, the larger-than-life characters, and the labyrinthine plots Ellroy seems to hold the patent of. In fact, because of their wider social context, it is precisely the supercharged, undoubtedly some would say exaggerated, nature of Ellroy's novels from *The Black Dahlia* on that allows us to read them as instances of late twentieth-century satire, comparable to, say Swift's commentary on the early eighteenth century.

The Black Dahlia (1987) is the first of the *L.A. Quartet* novels, both in terms of publication, and in terms of the period in which its action is set. It is a novel about the brutal murder of a promiscuous young girl and part-time prostitute in 1947 in Los Angeles. The girl, Betty Short – also known as 'The Black Dahlia' because she always wears short, clinging, tight-fitting black dresses – is found bisected, organs removed, face slashed ear to ear across the mouth so as to look like a clown, and all body parts washed clean of blood, in a vacant Los Angeles lot. Bucky Bleichert, the first-person narrator of the book, a one-time prize-fighter and at present an LAPD officer, is assigned the case, together with his partner and also ex-boxer Lee Blanchard. The novel is as much involved with detailing the complex relationship between these two men, and between them and Kay Lake, the woman Lee is living with in a 'white' relationship and who falls in love with Bleichert, as it is with unravelling Betty Short's murder.

The Black Dahlia, like *Blood on the Moon*, is heavily psychologized as to the motives and deeds of all characters. There are further similarities in the early histories of the killers, who all have suffered demeaning experiences and humiliations in childhood and early youth, in the gory descriptions of the killer's dens, in the harping on grievous physical injuries, and in the detailing of pictures of the victim. Finally, there is the attention to clinical detail in the descriptions of mutilation and violence. However, and this is where the difference between the *L.A. Noir* trilogy and the *L.A. Quartet* is most conspicuous, in *The Black Dahlia* the same kind of clinical attention also stretches to the physical description of the city of Los Angeles itself in the 1940s, complete with street details, car makes and models, and references to period events and personalities. The same attention to historical detail also marks the other novels of the quartet.

Ellroy's work shows a mounting complexity, and *The Big Nowhere* and *L.A. Confidential* are multi-layered novels, told from a third-person point of view, each of them chronicling a number of years during the 1950s. Especially *L.A. Confidential* is an extremely complex tale of murder, pornography, filial piety and betrayal. It is also a tale about 'absolute justice' and how it sullies everything it touches. Preston Exley, a 1930s famous hardline Los Angeles police inspector, raised his sons in a spirit of absolute justice, and it has made his son Ed(mond) into the emotionally cramped over-achiever, who plays everything strictly by the book, that he is at the beginning of the novel. Ed has joined the LAPD because he wants to emulate his father, as well as his older brother, an LAPD detective who died in the line of duty. Ed's counterpart is Bud White, another LAPD detective, who because of his own particular family history is not averse to taking the law into his own hands, especially when a woman's well-being is at stake. Emotionally, White, who is often prompted by excess of feeling, is Ed Exley's opposite. Even Jack Vincennes, the third detective and co-protagonist of *L.A. Confidential*, is in spite of his weakness and corruptness a better and more caring man than Ed Exley.

Still, it is Exley who transcends himself, learning from both White and Vincennes. It is not accidental that one of Exley's closest friends and colleagues at the end of the novel remarks that Ed comes to resemble Bud White more with each passing day, especially in his habits of speech. Their growing involvement with one another, to the point of almost becoming one another's double, is stressed by their sharing the same women. It is even underscored in the last scene of the novel, when White and his girlfriend drive off to Arizona after the ceremony where Exley has been promoted Chief of Detectives. Exley runs along with their car, pressing his hands to the car window, with White doing the same thing from inside the car.

Exley has not only emulated his brother and his father; he has outdone them. However, the price is high. As the final line of *L.A. Confidential* has it: 'Gold stars. Alone with his Dead.' (496) Alone also with the knowledge that his father's life gave the lie to his self-created myth of uprightness. In his own, and infinitely more corrupt way, Ed Exley will live a comparable set of lies, both with regard to his supposed heroism in the Vietnam War, and to his prowess as a detective. Alone, moreover, in the knowledge that all his father and his brother, and initially also he himself, stood for – law, order, the honor of the department – is perverted in present day America. Yet, unlike for White, for a man like Ed Exley there is no way out. At the end of the final volume of the *L.A. Quartet*, *White Jazz*, we find Exley running for governor of California, once again stepping into his father's tracks.

The Black Dahlia, the first novel of the *L.A. Quartet* (also as to historical period covered), shares with the other three novels, next to a number of recurring characters, an interest in serial killings – especially of prostitutes. What it shares with the L.A. Noir or Lloyd Hopkins trilogy is an interest in a link between white supremacism and psychosexual obsessions leading to repeated and often ritual murder. In the later novels of the *L.A. Quartet* the focus shifts from crackpot white supremacism to 'legitimate' right-wing politics in general. *The Big Nowhere* is at least in part about the Red Scare of the late 1940s, the tug between left and right within the movie industry, and the links between that industry, politics, and organized crime. *L.A. Confidential* in all respects is the pivotal novel of the *L.A. Quartet*: it is the one *The Big Nowhere* leads up to, and to which *White Jazz* serves as a sort of epilogue. *L.A. Confidential* also combines the psychosexual obsession and the prostitute murders from Ellroy's early novels. It is for the most part set in 1958, a fateful year in Ellroy's own life, as it is the year his mother was murdered. It is strong on political intrigue, both in and out of the police department. Finally, it continues the careers of some characters originally introduced in *The Big Nowhere*, and itself introduces a number of characters that will return not only in *White Jazz*, but also in *American Tabloid*.

In the *L.A. Quartet*, the corruption and crime rampant in Los Angeles are increasingly located as originating in the police department and in political intrigue rather than with organized crime. *American Tabloid* enlarges the scene to all of the United States. In *White Jazz*, LAPD lieutenant Dave Klein works as a part-time enforcer for the Mafia, but he also does odd jobs for Howard Hughes. At the end of the novel he is beaten to within an inch of his life at an order from Hughes, for having double-crossed the latter in a woman affair. In *American Tabloid*, Hughes returns in full force as the evil genius of America. Although he hardly ever appears in person, Hughes's power and his obsessions fuel the plot.

At the beginning of the novel, Pete Bondurant, one of the three protagonists of *American Tabloid*, watches Hughes shoot up in his Los Angeles hotel room, while on TV there is a news broadcast about Fidel Castro's rebellion against the Cuban dictator Batista. Bondurant is a giant of a man who was fired as Los Angeles County Deputy Sheriff after having killed a prisoner in his custody. He is now a licensed private investigator and serves as Hughes's handyman. Specifically, he is the latter's drugs-procurer and enforcer – it is Bondurant who beats Klein almost to death in *White Jazz*. Bondurant gets in deeper and deeper with organized crime via Jimmy Hoffa, the Teamster boss, and the latter's associates. The second protagonist of *American Tabloid* is Kemper Boyd, an FBI G-man who is also in the pay of the Mafia, but who also works for the CIA and for the Kennedy brothers. Finally, there is Kemper's colleague, Ward J. Littell.

Greed, political ambition, lust for power, voyeurism, and international politicking intersect in *American Tabloid*. Greed is the driving force for Bondurant and Kemper, as well as for the mafiosi they get involved with. Political ambition motivates the Kennedys, who want to crush organized crime as part of their election drive. Lust for power motivates FBI chief J. Edgar Hoover, who hates the Kennedys and – rightly – senses that they want to remove him from office. As a result he teams up with organized crime against the Kennedys. Voyeurism provides a strong lure for both Hoover, a homosexual, and Hughes, a crank who lives as a recluse but is keen on titillating tidbits, especially if they have racist overtones. International politicking takes the form of a drive to oust Castro, or to kill him, so as to get the Cuban exiles, who support American business and facilitate Mafia incursions in the island, back in the saddle.

In the course of the novel, the three main characters (Bondurant, Boyd, and Littell) shift allegiances as expediency dictates. Bondurant, and even more so Boyd, rise fast on the ladder of success. Yet, for various reasons, they lose favor with the Kennedys, as does Littell. Eventually it is Littell who comes up with the idea of assassinating Jack Kennedy, and who finds the necessary financial backing, initially from Hughes, and subsequently from the Mafia. In the end, though, the Littell–Boyd–Bondurant scheme is never carried through. *American Tabloid* implies that a rival scheme, with CIA and FBI backing, is effectuated in Dallas. The novel ends with Bondurant in Dallas on the morning of 22 November 1963, and Kennedy's motorcade approaching.

Towards the end of the novel, too, Littell goes to see Hughes, whom he has never yet met in person, although he has been working for him for some time now. He also observes Hughes shoot up, strapped in a cranked-up hospital bed in his hotel room, watching television cartoons and commercials, and sharing his bed with a dozen disassembled slot machines. This is the man who exercises a considerable hold on America via his money, which finances Mafia deals and political assassinations. Hughes is called the Vampire, and Count Dracula, by the paid help, and this is an apt indication of his personification of Ellroy's vision of America as racist and addicted, feeding on the life blood of others, on drugs, and on popular culture.

American Tabloid is a scathing denunciation of the intimate ties between politics, finance and organized crime in the United States. It brilliantly plays upon all received myths surrounding the Kennedy assassination, including the persistent rumors that there would have been more than one assassin, or that Kennedy was having an affair with Marilyn Monroe. In fact, in the novel Kemper Boyd puts the latter rumor into circulation as a diversion to mislead J. Edgar Hoover. At the same time, Ellroy also punctures popular myths, such as that alleging that Monroe was frigid. Ellroy has her – as overheard by FBI wiretap – have intercourse with almost any man she comes across, from famous actors and singers to the pizza delivery boy.

In *American Tabloid*, high-faluting political ideals are shown to be driven by the lust for money (Joe P. Kennedy), or sex (Jack Kennedy), or to result from personal hang-ups (Bobby Kennedy). There is not one really likeable character in the entire book. The three protagonists are each in turn first built up as potentially sympathetic, then systematically exposed as ruthless killers who maim, torture, and execute partly out of expediency, partly because they enjoy it. Boyd is potentially the most likeable of the three protagonists. Yet, he is the only one to die. In the end, Kemper is the only one to be fully taken in by the Kennedy charm. In the Kennedys, Kemper thinks he recognizes the America he himself, as the son of rich parents, once thought he would inherit. It was, however, a mirage to begin with. The 'reality' America lives by is that of the hype and gossip implied by the novel's title, *American Tabloid*.

Michael Connelly

Perhaps no other detective writer starting out in the 1990s, and certainly no other writer of police procedurals, has had so much praise heaped upon him as Michael Connelly. His first, *The Black Echo* (1992) won an Edgar for Best First Novel. It introduced Harry Bosch, a detective on the robbery and homicide table of the Hollywood branch of the Los Angeles Police Department. Bosch, we learn, used to be with the central LAPD homicide division, but has been demoted to the Hollywood branch because he killed an unarmed alleged serial killer. Instead of groping for a gun underneath a cushion, as Bosch thought, the man had rather ironically, and innocently, felt for his wig.

Bosch is notorious for not fitting in, for disobeying rules and regulations. Both his immediate superior, Lieutenant Pounds, and the chief of the Internal Affairs Division, Irvin Irving, would love to get rid of him. Regularly, Bosch is tailed by a couple of IAD men, who have to try and get something on him so that he can be fired. Equally regularly, of course, these IAD men screw up Bosch's investigations. As the series progresses, the character of Bosch fills out. We learn that his mother – a whore – named him after the Dutch late-medieval painter Hieronymus Bosch. He is loyal to his colleagues, until they prove themselves weak, cowardly, or crooked – whether by toeing the line, playing for promotion, covering their back, or crossing over to the criminal side. He lives all alone in a small house up in the hills above Hollywood, where a lone coyote roams at night. Bosch's image as loner is underscored by his being named Harry Haller on the one occasion that he meets his father, the successful Los Angeles defense lawyer Mickey Haller, whom his mother had an on-and-off affair with: Harry Haller is the name of the main character of Herman Hesse's *Steppenwolf*.

The Bosch novels powerfully evoke the contemporary American city-scape, primarily through detailed descriptions of Bosch's drives through Los Angeles. They equally powerfully address the social and political conditions of the contemporary United States, but always as mediated through the individual experiences of Harry Bosch. *The Black Echo* is heavily marked by the fall-out of the Vietnam war, which links all the characters. The novel begins with a man being found dead in a construction pipe at a dam site in Hollywood. Bosch recognizes him as a 'tunnel rat' from a platoon that cleared Viet Cong tunnels for the troops he himself served with in Vietnam. The man may have been involved in a major bank robbery, pulled off about a year before. Bosch is seconded to FBI-agent Eleanor Wish, in charge of investigating that robbery. He and Eleanor soon become lovers and he learns from her that she has lost a brother in Vietnam. The target of the original robbery was a former high-ranking South Vietnamese officer who is now a wealthy American businessman. Harry and Eleanor suspect that another robbery is being planned, targeting another former South Vietnamese, and they set a trap. When this misfires, Bosch pursues the robbers through the Los Angeles sewage tunnels – operating as a 'tunnel rat' on his home ground. He is about to be shot by the man who masterminded the operation, when Eleanor turns up to save him just in time. The criminal, as Bosch had already suspected, is Eleanor's immediate superior with the FBI, a man called Rourke who once held an important job in the American embassy in Saigon.

When checking the names on the half-sized replica of the Washington Vietnam Veteran Memorial that is erected in the veteran's cemetery in Los Angeles, Bosch cannot find that of Eleanor's brother. Confronting Eleanor, he finally learns that it is she who planted the idea for the robbery in her superior's mind, and who helped in its execution. She had hoped to have the man arrested in retaliation for the latter's involvement in the dishonorable discharge and the death, after his return to the US, of her brother. By shooting Rourke she has just as much saved her own skin as that of Bosch. Bosch forces Eleanor to turn herself in. Later, he gets a package through the post office:

> He didn't open it until he was home. It was from Eleanor Wish, though it did not say so: it was just something he knew. After tearing away the paper and bubbled plastic liner, he found a framed print of Hopper's *Nighthawks*. It was the piece he had seen above the couch that first night he was with her.
>
> Bosch hung the print in the hallway near his front door, and from

> time to time he would stop and study it when he came in, particularly from a weary day or night on the job. The painting never failed to fascinate him, or to evoke memories of Eleanor Wish. The darkness. The stark loneliness. The man sitting alone, his face turned to the shadows. I am that man, Harry Bosch would think each time he looked.
>
> (*Echo*, 412)

The Hopper picture pretty much sums up the atmosphere of the Bosch novels and its introduction in *The Black Echo* perfectly characterizes a series that since then has mostly gone from strength to strength. In the next novels in the series, the brooding figure of Harry Bosch is systematically elaborated. His essential loneliness, his resistance to authority, and his ambiguous susceptibility to alcohol, jazz, smoking, and women, make him into a 1990s reincarnation of the 1930s private eye reluctantly turned police officer, and relentlessly chafing against the yoke of rules, regulations, and procedures.

This is not to say, though, that every single aspect of *The Black Echo* is superb. It displays a powerful narrative style and a slightly larger-than-life but very credible protagonist. Eleanor Wish, though, comes across as a rather unlikely character. It is hard to credit her playing the double role she is supposed to play for such a long time, and to reconcile her apparent innocence and even naivety with the cunning with which she is supposed to have manipulated as experienced and ruthless a criminal as Rourke. In *Trunk Music* (1997) Connelly revives Eleanor to more satisfying effect, though in a novel that is less successful over all.

With *The Black Ice* (1993), Connelly turns to a set of different problems besetting America. In the first instance, this is a novel concerned with the whole-scale smuggling of the heroin derivative 'black ice' from Mexico into the States, and with the violent death of Cal(exico) Moore, a narcotics officer. However, it also emphasizes the sense of belonging to the *barrio* and its characters' personal pasts: broken homes, childhoods spent in motel rooms, with foster parents or in youth homes, the betrayal of children by their parents and of brothers by brothers. A *barrio* gang tattoo of a ghost with a halo, dubbed 'Saints and Sinners', plays an important role in the novel.

The question 'saint or sinner' extends to all the characters in the book. No doubt there are echoes here of the grotesque scenes from hell typical of the world Harry's last name refers to: that of Hieronymus Bosch. Harry Bosch himself, though he repeatedly 'sins' against all rules and regulations, is obviously a 'saint' at heart, in the sense that he transcends his foibles and has the right instincts where and when it matters. Before we think of Bosch as a latter-day Marlowe, though, we should consider that 'Chandler' is the name of the extremely successful civil rights lawyer who in *The Concrete Blonde* (1994) takes Harry Bosch to court for his shooting, four years earlier, of the alleged serial killer with the wig. The lawyer's first name is Honey, but she is nicknamed 'Money' because of her success in suing the city and authorities in general, gaining large legal fees every time she wins a case, even if the plaintiffs she represents are awarded only symbolic damages. Chandler is an extremely aggressive lawyer, digging into the unhappy boyhood that Bosch spent in an orphanage after his mother was killed, and drawing absolutely unwarranted conclusions from this. It is not only the legal profession that is lambasted in *The Concrete Blonde*, though. The press shares in the criticism. Connelly himself for years was a star police reporter for the *Los Angeles Times*. Judging by the vitriolic picture of Bremmer, the reporter who turns copy-cat serial killer in this novel, there is not much love lost between Connelly and his former colleagues.

The Concrete Blonde has a very effective unity of plot and time, both being bounded by the courtroom action of one week precisely. At the same time, and in multiple ways, this novel reaches back into Bosch's past. It does so in the form of the original Dollmaker case which is the subject of the ongoing trial. It also does so by way of Harry's involvement with Sylvia, the widow of the LA Police detective turned drug smuggler in *The Black Ice*. Finally, it unearths part of Harry's more remote past – notably his mother's murder 35 years earlier. As such, it directly leads into Connelly's next Bosch novel, *The Last Coyote* (1995).

With *The Last Coyote* Connelly's work more closely comes to shadow Ellroy's. The trip south of the border in *The Black Ice* is already vaguely reminiscent of that in Ellroy's *Brown's Requiem*. More significantly, there is the stark contrast between the hopes with which the victims in some of both Ellroy's and Connelly's novels come to the big city, and what they find there – especially the young women who aspire to be part of the movie industry and who often end up as porn queens and prostitutes, as in Ellroy's *The Black Dahlia* and Connelly's *The Concrete Blonde* and *The Last Coyote*. Then there is the similarity between criminal and detective in *The Concrete Blonde*, which resembles that of Ellroy's *Blood on the Moon*. Bremmer and Bosch share a past featuring a broken home and a destitute mother – a prostitute in Bosch's case, an alcoholic in Bremmer's. These mothers, moreover, were killed when their sons were still very young. Finally, Bremmer and Bosch both have names of Dutch origin starting with the same letter (in Ellroy's novels, by the way, many of the villains – such as Verplanck – have Dutch names). The murderers in both *Blood on the Moon* and *The Concrete Blonde* use poems to communicate with their pursuers and leave their signature on their victims. And of course Ellroy's own mother, like Harry Bosch's, worked as a prostitute and was killed on a Los Angeles street. While Ellroy comes closest to this real life trauma in *My Dark Places*, Connelly imaginatively elaborates upon this in Harry Bosch's biography in *The Last Coyote*, a novel that was nominated for an Anthony in 1996.

In each Bosch novel the criminal affair he works on immediately and strongly affects the life of Bosch himself. In *The Last Coyote*, though, is it Bosch's private life that determines the affair to be investigated. Everything seems to be falling in ruins around Harry at the beginning of this novel. He is suspended for having attacked his superior, Lieutenant Pounds; his house off Laurel Canyon has been hit badly during an earthquake, and is almost sure to be condemned by the building inspector; and Sylvia Moore, the woman he has been seeing for about a year, has left for Europe and their affair seems over.

The Last Coyote takes its title from the lone coyote – 'el tímido' – that Bosch regularly spots near his house. He dreams about the animal, and talks about it to Carmen Hinojos, the police psychologist. Obviously, he identifies with this animal to the point of assuming a comparable role in his own human society, longing for a simpler, straighter, more honest existence. The sessions with Hinojos open Bosch's eyes to the fact that there was a particular reason for his becoming so angry with Pounds. He realizes that his own anger at Pounds's interference in a murder case at least partially stems from his own mother's murder, in 1961. That case was never solved. Barred from doing his ordinary work anyway, Bosch decides to try and finally solve his mother's murder as a sort of self-therapy. In a telltale detail, the civilian clerk from whom Bosch gets the murder file on his mother is called Geneva Beaupre, which reminds us that the name of Ellroy's mother was Geneva Hilliker. Bosch's mother in the end turns out to have been killed accidentally by her own best friend and fellow call girl in a fit of jealousy. Although officially off-duty, during his investigation Bosch stirs up the cesspool of corruption and murder upon which LA's political and financial elite has built its empire.

When in *Trunk Music* (1997) Harry runs into Eleanor Wish again, the circle begun in *The Black Echo* is completed. This is a novel about various forms of love, but mostly that between men and women, and mothers and daughters. It is also about the shady sides of the movie industry and its collusion with the Mafia, particularly as a money laundering machine. *Trunk Music* offers some of the best police procedural description around, especially in its opening pages. Still, this fifth Harry Bosch novel seems less satisfactory, or perhaps simply more 'ordinary,' than its predecessors. Despite the return of Eleanor Wish, the personal or intimate angle is less urgent here than in the previous Bosch novels, especially *The Last Coyote*. While still very good, the writing in *Trunk Music* is on occasion plodding, with more explanation and stage setting – it is less vigorous, slacker somehow. Though one hates to think so, some of this may have to do with Connelly's political correctness in this novel. Jerry Edgar, Bosch's long-time detective partner, is an African American. Now Bosch is joined by Kizmin Rider, a light-skinned African American woman, reputedly on the fast track to promotion. Lieutenant Harvey Pounds, the Hollywood Station commander from the previous Bosch novels, has been replaced by a woman, Grace Billets. She not only is extremely efficient, she is also much more humane than Pounds in the way she runs the station. Moreover, she is bisexual, and has an affair with Rider. To top it all, the killer in *Trunk Music* turns out to be not only a frustrated cop, who blames affirmative action and equal opportunity employment for his own lack of career advancement, but also a white supremacist, a collector of 'nazi paraphernalia, white-power stuff' (*Music*, 374). Such schematic plotting comes with a price. At least part of the fun of the earlier Bosch novels arose from Bosch's altercations with Pounds, or with the sometimes caricatural Deputy Chief Irvin Irving. There is none of that in *Trunk Music*. Connelly's recent branching out with non-Harry Bosch novels such as *The Poet* (1996, winner of the Anthony Award and nominated for a Hammett), and *Blood Work* (1998) may well indicate a certain saturation with his original hero.

Perhaps it is indicative of the relative failure of *Trunk Music* that here Bosch is quite willing to compromise on his smoking. In the early novels, Bosch is a chain smoker, who will light a cigarette any time and anywhere, regardless of the company he is in, and certainly regardless of any rules or laws prohibiting smoking. To Bosch, this is a duty he owes not only to himself but to America: it is his way of ensuring that America remains the land of the free, the ultimate guarantor of individual liberty. In order to uphold this higher law, Bosch is quite willing to break its poor everyday relative. In *Trunk Music*, he still takes a drag now and then, and he will even do it where officially it is not allowed. Moreover, Eleanor Wish, who in *The Black Echo* did not smoke, does so in the later novel – a legacy of the three-and-a-half years she spent in prison. Yet, in contrast with the earlier novels, in *Trunk Music* smoking is not flaunted as a socially meaningful and liberating act. Harry and Eleanor do it because it makes them feel marginally better, but it is not the slap in the face of authority it was in the early Bosch novels.

In the earlier novels, Bosch's uneasy fit in 1990s America was signalled not only by his smoking habit, but also by Hopper's *Nighthawks*, as well as by Bosch's penchant for alcohol, and his preference for the powerful, soulful but moody jazz – more especially the great saxophone players – of the era prior to the onset of free jazz. All these are cultural icons also of the original hard-boiled detective novel and its period setting. In many ways indeed Harry Bosch comes across as a contemporary reincarnation of the classic private eye dropped into a contemporary police procedural. In *Trunk Music* there is almost none of this. Bosch even winds up in red swimming trunks on a Hawaiian beach, married to Eleanor Wish. The late 1990s have definitely tamed Bosch.

Angels Flight (1999) seems to confirm this. Eleanor leaves Bosch because she feels she cannot love him as much as he loves her. Loath to jeopardize a good thing, however, Connelly is careful not to make it a definitive separation. Eleanor merely goes away for a while to get her proper bearings. Bosch, predictably, seeks relief by focusing more than ever on his work. A famous black lawyer, Howard Elias, has been murdered on the eve of a much-publicized trial in which he was going to defend an alleged black child rapist and murderer. Los Angeles explodes in race riots. Bosch, fighting fatigue, alcohol and the searing pain of Eleanor's leaving, tracks down Elias's killer. Rather incongruously when it comes to motivation and plot, even if it vindicates Bosch's own unfair treatment at the hands of the man in the earlier novels, the killer turns out to be Chastain, the Internal Affairs Division detective who has been hounding Bosch from the first novel in the series. In a climactic scene Bosch hand-cuffs Chastain, and is about to bring him in, when the latter is pulled from Bosch's car by an angry mob, then trampled and beaten to death. Bosch himself only narrowly escapes harm.

In the aftermath, Bosch finds himself wandering about the lynching scene. Three things steady him: a cigarette he gets from the Asian owner of a looted liquor store, a message on a book of fortune matches reading 'happy is the man who finds refuge in himself', and 'the small bag of rice from his wedding' he finds in his pocket (*Flight*, 398). We may interpret these three articles as symbolizing the uneasy alliance which largely guide America's present: multicultural relations, self-reliance, and family values. Bosch's faith in this alliance is what enables him to face the inevitable: 'Bosch knew he would be co-opted. [Police Chief] Irving could get to him. Because he held the only thing Bosch had left, that he still cared about. His job. He knew Irving would trade that for his silence [about Chastain's corruptness]. And he knew he would take the deal.' (399) Bosch is finally beaten by the system. In fact, with *Angels Flight* the Bosch series begins to steer a course that again uncannily runs parallel to Ellroy's later novels. Corruption is seen to nestle in the very heart of the police force, of the legal and political system of the United States. However, the conclusions that both series come to – at least provisionally – are radically different.

Ellroy's characters, like Ed Exley in *L.A. Confidential*, consciously and cynically, implicate themselves in what they know to be a corrupt and even inhuman system. The alternative is that they opt out, like Bud White in the same novel. *American Tabloid* reverses the direction, and makes the 'system' the agent and the characters, however powerfully drawn, puppets-on-a-string, devoid of free will. At the end of *Angels Flight*, Bosch too hands in his freedom, in the scene with Irving we have just witnessed. However, and this is indicative of the opposite roads Ellroy and Connelly after all are traveling, Bosch finally resigns to an authority *beyond*. The moment he is about to fall to the mob in *Angels Flight*, the moment he is staring death in the face, he finds 'an essential truth ... he knew somehow that he would be spared, that the righteous man was beyond the grasp of the fallen.' Chastain's death scream is 'a wail so loud and horrible as to be almost inhuman ... the sound of fallen angels in their flight to hell', and Bosch knows that 'he could never allow himself to forget it' (400). With this epiphany befalling his detective Connelly adds faith to Bosch's inner strength.

Together, Ellroy and Connelly dominate the contemporary police procedural. Ellroy's work may well be deeper and more meaningful in the long run – in fact, with his later works, starting with the *L.A. Quartet*, and definitely with *American Tabloid*, Ellroy is no longer a genre writer, but has moved into mainstream American literature. Connelly basically takes up the same themes as Ellroy, but is careful to elaborate them within the self-imposed limits of his chosen genre, in fact partially recasting the police procedural as private eye novel through his maverick homicide detective Hieronymus Bosch.

7
Private Investigation in the 1990s

Marlowe at the end of the millennium

One of the most successful private investigators of the 1990s is Robert Crais's Elvis Cole – renamed from 'Philip James', after his mother had heard the 'King' Presley. *The Monkey's Raincoat* (1987), in which Cole made his debut, won an Anthony for Best Paperback Original and a Macavity for Best First Novel, and was nominated for Edgar and Shamus Awards. *Free Fall* (1993) was nominated for an Edgar. *Sunset Express* (1996) won, and *Indigo Slam* (1997) was cited for, a Shamus Award. In many ways Robert Crais comes closest to being the Chandler of the 1990s, a Chandler already modified by Robert B. Parker, with Elvis Cole in the role of a Marlowe who has been prepared for the late twentieth century by Parker's Spenser.

In Crais's debut novel *The Monkey's Raincoat* Chandler is omnipresent in the setting, in the tone, and in the character of Elvis Cole himself. Though there are excursions to the East Coast (*Lullaby Town* (1992)), Louisiana (*Voodoo River* (1995)), and, briefly, Seattle (*Indigo Slam*), Cole's natural turf is southern California. Cole narrates his own adventures. 'Dark steel knight's heraldry' lines his shelves, and the histories of King Arthur are his favorite reading (*The Monkey's Raincoat,* 152). Cole even quotes Chandler's famous *'Down these mean streets, a man must walk who is himself not mean'* (63). At the same time, in the way Cole handles these quotations, and by the context they function in, Crais ironically distances himself from Chandler.

Crais learned his trade in the 1970s and 1980s as a television writer for series such as *Hill Street Blues*, *Cagney and Lacey*, and *L.A. Law*. Small wonder then that his Elvis Cole series also shows an acute awareness of the American crime movie tradition. Yet, here too Crais keeps an ironical distance. In *Lullaby Town* Cole is bidden to ride with an Italian Mafia boss in the latter's Cadillac Eldorado. To the mafioso's question 'I'm *capo de tutti capo* ... you know what that means?' Elvis answers: 'You're Marlon Brando' (*Town*, 312). As this scene demonstrates, Crais's characters, primarily of course Cole, are also ironically aware of their being caught up in a 'Hollywood' world of *déjà-vu, déjà-lu, déjà-entendu*. Still, being located where he is, Cole more often than not has to make a living working for movie people.

Cole's relationship to his own world and his literary and celluloid ancestors, is summed up in the Pinocchio clock on the wall of his office and the Jiminy Crickett figurines on his desk. Jiminy Crickett watches over Pinocchio, and saves him when in trouble. This is also what Chandler's Marlowe does for the people he feels are worth saving. To the best of his ability, Cole does the same thing for the people he comes to care about. Cole knows that Chandler's novels and Carlo Collodi's tale, and the film versions based on them, are only make-believe. However, that does not make the feelings they express any less real for him, nor does it diminish the values they uphold. Cole's identification with Jiminy Crickett shows in the unease he feels when anyone visiting his office handles the figurines. People sometimes misjudge Cole on the basis of these paraphernalia. They most often live to regret it. In *The Monkey's Raincoat*, a Mexican criminal taunts Cole by fingering one of the figurines. Cole efficiently teaches him a very physical lesson. As he says to the man's partner, 'I didn't want you guys to think I was too easy' (90). Underneath the posturing, Cole is deadly serious about his business, and about its dangers as well as its responsibilities.

If Cole is a direct descendant of Chandler's Marlowe, quick to answer the call of wronged or abandoned women and children, he is an even more direct successor to Parker's Spenser. In many ways and regardless of the different locale – Los Angeles instead of Boston – Cole is a Spenser refurbished for the last decade of the twentieth century. When we first meet Cole in *The Monkey's Raincoat* he is 35 years old, 'five feet eleven and one-half inches tall ... one hundred seventy-six pounds, and ... licensed to carry a firearm' (2). For the past seven years he has owned 'The Elvis Cole Detective Agency'. Cole is a Vietnam veteran, a graduate of the 'two-year program' of the 'University of South-East Asia' (38). Like Spenser he has a rather mysterious, even sinister, partner: Joe Pike, an ex-marine and ex-LAPD officer, who now owns a gun shop in Culver City. Pike is an expert at at all weapons, but especially at hand-to-hand combat, who regularly serves abroad as a professional soldier. Pike invariably wears dark glasses and his supreme acknowledgement of glee is a barely perceptible twitch of the mouth. Like Hawk to Spenser, Pike is unwaveringly loyal to Cole; in almost every novel he saves Cole at least once. No pushover himself, Cole regularly beats or more likely kicks opponents into submission, and regularly leaves dead bodies in his wake. In their physical prowess, then, Cole and Pike resemble Parker's Spenser & Hawk duo, but again brought up to the present: whereas Spenser is an ex-boxer who keeps in training, Cole practises hatha yoga, tai chi, and tae kwon do, at times even comparing himself jokingly, and self-deprecatingly, to Bruce Lee.

The Cole novels are superbly plotted and full of suspense. *The Monkey's Raincoat*, for instance, is set in the movie world, as are a number of other Cole novels, and its plot centers upon the disappearance of a movie agent, Morton Lang, and his son. It ends with a classic shootout, in which the main criminal dies, together with a small army of mobsters. Pike is shot, Cole suffers major damage in a no-holds barred fist fight with a giant Eskimo bodyguard, but of course both heroes pull through. Still, Crais's particular forte is the portrayal of human relationships. Morton Lang's wife, Ellen, has to get a grip on herself and her life when she first has to learn to live without her husband. She also has to overcome her friend Janet's patronizing her. She even has to emancipate herself from her children, especially her older daughters, who treat her like a household fixture. Ellen begins to take charge by learning how to physically defend herself. She finally gets a firm handle on life again by shooting the master criminal, in legitimate self-defence. Now, she is ready to face the world on her own terms, and to make a new life for herself.

From *Free Fall* (1993) onwards Crais combines time-honored private investigation with more topical interests, in this particular case the Rodney King incident and the ensuing riots. Obviously, the novel is meant as a warning. The Rodney King case was bad in itself, but it is worse to let oneself be guided by the fall-out of such an event. In this particular case, a crack police team, and in particular its leader, are so jealous of their hitherto unblemished reputation that they are willing to commit far worse crimes to cover up the initial excessive use of violence of one of the team's members. A major theme of *Free Fall* is innocence, betrayed yet triumphant in the end. In the face of all appearances, Jennifer – the woman who calls in Cole – continues to believe in the innate decency of her fiancé, who belongs to the team in question, and the man finally justifies her trust. He denounces his fellow officers and his commander. Cole once again is a modern Marlowe, helping out the innocent and weak. In fact, these innocent prove rather tough in the end. In a move replicating what we saw in *The Monkey's Raincoat*, Jennifer firmly takes charge of the situation when she shoots a corrupt police officer about to kill her boyfriend.

Voodoo River marks a major development in Elvis Cole's character. In many ways, Cole is Mr Clean, and this undoubtedly explains much of his appeal. He does not smoke, does not drink much, only uses violence in self-defence, is extremely good looking, and generally qualifies as everybody's favorite son-in-law. In *The Monkey's Raincoat* Elvis has an affair, or perhaps rather a therapeutic relationship, with Ellen Lang, and a once-off encounter with another woman. Throughout the early Cole novels, though, Elvis basically is a man alone, with only a belligerent and jealous cat for company in his isolated house off Laurel Canyon. In *Voodoo River*, the stage is set very early on for an affair with Lucille Chenier, a 'petite' and extremely pretty Baton Rouge lawyer. In the next Cole novels, *Sunset Express* and *Indigo Slam*, the bond with Lucy will become ever more tight, and at the end of the latter novel, Lucy seems all set to move, together with her son Ben, to Los Angeles. At the same time, Elvis's involvement with Lucy also sets the stage for possible further intrigue, as her former husband obviously is not about to let her go so easily.

In *Sunset Express* the deepening relationship between Elvis and Lucy is thematized on all levels: Joe Pike and Angela Rossi, a policewoman falsely accused of tampering with evidence, turn out to have been lovers fifteen years earlier; Mrs Earle and Mr Lawrence, an elderly black couple, conduct a chaste courtship; even Elvis's cat has a fling. These happy relationships, however, stand in stark contrast with the main intrigue of the book. *Sunset Express* opens with the dramatic discovery of Susan Martin, clubbed to death and stuffed into plastic garbage bags, near a scenic overlook off Mulholland Drive, and less than a mile from her home. Her husband, 'Teddy' Martin, a famous millionaire restaurateur, is arrested for the murder. Martin claims that his wife was kidnapped, and that she was killed regardless of his having paid the required ransom.

Just as *Free Fall* seems at least partially inspired by the Rodney King case, *Sunset Express* reminds us of the O.J. Simpson case. And in both novels Cole in the end has to at least partially circumvent the law to get at the real villain. This ending is fully commensurate with both the prevailing public distrust in the legal system when it comes to punishing the true criminals, and with the typically American belief in the personal administration of justice. Lucy Chenier nicely sums up both beliefs when she remarks to Cole:

> The law is an adversarial contest that defines justice as staying within the rules and seeing the game to its conclusion. Justice is reaching a conclusion. It has very little to do with right and wrong. The law gives us order. Only men and women can give us what you want to call justice.
>
> (*Express*, 371)

As the Elvis Cole series grows, the idea of a true development from one novel to another is fostered by sometimes small but always telling references. In *Indigo Slam*, for instance, Edna Thornton, the African American woman from the Attorney General's Office with enough clout to authorize a risky operation involving counterfeit money, is willing to trust Cole because in *Free Fall* he helped another colored woman to clear her son's name. Also in *Indigo Slam* Cole is approached in the first place because of the publicity he gained from the Martin murder case in *Sunset Express*. At the same time, Elvis Cole's character continuously deepens. Even Joe Pike takes on more human traits. In fact, in *L.A. Requiem* (1999), Pike takes center stage. One of Pike's ex-girlfriends, Karen Garcia, has gone missing, and her father, one of the most powerful Hispanic politicians in the Los Angeles area, calls in the Elvis Cole Detective Agency. Karen is found dead in the Hollywood hills. When a second killing takes place, all signs begin to point to Joe Pike. Cole, who has blind faith in his partner, rushes to his aid, thereby jeopardizing his relationship with Lucy Chenier, who has arrived in Los Angeles to join him on a permanent basis.

Crais confronts Cole with a dilemma that Parker's Spenser never had to face. Lucy makes it quite clear that she must be the first person in Cole's life, if their relationship is going to have a real future, and that she finds it very difficult to accept that Cole's first interest, even temporarily, is Pike – who is, after all, almost a complete stranger to her. Although Cole does not really want to make a choice, his actions betray that loyalty is at least as strong as love: Pike's reputation and safety have priority. When Lucy's son is actually endangered she draws her conclusions and decides to go back to Lousiana. Although the novel does not overtly accuse her of anything, subtly we are invited to blame her for refusing to understand the depth of Cole's loyalty and of the friendship he feels for Pike. But Crais's decision to force a separation between Cole and Lucy in this particular way is far more interesting than the question of who is ultimately to blame.

It would seem that Crais, just before the turn of the millennium, reaches back into the past and revives an older tradition. Two truly manly, and almost infallible, males soldier on while the fallible woman – fallible because she cannot muster the stoic resignation demanded of her – is left behind. This traditionalist turn also betrays itself in the sections that for the first time reveal Pike's past and background. We read about Pike's authoritarian, loveless, and abusive father, his weak mother, his lonely childhood, his outstanding performance as a young Marine, the intense integrity and loyalty that cost him his LAPD-job and made him a social outcast. As a result of these experiences, Pike has not only developed superhuman self-control but also an extreme form of asocial individualism which has made him a moral law unto himself. In *L.A. Requiem* the old emphasis on male bonding and on a thoroughly masculine individualism reasserts itself with a vengeance. It is almost as if Crais has become uneasy with the prospect of a married private investigator – with a stepson thrown into the bargain – and at the last moment pulls his protagonist back from the brink of the disaster that is called marriage.

America as grotesque

An author who started out in the early 1990s, and who hitherto has won no major awards but instead enjoys a very solid 'underground' reputation, is George P. Pelecanos. Recently, his early novels have been reprinted to great acclaim not only in the United States, but also in Britain and elsewhere. In 1992, Pelecanos burst on the private eye scene with *A Firing Offense*, starring raw, gifted amateur detective Nick Stefanos. Born in Greece, Stefanos was brought to the United States at an early age, and raised in Washington DC by his grandparents. His grandfather and namesake, 'Big Nick', at one time used to be an enforcer for some bootleggers, and later invested his earnings in a Greek deli. At the start of the novel, Stefanos is an advertising manager for a consumer goods electronics company. He does not get on with his boss, and is not terribly thrilled with the job to begin with. At 30, he feels stalled in life. It is the memory of his grandfather that draws Stefanos into the private eye business when his help is called upon by an old man looking for his grandson.

A Firing Offense features the traditional first-person narrative, told by a reluctant private investigator with a definite drink problem, and set in a bleak late 1980s Washington DC cityscape, which from the opening paragraph sets the mood of the book:

> Torn lottery tickets and hot dog wrappers – the remnants of Georgia Avenue Day – blew across the strip. At the district line a snaggle-toothed row of winos sat on the ledge of a coffee shop. A poster of the mayor, a smiling portrait in debauchery, was taped to the window behind them. The coke sweat had been dutifully airbrushed from the mayor's forehead; only a contaminated grin remained. My Dart plodded south under a low gray cover of clouds.
>
> (*Offense*, 1)

Stefanos, who was born in 1958, is very much into music, and the names of singers, groups, albums, and tunes serve to situate events in time, but also to distinguish between *us* and *them*, between who belongs and who does not:

> This was late in '79 or early in '80, the watershed years that saw the debut release of the Pretenders, Graham Parker's *Squeezing Out Sparks*, and Elvis Costello's *Get Happy*, three of the finest albums ever produced. That I get nostalgic now when I hear 'You Can't Be Too Strong' or 'New Amsterdam', or when I smell cigarette smoke in a bar or feel sweat drip down my back in a hot club, may seem incredible today – especially to those who get misty-eyed over Sinatra, or even at the first few chords of 'Satisfaction' – but I'm talking about *my* generation. (116)

With music as with everything else, though, Stefanos definitely has the feeling that the best is long behind. His marriage has been over for some time, and while his ex-wife has moved up in the world, Stefanos seems to be sinking ever lower. In *A Firing Offense*, as in the later novels in the series, *Nick's Trip* (1993) and *Down By the River Where the Dead Men Go* (1995), he has some fleeting relations with women, but these always fizzle out, more often than not because the women move on to other men, better lives, whereas Stefanos stays behind.

In *Nick's Trip* Stefanos fathers a child at the request of a lesbian bar tender. As soon as she is pregnant, she moves to the West Coast with her partner, partly to prevent Stefanos from developing paternal feelings for the child. At the end of that novel, Stefanos starts an affair with Lyla, a pretty newspaper reporter, and things seem to be looking up. In *Down By the River Where the Dead Men Go*, however, it is pretty clear that both Stefanos and Lyla are drinking themselves into the ground. On a visit to Lyla's parents, her father (who used to be an alcoholic himself) tells Stefanos that he is probably a good man, but not for Lyla. The rest of the novel sees Stefanos unwinding his relationship with Lyla, much to her initial despair. At the end of the novel, though, when Stefanos dials Lyla, a man picks up the phone, and Stefanos has become history to yet another woman.

Nick Stefanos is an inveterate loner. In fact, he feels most at ease late at night, all alone behind the counter of 'The Spot', the bar he tends for a living. As in acknowledgement of this fact, *Down By the River Where the Dead Men Go* both starts and ends in 'The Spot', and with a drink – the drink that so often gets Stefanos into trouble but is his only friend and consolation in a bleak and downward-spiralling existence. At the end of *Down By the River Where the Dead Men Go* he has sunk so low that it is hard to imagine him going down any further.

Stefanos's steady deterioration, however, also reflects on the world he lives in. We get the impression that the United States is not a happly place to live in. The relationships between generations are almost never happy or close. Children, foremost Stefanos himself, never seem to live up to their parents' or grandparents' expectations. *A Firing Offense* closes with Stefanos toasting his grandfather's memory on Ocracoke Island, an island off the coast of South Carolina that he has visited in the course of his investigation. The men with whom he drinks have 'a startling island accent more northern European than American South' (215). These men, whom Stefanos soon calls his 'friends' (216), stand for European origins and earlier generations. For Theo, a friend of Stefanos's grandfather and a fellow Greek immigrant, America is better than the old country. Not so for Stefanos. *A Firing Offense* is a scathing critique of contemporary America, where innocence and youth are lost from the very beginning, and all is awash in drugs and alcohol, corruption and sales talk – where nothing is genuine nor anyone honest.

Nick's Trip focuses on the loss of youth, friendship and love. This applies first and foremost to Nick's relationship with Billy Goodrich, who was his best friend in high school. Although they eventually lost contact, he still thinks of Billy as a special friend. Therefore, it hurts him to find out that Billy – who murdered his wife and then hired Nick to cover his tracks – has simply tried to use him. What hurts even more, though, is that all the boyhood memories so dear to Nick mean absolutely nothing to his former friend. *Nick's Trip* is a nostalgic novel about the loss of illusions; about the past, too, with a smalltime mobster and erstwhile companion of Nick's grandfather setting the tone when he tells Nick: '"You have your grandfather's quick hands ... but you don't have his class"' (*Trip*, 63).

Child abuse is the red thread stringing together *Down By the River Where the Dead Men Go*. One night, just before Nick passes out in a drunken stupor, he witnesses a black boy being shot and shoved into the water. The boy turns out to have been mixed up in prostitution, pornography, and drugs, and to have been killed because he wanted out. Nick and Jack LaDuke, his partner in this novel, track down the source of all evil: an older white man, Samuels, very distinguished, and very depraved. In a scene reminiscent of hell, with bullets flying thick and fire madly leaping, Nick and LaDuke clean up the factory where Samuels does his dirty business. However, they cannot bring Samuels to justice. Nick ends up executing Samuels the way Calvin, the black boy, was killed: a gun in his mouth.

Though various clues could lead the police to Nick, he is never bothered. Boyle, an officer who hangs out at 'The Spot', tells Nick why: Boyle and the other officer who should have arrested Nick have themselves summarily executed a child molester some years before. LaDuke has become the weird character he is – half redneck, half fanatical preacher – because he was sexually abused by his father when still a child. In the end, that same father saves LaDuke's life when his son is grievously wounded in the Samuels factory shootout. The hideous and permanent facial disfigurement LaDuke carries away from this accurately reflects the psychological and social scar-tissue upon his and his nation's soul. Nick himself obviously is looking to atone for things when he decides to send the money this case earns him to California, to the child he fathered in *Nick's Trip*.

With *The Big Blowdown* (1996), *King Suckerman* (1997), and *The Sweet Forever* (1998), Pelecanos shifts gears. In these novels, Nick Stefanos features only as a minor character. These three novels, all third-person narratives, are in the James Cain tradition rather than that of Hammett or Chandler. Pelecanos had already tapped this vein with *Shoedog* (1994), a story about a liquor store robbery that goes shockingly wrong. In *King Suckerman* Pelecanos reaches back to 1976, America's bicentennial. *The Big Blowdown* goes even further back, to the 1940s, while *The Sweet Forever* is set in 1986, and is mostly a sequel to *King Suckerman*. Nick Stefanos or 'Big Nick' make brief appearances in each of these novels. At the end of *King Suckerman*, for instance, we see Nick going off on the trip, with Billy Goodrich, of *Nick's Trip*. Although violence erupts again and again in these novels, Pelecanos's real indictment of the US at the end of the twentieth century is to be found in the books featuring Stefanos as their major character. In particular in *Down by the River* Pelecanos gives us America as grotesque, as a hellish vision of almost uncontrollable perversion, greed, and weakness.

On the ball

Definitely lighter in tone than the fiction of Pelecanos is that of Harlan Coben. The impression of lightness is enhanced by the setting of Coben's fiction, the world of sports. Though not unique to Coben – Troy Soos, for instance, in the early 1990s initiated a historical detective series starring baseball player Mickey Rawlings – such a setting was still a novelty when *Deal Breaker*, the first novel to star Myron Bolitar, a sports agent and private investigator, appeared in 1995. This novel won the Anthony Award for Best Paperback Original, and was also nominated for an Edgar. The second Bolitar instalment, *Drop Shot* (1996), drew relatively little attention, but the third, *Fade Away* (1996) won both an Edgar and a Shamus Award, and was nominated for an Anthony. *Backspin* (1997) again won Coben a nomination. Coben himself is exceptionally tall, grew up in New Jersey, and used to play basketball – all things he shares with his hero Myron Bolitar. Though basketball features prominently in a number of Bolitar novels, football takes center stage in *Deal Breaker*, tennis in *Drop Shot*, golf in *Backspin*, and baseball in *The Final Detail* (1999).

Good-looking, charming, and wonderfully witty, Bolitar not only is a former pro-basketball player, but also holds a Harvard Law School degree. Now in his thirties, he runs a star sports agency in New York, together with his business partner, a bisexual former lady professional wrestler, and another female ex-wrestler. Providing Bolitar the backup Hawk provides for Parker's Spenser, and Pike for Crais's Elvis Cole, is Windsor Horne Lockwood III. *One False Move* (1998), the first novel in the series to make hardcover publication, calls 'Win' a 'financial consultant at Lock-Horne Securities, an old-money financial firm that first sold equities on the *Mayflower*' (*Move*, 15).

Lockwood is very well groomed, very rich, very blond, and very dangerous. In fact, he quite often is just a little too much of a good thing. The same, actually, goes for Bolitar himself, whose *bon mots*, and much-touted charm and wit, even if ironized, regularly start to grate. Given the inflated and often even almost cartoon-like nature of these characters, and considering that Coben's plots are often convoluted to the point of ricocheting, it is rather surprising that the Bolitar novels nevertheless succeed in striking a deeply human chord. Undoubtedly, this has a lot to do with the relationship between Myron, his friends, and, in particular, his parents, with whom he continues to live in the first couple of novels. What also helps is that the novels, though written in the third person, closely stick to Myron's perspective, focalizing things and events through him. Finally, and increasingly so as the series progresses, the link between the cases Bolitar becomes involved in and his own life, past and present, grows more intimate.

A peculiar strength of the Myron Bolitar series lies in its use of sports, perhaps a more pervasive social presence in the United States than anywhere else and, therefore, a powerful metaphor for the country, in order to reflect on recent American social and political developments. *One False Move* focuses on racial tension, discrimination, and multiculturalism. At the very beginning of the novel Myron drives through his New Jersey boyhood neigborhood, looking at the basketball playgrounds. Comparing his own days of practicing with black kids with what he sees now is a chilling experience:

> ... the looks of curious animosity he received back then were nothing compared with the dagger-death glares of these kids. Their hatred was naked, up front, filled with cold resignation. Corny to say, but back then – less than twenty years ago – there had been something different here. More hope maybe. Hard to say.
>
> (*One False Move*, 20)

The train of thought Myron here starts reaches an unexpected conclusion almost at the end of the novel when he goes to confront the novel's killer:

> ... he had been wondering lately about his own race issues. Now he saw the truth. His semi-latent prejudices had twisted on him like a snake seizing its own tail. Mabel Edwards. The sweet old black lady. Butterfly McQueen. Miss Jane Pittman. Knitting needles and reading glasses. Big and kind and matronly. Evil could never lurk in so politically correct a form. (314)

It does, of course. Once they get beyond the wisecracks and the antics of Bolitar's human entourage – Lockwood, the lady wrestlers – and start to concentrate on family intrigue and on how the past, including Bolitar's personal past, can come to haunt the present, Coben's novels assume tragic overtones.

High jinks in Trenton

Because of its mix of naivety and high spirits and its liberal deployment of screwball comedy elements, it is easy to mistake Janet Evanovich's Stephanie Plum series for a minor and facile take-off on a well-established genre. Instead, underneath the frolicking, Evanovich is redrawing the boundaries of that genre. She steers away from the almost exclusive concentration on high profile social issues that have come to dominate the genre over the last decade, especially so in the work of the majority of ethnic and female crime writers. At the same time, she does not avoid such issues.

With the appearance of her first Stephanie Plum mystery, *One for the Money*, in 1994, Janet Evanovich, who under both her own name and various others had already published a dozen books, most of them humorous romances, sounded an original PI note. She also immediately started a climb to the top of the bestseller list. The sequels, *Two for the Dough* (1996), *Three to Get Deadly* (1997), *Four to Score* (1998), *High Five* (1999), and *Hot Six* (2000), have only added to the popularity of Stephanie Plum. Most of these books also won awards, or were nominated for them. *One for the Money*, for instance, won the British Crime Writers' Association John Creasey Award and was also nominated for an Agatha and an Edgar, while *Three to Get Deadly* won the CWA's Silver Dagger. These are funny novels, skilfully combining the private eye and the romance, with fast and witty dialogues, and well-developed plots.

At the outset of *One for the Money* 32-year-old Stephanie Plum loses her job as a buyer of lingerie for a Newark department store. She turns to bounty hunting for her cousin Vinnie's bail bonding company. Stephanie thus goes from the most intimately feminine of female occupations straight to the most ruggedly masculine of male jobs. The tension between the two spheres Stephanie is thus linked to allows Evanovich to ironically undercut presentday mainstream detective writing. She does so in the character of Stephanie herself, and in her relationships with her family, friends, and colleagues. Still, the fact that the Stephanie Plum novels are to a large extent a send-up of currently fashionable women's detective writing does not prevent them from addressing the same issues as their more 'serious' counterparts. In *One for the Money*, for instance, Stephanie succeeds in putting a killer behind bars (from which he will return in *High Five*). In *Three to Get Deadly*, she uncovers a long-standing pornography business operating from the local candy-shop and ice-cream cone store. If the killer in *One for the Money* is portrayed as entirely loathsome, in *Three to Get Deadly* the pornographer turns out to be 'good', even 'saintly', uncle Moses.

Stephanie's typical theater of operations is the 'burg', the mixed, mostly Italian and East-European, ethnic neighborhood in Trenton, New Jersey, she originates from. Permanent members of the cast include Joe Morelli, Lula, Grandma Mazur, Ranger, and a host of minor characters, such as Stephanie's Hungarian-descended parents, and the colorful assemblage of elderly neighbors in her apartment building. Morelli is of Italian immigrant stock, and a police officer in the Vice department. Stephanie and Joe have known each other since childhood. In *Four to Score* – and in every other novel of the series – Stephanie tells us that when she was 16 Joe 'sweet-talked me out of my underwear, laid me down on the floor behind the eclair case [at the baker's where she was working] one day after work and relieved me of my virginity' (*Four*, 14). Though Stephanie always assures the reader, and herself, that 'the only way he'd get back into my pants would be at gunpoint' (14), she in fact experiences complete meltdown whenever Morelli is around. Though she suspects him of chasing every skirt in town, he in fact only seems to be waiting for her to make up her mind to stick with him.

In each novel Stephanie and Morelli find themselves working on related cases, though often from opposite ends. Part of the fun in these novels therefore results from their attempts to outwit each other. Stephanie usually wins, even though she is, as Morelli tells her in *Two for the Dough*, 'the worst bounty hunter in the history of the world' (*Two*, 301). To underscore that Morelli is quite correct in this evaluation, Evanovich has her heroine regularly take on what look like quick and harmless assignments. Invariably, these end up in scary encounters with homicidal maniacs and other raving lunatics. Equally invariably, Stephanie makes a mess of things. Her success at solving each novel's primary case, then, delivers an ironic comment on the machismo of classic male private eye fiction. At the same time, the way in which she arrives at her successes, and her obvious bumbling in most other circumstances, form an equally ironic comment on mainstream women's detective fiction, and especially on the professional efficiency that the heroines of this fiction take such pride in.

In *One for the Money*, Lula, a 250-pound black prostitute, gets hurt through Stephanie's fault. When she is 'reformed', through Stephanie's doing, she also gets a job as a filing clerk with the bail bond firm. From *Three to Get Deadly* on Lula starts to serve as backup for Stephanie. As such, Lula partially comes to replace Ranger. Initially, Ranger obviously is Evanovich's answer to Spenser's Hawk and Cole's Pike. A fitness freak of Cuban descent, he is also a weapons expert, master stalker, supreme bounty hunter, and the man who teaches Stephanie the essentials of the trade in *One for the Money*. Ranger habitually dresses in black, drives a black BMW, and is every woman's wildest dream. To have Ranger, even if only partially, replaced by Lula amounts to turning the classic private eye genre inside out. In order to press the point, Evanovich has Grandma Mazur, Stephanie's maternal grandmother, likewise develop an interest in Stephanie's bounty hunting activities. Grandma starts carrying a .45, and volunteers to accompany Stephanie on her forays. At the same time, neither Lula nor Grandma Mazur are anything like the female private eyes Sue Grafton or Sara Paretsky have familiarized us with. No one, of course, could be further removed from the likes of Kinsey Millhone or V.I. Warshawski than Stephanie Plum herself.

The difference already shows in the names of the various protagonists. Whereas both 'Kinsey' and 'V.I.' could refer to men as well as women, and imply a certain no-nonsense matter-of-factness and ruggedness, 'Stephanie' can only be the name of a woman, and definitely suggests a feminine sensuality. This impression is heightened by the family name of 'Plum', with its suggestion of fullness, ripeness, and sweetness. The name accurately prefigures the descriptions of Stephanie throughout the novels. 'Millhone' and 'Warshawski', on the contrary, sound straightforward and business-like. Like Kinsey and V.I., Stephanie has briefly been married – until, as she puts it in *Four to Score*, she encountered her husband 'playing hide-the-salami' with Joyce Barnhardt, 'bare-assed on [the] dining room table' (*Four*, 3). Joyce, a girl with fabulous breasts, and now also a bounty hunter for Vinnie, has been Stephanie's rival since high school. Joyce constantly lures Vinnie into cutting her in on Stephanie's cases. Stephanie, usually with the help of Joe, invariably succeeds in besting Joyce. By thus exploiting the theme of female rivalry in both the sexual and the professional field, Evanovich humorously, but no less obviously, goes against the drift of mainstream contemporary women's detective writing with its emphasis on female solidarity and bonding.

The same thing goes for Stephanie's relationship not only to Morelli, but also to her own family. Kinsey Millhone and V.I. Warshawski maintain no regular family ties. In this sense, they follow the tradition of classic male private eyes. Of course, at the end of the 1990s it has become almost a commonplace for crime writers to give their heroes a sense of family, and also to situate them in their personal relationships. Evanovich takes things somewhat further, though. Stephanie Plum has an extended family. She not only works for her cousin, there is always an uncle or an aunt somewhere in the background. Moreover, as a single woman, Stephanie is regularly expected to dine at her parents. These dinners are set pieces in each novel, and always feature Grandma Mazur looking to fix up Stephanie with eligible bachelors.

Evanovich's ironic undercutting of both male and female private eye conventions does not end with the character of Stephanie, and her personal relationships. It extends to most of the stock-in-trade of classic private eye fiction. Two examples in point are the use of cars, and of personal appearance. As we argued in our introduction, especially in male crime writing these elements often provide clues as to where and how to fit the various characters into their world. Contrary to what is the custom with her male colleagues – and undoubtedly also meant as such – Sue Grafton, in the very first novel of her Kinsey Millhone series, *'A' is for Alibi* (1982), makes a point of having her heroine downplay the importance of her car for her: a 1968 VW, 'one of those vague beige models with assorted dents ... it needs a tune-up but I never have time' (*'A'*, 5).

Evanovich is obviously well aware of the fetish role cars play in American crime writing, and she both skilfully adapts this convention, and ironizes it at the same time. Specifically, she turns Stephanie's relationship to her car into a running gag. At the beginning of *One for the Money*, Stephanie is allowed to drive Morelli's Toyota 4WD. It promptly gets blown up. In *Three to Get Deadly* she buys a Nissan pickup. This keeps stalling on her. When she finally has it fixed, it is blown away with a rocket-launcher. In *Four to Score* she has treated herself to a small, neat, sporty Honda CRX. Soaked with gasoline by a jealous lover, it is ignited by the mother of someone Stephanie pursues. In *Two for the Dough* Stephanie gets to drive her deceased uncle's powder blue 1953 Buick. Obviously, this is not the inconspicuous kind of car a bounty hunter on a stake-out wishes for. Yet, throughout the series this continues to be the only car that never stalls upon Stephanie, never lets her down, is solid as a tank, and effectively protects her from bullets and road maniacs. As things keep happening to her regular cars, Stephanie, much against her own wishes, is time and again reduced to fall back on the Buick. The message here, as with so many other elements in the Stephanie Plum series, is clear: it is the old, homely, and solidly 'American' values that carry the day, even if they look somewhat dated, or even dowdy.

Meticulous descriptions of the private eye's appearance have been part and parcel of the genre since its beginning. Chandler, for instance, has Marlowe present himself as follows in the very first paragraph of *The Big Sleep*: 'I was wearing my powder-blue suit, with dark blue shirt, tie and display handkerchief, black brogues, black wool socks with dark blue clocks on them' (*Sleep*, 9). In *Tunnel Vision* (1994) Paretsky has Vic Warshawski dress 'carefully for [her] meeting .... in black wool with a white silk shirt and ... red Magli pumps' (17). Crais ironizes hard-boiled tradition when in the opening paragraphs of *The Monkey's Raincoat* (1987) he has Cole hope that his client does not think Cole '*déclassé* in [his] white Levi's and Hawaiian shirt' (1). Evanovich does the same thing when she has Stephanie describe her typical daily wear as a 'black spandex sports bra ... matching spandex shorts and a sleeveless oversized Trenton Thunders baseball jersey' (*Four*, 1). Chandler's Marlowe and Paretsky's Warshawski deliberately dress up for work. Grafton's Millhone, in contrast, studiously avoids any particular attention to her wardrobe. Evanovich plays on both approaches: when she has Stephanie dress for the part, it is usually as a tart. In *One for the Money*, for instance, she poses as a hooker. In *Four to Score*, Stephanie needs to lure a gangster out of the funeral home where he is paying his respects to a deceased gang boss. Ranger tells her this will take 'smooth white skin barely hidden behind a short skirt and tight sweater' (*Four*, 39). Fifteen minutes later, Stephanie recounts,

> I was dressed in four-inch FMPs (short for 'fuck-me-pumps,' because when you walked around in them you looked like Whorehouse Wonder Bitch) ... I shimmied into a low-cut black knit dress that was bought with the intent of losing five pounds, gunked up my eyes with a lot of black mascara and beefed up my cleavage by stuffing Nerf balls into my bra. (40)

By carefully and systematically overhauling the conventions of the genre, Evanovich has created a hilarious subgenre all by herself. Rewriting the genre from within, combining and reconciling the various trends threatening to explode it, she returns it to its roots as popular entertainment.

8
The 'English Tradition' in Contemporary American Crime Fiction

When in 1962 P.D. James published her first novel, *Cover Her Face*, few readers will have suspected that James's work would give a new lease on life to the, at that point, moribund genre of the classic English mystery novel. *Cover Her Face* is not exceptional, and neither is its police protagonist, Adam Dalgliesh. That is to say, he *is* rather exceptional – tall, dark, moody, a published poet – but not compared to most Golden Age detectives created by the women writers who in this first novel are clearly James's inspiration. Reminiscent of Ngaio Marsh's Roderick Alleyn, Dalgliesh does as far as exceptionality goes not particularly stand out in the company of Dorothy Sayers' Peter Wimsey, Margery Allingham's Albert Campion, or, for that matter, Alleyn himself. As we can see now, however, James's mysteries developed into complex meditations on deception, guilt, and retribution – occasionally at the expense of their mystery element – while Dalgliesh became more enigmatic and reminded us less and less of his Golden Age precursors.

That an Englishwoman who had come of age in the aftermath of the Depression (James was born in 1920), and who had worked as a Red Cross nurse during the Second World War, would set the classic mystery on a new, more serious and darker course, is with hindsight perhaps not so surprising. What does come as a surprise is that since the early 1980s a number of American women writers have followed James's lead in revitalizing this particular genre, although not necessarily along her lines. I should emphasize that what I have in mind here is not the revitalization of the classic mystery *per se*, such as the donnish mysteries featuring Amanda Cross's Columbia-based professor Kate Fansler, but contributions to the revitalization of the specifically *English* version of the mystery, complete with English characters and English settings. If successful, or at least mostly successful, as is the case with the English mystery series developed by, for instance, Martha Grimes and Elizabeth George, such contributions are genuine *tours de force* that derive added interest from the fact that they have been created, so to speak, from outside. Whatever else they may be, because of their non-English origin they are inevitably self-conscious constructs that built upon a deep familiarity with the conventions of the genre.

Martha Grimes, Long Piddleton, and the twelfth Viscount Ardry

Martha Grimes, who published her first mystery in 1981, makes no attempt to hide her intimate knowledge of the classics of mystery and detective writing: references abound to both the male tradition – from Poe to Chandler – and the female one – Sayers, Christie, Josephine Tey, and the highly rated P.D. James. More in general, and in keeping with a prominent strand of the classic English mystery, Grimes's crime fiction is intensely literary. It invites us to revisit that pleasant realm of the English literary mystery created by Michael Innes, Nicholas Blake, Edmund Crispin and other highly literate writers in whose work literary history is never far away and who more than their less well-read colleagues emphasize the 'comedy' part of the comedy of manners that the classic mystery so often is. Especially Crispin's sense of comedy echoes in Grimes's novels, in which, as I have already suggested, literary allusions abound. We come across Shakespeare, Rimbaud, Marlowe, Browning, Trollope, Coleridge, Henry James, Grahame's *The Wind in the Willows*, and so on, in an impressive range of references, some of which are structurally functional. In Grimes's debut, *The Man with a Load of Mischief* (1981), a murder is made possible by the way a specific scene from *Othello* is staged. In *The Horse You Came In On* (1993) an early reference to Chatterton (which will resurface at various points in the novel) introduces a story that hinges on forgery. *Horse* is more generally a good example of Grimes's literariness: the novel contains fragments from a novel in progress by one of the characters (somewhat reminiscent of Djuna Barnes's *Nightwood*), offers a fake Poe story (which cleverly announces its own fakeness), and throws in an aborted scene from a mystery two other characters are trying to cook up. As if this is not enough, for the more academically oriented connoisseur Grimes presents a deconstructionist poet who is appropriately self-serving and talentless (Elizabeth George gives a similarly dismissive treatment to a Marxist literary critic in one of her novels), next to references to such unfrequented nooks in literary history as the Algonquin Round Table. Part of the pleasure of reading Grimes, then, is the pleasure of recognition: we encounter familiar themes, familiar locales – the village of Long Piddleton which returns in all the novels is of standard 'postcard' picturesqueness – familiar references, and familiar conventions. Clearly counting on our familiarity with the genre, Grimes conspirationally draws us into the game she is playing: her first novel, *The Man With a Load of Mischief* comes complete with the sort of map of Long Piddleton – not wholly appropriately designed in Tolkien-like fashion – that we associate with the heyday of the classic mystery.

Grimes's two main detectives are true to the classic convention. Like P.D. James's Adam Dalgliesh, her Superintendent Richard Jury reminds us of Roderick Alleyn: good-looking, tall, formidable in an unassuming, contemplative way, and yet compassionate and attentive. In many ways Jury, although a professional, resembles the highly literate and cultured amateur detective: there are books all over his apartment and, being a gentleman, he is essentially without ambition. His collaborator Melrose Plant, former twelfth Viscount Ardry and eighth Earl of Caverness, is a wealthy, fastidious, and somewhat diffident aristocrat who combines elements of Sayers's Peter Wimsey (the sartorial finesse and general knowledgeability), Allingham's Albert Campion (the diffident manner), and Crispin's Gervase Fen (the professorship in literature), even if Plant, unlike Wimsey, is always reluctant to leave his impressive country estate for the delights of the metropolis. But he comes complete with a gentleman's gentleman and the taste in cars we expect from his kind ('"Will you be requiring the Flying Spur or the Rolls, sir?"'). Even some of the comedy – one aspect in which Grimes easily outdoes her female predecessors – seems familiar: Jury's relationship with his formidable, and formidably attractive, co-tenant Carole-anne Pulatski reminds one increasingly, as the series develops, of the curious relationship between Albert Campion and the improbable Magersfontein Lugg. Like Lugg, she does not have a wholly reputable background, which includes a stint as a topless dancer, goes in for a sort of possessive mothering that includes the usual attempts at emotional blackmail, and treats her charge's possessions and rooms as if they are joint property: 'Carole-anne had decided three months ago that her favorite policeman should have [his flat] redecorated and (naturally without his knowledge) had called Decors, one of the swankiest outfits in London, to come round with their swatches' (*I Am Only the Running Footman*, 170).

In most of Grimes's novels the light mood that results from this sort of comedy, and that gives a self-conscious twist to the tradition, is never far away. In Jury's private life we have Carole-anne, in his professional existence there is the hypochondriacal Sergeant Wiggins and the feud between the cat Cyril and Jury's chief Racer, who is exactly as inferior to Jury as superiors are supposed to be, while in Melrose Plant's entourage there is the cast of Long Piddleton characters and the constant if not always convincing fuss they create. These novels are more than averagely entertaining: the comedy is woven into (sometimes too) ingenious, suspenseful plots. Grimes moves like a fencer around scenes and characters, offering a heady succession of angles and perspectives, and the language sparkles, the more so since the reader is always aware that here we have an American writer impeccably reproducing British idioms and accents. The odd ones out are *The Horse You Came In On* and *Rainbow's End* (1995) in which Grimes decides to use American settings: Baltimore and New Mexico, respectively.

Curiously, with American settings Grimes is out of her element. Although, just as Elizabeth George, she is good on American stereotypes like the awful Baltimore cabbie in *The Horse You Came In On*, she is inexplicably weak in imagining how the American cityscape must strike a fairly reclusive and utterly English upper-class character like Melrose Plant who finds it 'so difficult ... to make a trip, to bestir himself, to drag himself away from hearth and home and the Jack and Hammer' (*Horse*, 75). We never get the feeling of amazed and uneasy estrangement that we expect from Plant's confrontation with Baltimore. On the contrary, on his way from the airport to the city he reflects that 'there was nothing much to see on this typical airport-to-centre-city trip which could have been in London, Baltimore, New York, or anywhere except possibly Calcutta' (112). America simply does not register on Plant's consciousness. The best (and most implausible) example of this incomprehensible blindness on the part of Plant, who is otherwise fastidious enough, is his almost thoughtless putting on of the presumably not utterly clean clothes and cap of a dead bum. Perhaps we must conclude that while as an American Grimes is perfectly attuned to the 'strangeness' of England, and can, therefore, create a convincing fictional representation, she is too familiar with the American scene to imagine how 'strange' it still is in European eyes.

While in *The Five Bells and Bladebone* (1987) Grimes had already almost violated her readers' expectations by creating serious confusion with regard to a killer's identity, in a recent Jury and Plant novel, *The Case Has Altered* (1997), Grimes more fundamentally transcends both her own earlier novels and the limits of the classic English mystery. We have the usual comedy, although more low-key than usual, we have the usual problem of getting Plant convincingly into the action (at Jury's request he poses as a connoisseur of antiques), and we have the sly fun that Grimes in her more recent novels is fond of poking at her characters. Curiously, the narrator's irony at times strongly reminds us of Henry James's late novels: 'Plant's smile was, well, *dapper*'. (*Case*, 224)

Although no one would describe *The Case Has Altered* as the sort of mystery the late Henry James might have produced, the novel certainly shows us what Grimes can do in the way of serious writing. Arresting and precise descriptions abound: 'out in the distant pastures, the rime-caked sheep looked as if they were dressed in glass coats' (11); a house sits 'behind tall, thin trees that looked more like bars than trees, straight and evenly spaced' (21); a barmaid vigorously starts 'wiping down the bar. Having been left in charge, she was going to exert her limited authority and flaunt whatever sexuality she could muster.' (213) Melrose Plant, in the earlier novels often not much more than an observing consciousness, is given convincing insights into other characters:

> ... Melrose thought this must be the source of [Parker's] magnetism.... He did not waste time in small talk; he plunged right into the way he felt about life. Unlike many who gave the impression of divided attention – whose minds, you knew, were elsewhere – Parker's attention was wholly concentrated on the person he was with; he projected a sense of immediacy. He was not afraid to reveal things about himself, which invited whoever he was with to do the same. This was the source of the comfort Parker unknowingly and unselfconsciously offered. One felt at home. (183)

Grimes is also quite good on the complicated and delicate relationship between Jury and the defendant, the Jenny Kennington he has first met in *The Anodyne Necklace* (1983), a relationship that here founders on a mutual lack of trust and on the woman's secretiveness. Grimes catches all the strains and the subtle emotional shifts. We find the same subtle appreciation of mood and tensions in the interrogations that Jury conducts, that of the murdered girl's family, for instance, and in the novel's dialogues. On top of this, Grimes perfectly captures the desolate and wind-swept Lincolnshire Fens in winter.

In *The Case Has Altered* Grimes almost closes the gap with the serious novel. That she is well capable of this had already been illustrated by a non-series novel, the 1996 *Hotel Paradise* which, although driven by a number of mysteries and a sort of investigation, is only marginally a mystery. We have the enigmatic drowning of a young girl, over 40 years ago; a murder, some 20 years ago, of which the man who was found guilty is probably innocent; an unsolved murder in the present, and the unexplained appearances of a mysterious young woman; but the heart of the novel is its recreation of *temps perdu*. Central to *Hotel Paradise* is a strangely muted and innocent 1950s in an unidentifiable small town locale somewhere in the US – we may be in northern Pennsylvania or upstate New York, but Grimes is careful not to give away any definite clues. Television plays no role, there are no fast food franchises, and the local sheriff on his daily rounds slots dimes into parking meters to keep his flock from breaking the law. The magical hush that plays over everything and that gives the novel its timeless quality has to do with the voice and the limited perspective of its narrator, the 12-year-old Emma, whose discovery of who and what she is and of a wider world in which old loyalties must inevitably be redefined, is the foreground for Grimes's fascinating picture of small town life in the 1950s.

Elizabeth George, the eighth Earl of Asherton, and Acton, North London

Martha Grimes has done interesting things with the classic English mystery. Still, Elizabeth George (1949) must be considered the best of the writers who in the last two decades have revitalized the genre. Moreover, judging by the number of reprintings of her books – more than a dozen for her first novel – she is also the most successful, so that for once critical acclaim and popular success are not at odds with one another.

That first book, *A Great Deliverance* (1988), is a virtuoso performance. However, that is not what the reader expects after all the necessary introductions have been made. In fact, George's CID Detective Inspector Lynley, who will dominate the series that will develop from *A Great Deliverance,* initially has all the earmarks of a Lord Peter Wimsey replay, and his entourage is not much more promising. Our first glimpse of Lynley is that of a 'tall man who managed to look as if somehow he'd been born wearing morning dress.' In keeping with this, '[h]is move ments [are] graceful, fluid, like a cat's' (31). Lynley is not only the Eighth Earl of Asherton, with an Eton and Oxford background, he is also rich, living in posh Belgravia and with a Bentley to take him to the ancestral estate in Cornwall if he is so inclined. As we will find out in George's fourth novel, *A Suitable Vengeance* (1991), the estate comes complete with a smuggler's cove, an abandoned mine, and an old mill. He excels, moreover, at his job. In short, as policewoman Barbara Havers, who is assigned to work with him early in the novel – a partnership that will turn out to be a major variation upon the male/female partnership convention – tells herself somewhat sourly, 'He was the golden boy in more ways than one' (48). Lynley's inner circle reflects the exceptional (and improbable) qualities of the man himself. His close friend Simon Allcourt-St James is a brilliant forensic scientist and has in his early 30s 'known too much pain and sorrow at far too young an age' (36) and the women – St James's bride Deborah and Lynley's friend Lady Helen Clyde – are as impossibly attractive as the girls featuring in many classic mysteries (those of John Dickson Carr, for instance). After this, it cannot come as a surprise that Lynley easily matches his female companions in the looks department: he is 'the handsomest man' Havers has ever seen. But with Barbara Havers George has already laid a potential bomb under this paragon of looks and breeding and introduced a perspective to which Dorothy Sayers never exposed Lord Peter Wimsey: 'She loathed him.' (31)

Barbara Havers, who will become Lynley's permanent partner in the series, is in virtually everything his opposite. Her background and accent are definitely working class, her education is of the grammar-school kind, she is plain and dumpy and is, moreover, well aware of it. In her late 20s, she still lives with her parents in a 'wrong' street in Acton, North London, and fights an utterly depressing daily battle with her mother's at this point still rather serene madness and her father's addiction to betting and snuff – a habit which his doctor has expressly forbidden. As if this is not enough, the father has an aversion to bathing and has the equally unsettling, although less offensive, habit of referring to himself in the third person. Apart from the mental condition of her parents, but surely related to it, the most disturbing element in the Havers household is the shrine devoted to Barbara's long dead younger brother who died of leukemia at the age of ten: an elaborate, sick construction placed in such a way that the boy's picture can watch the 'telly'. Given such circumstances, we are not surprised to find that Havers has a more than average chip on her shoulder, the more so since her one experience with a man (as we learn in a later novel) has not even included the morning after. But, as Lynley realizes in *A Great Deliverance*, 'There was no question of angry virginity here. It was something else.' (118) It is this something else that has dogged Havers's police career so far. At one point promoted to Criminal Investigation she 'has proved herself incapable of getting along with a single DI for her entire tenure in CID' (24). As a result she has been demoted, a decision that has led her 'termagant personality' to explode in a memorable way. When *A Great Deliverance* opens, her superiors, aware of her undeniable ability, agree to give her one more chance, coupling her with the infallibly courteous and ever-patient Lynley, a gamble that unexpectedly pays off. This particular partnership is a brilliant innovation. While Grimes sticks to the standard combination of two males (who, in a minor deviation from tradition, are each other's equals), George makes a very uneasy male–female relationship part of her reworking of the classic format.

The Lynley–Havers relationship is a subtheme in all of George's books, but in *A Great Deliverance*, where its foundations are laid, it plays an exceptionally important role. George brilliantly creates correspondences between the case Lynley and Havers are sent out to investigate in the imaginary Yorkshire Dales village of Keldale and Havers's personal life, sometimes even in a literal sense, as when the shrine to her deceased brother in her parents' living room is mirrored by the shrine that a murdered Yorkshire farmer has apparently devoted to his long disappeared spouse. Inexplicably, George totally implausibly arranges for Allcourt-St James and his wife – with whom, to complicate matters, Lynley is in love – to be honeymooning in the same village. In fact, Allcourt-St James, like Lynley presumably the product of an infatuation on the author's part with either a certain type of Golden Age detective novel or with a certain sector of English society, will never find a natural place in George's novels, his presence usually unnecessary and always forced. Only Lady Helen Clyde, who gradually replaces Deborah Allcourt-St James in Lynley's affections and finally, after intense heart-to-heart talks in *For the Sake of Elena* (1992) consents to marry him (and actually does so in *In the Presence of the Enemy*, 1996), will become more or less integrated in the series.

But to return to Lynley and Havers. The case that takes them to Yorkshire is one in which a young woman has been found next to her father's decapitated body and has confessed to the crime only to completely shut up afterwards. The case is, however, by no means as straightforward as it seems. For one thing, the murder weapon has gone missing; for another, there seems to be no motive. Lynley and Havers succeed in unravelling an extraordinarily complicated mystery, in which one discovery leads to another. In a technique that she also uses to great effect in her other novels, and that suggests a parallel with archeological excavation, George allows her detectives to strip away layer after layer of deceptions and falsehoods until finally the terrible truth stands revealed.

In *A Great Deliverance* that truth is incestuous abuse, the systematic and prolonged abuse by a religious fanatic of his two young daughters, one of whom has years ago run away to save herself. This older sister, who is now in her mid-20s, is in the course of the investigation tracked down by Havers and is subsequently confronted with the sister she has last seen as a little girl. In the harrowing scene that follows she succeeds in breaking through the stupor that has overtaken her younger sister since their father's death. Her detailed description of the father's sexual demands provokes a response from the younger sister who in so doing finally returns to speech. It also has an enormous impact on Havers, who with Lynley and some others is watching the scene from behind a one-way glass panel. Havers crashes blindly from the room to find a restroom and is violently sick. The terrible form of abuse that has just been revealed to her and the overwhelming feelings of guilt experienced by the sisters – the younger turns out indeed to have murdered her father – forcibly bring home the total inadequacy of her own parents and confront her with her own feelings of guilt. We learn that Havers's parents never visited their ten-year-old son in hospital because they could not cope with his illness, leaving the daily visits to his sister, the emotionally vulnerable teenager Barbara, who has never forgiven herself for not being there when he actually died and who has ever since taken a subtle, insidious and rather disturbing revenge: the shrine in the Havers's living room is of her making, a way to daily remind her parents of their inadequacy and guilt, just as the shrine in the farm probably has been created by the older sister to remind her father of his failure as the husband of a runaway wife and mother. Confronting the fact that she has substantially contributed to the misery of her parents' lives and possibly even to her mother's feeble-mindedness, Havers 'put her head down on the porcelain and wept. She wept for the hate that had filled her life, for the guilt and the jealousy that had been her companions, for the loneliness that she had brought upon herself, for the contempt and disgust she had directed towards others.' When Lynley, who has followed her, 'wordlessly [takes] her in his arms', she weeps 'against his chest, mourning most of all the death of the friendship that could have lived between them.' (308)

As this makes clear, Havers's view of Lynley has dramatically changed. From slick, loathsome, and impossibly aristocratic womanizer Lynley has become a potential friend, a development made possible by the mutual respect that has grown in the course of the novel and by a shared sense of humour. But Havers is also aware that an earlier and ugly personal attack, triggered by the class bias and personal unhappiness that consistently lead her to completely misconstrue his behavior and feelings, may very well have destroyed that potential friendship.

This, however, is not the case. Lynley has not only in the meantime realized that Havers's unreasonable aggressiveness has more to do with her personal problems than with anything he might do or not do, he also knows that her anger, although totally off its immediate target, is not wholly misplaced: '... beyond Havers there was truth. For underneath her bitter, unfounded accusations, her ugliness and hurt, the words she spoke rang with veracity.' (243) Lynley, who in the later novels repeatedly shows an intense self-awareness, is willing to redirect Havers's anger and to hook it up with his real shortcomings: his sexual encounter with a Keldale witness that Havers has overheard and, more mysteriously, sins that are only hinted at when he briefly reflects on his reasons for having chosen this particular profession: '*It's a penance ... an expiation for sins committed ....*' (128) Considering that he is not in a position to cast the first stone – the reasons for which are spelled out in *A Suitable Vengeance* – Lynley is able to make allowances for Havers's personal demons and ends by giving her a chance to redeem herself and by offering the moral support that she now has come to appreciate. Fully aware of the limitations of Havers's social graces and of the fact that easy personal relationships will probably be forever beyond her, he has also come to value her honesty, her courage, her ability, and her devotion to the job.

With its unexpected twists and revelations, *A Great Deliverance* is a wholly satisfying mystery in the Golden Age tradition. But it is more than that. George gives an unprecedented depth to the conventional figure of the aristocratic detective, who in her hands, unlike earlier versions like Albert Campion and Peter Wimsey, loses every trace of P.G. Wodehouse's Bertie Wooster. Lynley is a man of great seriousness who has his own demons – which are spelled out in *A Suitable Vengeance* – and who occasionally, as in an ugly scene in *In the Presence of the Enemy*, allows his anger to run away with him. This seriousness is not limited to Lynley. *A Great Deliverance* is more generally a serious book. Havers's pain and guilt are terribly serious and so is the series of interlocking crimes that is revealed. What is perhaps worse is that there is no real deliverance. A daughter is reunited with her long lost mother but will never forget that she has been betrayed and deserted, just like she herself has deserted her younger sister. The priest who, through the confessional, was aware of the abuse, must live with the knowledge that his silence has effectively condoned the practice and has ultimately led to murder. The woman who seduces Lynley stands accused of what within the context of this novel almost constitutes a crime: a wilful superficiality that must serve to protect her against responsibility. *A Great Deliverance* is about the evasion of moral responsibility, an evasion so general and so diffuse that no character fully transcends it. Only Lynley, who is atoning for earlier evasions and Havers, in her painful recognition of what she has done to her awful parents, come close.

It is this moral seriousness that marks George's distance from the classic tradition. We are of course meant to recognize her borrowings: the brother suspected, and cleared, of murder in *A Suitable Vengeance* reminds us of how Sayers has Peter Wimsey exonerate his brother Denver; we have the murder in the isolated country house (in *Payment in Blood* (1989), in which, incidentally, the relationship between Lynley and Havers is already a good deal more balanced); we have the world of Cambridge colleges in *For the Sake of Elena* (1992), and so on. George's novels, however, always convey a moral judgment that goes much further than anything the classics ever offered. The widespread moral irresponsibility that is inevitably revealed, and of which the actual culprit is occasionally less guilty than a good many others who will get off scot-free, reminds one of the bleak world of the classic private eye. Whereas in classic private eye fiction much of that irresponsibility is suggested, a result of metaphors and mood rather than detection, in George's fiction it is actually shown, an effect of her habit of offering a variety of characters and multiple points of view. On the other side of the spectrum we find characters who, with equally disastrous results, more or less monopolize responsibility, who are unwilling to share their burden either out of pride or out of love – as in the more recent *In Pursuit of the Proper Sinner* (1999) in which a husband commits suicide to keep hidden from his wife what she is already fully aware of.

Apart from her complex plots, this panoramic strategy, reminiscent of mid-nineteenth-century realist fiction, is George's great strength, not in the least because it also allows her to maintain a constant level of suspense by switching perspectives (and thus cutting off the flow of information) at exactly the right cliff-hanging moment. Still, in her more recent fiction, this strength begins to develop into a weakness, paradoxically because she sets her sights too high. Although *A Great Deliverance* is very good on its Yorkshire setting, it focuses almost exclusively on the investigation. The result is a taut novel – in spite of its considerable length – that has the reader walking an emotional tightrope. With *For the Sake of Elena* we arrive at something of a turning point. The novel is very good on the cowardly self-centeredness of the Cambridge don who is the father of the main victim; on the relationship between Lynley and Lady Helen Clyde; on the depressing sexism of a number of minor male characters; and on the hatred an ex-wife feels for her former husband and his new wife. It is even better on Havers, who after the death of her father is now solely responsible for a mother who has slid into dementia and can no longer take care of herself. Especially chilling is the scene in which Havers's mother has 'messed' herself because she is too scared of the hose of the vacuum cleaner – which she takes to be a snake – to leave the sofa. Livid with the woman who is supposed to look after her mother and who has deliberately left the hose on the floor to make sure that her charge would not wander off, Havers fires her and, racked by guilt, finally decides to place her mother in a home. This is what the 'literary' George – the George giving us material that is not related to an investigation – does brilliantly: relatively brief scenes of great emotional intensity and power that substantially contribute to the seriousness of her fiction.

In her most recent novels George's affinity with realism is both a liability and an asset. What works against her is her desire to provide too many minor characters with a believable perspective and a matching psycho-social background. As a result *In the Presence of the Enemy*, published in 1996, runs to 630 pages while the 1997 *Deception on His Mind* in which, interestingly, Havers is given a solo performance, adds another 120 to clock in at 750 pages. Keeping the reader's interest alive for such marathon runs would tax any novelist. George does not quite bring it off because not all of the perspectives that she offers are equally interesting; in fact, with regard to some she would seem to be on automatic pilot, working out stereotypes along all too predictable lines, sometimes even to the point of caricature. (In *Deception* we have a German whose English is quite good, but who yet begins every other sentence with '*Ja*'. Germans do not have this particular affliction, not even when they speak German.)

A positive development in the recent novels is their overt interest in politics, an interest that is of course wholly absent from the classical tradition. Right from the start George has been a political writer in the sense that the personal in her novels always has had political overtones. Although she is obviously not a radical feminist novelist, there is always a feminist undercurrent in her fiction. Even in those cases where the criminal is a woman there is a strong suggestion that the fact that this is a world in which males still dominate virtually everything has either directly or indirectly contributed to the crime. This is not to say that all of George's women are blameless victims. It is clear, however, that they must cope with both individual and social pressures that the male characters who are the instruments of these forces are largely ignorant of. Lynley is one of George's few males who at a certain point becomes aware of this. As he puts it in a conversation with his future wife: '"All I can say right now is that I finally understand that no matter how the load is shifted between partners, or divided or shared, the woman's burden will always be greater. I do know that."' (*Elena*, 382)

In *In the Presence of the Enemy* and even more so in *Deception on His Mind* the major crimes, although as personally motivated as the murder in her first novel, are embedded in a much larger political framework. *Presence*, published when John Major still headed a British Conservative government, pits a junior minister who with her espousal of family values, her limitless ambition and uncompromising inflexibility (with regard to the IRA, for instance) is roughly modelled on Margaret Thatcher, against the editor of a leftist tabloid with whom she once had a brief and exclusively physical affair. This set-up enables George to bring in the hypocritical and sleazy dealings of a number of Conservative politicians and the equally unsavory practices of British tabloids. (The only indication that her sympathy lies with Labour is that her tabloid editor wakes up to his basic immorality while the Minister does not: 'One couldn't walk the path he'd chosen so many years ago upon coming to London and still remain a sentient creature. If he hadn't known that before, he knew now that it was an impossibility. He'd never been so lost.' (*Presence*, 442)) Unfortunately, the novel is marred by a wholly superflous first part in which Allcourt-St James, his wife Deborah and Lady Helen Clyde try to trace a missing child. For whatever reason, George, for all her realism, finds it hard to cut this particular tie with the Golden Age. (Lady Helen tells Deborah,

'"Darling ... just think of Miss Marple. Or Tuppence. Think of Tuppence. Or Harriet Vane."' (163) Unfortunately, neither Deborah Allcourt nor Helen Clyde come close to Harriet Vane in terms of intrinsic interest.) Lacking the anger and drive of Barbara Havers, Deborah and Helen are plucky girls in the young Tuppence mold rather than the mature and serious women that one expects a mature and serious version of Peter Wimsey to associate himself with.

It is the political factor plus the absence of the Lynley entourage – even more than the absence of Lynley himself – that makes *Deception on his Mind* so convincing, even if here, too, George errs on the side of comprehensiveness: we simply get too many perspectives, not all of which are relevant to the story that she is telling and with regard to some of which her imagination lets her down. But that story is gripping enough, beginning with the discovery of a dead Pakistani on the beach just north of Balford-le-Nez, an Essex seaside resort not too far from Clacton-on-Sea (the Nez in question looks suspiciously like the real-life Naze – also not too far from Clacton – in the map that George provides with a tongue-in-cheek reference to the classic tradition). To the local Pakistani community, led by a firebrand political activist, the murderer must have been motivated by racial hatred. Since this implies a white murderer the Pakistanis, whose anger explodes in a small-scale riot, suspect a cover-up. At this point Detective Chief Inspector Emily Barstow, in charge of the investigation, invites Barbara Havers, who has rather implausibly come to Balford to keep an eye on a Pakistani neighbor and his little girl, to liaise between the Pakistani community – represented by the activist and Barbara's London neighbor – and the investigating officers. Before long Barbara drifts into the investigation itself, allowed to do so by Barstow, whom she has met at a police course and for whom she has immense admiration. Emily Barstow openly defies convention with her 'jet black hair, dyed punk and cut punk', is as matter of fact about sex (which is 'a regular bonk with a willing bloke' (*Deception*, 84)) as about anything else, has the figure of the 'dedicated triathlete' that she is, and is in Barbara's eyes dazzlingly good at her job: 'nowhere was there a woman more competent, more suited to criminal investigations, and more gifted in the politics of policework than Emily Barlow' (66).

What she is definitely not good at, however, is race relations. There is a good deal of racism in the novel, even if, as Barbara at one point tells herself, by no means all of her compatriots are racists. We have the almost intangible segregation in Barbara's hotel, for example, but also shockingly crude and mean incidents of overt racism. Gradually,

Barbara's hero is exposed as a hardline racist. For a while, Barbara is able to ignore Emily's references to 'those people' and her derogatory generalizations: '"none of these yobbos can be trusted half an inch"' (609). But when Emily is fully prepared to let a '"Paki brat"' – the ten-year-old daughter of Barbara's neighbor – drown in order to catch a Pakistani criminal who is trying to make his way across the North Sea to Germany and has thrown the child overboard, Barbara is squarely confronted with Emily's refusal to see Pakistanis in human terms. Holding a gun on Emily, she tells her to turn the boat in which they are chasing the fleeing Pakistani and to pick up the foundering child. When Emily does not immediately respond she fires the gun but fortunately misses after which a badly shaken Emily allows her and the (male) detective who is also on board, and who clearly sides with Barbara, to save the child's life.

Race and the differences between Pakistani and English culture constitute the dominant themes of the novel. Race determines the relations between the Pakistani community and the police (ironically, and in typical George fashion, the activist turns out to be right with regard to Barstow's racism, while she is right concerning his criminal activities), while the enormous cultural differences greatly complicate the investigation and for a long time divert the suspicion from the actual murderer. It is Barbara, who is a good deal more attuned to these differences than her temporary superior who is blinded by her own prejudices, who finally tumbles to the truth. Moreover, the issue of race is instrumental in Barbara's unprecedented pulling of a gun on a superior officer. They seem to hold each other hostage: Emily may report Barbara's insubordination leading to attempted murder while Barbara, as she is well aware, is in a position to report Emily's racism and willingness to sacrifice the life of a child to the pursuit of a personal vengeance. But there is no doubt that Emily holds all the cards: she not only outranks Barbara but she is also completely ruthless and unforgiving where Barbara is willing to make allowances. It is the fact that Barbara finally sees through Emily's 'professionalism' – built to a considerable extent on self-deception and the resolute denial of personal relationships – that allows her to see that Emily's apparent strength is her major weakness and that topples Emily from her intimidating pedestal: 'Don't think [your solution of the murder] changes a thing between us, Emily was telling her. You're finished as a cop if I have my way. Do what you have to do, was Barbara's silent reply. And for the first time since meeting Emily Barlow, she actually felt free.' (740)

In the course of the novels Barbara Havers gradually overcomes her crippling insecurity and pathological and often aggressive defensiveness. She frees herself first of all from Lynley. When they start working together, in *A Great Deliverance*, she tries to hang on to her instinctive loathing of him in order to protect her cut-and-dried, class-based view of everything he stands for. Eventually Lynley's competence and compassion break down her defenses and force her to revaluate her prejudices. Equally important is that Lynley, for all his easy superiority, is not infallible and occasionally allows his judgment to be affected by emotional involvement. '"Stop lying to yourself",' Havers tells him in *In the Presence of the Enemy*. '"You're not after facts. You're after vengeance. It's written all over you."' (261) And when he does not see reason, she adds for good measure: '"Holy hell ... You can be a real prick."' (262) Because Lynley encourages her to speak her mind, instead of pulling rank as Emily Barstow does when Barbara sins against police hierarchy – '"You're out of line, Sergeant"' – Barbara can be her prickly, outspoken self.

In a parallel development, Barbara learns to cope with her suffocating feelings of guilt, which is to say that she finds a balance between her responsibilities with regard to her parents and, more in particular, her increasingly demented mother, and her responsibilities with regard to herself as an adult woman with a life of her own. Although she never overcomes her guilt – not to be confused with responsibility – she finally realizes her wish to go and live by herself. Finally, in *Deception on His Mind*, she learns to see through another false image: that of Emily Barstow, female supercop. Like Eve Bowen, the Conservative junior minister in *Presence*, Barstow stands for the female who has adopted the worst male traits: ruthless ambition, emotional distance, complete self-sufficiency, sexuality without affection. Realizing that Barstow's limitations far outweigh her own, Barbara is free to be her competent and compassionate, if dumpy and rather unprepossessing self.

With Barbara Havers, we are a long way from the classic tradition. And even if Lynley is closer to some of his Golden Age predecessors, there is an awareness of human frailty and of man's self-serving stupidity that is almost wholly absent from the tradition (Dorothy Sayers's *Gaudy Night* in which, appropriately, Harriet Vane plays the leading role, comes to mind as an exception). In one of the last scenes of *Presence*, watching the murderer and 'casting the observation into the light of what he'd learned about his background, Lynley fe[els] only a tremendous defeat' (620). Here the mood fuses with that of the more serious version of the private eye novel, just as it does at the end of *Deception* when Barbara feels equally 'weighted down by the case' (746) – a phrase one associates with Philip Marlowe or Lew Archer rather than with an English policewoman. But, then, that policewoman has in *Presence* been badly battered by the killer she attacks to save a young boy's life and has only a couple of weeks later, still hurting from her bruises and broken ribs, fired a gun at her superior officer to save another child from drowning. Not only the mood of the private eye novel, including its inevitable defiance of authority, but also its dramatic action and the self-sacrificial interventions of the classic PI, have entered George's reworking of the tradition.

9
Historical Mysteries

One of the more remarkable developments in crime writing since 1980 has been the veritable explosion of crime fiction placed in a historical setting. Of course, earlier decades too knew this particular subgenre. In the UK, for instance, during the 1970s Peter Lovesey ran a series set in the late 1800s. In the 1990s he returned to this period with as his detective the then future King Edward VII, affectionally nicknamed 'Bertie'. Also during the 1970s, but less famous than Lovesey, Derek Lambert, writing under the pseudonym Richard Falkirk, created Bow Street runner Edmund 'Beau' Blackstone, hero of a series set in early nineteenth-century London. Turning to exotic as well as historic settings, from the late 1950s on and throughout the 1960s, Robert van Gulik, a Dutch diplomat writing in English, published his Judge Dee mysteries, set in seventh-century China.

On the American side, James M. Cain, famous for *The Postman Always Rings Twice* (1934), tried his hand at historical crime fiction with *Past All Dishonor* (1946), set in mid-nineteenth-century California. Starting in 1950, with *The Bride of Newgate*, and ending in 1972, with *The Hungry Goblin: A Victorian Detective Novel*, John Dickson Carr wrote a number of mysteries with settings ranging from seventeenth- to nineteenth-century England. *The Hungry Goblin* has as its detective-protagonist Wilkie Collins, the Victorian novelist often regarded as one of the inventors of the detective novel with *The Moonstone*, published in 1869, the same year in which Dickson Carr's novel is set. In an earlier story, Dickson Carr had already featured Edgar Allan Poe as detective. Of crime writers active to this day, Joe Gores in 1975 made writer–detective Dashiell Hammett the hero of an eponymous detective novel set in 1928, and two years later Stuart Kaminsky created Toby Peters, the bumbling private eye of a series set in 1940s California.

The event that marks 1980 as the take-off year for historical crime fiction on a large scale is undoubtedly the publication, and subsequent mega-success, of Umberto Eco's *The Name of the Rose*, in which the English monk William of Baskerville investigates a series of murders in a fourteenth-century north Italian monastery. In 1986 Eco's novel was turned into a highly praised and successful movie starring Sean Connery as this Sherlock Holmes-derived protagonist. A contributing factor to the sudden visibility of historical crime writing may well have been the initially far more modest success of British writer Ellis Peters's Brother Cadfael, the medieval Benedictine monk, who had solved his first case in *A Morbid Taste for Bones: A Mediaeval Whodunit* (1977) and had returned for a second in *One Corpse Too Many* (1979). Throughout the 1980s Peters published new Cadfael novels at the rate of one, and sometimes two, a year. Perhaps even importantly, the series was successfully adapted for television.

Historical novels often say as much about the present as about the past. The same thing is true for their counterparts in crime writing. Indeed, the crime plot is an ideal frame to touch upon past as well as present injustices, their backgrounds and explanations. This is easy to see in the case of novels featuring what in Chapter 11 we call 'other' detectives, which are particularly concerned with racial and gender discrimination, and some of which – like Walter Mosley's Easy Rawlins or Robert Skinner's Wesley Farrell mysteries – are historical novels as well. However, it is also true of quite a number of series that at first sight seem to be nothing more than, at times superbly executed, historical costume dramas. For an example I turn to a little-known series set in what at first sight seems the lighthearted world of early twentieth-century professional baseball, Troy Soos's Mickey Rawlings novels.

Rawlings moves from one famous baseball team to another (the Chicago Red Sox, the New York Giants, the Chicago Cubs, the Detroit Tigers, the Cincinnati Reds) over the course of the series, and over a period spanning 1912 to the 1920s. The series is thick with real life historical characters, most of them legendary baseball players. There is a good deal of baseball lore, and the games Rawlings plays are vividly described. In each novel, Rawlings gets mixed up in a murder case. Usually, the murder in question has something to do with baseball politics. Beyond this, though, wider social issues are touched upon. In *Hunting a Detroit Tiger* (1997) for instance, Rawlings investigates the murder of a former baseball player who also was a union organizer, while at the same time the owners of the team he himself plays for press him to take a stand against the unions. Via a historical detour Soos touches upon subjects that he obviously considers relevant also for the present, but which the present would rather disregard. This series does what the best of historical crime fiction does very well indeed: via the experiences of a number of interesting characters interacting with historical figures, it vividly portrays an era gone by, yet at the same time also speaks to our own age.

From 1980 on we see a veritable boom of historical crime fiction, spanning all periods and most continents. Some authors are incredibly prolific at this trade. An extreme example of this industriousness, the British writer P.C. Doherty, who also writes under the names Paul Harding and C.L. Grace, has since 1990 averaged at least two to three medieval mysteries featuring various investigators a year, while he also writes ancient Greek mysteries as Anna Apostolou, ancient Egyptian novels under his own name, Renaissance mysteries as Michael Clynes, and nineteenth-century mysteries as Ann Dukthas.

Regardless of whether their authors are British or American, by far the majority of historical series are set in England, with single novels occasionally moving to different, usually European, locales. Exceptions are American writer Laura Joh Rowland's Sano Ichirō series, which is set in seventeenth-century Japan, and the Amelia Peabody series by fellow American Elizabeth Peters that uses Victorian Egypt as its backdrop. In 1998 Peters, whose real name is Barbara Mertz (1927), and who also writes under the pseudonym Barbara Michaels, received the Grand Master Award for her entire production.

Over the last decade the number of American crime writers opting for an American decor for their historical fiction has steadily grown. Most of these authors favor the nineteenth and early twentieth centuries. Still, there are a number of novels set in early American history. One of these, Margaret Lawrence's *Hearts and Bones* (1996), the first novel in a subsequently highly successful series, was even nominated for both the Edgar and Agatha awards. At the same time some American authors continue to situate their mysteries in England, even when their time of action is the early twentieth century. Laurie R. King, for instance, runs a successful series featuring Mary Russell, alleged female companion to a more than middle-aged Sherlock Holmes. Russell acts as Holmes's collaborator, and later becomes his wife.

We will concentrate here on some of the more successful exponents of the genre, taking care to observe a certain spread by historical era. In our trip into the past we will bypass the most immediately historical period, the decades following the Second World War. This is not to say that there are no good crime novels set in this period. In fact, the work of some of the most interesting of contemporary crime writers is set in the years following the war. Both Walter Mosley's Easy Rawlins mysteries and James Ellroy's LA novels cover the period 1945–1972. However, as we discuss these writers elsewhere (see Chapters 11 and 6) we do not include them here. Another reason not to deal with the work of Mosley, Ellroy, and others like Robert Skinner (see Chapter 11) in this chapter is that they focus primarily on character and plot, whereas the historical mysteries we want to discuss here give priority to the historical environment itself – without neglecting character or plot. The historical crime writers we will examine in some detail are Steven Saylor, Maan Meyers, Margaret Lawrence, Myriam Grace Monfredo, and Caleb Carr.

Ancient Rome

Gordianus the Finder, the hero of the 'Roma Sub Rosa' series of Steven Saylor, makes his debut in *Roman Blood* (1991). In the spring of 80 BC, Gordianus, in his mid-30s, and owner of one Egyptian slave girl, Bethesda, who also happens to be his mistress, is engaged by the aspiring young lawyer Marcus Tullius Cicero ('little pea') to investigate the murder of a Roman citizen, Sextus Roscius – a murder allegedly committed by his estranged son. The punishment for parricide is horrific, as this is a crime that endangers the patriarchal order and authority upon which Rome is founded. Somewhat hesitantly, Gordianus accepts the commission – he knows that a far more experienced lawyer than Cicero has already given up on the case, which is to be pleaded shortly on the Forum, before the Rostra, and a jury of Roman citizens.

The immediate strength of *Roman Blood* and its successors, *Arms of Nemesis* (1992), *Catalina's Riddle* (1993), *The Venus Throw* (1995), *A Murder on the Appian Way* (1996), *Rubicon* (1999), and *Last* seen in Massilia (2000), lies in its superb portrayal of Rome in the earlier half of the first century BC. Through the entire series, the life of the sprawling metropolis that Rome was under the late Republic down to the eve of Julius Caesar's accession to power, is pictured in brilliantly vivid colors with what convincingly passes for historical accuracy. We hear the orators in the Forum, we enjoy the luxuries of the stately homes on the Palatine Hill, we smell the stench of the Subura, the popular quarters at the foot of the Esquiline Hill. In *Roman Blood,* we follow Gordianus into the countryside of Latum and Umbria. In *A Murder on the Appian Way,* we first follow Gordianus along this most famous of Roman roads, and later we accompany him up to Caesar's headquarters at Ravenna in 52 BC, the year in which this particular novel is set.

Gordianus's unusual calling as a private investigator *avant-la-lettre* brings him into contact not only with such famous historical figures as Cicero and Caesar, Pompey and Marc Antony, but also with Rome's criminal element. In *Roman Blood* he mingles with the prostitutes of the numerous houses of pleasure catering to the tastes of the Romans, and adopts the street urchin Eco, a dumb boy abandoned by his widowed mother, who lost her mind after being gang raped by thugs hired to prevent her from revealing what she had seen of Sextus Roscius's murder.

Each of the 'Roma Sub Rosa' books take its cue from one of Cicero's orations or other writings. *Roman Blood,* for example, builds upon 'Pro Sexto Roscio Amerino', and *A Murder on the Appian Way* is based on 'Pro Milone'. *Catalina's Riddle* takes off from Cicero's famous orations against Catilina. For the rest, Saylor draws upon the works of Sallust, Plutarch, and literally scores of other Latin authors, as well as contemporary secondary sources. Occasionally, the desire for historical accuracy also leads to somewhat articifially contrived scenes as when, for instance, in *A Murder on the Appian Way* Gordianus's daughter asks what an 'interrex' is, and Gordianus holds a long disquisition on the subject. All in all, though, what emerges from these books is a remarkably detailed and believable picture of late Republican Rome.

However, Saylor is not only good on historical accuracy, or when it comes to tight plotting and the creation of credible and humane characters. He is also superb at dressing his books with a rich symbolic texture. This symbolism usually suggests further layers of meaning. To offer one example, in *Roman Blood* the novel's title refers to the stain Sextus Roscius's blood left on the flagstones of the alley in which he was murdered and the smear his hand made on the door of a grocer's shop, both of which provide clues to Gordianus. It also refers to the blood of Gordianus and Bethesda's dog, killed by thugs out to scare Gordianus off the case, to the blood of Sextus Roscius's son after his violent death, and to the blood of the latter's daughter when he first forced her to have incestuous incourse with him. To pick up the latter element first: incest is a hot topic in the 1990s, and by way of his fictional historical characters Saylor clearly wants to participate in an ongoing debate.

Beyond this, Saylor's title also refers to the issue of citizenship itself, to the question: who can legitimately claim 'Roman blood'. Is this privilege reserved for the patricians and their descendants, like the Roscii, or for native-born Romans like Gordianus himself? Does it extend, or can it be extended, to manumitted slaves like Chrysogonus, dictator Sulla's favorite and the villain of the piece? To Tiro – Cicero's slave secretary – when freed by Cicero in *A Murder on the Appian Way*? To Gordianus's adopted children in the later novels in the series? To Bethesda after her marriage to Gordianus? Or to Davus, Gordianus's bodyguard and slave, who fathers a child upon his master's daughter?

In its answer to these questions, Saylor's series takes a political stance. In *A Murder on the Appian Way*, for instance, Eco, the once mute boy whom Gordianus rescues at the end of *Roman Blood*, and whom he later adopts as his legal son and heir, has grown up to become an officer in Julius Caesar's army, and is himself the husband of a Roman wife, and father to legal Roman citizens. Gordianus himself is obviously on the side of the have-nots. He is also dead against empire, as becomes clear from a conversation with Cicero early in *Roman Blood*. Through his characters, their conversations, and their experiences Saylor, though ostensibly writing about the first century BC, in reality is also taking a stance with regard to present-day America. Indeed, the United States, the ruling empire of its era, is facing the same issues as Rome in its own period of domination – issues that center around citizenship, legal and illegal immigration, and so on.

Historical New York

The multiculturalism *avant-la-lettre* that we find in Saylor's novels also plays a major part in *The Dutchman's Dilemma* (1995), the fourth of the 'Dutchman' series by Maan Meyers, actually the husband-and-wife team Martin and Annette Meyers. Each of these writing partners also publishes mystery series under his or her individual name. The *Dutchman's Dilemma* is set in New York, some ten years after the takeover of New Amsterdam by the English in 1664. The action of the first novel in the series, *The Dutchman* (1992), takes place during the surrender of New Amsterdam, and recounts how Pieter Tonneman, the Dutch schout (police constable) of New Amsterdam who stayed on as the first sheriff of New York, falls in love with a young Jewish widow, Racqel Mendoza. At the start of *The Dutchman's Dilemma*, Tonneman has resigned his commission, because his marriage to Racqel is not looked upon with favor by New York's Christian citizens.

Racqel herself is ostracized by the Jewish community for having married outside of her faith. However, Tonneman is pressed into service again to investigate the brutal slaughter of a stallion, a gift from King Charles II to the English Governor of New York. At first he is reluctant. During the Sunday service, however, the stallion's penis is found in the preacher's Book of Common Prayer. Rumors start circulating about religious conspiracies. Inevitably, suspicion centers upon the Jews. When Racqel is accused of witchcraft by both Christians and Jews, it suddenly becomes urgent that Tonneman solve the case.

The Dutchman's Dilemma can easily be read as one long indictment of religious extremism, and of the prejudices it fosters. There is not just the rift between Christians and Jews, but also that between Protestants and Catholics, and between various Protestant sects. Of course, there is also the distrust of the native Americans, their customs and their lore. Beyond that, there is the division between the various groups, of different geographical and linguistic affiliation, that inhabit New York: English, Dutch, New England, Sephardic Jewish, native American. *The Dutchman's Dilemma* is a plea for tolerance in all things, and for respect for difference: cultural, religious, or linguistic. The same theme, couched in much the same terms, returns in the other novels in the Dutchman series, *The Kingsbridge Plot* (1993), *The High Constable* (1994), *The House on Mulberry Street* (1996), and *The Lucifer Contract* (1998). These novels are set, respectively, in 1775–78, 1808, 1895, and 1864, and in each of them we are witness to the exploits, in detection or law enforcement, of a descendant of the original Pieter Tonneman.

The Dutchman's Dilemma includes a map of seventeenth-century New York, situating the houses of the characters as well as other relevant locations. In a 'footnote', the historical accuracy of some of the characters, their physical surroundings, and the medical lore that the novel presents, is accounted for. There are detailed descriptions of period dress, food, customs and laws, both Christian and Jewish. In all, these elements succeed in establishing a credible historical setting for the novel, even if its plea for tolerance would have been most uncommon in the time in which it is set. Obviously, this plea belongs to our time. This would seem to be even more the case with some of the characters, and particularly with Pieter Tonneman himself. His teetotalling and his aversion to pipe-smoking strike us as peculiarly late twentieth-century. The former might still be accounted for by the fact that Tonneman used to be somewhat of a drunk himself, who has mended his ways. The latter, however, seems rather out of place in the mid-seventeenth century, particularly in a pioneer environment. Add to this Tonneman's exemplary behavior toward Racqel – loving, caring, never overbearing, passionate yet always full of respect – and this seventeenth-century detective turns into a true hero of our own times: sanitized, sensitized, civilized.

New England

Though one would hardly say so at first sight, Margaret Lawrence's *Hearts and Bones* (1996) is also just as much about our own times as about the period of its setting, the late eighteenth century. The time of action is February 1786. Hannah Trevor, a 38 year old midwife in Rufford, a small town in Maine (then still part of Massachusetts) discovers the body of a young woman, Anthea 'Nan' Emory. The woman has been raped and strangled in her own bed. Examining the body together with Town Constable Will Quaid, who is also the local blacksmith, Hannah to her dismay notices from the impressions on Anthea's throat that the murderer has two fingers missing on his left hand. Only one man in town fits this description, and Hannah knows him all too well: Dan Josselyn, the English officer who sided with the Americans during the Revolution, eight years earlier, and who is the father of Hannah's deaf and dumb child, Jennet.

The atrocities committed during America's war of independence also hold the key to Nan's death. Then 13 years old, she was raped – like all the women of her village – by a band of Rufford men, intent on avenging the death of one of their number. Present at the rape was Will Quaid. An immensely strong man, Quaid has been unable to have relations with women because of a humiliation his own father made him undergo when he was still a child, and which was repeated when he was in the army. Enraged at his own impotence, Will kills the men that raped Nan. Years later, Nan seeks out Will as the instrument for her vengeance. Through her war experiences intimately acquainted with pain and fear, and full of self-loathing, Nan uses her knowledge to seduce Will, who for the first time finds himself able to physically love a woman. Nan makes sure she is with child by Will, then persuades him to kill her as an act of mercy, forcing him to rape her in the process. She also makes him promise to kill the surviving Rufford company men in retribution for what was done to her, regardless of whether they were actually involved in her own humiliation or, like Josselyn, had no responsibility for the crime. Hannah slowly and painfully figures all this out. The novel comes to a climactic close with a scuffle in which Quaid is shot to death. During Will's final moment, he and Josselyn embrace, in a clear repetition of Will and Nan's final embrace. In the end, killer and victim are one.

Hearts and Bones is historically accurate in its description of New England town life at the time of the Revolution, particularly with regard to women: midwifery, quilting (from a popular pattern of which the book takes its name), recipes, and so on. At the same time the novel is very contemporary in its psychology. It sketches the traumas of war for both men and women involved in atrocities, whether as perpetrators or as victims. It also addresses issues of equality between men and women, as in the relationship between midwives Hannah and Julia, and the physician Clinch. The latter obviously wields more authority, and represents the claims of scientific rationalism. Yet, he is equally obviously catastrophically wrong in his treatment of pregnancy and his handling of childbirth. Julia and Hannah, on the other hand, have the advantage of personal experience, of centuries of folk remedies, and of plain common sense. It is because of the skewed power relations between men and women that Hannah decides not to marry again after her first husband's departure. Instead, she opts for single motherhood – a decidedly late twentieth-century possibility – seducing Josselyn to gain her aim. Hannah has personally experienced the fact that women at the end of the eighteenth century in the eyes of the law do not exist as responsible agents, and she would rather be subject to her kind and caring uncle than to an indifferent husband.

Seneca Falls and the rights of women

Three quarters of a century later things have not changed much, we learn from Miriam Grace Monfredo's *Seneca Falls Inheritance* (1992). The novel's amateur investigator, Glynis Tryon, the town librarian of Upstate New York Seneca Falls, chooses to stay unmarried for much the same reasons as Hannah Trevor. This first novel in the Glynis Tryon series, covering the period immediately running up to the first ever Woman's Rights Convention, held in Seneca Falls in 1848, is primarily concerned with women's rights. Subsequent novels in the series invariably link women's emancipation to other issues topical to the nineteenth-century age of reform as well as to our own era of equal rights and opportunities. In *North Star Conspiracy* (1993) Glynis becomes involved with the Underground Railroad helping fugitive slaves escape to freedom. *Blackwater Spirits* (1995) sees her battling the discrimination of native Americans. The temperance movement also plays a role in this novel. In *Through A Gold Eagle* (1996) abolitionism provides the key to the novel's plot.

The intrigue of *Seneca Falls Inheritance* revolves around the murder of a woman, Rose Walker, who has come to Seneca Falls to claim half of the inheritance of the richest man in town, Steicher, whom she says was her father by an earlier wife. Though suspicion first settles on Steicher's son and designated heir, in the end Rose's husband Gordon turns out to be the real murderer. Ironically, his deed has been provoked by a law then only recently passed in New York – the Married Women's Property Act – which stipulated that, contrary to earlier legislation, women could keep control of their poperty even when married. If Rose had left her husband, he would have received nothing from whatever she had inherited. With Rose dead, however, her husband can rightfully claim his deceased wife's property, including her inheritance.

The female voice comes through very strongly in *Seneca Falls Inheritance*, and in Monfredo's entire Glynis Tryon series. First and foremost, of course, there is the Woman's Rights Convention, with the presence of such historical luminaries as Elizabeth Cady Stanton, Lucretia Mott, and Frederick Douglass. A set of 'historical notes' at the end of the novel informs us about these characters, the role they played in the Woman's Rights Convention, and the situation of women in the mid-nineteenth century in the United States in general. In the novel itself, Monfredo also takes care to highlight the plight of nineteenth-century women, and particularly of married women, in her descriptions of the eternal drudgery of household chores, the continuous childbearing and rearing, and the sexual subservience to a husband. By choosing to stay unmarried, Glynis Tryon deliberately opts out of this. Monfredo insists that quite a number of nineteenth-century American women made a similar choice.

Like Glynis, a considerable number of nineteenth-century women – at least in the United States – preferred developing their minds, and their artistic and aesthetic sensibilities, to marriage. Here too, though, the nineteenth century raised formidable obstacles. Glynis is virtually ostracized by her family for having pursued a college education, and for the same reason the Seneca Falls townspeople think her a very odd creature indeed. Monfredo makes the same point via Elizabeth Blackwell, one of the historical characters in the novel. Blackwell was the first woman to become a qualified physician in the United States, obtaining her medical degree from Geneva Medical College in 1849. Ironically, Geneva College was deeply unhappy about Blackwell's medical studies, and after her graduation changed the rules of admission in order to exclude other female students.

One of the strongest points of *Seneca Falls Inheritance* is how the Woman's Rights Convention, and the historical conditions of women in the mid-nineteenth century, meaningfully inform the crime plot, as in the following passage:

> 'It was the convention', [Glynis] said.
> They all stared at her. Quentin Ives finally said, 'The Woman's Rights Convention made you suspect Gordon Walker?'
> Glynis nodded. 'It was a tangled skein of connections, really'. She sat down at one end of a wicker sofa, curling her feet beneath her. 'I sat in the Wesleyan Chapel [the place where the Convention was held] wondering just what we women started', she explained. 'What we would be leaving the next generations: my nieces, and grandnieces to come, and Elizabeth Stanton's daughters and granddaughters not even born yet. Would what they inherited be a benefit to them as we hoped – or a loss for some that we couldn't foresee? And that, in one of those twists the mind sometimes takes, made me think of the Steicher inheritance, and Rose Walker. Who, besides Karl [Steicher's son], would lose if she lived?'
> 'Later ... I remembered the Married Women's Property Act. You know, it was the passage of that law just a few months ago that encouraged Elizabeth Stanton to call a convention about women's rights. I suddenly thought what a terrible irony it would be if that law, designed to protect women, had caused a woman's murder?'
> (*Inheritance*, 276)

Seneca Falls Inheritance aims for historical accuracy in its depiction of daily life in nineteenth-century America. Rail time tables, for instance, play a major role in the solution of Rose's murder – the railroad having come to Seneca Falls in 1846.

New York revisited

With the late nineteenth-century mysteries of Caleb Carr we return to New York City. In *The Alienist* (1994) and *The Angel of Darkness* (1997), Carr concentrates on serial murders and on the psychological motivation behind them. His narrator, John Schuyler Moore, is a police reporter for the *New York Times* who is in his late 30s. In *The Alienist*, Moore late one night in 1896 is called out by Dr Laszlo Kreizler, a controversial 'alienist' – the contemporary term for 'psychiatrist' – and specialist in forensic psychiatry. A boy has been found murdered and horribly mutilated near the East River. At the crime scene, Moore meets Theodore Roosevelt, then Police Commisioner of New York. The murder victim is an immigrant Italian boy, working as a transvestite prostitute in one of New York's innumerable houses of vice. Moreover, he is not the first such boy to have been murdered in recent years. As ordinary police investigations have not yielded results in the matter, Roosevelt now decides to set up a task force consisting of Kreizler, Moore, Sara Howard – as a policewoman a controversial novelty in the 1890s – and the detective sergeants Lucius and Marcus Isaacson. Hovering around the edges of this little group are Kreizler's two servants, Stevie Taggart, a young small-time criminal whom Kreizler has rescued from the reformatory and whom he has virtually adopted, and Cyrus Montrose, a black giant and former patient.

Each of the members of this unit brings his or her particular expertise to the investigation. Sara makes some crucial inferences about female pyschology when it looks as if the investigation is about to stall. Cyrus, a murderer himself, can fall back on his own experience when the group tries to come up with a psychological profile for the man they are looking for. Stevie Taggart has his underworld contacts. The Isaacsons are trained in forensic medicine and in the then most modern techniques of detection – like fingerprinting. Kreizler himself puts it all together and provides the psychological underpinning to the investigation. Indeed, a lot of the interest of *The Alienist* derives precisely from the meticulous description of the techniques followed by the then nascent disciplines of forensic psychiatry and medicine, and of police detection.

As one possible suspect after another is cleared, we follow Moore, Sara and the Isaacsons on their rounds of New York, checking an alibi or establishing the whereabouts of a witness. Carr is a trained historian, and he is particularly good at conveying a sense of late nineteenth-century New York. We are made to see, feel and smell life, particularly lower class life, in a busy metropolis: the crowded tenements teeming with immigrants, the gin palaces and whorehouses, and the insane asylum Bellevue. The appearance of historical figures such as Theodore Roosevelt, but also Jacob Riis, the Danish-born journalist and reformer, author of *How the Other Half Lives* (1890), only adds to the realism of *The Alienist.*

In a dramatic sequence of events on the ramparts of the great Croton water reservoir, then occupying the place where we now find the New

York Public Library, the drama reaches its climax, and the serial murderer is killed. Spurred on by scientific curiosity, Kreizler dissects the man's brain, looking for physical indications of madness. As he already had surmised, he finds none. Kreizler, after all, is an alienist who believes that our behavior has a psycho-social explanation. If we are prepared to bend the meaning of the term a little, we find Kreizler also an 'alienist' in the sense that he locates the roots of criminal behavior in the criminal's 'alienation' from society:

> 'If the average person were to describe John Beecham in light of his murders, he'd say he was a social outcast, but nothing could be more superficial, or more untrue. Beecham could never have turned his back on human society, nor society on him, and why? Because he was – perversely, perhaps, but utterly – tied to that society. He was its offspring, its sick conscience – a living reminder of all the hidden crimes we commit when we close ranks among each other. He craved human society, craved the chance to show people what their 'society' had done to him. And the odd thing is, society craved him too.'
> 'Craved him?' I said, as we passed along the quiet perimeter of Washington Square Park. 'How do you mean? They'd have shot him through with electricity if they'd had the chance.'
> 'Yes, but not before holding him up to the world', Kreizler answered. 'We revel in men like Beecham, Moore – they are the easy repositories of all that is dark in our very *social* world. But the things that helped make Beecham what he was? Those we tolerate. Those, we even enjoy ...'
>
> (*Alienist*, 592)

In the debate that raged at the end of the nineteenth century between those that believed that crime was congenital to certain people, families, classes, or races, and those that turned to the individual's social environment and personal past for an answer, it is clear which side Kreizler is on. It is equally clear which side Kreizler's creator is on at the end of the twentieth century, when the same debate threatens to flare up once again. The contemporaneity of the issues Carr addresses in *The Alienist* becomes all the more clear if we consider that the late nineteenth-century social conditions in which he grounds his plot and characters, risk repeating themselves in our times, and not just in the United States. We once again see mass migration for economic and political reasons and countless 'illegal aliens' who are as often as not economically and sexually exploitated.

There is no obvious explanation for the sudden popularity of historical crime writing at the end of the twentieth century. Perhaps it is exactly the approaching end of the second millennium that has triggered the interest in history and the awareness that the past is still usable that we see displayed in these novels. The past is relevant to us in historical crime fiction because it allows us to draw parallels with the contemporary world and to illuminate contemporary issues and problems. Although not all historical crime writing presents the past as 'usable' in this particular sense – Peter J. Heck's series featuring Mark Twain as detective is for instance not much interested in its social and moral relevance – many representatives of the genre intelligently and subtly avail themselves of the possibilities it offers. Let us hope that now that the third millennium has rather unspectacularly arrived this interest in the past will not fade away.

10
In Waco's Wake: Patricia Cornwell and Mary Willis Walker

In the 1990s crime fiction by women writers has followed the more general trend towards increased levels of suspense, shock, and terror that characterizes the popular culture of the late twentieth century. In female crime writing, too, we see new levels of violence and an increased exploitation of the sort of terror that is characteristic of the thriller. This chapter will look at that often highly successful combination – successful in terms of awards and sales – and will do so by focusing on four megasellers of the mid-1990s: the first two Molly Cates novels by Mary Willis Walker (*The Red Scream*, 1994, and *Under the Beetle's Cellar*, 1995) and Patricia Cornwell's *Postmortem* (1990) and *Cause of Death* (1996), two of her Kay Scarpetta books. As will become clear, there are good reasons to discuss especially *Under the Beetle's Cellar* and *Cause of Death* within one single framework. *Postmortem* and *The Red Scream* are not only thrown in for good measure, but also because they too so clearly illustrate what in these and other massive sellers of the 1990s would seem to be a persistent view of crime and, more in particular, the criminal.

A major reason for picking Cornwell and Walker out of at least a dozen women crime writers who have been extraordinarily successful in terms of sales, is that their sales are matched by critical appraisal. Cornwell's first Scarpetta novel, *Postmortem*, won virtually every best first novel award around (the Edgar, the Anthony, the Macavity, and the John Creasey) plus the French *Prix du Roman d'Aventure*, while her *Cruel and Unusual* (1993) won the Gold Dagger Award of the British Crime Writers Association. Mary Willis Walker's debut *Zero at the Bone* (1991) won Macavity and Agatha awards for best first novel, while *The Red Scream*, her first novel featuring Molly Cates, won the Edgar, and its sequel, *Under the Beetle's Cellar*, won the Macavity, the Anthony, and Hammett awards. In short, Walker and Cornwell have fared extraordinarily well with their peers and other connoisseurs.

This suggests that we should read the new standards of violence and perversion that we find in these and other recent novels by women writers as a sign of the times, and not simply as the personal preference of two of the most prominent new female crime writers of the 1990s. Such a view of things is supported by a similar upping of the ante in the work of a number of well established authors. See, for instance, the discussion of Marcia Muller's mid-1990s novels earlier in this book. Surely not accidentally, Muller also happened to find herself in the awards sphere with a couple of mid-1990s thrillers. Her 1993 *Wolf in the Shadows* was nominated for the Edgar and won the Anthony while *A Wild and Lonely Place* (1995) was nominated for the Macavity. This is not to say that all crime writing by women has chosen to present ever higher levels of violence and terror. 'Cozy' detective novels still abound and the majority of female PIs do not overtax the reader's credulity. There is no denying, however, that the strategy pursued by Cornwell, Walker, and other female crime writers such as Barbara D'Amato (*KILLER. app*, 1996) or Edna Buchanan (*Miami, It's Murder*, 1994) is a popular success. That success, however, has a price. On the surface, it presents an enormous boost for female crime writing. But if we look a little closer we see how much of what female crime writers had gained the authors in question are prepared to give up. What we see is basically a return to an older, discredited ethos and it is an unpleasant idea that there must be a connection between weeks on the bestseller lists and the conservatism that ultimately characterizes these novels.

Mary Willis Walker

Mary Willis Walker's series heroine Molly Cates is firmly anchored in the recently established tradition of the independent female professional-cum-investigator. Cates, who makes her first appearance in *The Red Scream*, is a 42–year-old reporter with what would seem to be a rather upmarket Texas monthly. Apparently, she habitually seeks out the extreme in her pursuit of stories, specializing, according to her editor, in 'the more bizarre and high-profile crimes' and in 'religion, especially our home-grown religious extremists'. (This interest in religious cultists, which is nowhere in evidence in *Scream*, is invented for the occasion in *Under the Beetle's Cellar* where it enables Cates to get into the act.) Walker makes sure that we cannot attribute Cates's unmarried state to a general unattractiveness. She has been married three times (with decidedly poor results), has had 'more lovers in between than she had ever counted' (*Scream*, 117), and in the course of *Scream* rekindles the torch that her first husband, Lieutenant Grady Traynor of the Austin Police Department, used to carry for her.

Walker suggests that Molly has rather outspoken liberal views. She is against capital punishment, is not religious, and hates condescension from men. More in general, she follows her own judgment, which has at least once led to irreparable damage. During her marriage with Traynor, now over 20 years ago, she has slept with an 'old tobacco-chewing county sheriff' in the hope of trying to discover who murdered her father a few years earlier. Not surprisingly, this as it turns out futile act has wrecked the marriage. It is the only thing she regrets – but only because she has in the meantime come to see her behavior as obsessive. As she now tells Traynor, she would do it again if that would lead her to the murderer. (Surely *All the Dead Lie Down* of 1998, in which Molly successfully reopens the case, must at that point already have been a gleam in Walker's novelistic eye. In any case she takes care to emphasize Molly's determination: 'Nothing in the world gave her the motivation that opposition did.' (18))

The encounter with her ex-husband soon leads to an affair, but Molly fiercely guards her independence, even if, as she later admits to her and Traynor's 24–year-old daughter, he is the love of her life: 'She'd enjoy a good man in her life, but not in her house. One of her goals in life was never again to share a bathroom with a man.' (139–40) In *Cellar*, when Traynor becomes increasingly insistent in his attempts to get Molly to live with him, she repeats that she will 'never set up housekeeping again' and tells him to have no expectations: '"I eat when I feel like it. I read all night when I want to. I never cook. I still do vigils. I don't hang up my clothes. I keep some bad company. I follow my obsessions. I work all the time – it's what I love",' adding, in case he has not got the point: '"I live like a man."' (*Cellar*, 260). Traynor would by the way seem to support her claim to masculinity: she is the only woman he has ever known who is not a 'silly romantic' – a view which does not do much to hide his gendered attitude to things.

Molly's description of her masculine lifestyle merits attention because it, too, is so completely gendered and so at odds with how most men really live. Walker, who more generally holds up Molly's life style as admirable, accepts the male gendered myth of idealized total freedom that is characteristic of the hard-boiled tradition and that is as silly for women as it has always been for men. Curiously, what we see of Molly's actual life is strangely at odds with this description. In both novels the only man in her life is her ex-husband Traynor, whom she loves 'desperately and forever' even if she does not want to live with him. Her apparently turbulent love-life of the past 20-odd years is only mentioned in passing and is not in evidence at all while the 'bad company' she herself mentions, and the 'cold part of her mind that [is] always hunting for a good story' (*Scream*, 103), never make an appearance. Walker takes care not to alienate a reading public that may well be impressed by such hints at total independence but that may equally well take offense at a heroine who actually enjoys promiscuity and bad company.

Walker clearly wants to present her protagonist as the equivalent of tough masculinity and as subscribing to the same sort of private morality that has traditionally been the privilege of crime fiction's tough males. In *Cellar*, for instance, Molly lies, breaks 'most of the ASNE ethics for journalists', takes advantage of an old drunk, is pepared to trample all over an old woman, and so on. Of course she has her eye firmly on a higher moral purpose: the rescue of 11 primary school children who have been kidnapped by a crazed cult. Interestingly, its leader recognizes the steely moral fibre under Molly's veneer of petty sins:

> He sees you as ungodly, unfeminine, wrongheaded, and doomed. But he also sees you as ruthlessly honest and struggling to tell the truth as you see it. More honest than the people who call themselves Christians and do nothing about it. He thinks your interest in exploring faith is more religious than most people's watered-down or fake belief.
>
> (*Cellar*, 253)

What he does not see, ironically, is that this ruthless morality for which the end justifies the means could well turn against him. In an act of personal betrayal Molly enables an FBI markswoman to kill the man and thus makes it possible to rescue the children. However, what would normally be treachery is here fully justified by the circumstances. Walker plays it safe. Molly may follow a private moral vision, but in the end very few readers will question the course she takes.

Although Molly Cates, then, is rather traditional, the novels in which she features are not. As I have already suggested, Walker is one of those new writers of the 1990s who have introduced a new level of terror and perversion in female crime writing. *The Red Scream* and *Under the Beetle's Cellar* present villains whose sheer inhumanity serves to condone all the moral lapses that Molly Cates could ever be accused of. In *Scream* the major villain is serial killer Louie Bronk who, after murdering his female victims, rapes them and shaves their heads. (Rather appropriately, the prison authorities have him trained as a barber while serving time for his first murder.) Bronk is on Death Row in Texas' Huntsville prison and his time is running out. On Death Row Bronk has taken up writing poetry and the red scream of the novel's title is his metaphor for the terror that lies in wait in the final hours before execution.

The novel revolves around Molly's increasing suspicion that Bronk, who has been tried before serial killing became a capital charge, may not have been guilty of the one murder that got him the death penalty. This particular murder has, at least technically, been committed in the course of committing another felony, which has opened the door to the death penalty. Although Molly has come to dislike him intensely in the course of several interviews and has no doubts that he is indeed a serial killer – at one point she tells her daughter than she '"can't wait to see that sneering, smug, murdering, evil son of a bitch dead"' (39) – she sees it as her moral duty to save him from a fatal miscarriage of justice. Part of her motivation may derive from her feeling that Bronk himself, with his 'rotten childhood [that had] sent him forth determined to kill and rape' (66), is in some ways a victim, a feeling apparently intensified by Bronk's underdog position: '"the entire criminal justice system [is] like an inexorable steamroller out to flatten one miserable wretch"' (72). Her primary motivation, however, quixotic as it may appear in this particular case, is her strongly developed and rather abstract sense of justice. This situation clearly has novelistic potential, but it cannot really be said that Walker develops its contradictions – a point to which I will return.

Molly Cates's problem is how to convince the relevant authorities that Bronk is innocent of this particular murder and, therefore, should not be executed. Moreover, the investigation she undertakes on Bronk's behalf is sabotaged at every point by those who want to protect the real killer, who by that time has killed again, and in a final confrontation will almost succeed in killing Molly herself. Neatly side-stepping our expectations, Walker has Molly fail in her self-imposed task. Molly does not obtain a stay of Bronk's execution, even though she can at one point present his case to the governor in person. (Also rather neatly, Walker gives us a female Texas governor.) Molly's fallibity is further emphasized by her failure to identify the real killer responsible for the novel's murders until the latter actually attacks her. Such lapses, along with the 'early morning terrors' that she has suffered since her father's death, 26 years ago, and other minor foibles, such as the 'incipient panic' with which she usually reacts to mistakes, put Molly among the tough-but-humanly-fallible and emotionally vulnerable protagonists that contemporary female crime writers have created. Still, Walker apparently feels she has to give her heroine a final victory of sorts. In the two last pages Molly finally succeeds in doing the 25 push-ups she has set herself as a standard – with physical fitness functioning as a form of self-empowerment – and is allowed to write the article on Louie Bronk that her editor has repeatedly refused to consider. What is more, she can present the true story of the murder for which Bronk has in the meantime been executed and thus posthumously rehabilitate him – at least in this respect.

In a more important sense, however, he is not rehabilitated at all. Bronk is a 'small, insignificant man', wholly unprepossessing. He has an 'unpleasant-looking hard paunch' and 'stringy arms'; his hair is 'sparse and limp', his lips are 'mere gray lines', his eyes are 'squinty and narrow, close-set, with no lashes or eyebrows' and he has a 'sharp beaky nose' (198). As if this is not enough, Walker has him sweating profusely, even under ordinary circumstances, while his breath is 'rotting' and his eyes never blink. This last characteristic, together with images such as 'cords in his neck [that stand] out like snakes' (226) and similar descriptions, clearly functions to suggest that Bronk is as reptilian as he is human. More subtle, since they convey a state of mind and do not describe an outward appearance that Bronk has little effective control over, are Bronk's poems, with which Walker opens her chapters. Some of them are, in fact, chillingly well done:

> Pretty gal all alone
> On the highway, car broke down.
> You pull behind her real quick.
> She gets to looking sick,
> Mouth all dry
> Starts to cry
> Like a flood,
> Sweating blood.
> Please, please don't.
> Honey I won't
> Won't hurt you none.
> There it's done.
> Weren't that fun?
>
> (*Scream*, 196)

Bronk's appearance, the demonic cat-and-mouse mentality that is expressed by this and other poems, his habit of raping his victims after their death and then shaving off their hair, effectively relegate him to the subhuman, as does Molly's remark that in 20 years of interviews with criminals Bronk is the first one in which she has not been able to see 'our common humanity' (217). Since Bronk's voice is only heard in his poems, which do not do much to counteract this claim, the reader has not much chance of arriving at a different conclusion. Needless to say that Molly's stubborn desire to do such a man – and his memory – justice can only highlight the curiously abstract and absolutist character of her sense of justice.

In striking contrast with Molly's attitude is that of her creator, who presents Bronk in the worst of lights. None of the murders he has committed is described in any detail and since he is not responsible for the violent deaths that occur in the novel, Bronk's subhumanity is not so much demonstrated as suggested. His repulsive appearance, which is calculated to prejudice us against him, and the virtual absence of his voice, seal his fate. One obvious effect of turning Bronk into a subhuman is that it indirectly exonerates the system. As a matter of fact, the paradoxical effect of the system's failure is that a monstrous serial killer gets what he deserves. No wonder, then, that *Red Scream* sends out strangely contradictory signals. Bronk's monstrosity guarantees that the miscarriage of justice that sends him to his death is not an issue in the novel, even though Molly has spent a good deal of energy and time trying to save the man's neck. It never leads to questions concerning the system's premises. On the contrary, once the governor has refused to stay Bronk's execution, everything that follows is simply taken for granted.

Walker effectively avoids such contradictions in the second Molly Cates novel, *Under the Beetle's Cellar*, in which the criminal is the stunningly handsome Donnie Ray Grimes, now known as Samuel Mordecai, leader of the Hearth Jezreelites, an obscure religious cult. Since we not only hear Grimes's incoherent ramblings – in which, rather innocently, the Beast announced in the Book of Revelation turns out to be the personal computer – but also witness his total disregard for suffering and extreme cruelty, he becomes a truly inhumane character whose apparent madness in no way exonerates him. Grimes, convinced that he is one of God's elect, is indeed almost totally inhuman.

The Hearth Jezreelites have settled in a fortified compound near Jezreel, Texas, presumably because the Book of Revelation tells us that

Armageddon, the final battle between the forces of good and evil which will herald the Apocalypse, will take place in the Valley of Jezreel. In any case, Grimes and his sect are convinced that the Apocalypse is near. They have, in fact, started to count down: when the novel opens it is the 46th day of the 50-day period of purification which according to Mordecai must be observed in anticipation of the Apocalypse. Although somewhat unusual, in this day and age the Jezreelites' expectations are not exactly startling. His god has revealed to Mordecai, however, that he and his followers must not only prepare themselves for the Apocalypse by way of this period of purification, but also that the Apocalypse demands the literal sacrifice of 50 innocents. In order to meet this divine demand the Hearth Jezreelites have kidnapped a schoolbus driver and 11 of his young wards and keep them imprisoned in an old bus which is buried in the dirt under the floor of a large barn. This unlikely hiding place derives from another of Grimes's visions in which he has received the message that the earth is the element in which the purification of the innocents must take place. (It has the additional advantage of making it impossible to rescue the children in a surprise attack and of allowing Walker to create a stand-off that will last long enough for a substantial novel, and that reminds us – as do the Hearth Jezreelites themselves – of the Branch Davidians and their stand-off with the federal authorities in Waco, Texas.)

Walker makes the most of the possibilities in this eerie, badly lit underground prison, especially of the buried-alive theme that is always close under the surface (no pun intended): '... the strangest part, the worst of it, was the windows. They were black with the earth pressing in on them ... A thick white grub worm wiggled against the glass and a dark beetle was inching its way through a tiny burrow' (*Cellar*, 2). Since Walker has to take us inside the bus for maximum effect, Molly's point of view – the only point of view in *Scream* – here alternates with that of Walter Demming, the bus driver who has been imprisoned with the children and who is all along aware that none of them will survive their ordeal. Demming's point of view also allows us to witness the death of one of the children, a development that increases the terror we feel and that simultaneously serves to further indict Grimes, who has refused to pass on the inhalers the outside world has sent for the asthmatic boy in question, because 'drugs' are not allowed during 'purification'.

Grimes's apparently nonchalant waste of the life of one of his 'innocents' carries a grisly explanation when we learn that he only needs eight of them since he has already sacrificed 42 others. He has personally killed – with a sickle – the 42 babies born in the compound over the least three years, including his own, after keeping them in underground boxes for 50 days. As if this is not enough to convince us of the man's utter madness and perversion, Walker creates the 'Sword Hand of God', Jezreelites who operate undercover in the outside world and who function as Grimes's death squad, turning defectors, Grimes's own wife among them, into so-called 'blood statues': the victims are tortured, stripped naked, and hung upside down with their throats slit.

We clearly must believe that, like Bronk, Grimes constitutes a category all by himself. While with Bronk Molly never could 'see a common humanity', Grimes has completely overpowered her during their one and only meeting:

> But something happened when I was out there at Jezreel, something extremely upsetting to me. There is this ... quality about Samuel Mordecai .... He has this ... well ... I really am at a loss of words here. He has something – some force – that caused me to sit down and shut up, even though sitting down and shutting up is something I haven't done very well since the third grade and even then I didn't do it very well.
>
> (*Cellar*, 45–6)

However, Walker's actual presentation of Grimes fails to live up to this. It is not that the madness and hatred of Grimes and his equally deluded followers are unthinkable, but it is hard to accept the particular expressions of madness and hatred that Walker presents, particularly the cold-blooded execution of 42 infants. In fact, her strategy of demonizing the main villain is taken so far that it almost backfires.

This conscious demonizing of both Bronk and Grimes must be linked with Walker's presentation of Molly as an honorary male, the fact that she has Molly take at face value that male myth of total freedom. The monstrosity of Bronk and Grimes belongs to an old-fashioned world of heroes – either male or male gendered – and monsters rather than to the far more subtle and empathic world of most contemporary female crime writers. With its privileging of maleness that world is ultimately mysogynistic. It is, in the final analysis, not really a surprise to find women at the root of the evil of these novels. Bronk is motivated by a deep hatred for his mother and his sisters – one of whom is his first victim – who have neglected, abused, and finally abandoned him. Grimes has been abandoned as a new-born infant by his unmarried mother, has then first been raised by a mother who deserted him when he was still a boy for a life of prostitution in Las Vegas and later by a cold, unloving, fundamentalist grandmother. The culpability of their fathers, natural or otherwise, who have also abandoned them and who have, moreover, left their wives or girlfriends to cope, somehow manages to escape notice.

The Red Scream and *Under the Beetle's Cellar* present a world that with its seemingly strong and independent heroine is at first sight more or less feminist in orientation. Under that surface, however, we find much that belongs to the illiberal, strongly gendered world of the thriller. There is little doubt that biologically Molly Cates is a female, but Walker works hard at making her an old-fashioned male in an old-fashioned male world, creating a framework within which Traynor's remark that Molly is the only woman he has ever met who is not a 'silly romantic', can be offered, and accepted, as a compliment.

Patricia Cornwell

While Walker, although on the verge of lapsing into unintentional parody, arguably keeps things under control in *Cellar*, Patricia Cornwell's *Cause of Death* (1996), which like *Cellar* echoes the Branch Davidians tragedy, fails to do so. Ever after *Postmortem* (1990), which introduced Dr Kay Scarpetta, chief medical examiner of the Commonwealth of Virginia, Cornwell's self-inflicted problem has been to generate more tension and excitement than she did in her first novel. Since *Postmortem* already seriously taxes our credulity, raising the ante has not been the easiest thing to do.

In *Postmortem*, Scarpetta, who in spite of her official status operates not unlike a private investigator, is after a sadistic serial killer, who eventually breaks into her house and is shot dead by the police detective who fortunately has followed him. Incredibly, it turns out that Scarpetta, although believing that she herself may be the killer's next target, has not only failed to check her windows, allowing the man easy access to her house, but has also forgotten to load the gun that she has put under her pillow by way of precaution. Both acts of forgetfulness are totally at odds with the competence she shows in her job and would invite psychoanalytic attention if it were not so obvious that Cornwell arranges these lapses to further increase the novel's level of terror. At that point we have already been exposed to a whole range of unsettling scenes and events. The crimes are unusually violent and

Cornwell gives us rather graphic descriptions of the victims' bodies. Moreover, the novel, as its title suggests, takes the reader into the autopsy room, although in not nearly as much detail as the later novels do. Still, even if Cornwell does not really exploit Scarpetta's autopsy scenes in *Postmortem,* they certainly have an inherent shock value. (In the later novels Cornwell is more exploitative and not averse to offering irrelevant but spicy details: 'biology had dealt him an earlier blow called hypospadias, which meant his urethra opened onto the underside of his penis instead of in the center'; *Cause,* 35.) On top of this, Scarpetta's boss tries to undermine her professional reputation by breaking into her computer and altering important data, while another high-ranking authority, the Commonwealth's attorney, turns out to be a rapist who has designs on Scarpetta herself. As if to add to the mistrust of (male) authority that the novel inspires, Cornwell has her killer work as a member of the communications staff at 911, selecting his victims on the basis of their voices.

Like Walker's novels, *Postmortem* at first sight suggests a fairly strong liberalist feminist perspective. The novel's protagonist is an extraordinarily competent, high-ranking professional who values her independent stance and is easily equal to the males that surround her. Moreover, the criminal element – not only the killer, but also, in their own way, Scarpetta's boss and the attorney – is exclusively male. To top things off, the police sergeant who is assigned to the case is a sexist redneck so that in the final analysis Scarpetta is the only sympathetic major character. But a reading in terms of feminism is too simple. As in Walker's novels, the criminal is presented as a monster – he is not only a murderous psychopath, but has a strange body odor because of a rare metabolic disorder. *Postmortem* sets up an absolutist, black and white framework that reminds us of an earlier, more conservative age; a framework which allows the police sergeant to shoot the rapist, whose only weapon is a knife, four times from close range: 'Marino didn't have to kill him. No one would ever know except the two of us. I'd never tell. I wasn't sorry. I would have done it myself.' (*Postmortem,* 394) Another disturbing sign is the sudden incompetence that almost allows the killer to get at Scarpetta, plus the fact that it is the redneck cop – a male – who ultimately saves her life. In the last part of the novel Cornwell pulls the rug from under her heroine's feet, sacrificing Scarpetta's credibility to the thriller ending she wants to have (although she herself does not seem to notice her heroine's diminished status). This is all the more regrettable since it is so unnecessary. *Postmortem* may have its defects – Cornwell's style being the most conspicuous of them – but it is an undeniably effective and innovative piece of crime writing. Cornwell makes brilliant use of recent advances in forensic science so that we have an exciting mixture of police procedural, private investigation, and Holmesian clue hunting (and examination). Cornwell's decision to attach a thriller ending to such an in itself more than satisfactory mix leads to an overkill that damages her protagonist and the novel as such.

Motivated, no doubt, by the same urge that made her go for a thriller ending in her first novel, Cornwell opts for a flight forward in the later Scarpetta novels. While much of *Postmortem* returns in these novels – the autopsies (now more detailed and with the sort of irrelevant detail mentioned above), the acts of sabotage on the part of male rivals, the killer who targets Scarpetta herself – their coherence and plausibility are increasingly sacrificed on the altar of suspense and terror. By the time of *Cause*, the seventh Scarpetta novel, Cornwell would seem to have written herself into a corner and the reader begins to wish that she would every now and then follow Scarpetta's strategy for coping with apparently insoluble problems: 'When all else fails, I cook' (*Postmortem*, 150).

Like *Under the Beetle's Cellar*, *Cause of Death* is clearly, even if only partly, inspired by Waco's Branch Davidians (as is Stuart Woods's *Heat* (1994) and a number of other crime novels of the mid-1990s). Its beginning, in which a diver is found dead near an inactive submarine in Norfolk, Virginia, is promising enough. Scarpetta, who happens to be in the neighborhood, gets a strange phone call, is treated with inexplicable condescension and hostility at the scene of what seems to be an accident (where we find that Cornwell has added diving to Scarpetta's already unlikely accomplishments), and is not satisfied with the cause of death, a suspicion that is borne out when during the autopsy she smells cyanide. The autopsy, by the way, also brings out Scarpetta's sense of self-importance, which ever since *Postmortem* has been on the increase and which in *Cause* reaches disturbing proportions. 'The ability to smell cyanide is a sex-linked recessive trait that is inherited by less than thirty percent of the population. I was among the fortunate few' (*Cause*, 40), Scarpetta tells us in all seriousness, apparently not realizing that these 'fortunate few' in the US alone must come close to 80 million. (Later, in England, she reflects that if there was a nuclear disaster in England or Europe, 'chances were I would be brought in to help handle the dead' [277], as if in such circumstances, with the cause of death absolutely clear, the British, or the Europeans for that matter, would think it necessary to call on the expertise of Virginia's chief medical examiner.)

However, what unhinges Cornwell's novel is not Scarpetta's absolutely monumental self-preoccupation but the plot line that introduces the New Zionists and their leader Joel Hand. Like Grimes and his Hearth Jezreelites, Hand and the New Zionists live in an isolated and closely guarded compound, and have the nasty habit of tracking down and killing defectors. Still, compared to Grimes and his cult, the New Zionists are relatively harmless. What we see are some ordinary murders and an attack on a nuclear power plant that leads to more deaths. What must convince us of the utter depravity of Hand and his Zionists is the *Book of Hand*, written by Hand under the apparent guidance of God himself:

> Like the Christian Bible, much of what the manuscript had to say was conveyed in parables, and prophesies and proverbs, thus making the text illustrative and human. This was one of the many reasons why reading it was so hard. Pages were populated with people and images that penetrated to deeper layers of the brain. The Book . . . showed in exquisite detail how to kill and maim, frighten, brainwash and torture. The explicit section on the necessity of progroms, including illustrations, made me quake.
>
> (*Cause*, 76)

The Book's extraordinary, scripture-like status is underscored by a description so outlandish that it must be meant to make us sit up and be impressed: 'Written in Renaissance script on India paper, it was bound in tooled black leather' (75–6). Are we supposed to believe that Hand has mastered Renaissance writing (whatever that may be)? Such frenetic straining for effect is what we often find in Cornwell, especially in the later books. For good measure she has Scarpetta refer to the Inquisition, although Hand's book, with its reference to progroms, sounds more like a homespun version of the Protocols of Zion, and a moment later Scarpetta talks of the 'runes' she is reading, as if runes and Renaissance script have any sort of connection. This pseudo-learning, however, cannot hide that Cornwell does not really know what to do with her cult. Why are the New Zionists so bent on torture and murder? What motivates them? We never learn.

In line with this we also never get to understand the reasons for the New Zionists' major action: the violent takeover of a nuclear plant. What begins as the sort of Scarpetta mystery that we have come to expect suddenly develops into a thriller about nuclear terrorism. It soon appears that Hand and a group of his followers have taken over the power plant to ship plutonium and 'fuel assemblies' to an Arab nation, presumably Libya, while simultaneously other followers, or perhaps Libyan agents, have succeeded in stealing an inactive submarine that can be retrofitted with nuclear arms. Cornwell sets up a disaster scenario in which a rogue submarine will be able to effectively threaten the whole world and will no doubt in first instance target the US. (When Scarpetta learns about the takeover, her 'thoughts' immediately start 'flying through lists of what [she] must do' [250], as if the responsibility for this sort of thing rests exclusively on her shoulders. Needless to say that Cornwell indeed gives her a central role in defusing this nuclear time bomb.) It is a mystery why a religious sect, even one as given to fantasies of violence and torture as the New Zionists, would lend itself to the purposes of Libya or any other nation. What is in it for Hand and his fellow cultists? Again, we never know.

In her breathless pursuit of maximum impact, Cornwell surely alienates all but her most gullible readers. It is not just that the US government would never allow the ship the New Zionists are loading to sail, so that the nuclear threat is never real – not even if we grant Cornwell's apparent assumption that all you need to create a realistic threat out of the combination of plutonium and an old submarine is a couple of hours with a good screwdriver. Cornwell consistently damages her case, as she in fact started to do in *Postmortem*, by giving the most ordinary things and occurrences emotional charges that they simply cannot bear and by distorting characters beyond recognition. It is not just the villains who are distorted into monsters. Scarpetta's niece, for instance, is consistently presented as a genius of Nobel prize quality. It clearly does not occur to Cornwell that the depressions, drinking bouts and general instability that she uses to further emphasize the girl's uniqueness make the reader wonder how she ever made it into a hardcore FBI outfit.

The all-round implausibility of *Cause of Death* plus the conservative black and white scheme Cornwell employs severely damage what otherwise might be construed as Scarpetta's feminist independence and pride in her achievements. Scarpetta experiences just too many instances of male supremacist sabotage – she is now sure that even her fellow medical students at Johns Hopkins and her male colleagues in law school tried to wreck her career because she was a woman – and is too infallible, even in the kitchen. (Ordinary cooking is out in crime novels with feminist pretensions but *haute cuisine* stuff, which is linked with status, is rather popular, even with male protagonists, witness

Robert Parker's Spenser.) Although not exactly an honorary male, Scarpetta's infallibility and her fantasies of omnipotence do not qualify her as a feminist either. Neither does her self-chosen isolation: 'My stone house was set back from the street . . . the wooded lot surrounded by a wrought-iron fence neighboring children could not squeeze through. I knew no one on any side of me, and had no intentions of changing that.' (92)

The way writers like Walker and Cornwell seek to create suspense and terror brings in by the back door the attitudes and perspectives of the self-absorbed and rigid masculinity of the cold war thriller and of now widely discredited PI writers such as Mickey Spillane. What is especially unfortunate is that that normative masculinity is strongly associated with their female protagonists. Female crime writing has since the early 1980s shaken up the genre and introduced fascinating new elements. With the female thriller-heroine of the 1990s we travel back to the paranoid mentality of the illiberal 1950s.

11
'Other' Detectives: the Emergence of Ethnic Crime Writing

Popular literature often addresses hopes and fears affecting large sections of a nation's population, especially when in the throes of social, political, and economic change or upheaval. In the case of the detective this is very clear. The genre originated in early and mid-nineteenth-century France and England, closely upon the creation of the first modern and professional police services. This development itself marked the middle-classes's determination to safeguard its own only recently won hegemony *vis-à-vis* both the arrogant arbitrariness of aristocratic rule and the growing 'greed' of the have-nots (see, for instance, Knight 1980; Mandel 1984; Porter 1981).

In the classical ratiocinative detective novel, first codified by Edgar Allan Poe, the solution of the mystery signals the restoration of law and order, after which the world resumes its course and the body social and politic can return to business as usual. This kind of fiction, which had its 'Golden Age' between the wars in England, is typically set in middle-class milieus, from the rural modesty of the village of Agatha Christie's Miss Marple to the upperclass manors in which her Poirot performs. It equally typically features drawing-room mysteries bordering on intellectual games not unlike *The Times* crossword puzzle featured in so many samples of the genre. With its inevitable re-establishment of social and moral order this form of fiction served to counter the social and political threats of the interbellum by conjuring up an idyllic, unchanging, almost pastoral England. Implicitly it sought to perpetuate the political system enabling such a vision.

At the same time, the American hard-boiled private eye novel arose to serve a similar need, but tailored to American circumstances. Specifically, it addressed the fears of America's white middle class in a period when this felt itself threatened by a combination of developments both abroad and at home coming to a head during the two world wars: the rise of the Soviet Union leading to the first 'red scare' of the early 1920s, massive waves of immigration from southern and eastern Europe between 1880 and the First World War leading to the establishment of a quota system for future immigration, the Crash of 1929, and the outbreak of the Great Depression. It is especially in the pulp fiction of the period that these threats are openly identified. Yet, they also speak from some of the work we now consider as marking the high point of hard-boiled crime fiction, and written by authors who considered themselves – and are considered by others – as definitely on the left side of the political spectrum. In Dashiell Hammett's *The Maltese Falcon* (1930), for instance, white Anglo-Saxon Sam Spade is pitted against a homosexual oriental, a foreign moneyshark – British but with a German-Jewish name – an Irish immigrant hussy, and a low class gangster punk. In other words, Hammett, in spite of his political sympathies, presents a negative picture of what conservative middle America thought of as 'undesirables'.

At the same time, the interbellum also saw the creation of some ethnic detective series, though typically these were not written by writers who belonged to the ethnic minorities in question but by w1hite writers. One of the most successful series was that featuring Honolulu-born Chinese American Charlie Chan, written by the Ohio-born and Harvard-educated Earl Derr Biggers (1884–1933). Because of his early death Biggers only completed six Chan novels. However, from 1926 on Chan starred in numerous movies, though always played by white actors. Rather predictably, in recent years the Charlie Chan series – the movies rather than the novels – has been decried as racist because of its alleged stereotyping of Asian Americans. The same charge has been brought against the Florian Slappey short story series, first serialized – like the early versions of the Charlie Chan novels – in the 1920s and 1930s in *The Saturday Evening Post*, and later collected as *Florian Slappey Goes Abroad* (1928) and *Florian Slappey* (1938). Slappey is an African American detective, created by white Charleston-born Octavus Roy Cohen (1891–1959), who also authored various other mystery series featuring white detectives.

Contemporary ethnic detectives

A more contemporary example of ethnic detective writing undertaken by a white author is the extremely successful Lieutenant Leaphorn and Detective Jim Chee series, featuring two Native Americans – one part, the other a full-blooded Navajo. The series author, Tony Hillerman, is definitely white, even if raised among native Americans. Hillerman is often considered the 'founding father' of 'serious' ethnic detective writing other than African American. Hillerman's example has been followed by a number of Native American crime writers. Unfortunately, none of these seem to share Hillerman's writing talent.

Aimée and David Thurlo's Ella Clah mysteries, for instance, are routinely compared to Hillerman's Leaphorn and Chee novels. They themselves explicitly dedicate the third Ella Clah mystery, *Blackening Song* (1995), to Hillerman. In a sense they even try to outdo the master by making their FBI Special Agent Ella Clah not just a Navajo but also a woman. In the end, though, the Thurlos are merely weak epigones of the master. The characters in the Ella Clah mysteries are wooden, and so is the dialogue, which fails to distinguish the characters from one another. The descriptions of the majestic southwestern landscape are no match for those in Hillerman's novels. The plots are farfetched, and ultimately unconvincing, as they tend to rely excessively upon the supernatural. *Blackening Song*, for instance, prominently features the 'skinwalkers' that are a staple also of Hillerman's fiction. Hillerman, though, takes great care never to claim that these evil Navajo 'witches' – supposedly able to turn into coyotes – actually exist. With him, they are part of Navajo belief, and this belief can be exploited and manipulated with evil intent. Or, as in *The First Eagle* (1998), it can lead an old Navajo woman to erroneously interpret what she saw. With the Thurlos, in contrast, we find people literally changing into coyotes. We are even made to 'witness' a gathering of skinwalkers practising their rituals.

Much more interesting, yet less squarely within the detective genre, is Mardi Oakley Medawar's *Death at Rainy Mountain* (1996), the first of a series starring mid-nineteenth-century Kiowa investigator Tay-Bodal or 'Meat Carrier'. Frankly, the detective story here merely serves as a coathanger for the odd characters, and for a description of the customs of the Kiowa at the end of the American Civil War. This is also the avowed intention of Medawar, a Cherokee herself. In her 'author's note' to *Death at Rainy Mountain* she stresses the historical accuracy of much of what she writes about in this novel. 'During the course of telling a story', she claims, 'I can give my people back their heroes ... I can restore to these heroes their names.' Via her detailed descriptions of her people's customs and rituals, she can write her people back into history. Medawar's intention is shared by many contemporary 'other' detectives. These detectives include a variety of ethnic and gay private eyes. We will begin our discussion of such 'other' detectives with

African American crime fiction, arguably the earliest form of 'ethnic' crime writing.

African American crime writing: Walter Mosley's Easy Rawlins

Until not long ago it was customary to label Chester Himes, with his hard-boiled Harlem detectives Grave Digger Jones and Coffin Ed Johnson, the first practitioner of African American crime fiction. More recently, however, research has unearthed various earlier black mystery writers. Paula L. Woods, in her introduction to *Spooks, Spies, and Private Eyes: Black Mystery, Crime, and Suspense Fiction of the 20th Century* (1995), credits Harlem Renaissance author Rudolph Fisher with being the first African American author of a mystery novel also featuring African American characters. With *The Conjure-Man Dies: A Mystery Tale of Dark Harlem* (1932), Woods claims, Fisher 'was the first [black mystery writer] to set his story in the black community and to address issues important to American negroes, including their relationship to their African ancestry, color prejudice, and superstition' (Woods, xv). Around the same time as Fisher, another Harlem Renaissance writer, George S. Schuyler, published some detective stories focusing on some of these same issues. Yet another Harlem Renaissance author, Alice Dunbar-Nelson, also ventured into the detective genre, but she concentrated on white characters. Woods credits Frank Bailey with having pushed, in *Out of the Woodpile: Black Characters in Crime and Detective Fiction* (1991), the genealogy of African American detective writing back to Jamaica-born W. Adolphe Roberts, who in the 1920s published several mystery novels. She herself unearths even earlier examples, such as a 1900 story by Pauline E. Hopkins (1859–1930), and a 1907 story by J.E. Bruce (1856–1924). None of these, however, featured African American detectives, or were set in African American communities. Still, 'Talma Gordon', the 1900 Pauline Hopkins's story anthologized in *Spooks, Spies, and Private Eyes*, clearly thematizes the issues of miscegenation and 'passing'.

In *The Blues Detective: A Study of African American Detective Fiction*, a critical study that appeared one year after Woods's *Spooks, Spies, and Private Eyes*, Stephen F. Soitos firmly grounds black detective fiction in Pauline Hopkins's *Hagar's Daughter*, a novel serialized in 1901–02 in the *Colored American Magazine*, of which Hopkins was one of the editors. *Hagar's Daughter* features not one, but two black detectives, one of them, and arguably the more important, a female, Venus

Johnson. As with 'Talma Gordon', miscegenation and passing play important roles. J(ohn) E(dward) Bruce's novel with the telling title *The Black Sleuth* was serialized in 1907–09 in *McGirt's Magazine*, but remained unfinished. It features an African-born detective, Sadipe Okukenu, and the relationship to Africa and the African past looms large.

Both Hopkins and Bruce were active in movements for the advancement of African Americans and used their literary skills to support the black struggle. The same is true of Rudolph Fisher's *The Conjure-Man Dies*, the crime fiction of Chester Himes and, later, the postmodern anti-detective novels of both Ishmael Reed – particularly *Mumbo Jumbo* (1972) and *The Last Days of Louisiana Red* (1974) – and Clarence Major – specifically *Reflex and Bone Structure* (1975). It still is true of the most recent African American author to successfully enter the lists of hard-boiled detective fiction: Walter Mosley.

Mosley's 'Easy' (from Ezekiel) Rawlins series combines strands of the classic hard-boiled detective novel in the language and character of Rawlins himself, and in the intrigues he gets involved in, and of the adaptation of this tradition in African American fiction, as Soitos has outlined it. Soitos isolates four 'tropes of black detection'. First, 'the black detective's identity is directly connected to community' and black detectives 'are aware, and make their readers aware, of their place within the fabric of their black society' (Soitos, 29). They also always 'delineate the color line as primary in any case or social relation' (31). Second, black detectives, like all African Americans, operate from a typical double-consciousness background. This involves role-playing, the adopting of masks and disguises, and the assumption of a trickster identity. Then, there is what Soitos calls 'blackground'; the interweaving into the text of references to a number of 'black vernaculars' such as 'music/dance, black language, and black cuisine' (37). Finally, Soitos also lists the use of hoodoo, as the expression of specifically black religious and sociophilosophical beliefs, or of a specifically black world view, as distinctive of African American detective fiction.

Hoodoo is absent from Mosley's fiction. Soitos's other tropes, though, are certainly prominently present. There are frequent references to jazz, including the mention of famous performers, such as Billie Holiday, passing through the black bars of Los Angeles. Southern dishes are featured on Rawlins's visits to friends and acquaintances, most of whom, like Rawlins himself, originate from East Texas. The black vernacular is also very much in evidence, especially in the speech of Raymond 'Mouse' Alexander, Easy's boyhood friend. However,

Mosley's Rawlins most conspicuously answers to Soitos's tropes one and two. Different from what Soitos claims with regard to black detective fiction, though, the Easy Rawlins novels are not third-person narratives. Easy tells his own story, in the typical hard-boiled idiom.

When we first meet him, in *Devil in a Blue Dress* (1990), Rawlins is a tough East Texas-born ex-GI, who after the Second World War has removed to California. The reasons for his move have to do with the labor market, and with the racial attitudes of the south. In this, the fictional Rawlins joins in a trend shared by many historical African Americans in the same period. However, Rawlins also has another motive for leaving his birthplace: through no fault of his own, he is implicated in a murder. His best friend 'Mouse' has shot and robbed his own stepfather, with Rawlins as an unwilling witness. Mouse is slight of build, but deadly. Rawlins, who has been involved with the woman Mouse wants to marry, and who fears he may now know one secret too many about Mouse, hops on the bus for California. This episode in Rawlins's life is regularly alluded to throughout the 'color' novels – *Devil in a Blue Dress, A Red Death* (1991), *White Butterfly* (1992), *Black Betty* (1994), and *A Little Yellow Dog* (1996) – making up the regular Rawlins-series, and is described at length in *Gone Fishin'* (1997). In each novel, Mouse makes an appearance, often as a deus ex machina saving Easy's life, committing the violence Easy himself is apparently incapable of, or which he is simply unwilling to perform. At the same time, Easy is never quite sure whether Mouse will not eventually turn on him.

'Color' not only features prominently in the titles of the Rawlins novels, it is also, though in a different sense, what the series is about. From its very opening sentence, *Devil in a Blue Dress* is literally all about the color line: 'I was surprised to see a white man walk into Joppy's bar.' The man in question is not just white of skin, he also wears a white suit and hat, has light-blond hair, and is called DeWitt Albright. He will become Rawlins's new employer. Rawlins used to be a mechanic at Champion aircraft, but has been fired by the white team boss, ostensibly for being lazy, but in reality because he dared to stand up for his rights. Albright will also almost become Rawlins's nemesis.

Albright wants Easy to find a beautiful white girl, Daphne Monet, who has a preference for 'dark meat' and is rumored to frequent black jazz bars. Here, as in most of the cases he reluctantly gets involved in, Easy's color allows him access where whites, including the police, dare not go, or would be ineffectual anyway: the black community of Watts, Los Angeles. In *A Red Death*, for instance, Rawlins is pressed by the FBI to infiltrate an alleged communist ring operating from a black church. In *White Butterfly* he is pressured into assisting the police with the investigation of the murder of a white girl. The trail leads to the black community, where similar murders have also been taking place. Hitherto, nobody very much cared about these murders, precisely because they happened among blacks. In *Devil in a Blue Dress*, Daphne's 'whiteness' is all-important – or, rather, the secret of her 'passing' for a white woman is all-important, since in reality she is the 'black' Ruby Hanks. As the fiancée of a rich white business tycoon with political ambitions, Daphne/Ruby and her ancestry have become pawns on the political chessboard.

At the end of *Devil in a Blue Dress*, Daphne/Ruby has disappeared from Easy's life, and DeWitt Albright, Joppy, and a host of other characters are dead, not least thanks to Mouse's interventions. When Easy accuses Mouse of committing murder unwarrantedly, Mouse teaches Easy a little lesson from the black point of view:

> 'You just like Ruby', Mouse said.
> 'What you say?'
> 'She wanna be white. All them years people be tellin' her how she light-skinned and beautiful but all the time she knows that she can't have what white people have. So she pretend and then she lose it all. She can love a white man but all he can love is the white girl he think she is.'
> 'What's that got to do with me?'
> 'That's just like you, Easy. You learn stuff and you be thinkin' like white men be thinkin'. You be thinkin' that what's right fo' them is right fo' you. She look like she white and you think like white. But brother you don't know that you both poor niggers. And a nigger ain't never gonna be happy 'less he accept what he is.'
> (*Devil*, 209)

The lesson Mouse here teaches Easy trickles down through the entire Rawlins series. In *Devil in a Blue Dress* Easy tells himself, and his readers, that he is no longer afraid of white men. In fact, he has killed plenty of fair-skinned, blond-haired, blue-eyed German boys in Europe. In order to prove himself, both to himself and to his white fellow-GI's, he even volunteered for the Battle of the Bulge. At the end of the novel Easy bests the police, and the DA's office, by selling them an acceptable version of what happened, exonerating himself and everyone he cares about. He even is able to hold on to part of the small fortune Daphne/Ruby had stolen from her fiancée, and which Mouse divides between himself, Easy, and the girl. With the money, Easy sets up as the landlord of a small block of apartments. At the same time, he resorts to typical double-consciousness behavior when he hides his new status from the world, and especially the white civic authorities, foremost among them the IRS, and poses as merely the caretaker and janitor of his own property. Similarly, whereas Easy is perfectly capable of using 'standard' American English, both as to vocabulary and grammar, he resorts to 'black' speech in his dealings with whites, and strikes the pose of a 'dumb negro' as part of his trickster disguise.

The Easy Rawlins series is historical in conception, giving us an extended view of Rawlins's life in 1948 (*Devil in a Blue Dress*), 1953 (*A Red Death*), 1956 (*White Butterfly*), 1961 (*Black Betty*), and 1962 (*A Little Yellow Dog*). We follow both his own development as a character, and his changing relationship to American society. This relationship gradually darkens as Rawlins, outsmarted and outmaneuvered by white businessmen, over the years loses not only his block of flats, but even the little house he owned in *Devil in a Blue Dress*. The marriage he enters into breaks up in *White Butterfly*, when his wife, with their little daughter, leaves him for a friend and former colleague. In *A Red Death*, he adopts an orphan boy, Jesus, and in *White Butterfly* a little girl, Feather. With them he moves into another small house he buys in a black middle class neighborhood in West Los Angeles. In all, Rawlins finds that, as Mouse predicted, he has to curtail considerably his ambitions with regard to 'liberty, and the pursuit of happiness' if he wants to keep a 'life' in a world ruled by racial prejudice.

A Little Yellow Dog is perhaps the most entertaining Easy Rawlins novel as far as its action goes. At the same time, it also sees Rawlins reduced to bare essentials, with few illusions left. He now works as 'supervising senior head custodian' in a junior high school, and tries to lead as inconspicuous a life as possible with his two adopted children. Fate comes knocking in the form of Mrs Idabell Turner, a teacher, who seduces Rawlins one morning when she asks him to take care of her little yellow dog for just one day. Predictably, things spin out of control, and once again Mouse's little lesson from *Devil in a Blue Dress* proves only too true. In all previous Easy Rawlins novels shooting people was the job of Mouse. Now, Rawlins himself shoots several people, one of them being Mouse himself. Easy also gets romantically involved with a murderess, and ends up acknowledging the fact. Most importantly, *A Little Yellow Dog* ends after Kennedy has been assassinated, an event that spells the loss of hope for Rawlins and for the nation. In *Black Betty*, when having a nightmare, he still 'tried to think of better things ... about our new young Irish president and Martin Luther King; about how the world was changing and a black man in America had the chance to be a man for the first time in hundreds of years' (*Black Betty*, 2). With hindsight, we know that Rawlins's high hopes for King too are to be dashed soon after the time in which *A Little Yellow Dog* is set. In interviews and articles Mosley himself has become increasingly sombre and militant about race in America.

Dale Furutani's Ken Tanaka

Unlike Mosley's Easy Rawlins series, many other novels featuring ethnic detectives tend to avoid violence. In order to make their point, they often also provide extensive backgrounds to their stories. Hence, in some of these novels the emphasis partly shifts from plot and character to social and historical explanation. This is particularly the case in newer ethnic detective fiction, like Dale Furutani's Ken Tanaka mysteries. Indeed, in *Death in Little Tokyo* (1996), and even more so in its successor, *The Toyotomi Blades* (1997), the author regularly presents disquisitions on Japanese, and in particular Japanese American history, with specific emphasis on moments or instances of ethnic discrimination.

The pedigree of Asian American crime writing is much less firmly established than that of its African American counterpart. As a matter of fact, Ken Tanaka may well be the first Japanese American private eye, and Furutani may well be the first Japanese American detective author. In fact, Furutani's hero is a rather unlikely private eye. Tanaka is a 42 year-old Hawaiian-born computer programmer. He has a failed marriage to a caucasian behind him; so does his present girlfriend Mariko, an aspiring Japanese American actress in her 30s, and an ex-alcoholic. Tanaka and Mariko blame white racism for their failure to get ahead in their respective careers. Mariko invariably is cast in minor 'Asian' roles; Tanaka himself has been laid off in a recent 'downsizing' operation.

Tanaka and Mariko are both members of a mystery club. When it is Tanaka's turn to stage a fake crime for the benefit of his fellow club members, he does this so realistically that he snares an actual client. From there on, the plot of *Death in Little Tokyo* starts echoing Hammett's *The Maltese Falcon*. To be fair, Tanaka has in the first chapter announced that the mystery he will provide will take its cue from Hammett's novel. So when a woman calling herself Rita Newly presents herself to him with the request that he take delivery of a package for her, he at first assumes that someone is turning the tables on him. However, when the Japanese man Tanaka collected the package from is found murdered, things turn serious. In the end, both the murderer and his victim turn out to be Japanese Americans. The root of their murderous conflict lies in the period the two men spent in the 'relocation' camps the United States government set up for its citizens of Japanese descent during the Second World War, and in the division between those Japanese Americans that took the loyalty oath imposed upon them by the United States authorities, and those that did not. Ultimately, then, it is white prejudice and paranoia that are to blame for the tragedy that occurred.

The fame Ken Tanaka gains from solving his first case earns him an invitation to appear on a Tokyo talk show. In Japan, he is called upon to help investigate the mysterious disappearance, from museums and private collections around the world, of some famous seventeenth-century samurai swords: the Toyotomi blades that feature in the title of the second Ken Tanaka mystery. In fact, Tanaka himself owns one of the six blades in question – bought, perhaps somewhat implausibly, at a Los Angeles garage sale. The sword was featured in a photograph of his that has appeared in the Japanese press, and all at once a new light is thrown upon the invitation to come to Japan. The Toyotomi blades put together form a map pinpointing an ancient treasure. Tanaka, aided by Mariko and his own computer skills, of course succeeds in locating the treasure. However, he has been beaten to it first by ancient robbers, and more recently by the Japanese traditionalists who have been after the swords and who had hoped to use the treasure for their own purposes. In the end, the treasure turns out to consist of bales of silk and brocade – priceless at the time they were stored, but now rotting and turning to dust. *The Toyotomi Blades* really is one long meditation on what it means to be a Japanese American in terms of ancestry and loyalties, and on the relationship of Japan to the Western world and modernity in general, and to the United States in particular.

At the end of *The Toyotomi Blades* Tanaka decides to look into the possibility of applying for a legitimate private investigator license. It is difficult to see, though, how much further Furutani can take his protagonist without toughening him up considerably. After all, he is probably not always going to have the good fortune, as in *The Toyotomi Blades*, of having the disinterested assistance of a Hawaiian Sumo-wrestler. Admittedly, there is some enjoyable tongue-in-cheek reflection on the conventions of hard-boiled fiction and on how Tanaka's own exploits relate to this. There are also the regular references to Japanese cinema, especially Akira Kurosawa and Toshiro Mifune, and to American movie classics. In all, though, *The Toyotomi Blades* calls for an awful lot of coincidence to construe a workable plot. Perhaps that is why Furutani with his latest novels, *Death at the Crossroads* (1998) and *Jade Palace Vendetta* (1999), has turned to writing 'Samurai mysteries', featuring roaming samurai warrior Matsuyama Kaze, and set in the early seventeenth-century Japan of the making of the Toyotomi blades. With this, Furutani joins the vogue for historical detective fiction, and more in particular meets the interest in feudal Japan that we also see in Chinese-Korean American Laura Joh Rowland's highly succesful *Shinjū* (1994) and *Bundori* (1996), which star a 'special investigator' of Edo (that is, Tokyo before the 1868 Meiji Restoration).

Twice marginalized: ethnicity and sexuality

A particularly interesting example of non-mainstream crime writing is the pairing of ethnicity and sexual 'otherness' that we find in the Henry Rios novels of Michael Nava, five times winner of the Lambda award for Best Gay Men's Mystery, and in the first Benjamin Justice mystery of John Morgan Wilson. Nava is a Mexican American lawyer and a gay rights activist who, with Robert Davidoff, is the author of *Created Equal: Why Gay Rights Matter to America*. Not surprisingly the Rios novels feature a Mexican American lawyer and focus on ethnicity and homosexuality. *The Hidden Law* (1992) refers to the title of a W.H. Auden poem rather cryptically describing the workings of fate. Nava applies this theme to the Chicano community. Specifically, he details how the lives of fathers determine those of their sons. In spite of whatever success they may achieve, minority fathers always remain aware that they continue to be second-class citizens in the Anglo world. Often, they take their hidden rage at that world out on their wives and children. They also tend to take it out on themselves in the form of self-destructive drugs or alcohol abuse. The sons revolt. Sexually, Nava seems to imply, they may do so by turning gay. Professionally, they try to turn themselves into what they think to be successful opposites of their fathers. Rios himself is a good example of this filial rebellion, because as a gay lawyer he champions all the 'permissive' causes his macho policeman father abhorred. His client Michael Ruiz finds himself in a similar position: he feels unloved by his successful Chicano parents, and is being over-protected by his Chicano grandmother. Partly as a result of the psycho-social pressure he experiences, Ruiz allows himself be to be put forward as the murderer of Gus Peña, a Chicano California state senator who perfectly answers to the type of minority father sketched.

Rios eventually finds out that the real murderer is Peña's son. The latter's mother and sister consented to the murder because of the domestic violence rampant in the Peña household, because of Peña's unrelenting alcoholism, and his forceful opposition to his son's relationship with an older Anglo woman. They are all speculating on Ruiz being acquitted for lack of evidence. As it turns out, Rios's intervention puts both Peña's son and Ruiz behind bars – they will have to face up to what they are. So will Rios himself. In the course of his investigation Rios has come to realize how 'the hidden law' rules his own life, and that of his community, and how his being gay relates to all this. In the end, Rios closes his law practice in order to take stock of his life and to finally do himself some good, as his psychologist had urgently counseled him to do.

The Hidden Law, like the Henry Rios novels in general, provides a panoramic picture of multi-ethnic Los Angeles. Curiously, Nava is exceedingly sparse with physical desciptions of Rios. Still, on the rare occasions when we do get a glimpse of Rios's appearance – often through the reactions of other characters – the emphasis invariably is on his mestizo, Mexican-Hispanic traits.

Next to the ethnic, there is the gay interest. In *The Burning Plain* (1997) Rios gets involved with a young actor in whom he sees Josh, his lover from the earlier novels in the series, reincarnated. The man is promptly found murdered. When a number of other gay young men about town are also killed, Rios himself becomes a prime suspect. Working to clear his name, Rios uncovers sexual depravity, corruption, blackmail, and murder rampant in the highest political offices, as well as in the movie studio boardrooms. A casual remark about a woman at a poetry reading comparing Los Angeles to the hell of Dante's *Inferno* reveals the full extent of Nava's ambitions. *The Burning Plain* is a rewriting, many times removed, of Dante's masterpiece. It was Dante who described the seventh circle of hell, the one to which homosexuals were assigned, as a 'burning plain'.

In *Simple Justice* (1996), which won an Edgar for best first novel, John Morgan Wilson likewise pictures gay Los Angeles as a contemporary hell. At the age of 17, Ben (Benjamin) Justice catches his father in the act of raping his 11-year old sister. He kills his father, a police officer with a history of violence especially toward his wife and son. The incident destroys the family. Years later, when Justice is a star reporter on the *L.A.Times*, and his lover Jacques lies dying from Aids, a story that Justice writes on the disease wins him a Pulitzer Prize. However, when it is rumored that the gay couple he wrote about is fictional and he does not reveal their identity, he has to return the prize and loses his job. Now, after having almost drunk himself into the grave, Justice lives alone in his former lover's garage apartment, cultivating his memories.

Justice is invited by his former editor at the *L.A. Times*, who is now employed by the rival newspaper the *L.A. Sun*, to work as a gofer for one of the *Sun*'s crime reporters, Alex(andra) Templeton, who is preparing a story about a murder outside a gay bar. A Chicano boy, Gonzalo Albundo, with blood on his hands, was caught bent over a dead white boy, Lusk. Gonzalo readily confesses to the killing. In the course of his duties, Ben meets Paul Masterman Jr, a conservative senator's son, in whom he becomes sexually interested. Paul is orchestrating his father's bid for re-election and arranges a TV spot aimed at the votes of the gay electorate on the site of the Lusk killing.

As the story unfolds, Wilson deftly weaves in the ethnic theme. Justice is white. Templeton is African American, and so is Jefferson Bellworthy, a gay ex-football star who now is a bouncer and barman for the club in front of which Lusk was killed. Lusk himself was Jewish, and so is Derek Brunheim, Lusk's longtime lover. Gonzalo Albundo is Hispanic. Jim Jai-Sik, alias Jim Lee, and briefly Ben's lover, is Korean American. Wilson is equally skilful with regard to the psychological dimension of his characters. Paul Masterman, who turns out to be the real killer, but also Lusk and Ben himself – just like Nava's characters – at least partially seem to have become gay because of serious relational problems with their fathers. These problems intersect with social pressures specifically linked to their respective ethnic backgrounds.

A lot of the action and motivation of *Simple Justice* is fueled by the fear of coming out. Gonzalo Albundo rather confesses to a murder he did not commit than to being gay. Paul Masterman rather commits murder than confess to a youthful homosexual one night stand. Ben himself, finally, preferred to return his Pulitzer Prize to 'coming out' with his own personal tragedy – the 'fictional' couple in his prize-winning story has, after all, been real enough: Ben himself and his lover Jacques. *Simple Justice* paints a heartbreaking picture of the gay community of Los Angeles, throbbing with sexual energy, but also with hurt and desperation. And always, in Nava's Henry Rios series as in Wilson's Benjamin Justice novels, the threat of Aids is palpably present, and the ravages the disease causes in the lives of the protagonists, and in the gay community at large, are movingly detailed.

The past revisited: Robert Skinner's *Skin Deep, Blood Red*

An original perspective on the ethnic issue, and one that takes us right back to the beginnings of both ethnic and hard-boiled crime writing in the United States, is provided by Robert Skinner's *Skin Deep, Blood Red* (1997). The novel definitely claims a place in the Hammett tradition. In fact, it initially reads like a straightforward calque of *The Maltese Falcon*. There is the smuggling into the United States of a valuable item – a suitcase full of uncut diamonds fresh from South Africa. We meet an enticing blonde with an Irish surname, or at least alias, Miss Flynn. The villain is a highly cultivated but at the same time unspeakably evil and more than slightly sinister Jewish businessman: Mr Ganns. The hero is an unflappable, attractive, but playing hard-to-get investigator: Wesley Farrell. Even the physical description of Farrell reads like a cross between the Sam Spade of *The Maltese Falcon* and the Ned Beaumont of *The Glass Key*. Also the period in which *Skin Deep, Blood Red* is set is close enough: the late 1930s. Obviously, there are also some twists to the plot that distinguish Skinner's novel from its predecessor. To begin with, the locale is not San Francisco, but New Orleans. Then, the murder that sparks off the story is not that of the investigator's partner in detection, as in *The Maltese Falcon*, but rather that of a corrupt police officer. Farrell is not a professional private eye, anyway, but rather a nightclub owner accidentally drawn into sleuthing. The novelty of *Skin Deep, Blood Red*, however, and at the same time its main interest, lies in its treatment of race, and particularly 'passing'.

Farrell turns out to be part Creole, and therefore black in the eyes of 1930s America, particularly so in the south. He has passed as white for most of his life, and wants to keep it that way in order to safeguard his position both in the underworld of New Orleans and in the city's regular society. Over the course of the novel Farrell's past is gradually revealed, along with his acceptance of his mixed heritage and his final assumption of a Creole identity. In the process, he is transformed from a typical hard-boiled 'lone ranger' into a man assuming family responsibilities. To begin with, there is the re-established relationship with his long-lost father, the white New Orleans police detective Frank Casey. Ironically, the blame for the separation of Wesley's parents rests with his mother's upper-crust Creole family. They deemed Casey, though white, socially inferior because of his Irish immigrant origins. The social prejudice practised by Creole society proves to be just as devastating for the individuals caught up in it as the racial discrimination prevalent among whites. Skinner explicitly holds out an alternate model when he depicts how Casey and his Creole wife live the early years of their marriage in Cuban Havana, free of racial prejuduce. However, Farrell also recognizes his love for the black singer he has been having an affair with for years. Finally, he assumes the guardianship of a young black cousin whose childhood experiences strongly resemble Farrell's own. Farrell's assumption of his Creole identity, with all the risks this implies, obviously amounts to a plea for hybridity and tolerance on the part of his creator. The second novel in the series, *Cat-Eyed Trouble* (1998), conveys a similar message.

If all this smacks of a particularly contemporary and modish political correctness, so be it. The fact remains that Skinner has succeeded in putting a novel spin on some of the oldest clichés in the genre, thereby proving their resilience and their usefulness in ever new circumstances. Specifically, by rewriting *The Maltese Falcon* for the 1990s, he has not only retuned one of the earliest classics in the hard-boiled tradition, but also has refashioned a story that originally conveyed white America's fear of 'undesirables' into an advertisement for ethnic and cultural tolerance.

12
Black Female Crime Writing

African American women writers have until fairly recently virtually ignored crime fiction. In 1988, Maureen Reddy could still declare that 'despite a great deal of searching, I have yet to find a crime novel written by a woman of color' (Reddy 1988, 16). Although later researchers have shown her to be mistaken (see Soitos 1996), it is not until the 1990s that African American women have had an impact on the crime writing scene. This is not much of a surprise. Since female black police officers were until recently pretty scarce, police procedurals featuring black women were not the obvious thing to do. The same is true of the private eye novel. Although there must now be African American female PI's in major American cities, a novel featuring one would until recenty have been regarded as too implausible. Apart from these considerations, the conservative and male-oriented nature of the traditional private eye novel and police procedural cannot have endeared itself to the inevitably disempowered female African American writer, even if she happened to find herself attracted to the format. It is surely not accidental that most black women crime writers have created amateur detectives. One result of this strategy is that, as a group, black women writers – with lesbian writers, who have an equally compelling reason to avoid institutional settings – come closest to integrating crime writing with mainstream realistic fiction. Not all of them present amateurs, however. Dolores Komo's *Clio Brown: Private Investigator* (1988) – according to Sally Munt 'the first crime novel written by a Black woman featuring a female detective' (Munt, 111) – follows the traditional private eye formula. Eleanor Taylor Bland's *Dead Time* (1992), the first of a rather successful series, is a police procedural featuring Marti MacAlister, an African American female police officer in the small town of Lincoln Prairie, 60 miles north of Chicago (the main setting of the 1995 *Done Wrong*). Perhaps the most interesting professional has been created by Valerie Wilson Wesley. Her self-employed Tamara Hayle is a plausible mix of private eye and amateur elements and is, perhaps because of that, the first female black private eye whose exploits are published by a mainstream press.

All in all, the amateur formula has so far produced the best writing, not in the least because it allows its practitioners a greater range than fiction that features a professional investigator or detective. I will therefore concentrate primarily on the amateur detectives, more particularly on the work of Barbara Neely and Terris McMahan Grimes, and on one of Nikki Baker's novels, *Long Goodbyes* (1993). I will close the chapter with a discussion of the most prominent female black PI, Wesley's Tamara Hayle. This does not exhaust this first generation of African American female crime writers but reasons of space make it impossible to deal with Chassie West, Yolanda Joe, Penny Mickleburg, and others who also debuted in the 1990s.

South and north: Barbara Neely's Blanche

Barbara Neely's *Blanche on the Lam* (1992) is in one sense one of the most successful first crime novels ever written, almost achieving a grand slam on the awards scene: Agatha Award for Best First Mystery Novel, Macavity and Anthony Awards for Best First Novel. Neely's novel does indeed stand out, if only because of its protagonist, the ironically named black domestic worker Blanche White.

Forty years old, with big bones and hips, and 'breasts and forearms to match', Blanche is a wonderfully independent spirit and sharp social observer whose first brush with crime is the indirect result of her being sentenced to 30 days in jail on a bad-check charge in her home town of Farleigh, North Carolina. Outraged because her checks have only bounced because four of her employers have (temporarily) left town without paying her and also, at a deeper level, because she works six days a week and is still so low on funds that this can happen to her, she deceives the matron who is supposed to keep an eye on her and becomes, at least technically, a fugitive from the law. In an at first sight implausible manoeuver, Neely then has her run into a white woman who is waiting for the help that an agency has promised to send her, allowing Blanche to assume the help's identity and to follow the woman and her family to their country home, away from Farleigh. This is all the more implausible since the woman has employed the help she is waiting for before and surely must see that Blanche is new. But she does not and we are made to see why: blacks are invisible and black domestics are doubly invisible. Blanche's unproblematic acceptance introduces a racial theme that competes with the unfolding mystery for the reader's attention.

Blanche's name is doubly ironic. Not only because her first name also means 'white', but also because even among African Americans her blackness stands out. To defend herself against the taunts of other kids – 'Ink Spot', 'Tar Baby' – she has as a child transformed herself into 'Night Girl', who could roam around the neighborhood unseen after nightfall. It is this early, socially induced self-empowerment that has made her what she is: 'A Night Girl kind of woman' (*Blanche*, 60) who when necessary can self-confidently take charge of her own life. This self-confidence has enabled her to go against the wishes of her formidable mother Miz Cora in leaving Farleigh for the larger world, to openly refuse to have children – a sure sign of female independence – but also to return to Farleigh to take care of her deceased sister's two kids, to reject Christianity (for which Neely compensates her with a sort of extrasensory sensitivity), to take genuine pride in her cleaning and cooking, to counter the impudence of 'teenage white boys working up to being full-fledged rednecks' (37), and so on. Her self-confidence is a great source of strength in her dealings with whites in general – a strength she slyly reinforces by regularly spitting at the local Civil War monument – and with white employers in particular:

> Blanche had never suffered from what she called Darkies' Disease ... What she didn't understand was how you convinced yourself that you were actually loved by people who paid you the lowest possible wages; who never offered you the use of one of their cars, their cottage by the lake, or even their swimming pool; who gave you handkerchiefs and sachets for holiday gifts and gave their children stocks and bonds. It seemed to her that this was the real danger in looking at customers through love-tinted glasses. (84)

Needless to say, Blanche has no illusions about her newfound employers, and quite rightly so, as it turns out. She has stumbled into a situation involving fraud and murder, and will eventually have to fight for her life, a feat that substantially adds to her self-confidence – 'She would always be a woman who'd fought for her life and won' (215) – so that, at the end of the novel, she negotiates with the family's lawyer a revision of her trial and sentence and a trust fund for the education of her sister's children. She is all the better at this sort of thing because of her thorough understanding of race relations in the south, even to the point that she can play around with its stereotypes, for instance the childlike but oh so loyal black domestic: '"Oh, Lord!" Blanche lifted her apron to her face as she'd seen Butterfly McQueen do in *Gone With the Wind* ... It was the kind of put-on that gave her particular pleasure.' (153)

What is perhaps most remarkable about *Blanche on the Lam* is that Blanche's world is so overwhelmingly female. This is not to say that males are unwanted – it is a decidedly heterosexual world – but that in a number of ways they are decentered. True intimacy and true emotions are reserved for other women and for children. Blanche and her friend Ardell, for instance, have over the years 'supported and encouraged each other with an intensity and constancy that had often made their men jealous and suspicious' (19). Men come and go, but women offer stability and continuity. Throughout the novel Blanche is in touch with both Ardell and Miz Cora – who in Blanche's forced absence takes care of the children – and through them with the whole of the African American female community which, through its domestic worker members, turns out to be a virtually inexhaustible source of information on Farleigh's upper middle-class white families (who no doubt have no idea that Farleigh's black working-class women know more about their marital problems and other well-guarded secrets than their best friends).

This extended network, which is as reliable a back-up force as one could wish, is a major source of comfort. More important, however, is Blanche's inner strength, which manifests itself in her comfortable relationship with her body (including her sexuality), her easy way with emotions – unlike Miz Cora, who belongs to an older, grimmer generation, she knows the value of a good cry – and her ironic directness: '[on the radio] a woman with a husky voice tried to sell seaside condos by implying they came with a year's supply of pussy' (148). (Blanche's voice is not the least of the novel's pleasant surprises.) When at the end of the novel she leaves Farleigh for Boston, that inner strength will have to do double duty in what she considers 'yet another enemy territory' (215).

Interestingly enough, it is not the white northeast that causes her trouble in the sequel, *Blanche Among the Talented Tenth* (1994), but an elitist all-black resort on the Maine coast called Amber Cove. In this second novel, Neely makes Blanche even more intensely aware of her identity as an African American woman: 'She could picture herself a hundred shades lighter with her facial features sharpened up; but she couldn't make the leap to wanting to step out of the talk, walk, music, food and feeling of being black that the white world often imitated but never really understood' (20). To emphasize the extent to which Blanche has rejected mainstream culture, with its suggestion of color-blindness, Neely now has her adopt a 'haphazard', but decidedly non-Western, 'spirituality', which includes the 'occasional bone casting by a Yoruba priestess' (60) and regular prayers to her ancestors. Africa, too, has become a theme, and its life-giving abundance as the Mother of the human race is repeatedly contrasted with America's petty lack of vitality: 'She knew she was attractive to the kind of black men whose African memory was strong enough for them to associate a big butt black woman with abundance and a smooth comfortable ride, men who liked women who ate hearty and laughed out loud.' (56)

Like Neely's earlier novel, *Blanche Among the Talented Tenth* is deeply concerned with racial themes, but in a way that comes as a complete surprise: the focus is on color prejudice *within* the black community, a prejudice that victimizes its blacker members – '"black folks puttin' each other down for being too black"' – even if the novel also presents a case of a father virtually disowning his son because he is not black enough. Although Neely suggests at one point that this black prejudice against blackness derives from white prejudice against African Americans in general, she holds blacks fully responsible for the discriminatory attitudes that are rampant inside and outside Amber Cove. Wherever Blanche turns, she runs into prejudice and its effects. While in the 1960s women of her own deep blackness were 'status symbols', black men now ignore them in favor of 'lighter women'. Parents actively try to prevent their children from marrying darker mates. We hear that some black fraternities and sororities are 'really sick around color' and in the black private school that Blanche's niece and nephew now attend color is a serious concern. The residents of Amber Cove pride themselves on their light skin (not to mention their social standing). Amid all this unpleasant social climbing, Blanche presents authentic blackness. To her, in Amber Cove 'the things, beside color, that made a person black were either missing or mere ghosts of their former selves' (58). Black authenticity is not only bound up with a certain lifestyle, but also with caring and responsibility. To Blanche 'boys in dreds with their pants hanging off their butts' who rap about what bitches black women are do not constitute a contribution to African American culture. Neither does the grand old lady of the novel, one of the earliest black feminists, who in the end turns out to have abused Blanche's friendship. Perhaps her marriage with a white college professor should have warned us: an African American woman who has voluntarily given up at least part of her identity is not to be trusted.

Blanche Among the Talented Tenth – W.E.B. Dubois's term for the black elite – seeks to establish authenticity in the communal ethos of lower middle-class African American women, even if Blanche gives that ethos her own Yoruban twist. Blanche's one help and stay is still her friend Ardell in faraway Farleigh, whom she consults several times a week. Like the mystery that it presents the novel's tone is low-key rather than radical and disturbing, and so appeals to its readers' capacity for tolerance rather then their potential as revolutionaries.

Neely's most recent novel, *Blanche Cleans Up* (1998), in which Blanche lives with her two adopted children in Boston's Roxbury, is a good deal less low-key than the earlier books. Neely's new and more transgressive stance expresses itself in a variety of ways. The cast of characters now includes the socially marginal – we have, for instance, a self-assured black lesbian and an equally self-confident black 'sex worker' (which is how she introduces herself to Blanche); as a character, Blanche is more directly sexualized than she was in the earlier books (describing herself at one point as 'a masturbation champion'); we have vigilante justice, with a group of reformed and socially responsible ex-cons almost professionally eliminating a killer; and we see the successful white politician who is morally speaking the absolute low of the novel, engage in all sorts of deviant sexuality in one single session (dressed up in a pinafore and knee socks, he gets a spanking with a hairbrush, is penetrated anally by a German shepherd, and is finally transported to the heights of pleasure by three little girls). Naturally, this radicalization also expresses itself in the novel's (and Blanche's) view of race and race relations.

While *Blanche Among the Talented Tenth* was severely critical of certain sectors and tendencies within the African American community, *Blanche Cleans Up* consistently sides with blacks, with the one exception of the minister who has sold himself to the white establishment. (It is surely not accidental that the man is a minister. Even more than in *Tenth* Neely has Blanche reject Christianity and replace it with African beliefs and rituals.) The 'Ex-Cons for Community Safety' are rather unexpectedly 'polite, quiet, formal' (*Cleans*, 223); the violence and/or irresponsibility of the Black youths in the novel turns out to have been caused by lead poisoning (for which the authorities are ultimately responsible) or is the result of a self-fulfilling prophecy on society's part: 'Pooky was trying to be exactly who America told him he was: everybody's worst nightmare' (145); the CIA is indirectly accused of being involved in shipping drugs into African American communities ('like black folks hadn't known that for years' [41), even the black hatred of gays that Blanche encounters in the novel is traced back to slavery. That the gulf between black and white has widened is, apart from the way the novel's white characters are portrayed, also clear from a number of rather casual asides. For Blanche, for instance, black men who are sexually interested in white women have the 'pink pussy jones' and she applauds the new habit of African American parents to make up their own names for their children instead of using 'European' names.

In *Blanche Cleans Up* Neely's protagonist is far more consciously political than she was in the earlier novels where her independence and political awareness seemed to be an almost natural product of an independent, compassionate, and proud character. In this third novel Blanche is burdened with what looks like a new-found political correctness on the part of her creator. We have the socially marginal, an interest in the creativeness of the working class (at one point Blanche reads poems and stories by hospital laundry workers), environmentalism, community self-help, and so on. Roxbury is not doing Blanche much good: she is turning into an author's mouthpiece. Fortunately, the end of the novel holds out an interesting promise. We hear that a fire in police headquarters in Farleigh has destroyed all records. Blanche is free to leave Boston, where she has never felt welcome, and to return to North Carolina. Her return there may well allow her to find her old self.

Middle class detection in Sacramento

In 1997 Terris McMahan Grimes' *Somebody Else's Child* (1996) almost equalled the achievement of Neely's *Blanche on the Lam*, winning Anthony Awards for Best First Novel and for Best Paperback Original and being nominated for the Agatha Award for the Best First Mystery Novel. Grimes also collared the Chester Himes Award. As dense in its description of the African American community as Neely's work, the novel combines a strongly conveyed social setting with a convincing crime story. An interesting difference with Neely's work, and one which allies Grimes's novel with the PI tradition, is that Grimes's protagonist tells her own story as a first-person narrator.

The protagonist of *Somebody Else's Child* is Theresa N. Galloway, 38 years-old and size 16, wife of a rather irascible husband and mother of two children, who at ages 16 and 11 constitute something of a natural force in the Galloway home. She is a graduate of Sacramento State and is employed as a personnel officer by a state agency in Sacramento, where she grew up and now lives with her family in what is clearly an affluent middle-class neighborhood.

Appropriately, the novel opens with what surely is the major force behind Theresa's social success, her mother, fairly recently widowed and in her early 70s: 'Mother has always been rather excitable. What can I say, she's my mother and I love her. But the truth of the matter is, she gets into other people's business and she gets carried away in the process.' (9) As will appear in the course of the novel, Theresa, without admitting so much to herself, is very much like her mother – in fact, without her getting rather single-mindedly involved in other people's affairs there would be no mystery. Although there are some caricatural elements in Grimes's presentation of Theresa's mother: 'She simply starts talking when someone answers [her phone call] and stops talking when they hang up' (9), she is on the whole a formidable old lady whose behavior is dictated by a religiously inspired compassion and a strong sense of dignity. As Theresa says of her mother and the latter's neighbor – 'Sister Turner' to her mother – 'They were two genteel colored ladies from the South; graciousness was a way of life for them, no matter how mean their circumstances.' (17) Underneath this gentility we find great determination. Having come to Sacramento from Shreveport, Lousiana, in the early 1940s to work in the war industry, Mother has after the war held a long-term job with Campbell's Soup that, together with her husband's employment as a city garbage man, has propelled the family into the black middle class. The result is not only a college education for her daughter, but also a different attitude toward race on the part of her children. Whereas Mother lives in a black neighborhood and only associates with black people, most of them old friends, her son, who is with the army and is stationed in Germany, is married to a white woman, and Theresa would seem to be largely oblivious of race and racial issues. Alone in the dark with a white man she has known since high school, she asks the Lord to 'give [her] the strength to cripple his sorry behind' in case he starts acting 'funny' (175). The fact that his whiteness might complicate matters simply does not enter her mind. Not surprisingly, we get to know that she more than once has been accused of thinking she was white and of 'sounding white'. And it is surely not accidental that the one African American woman who is very much aware of race – Theresa's assistant – is presented as an almost professional trouble-maker whose accusations, no matter what the issue happens to be, cannot possibly carry much weight. Whereas in Neely's novels race is always a central issue, *Somebody Else's Child* steers us away from race.

As a matter of fact, even if racism finally enters the novel through the person of the killer, the real issue is class. In the course of her investigation, Theresa comes across a fair number of people that her socially aspiring background has not prepared her for: addicts, physically abusive husbands, teenage bystanders who cheer on vicious fights. Perhaps the most unsettling scene involves a woman – 'Her pants were so tight, I could see all her stuff, her lips, everything' (85) – who physically forces herself upon Theresa in order to kiss her for what a moment later turns out to be a bet:

> She slapped five with one of the men and said, 'Gimme my money, nigger.'
> 'Yeah, but did you stick it all the way in?' he asked.
> 'To her tonsils, mothafucka. I could have fucked the 'ho if I wanted to.'
>
> (*Child*, 88)

Wisely, Theresa decides that the streets are 'just too mean' for her.

Somebody Else's Child effectively contrasts the 'street' – black, lower class, and as often as not criminally inclined Sacramento – with the middle-class respectability of Mother and Theresa, symbolized by Mother's 'large, well-tended garden' and by Theresa's lavish bathroom with its sunken, jetted tub, the one room she considers her own. There is one point at which Theresa almost loses control and just misses shooting a man who a moment before has seriously battered her and would seem to be intent on finishing the job. Significantly, however, she can later only recollect the urge to shoot with guilt and shame. Although both subscribe to middle-class values, this creates an interesting distinction between mother and daughter. Just prior to the scene in question Mother has to Theresa's utter astonishment produced a gun and handed it over to her daughter, to 'protect' herself with (not the gun that Theresa almost fires, by the way). Theresa's middle-class sense or order and normality – 'In my way of thinking, there's an explanation, a reason, for everything' (188) – has never been seriously challenged, not even after she has graduated from college. As she tells us in *Blood Will Tell* (1997), 'I'd lived a rather charmed life for a black person in state service; promotions had come relatively on time, I had a decent boss, I liked my job, I'd never been in the position of having to fight for my survival.' (145) Mother's equilibrium, however, has been won the hard way and as a result she is prepared to defend what defines the meaning of her life. Consequently, when that meaning is threatened and her sense of morality offended she is not above considering an Old Testament retribution in the form of putting out a contract on an alleged killer. As a matter of fact, in *Blood Will Tell* she is not above shooting and wounding a killer herself.

It is the women who guard the staunch middle-class morality that is the novel's norm and who are, consequently, the hardest on those who violate it. Theresa's mother, solidly supported by her old friends, provides a stable anchor, and is not averse to giving her daughter a piece of her mind when strongly voiced advice seems in order: '"You tell that child, the easiest thing in the world is to get a boy to lay down with you, and the hardest thing in the world is to get a man to stand beside you"' (*Child*, 149). Within her own family, Theresa personifies morality. While '[t]he street runs close to the surface in [her husband] in the best of times' (213) and she is by no means sure of his unswerving devotion to her, for her infidelity is 'out of the question'. In *Blood* , where racism occasionally comes to the surface, we get a fine example of her moral optimism when her son has been suspended from school for attacking a classmate who has called him 'nigger'. While her husband wants to encourage the boy to defend himself physically against verbal abuse, Theresa is the voice of middle-class reason and restraint: '"Every time Shawn reacts as he did, there's a shift in power. He ends up having his chain jerked left and right, being manipulated. That's what I expect you to say to Shawn."' (139) Even the mother of her streetwise husband belongs to this solid front of black respectability. When he spends the night at his parental home because of one of his fights with Theresa, he finds himself painting his mother's garage in the morning.

This neatly captures the matriarchal undercurrent in Grimes's portrayal of the African American middle class. This is not a world in which men slap women around in between pool games and snorts of coke. If anything, Grimes's middle-class women are protective regarding their men. *Blood* makes this point very subtly. Theresa refuses to believe that her mother has for some time been aware of the fact that the man who presents herself as her husband's natural son is an impostor, and that she has simply played along, until Mother reveals what up till then has been a perfectly guarded secret: the letters that the impostor claims to have been written by her husband cannot possibly have been written by him because he was illiterate, only able to write his own name. Even after his death, Mother is reluctant to reveal what, with her help, he has always been able to hide from his children, and reminds Theresa that he '"was smart enough to see to it that each one of you got an education"' (260). As in Nancy Pickard's *I.O.U.*, involvement in crime here leads to revelations that have personal ramifications.

The fearless sense of moral and social responsibility that we see in Grimes's middle-class women also informs the males of Mother's generation. In *Blood Will Tell*, after Mother's house has badly suffered from the proceedings, her new friend Brother Cummings calls in 'the brothers from the lodge.... By nightfall they had all the damage ... cleaned up, patched up, and painted' (257–8). With Theresa's husband, however, we are on different, perhaps more contemporary ground. While she herself is not so sure what were to happen if his fidelity would be put to the test, we have ample evidence that his sense of responsility in general is not overdeveloped. Although Theresa typically blames herself for asking too much of him during her adventures with Mother, not in the least because he takes the lead in doing so – it's not easy to determine Grimes's position here – it is obvious to the reader that she is the one who holds two jobs: her job at the agency and the job of running a household. The mercifully often absent husband has a spoilt-brat quality that makes him far less attractive than the ever, well-almost ever, sanguine Theresa. Perhaps the ultimate victory for stability and the family, not to mention private enterprise, is that at the end of *Blood* Mother buys a twenty-five percent stake in her son-in-law's struggling business.

Like Barbara Neely's novels, *Somebody Else's Child* and *Blood Will Tell* manage to create a very believable social environment in which family and the idea of an African American female community play major roles. As a matter of fact, in *Blood* Mother is running for president of the 'Negro Women's Community Guild'. Men, although indispensable and, not to forget, also to be appreciated for their own sake, invariably hover on the margins. It is surely not accidental that Grimes has dedicated her first novel to her mother – her 'champion and inspiration' – and her mother-in-law. Since the themes of family and community are worked out so convincingly and are fully integrated with the mystery component of these novels – as is the case with family and mystery in Baker's *Long Goodbyes*, which I will turn to in a moment – the social environment reinforces rather than distracts from the mystery, offering the sort of stable, familiar background against which crime seems all the more disruptive. Family and community are important forces in the work of virtually all black female crime writers. The life of Eleanor

Taylor Bland's Marti MacAlister, too, is absolutely centered around her two teenage children, memories of her dead husband – whose murder she solves in *Done Wrong* (1995) – and the example of her much admired mother ('Momma's strong'; *Done Wrong*, 152). Given the strength of family and community ties in African American crime writing, it is not surprising that the traditional private eye format, with its lone dispenser of a more or less private justice, has found few followers among black female writers. As we will see, even those who employ it, like Valerie Wilson Wesley, only use certain features of the genre and as often as not with untraditional ends in mind.

Reunion in Blue River

As in Grimes's novels, or in Bland's Lincoln Prairie, race is not really an issue in Nikki Baker's *The Long Goodbyes* (1993), the third novel in a series that started with *In the Game* (1991; see Munt 1994 for a discussion). Once again, however, family is a central element. Baker's protagonist Virginia (Ginny) Kelly is a security analyst in a Chicago investment firm who ten years after her graduation returns home to the small midwestern town of Blue River for a high school reunion. What really draws her back to Blue River, however, is the momentous five minutes during the graduation party when her glamorous, blonde-haired classmate Rosalee tried to seduce her – 'a loser with Coke-bottle glasses and a shy kind of awkwardness' (*Goodbyes*, 57–8) – and for the first time made her 'feel proud', even if after the first kisses she got scared and made Rosalee stop. Having been asked to attend by Rosalee, whom she has not seen since leaving Blue River, her hidden agenda is to repeat those five minutes or, better, finish what was begun ten years ago. She does, but finds no satisfaction in the deed: 'Rosalee rocked back and forth against my face ... it was a bitch that she could look past the grand significance of this fantasy event for me in search of nothing more intimate than the proper rhythm, the most effective speed.' (7-8)

As this brief introduction shows, *Long Goodbyes* is much more than a mystery novel; it is as much about coming to terms with a personal history as it is about crime. As a matter of fact, apart from the description of a murder with which the novel opens and whose only function surely is to establish the novel as a murder mystery, there is nothing mysterious until we are halfway through. There is no real sleuth either, because as so often in novels with a female protagonist, and certainly in these novels featuring a black female protagonist, the personal element is completely interwoven with the mystery. Ginny acts as a detective first of all because she cannot let go – still longing for 'the sexual act I thought would define me' (160) – and wants to find out certain things about Rosalee. She does, in fact, not even know that a murder has taken place until the murderer tells her so in the wholly mistaken belief that she is on to him. This would seem to be a recurrent pattern in these novels. In *Blanche on the Lam,* for instance, Blanche suspects the wrong person until the real killer gives up all subterfuge and the same goes for Theresa Galloway in *Somebody Else's Child.* These protagonists get accidentally involved in crime and their involvement never goes beyond the accidental: the mere fact that they encounter crime quite rightly does not turn them into professional detectives. (The fact that such accidental involvements keep recurring is of course less easily explained.) Even the professionals among female black detectives more or less accidentally solve their cases – witness Valerie Wilson Wesley's Tamara Hayle novels. If this is not poor plotting (which should not be ruled out), it must point to an attitude on the part of these protagonists that is basically different from that of the classic sleuth. These women poke around, in the words of Sandra West Prowell's Phoebe Siegel, because detecting is not a profession but a situationally determined and strictly temporary activity. They lead full lives in which there is no room for the single-minded pursuit of truth that characterizes the traditional highbrow amateur.

But to get back to *Long Goodbyes,* with its Chandleresque title. The novel portrays not only a failed trip down memory lane from which Ginny returns with an emotional hangover and a bad conscience, it also presents a convincingly detailed confrontation of a young black lesbian woman with her not unloving, but deeply disappointed parents who still keep hoping that her lesbianism is only a 'phase'. (It is an enigma why Baker never won an award with this novel, which, like her other work, is stylistically so much better than the vast majority of crime novels.) Because of her lesbianism or, rather, because of the resistance it generates, Ginny is an outsider – a rarity in crime writing by African American women. She may occasionally feel herself 'succumbing to [her] middle-class surburban programming', but black middle-class values, which for years made her mother try to straighten her daughter's hair, do not hold much charm for her. We even get an unexpectedly nasty swipe at Martin Luther King, the man who once personified the aspirations of the African American middle class: 'all we had was a bourgeois savior who liked his women white and wore silk pajamas like Hugh Hefner' (175). Realizing towards the end of the novel that Rosalee's hold on her imagination originates in the fact that she is 'another connection with that kinder, gentler time' when their graduation pictures were taken, before disenchantment set in, she is finally able to let go because disenchantment was inevitable. She could never belong in a social environment that rejects her sexual orientation. In *Long Goodbyes* Baker perfectly balances the personal and the public – crime being always a public matter. It testifies to her abilities as a writer that ultimately the personal is more interesting.

Black female PI in Newark

While the female black amateur detective is gaining ground, the black female PI is still rare and it is clearly too early to talk of recurring patterns. If we might go by the work of Valerie Wilson Wesley, who is surely the most prominent female black private eye novelist, the female black PI will feel most comfortable somewhere in between the solitary outsider position of the traditional private eye and the social network that is so important in Neely's and Grimes's novels.

The traditional private eye role is established in a number of ways. Wesley's private investigator, Tamara Hayle, who makes her first appearance in *When Death Comes Stealing* (1994), is a divorced woman in her mid-30s who is not involved in a permanent relationship, whose parents are deceased, and whose only brother committed suicide when she was aged 20. She works out of a 'tacky' office in a 'sad-sack' building in an urban environment – Newark, New Jersey – and is permanently low on funds so that she drives the mandatory beat-up vintage car (a diesel Jetta, in her case). Like so many other private eyes she is an ex-police officer, having spent a number of years on the Newark force. Not unexpectedly, her reasons for leaving the force have to do with race. As she tells us: 'I hadn't heard a white person say ["nigger"] since I'd left the [Police] Department and heard it every day' [sic] (*When Death*, 87). True to PI form, she is contemptuous of the rabbitty law-abiding bourgeoisie, especially of 'Goody Two-Shoes sisters – the kind who make their own pie crusts and never give their lovers head.' (43) Unlike so many other private eyes she is outspoken about her reasons for setting up her own investigative outfit: 'I have always been drawn to danger – that part of me that wanted to become a cop, that likes to drive fast, that plays it on the edge' (100). In line with this, she as often as not feels attracted to men she does not trust (and who, as it turns out later, should indeed not have been trusted).

But this is only one side of the coin. The other side establishes Tamara firmly within a social network and provides her with the sort of personal history that never comes with the traditional private eye. Tamara may stand alone, but she is also a parent, responsible for a teenage son and, like other single mothers, struggling to cope with the demands a child makes on a single parent's time and energy. Born and bred in Newark's Central Ward, she is 'a Newark girl at heart, always will be' (even if the older, pre-riot Newark comes more alive in the novels than the contemporary city). The absence of immediate family (excepting her son, of course) is compensated for by her friendship with her life-long friend Annie and by her cordial relationship with the beautician Wyvetta, whose salon occasionally plays a role that one does not expect in a private eye novel: in *No Hiding Place* (1997) Tamara treats herself to a visit to Wyvetta's salon and picks up invaluable information from the other patrons. And in the background there is always that female African American community and the support (plus its token, food) that it has to offer: 'Black women and food, sisterly comfort when you need it – brothers may fail you, money may fly, but there's always good food and the grace to offer it.' (*When Death*, 241) In *No Hiding Place* a family's kitchen counters are 'already piled high with food dropped off by caring neighbors and friends' (*Place*, 212) within hours after a daughter has been killed.

Moreover, while the traditional white PI's lack of embeddedness in the absence of personal and social histories allows an exclusive focus on a case that is often as detached from history as the investigator himself, Tamara's blackness effectively precludes such a perspective. Crime always has a socio-historical dimension. This is not to say that the crimes that Wesley presents are never motivated by personal greed or jealousy, but somewhere along the line race will have played its part. The murderous events in *When Death* have their origin in the fact that long ago Tamara's ex-husband has falsely accused a child of having accidentally killed the baby that he himself had let slip and fall to the floor. Defending himself against her accusations, he points to the historical situation: '"They would have tried me for manslaughter, Tammy. I would have spent ten good years of my life in jail. They didn't care nothing about no justice for a black man, but a little girl? They'd forgive her, coddle her, feel sorry for her."' (287) Tamara still despises him for his general weakness and self-centeredness, but cannot deny that he has a point. Likewise, while Wesley's portrait of young inner-city blacks is not exactly flattering – her own values make a brief appearance when she has Tamara tell her son '"Don't say ain't"'

– she also makes it abundantly clear that they are fighting an uphill social battle that as often as not is made more difficult by police obstruction. Young black males are the prime victims of the racism that has driven Tamara herself from the force. For Tamara, then, the classic stance of uninvolved objectivity is not only impossible but would be manifestly false. One noteworthy result of this is that we do not get the standard wisecracks: since she does not need to establish the necessary distance between herself and the outside world, Tamara can do without the verbal armament. As I have noted above, Tamara is in some ways modeled after the traditional private eye. Her undeniable hesitations with regard to more than superficial emotional relations, however, are not so much the product of a professional code as the result of childhood trauma, of having been caught between a 'happy drunk' of a father and an unpredictable, violently aggressive mother. In particular her relationship with her mother, in which 'love and yearning for her approval [were] coupled with the disgust and anger at her cruelty' (*No Hiding Place*, 126), has clearly resulted in a fear of emotional involvement that resembles the supposedly self-willed uninvolvement of the classic PI. (Interestingly, Wesley's first novel, like Grimes's, is dedicated to her mother, so that we are tempted to read a certain adjustment to the PI format in the way Wesley portrays her protagonist's relationship to *her* mother.)

If Tamara Hayle is at all representative, the female Black PI would seem to position herself halfway between classic, godlike uninvolvement on the one hand and emotional empathy and social support on the other. Her toughness is the PI's toughness – at the end of *When Death Comes Stealing* she kills the murderer with one superb shot in order to save her son – but her vulnerability, her persistent sense of guilt, her emotionality and her strong sense of solidarity with especially the female African American community make her a very contemporary, very female PI.

13
The Persistence of Gender: the Private Investigators of S.J. Rozan

Female protagonists have become common in all forms of crime writing and female crime writers now routinely work with female protagonists. This does not mean that women writers have completely given up on male investigators, witness the work of Martha Grimes and Elizabeth George. However, Grimes and George work in a subgenre in which the female-created male investigator has a long and impressive tradition, and on which they consciously draw. One can see why they might want to continue a formula that has served so well Agatha Christie, Dorothy Sayers, Margery Allingham, Ngaio Marsh, P.D. James, and other prominent predecessors. Outside the specific subgenre of the English mystery, the female-created male investigator has a hard time surviving. A number of them, like Chris Wiltz's Neal Rafferty, who debuted in 1981, are still around, but there are few recent additions. For my purposes in this concluding chapter, the most interesting of these newcomers is S.J. Rozan's prosaically named Bill Smith.

Smith will be the focus here, but not all by himself. With Smith, Rozan also introduced his female business partner: the Chinese American investigator Lydia Chin. Since 1994, when *China Trade* appeared, Rozan has published six Smith/Chin books, of which I will discuss *China Trade* and its follow-up *Concourse* (1995) in some detail, while using numbers three – *Mandarin Plaid* (1996) – and four – *No Colder Place* (1997) to further emphasize the points I want to make. Partnerships such as the Smith/Chin one are nothing new. Rozan, however, has hit upon a new narrative strategy for the series as a whole which she so far has brilliantly exploited: Chin and Smith more or less alternate in the novels, with Chin narrating and, because of that, dominating, the action of *China Trade*, Smith taking the honors in

Concourse, Chin again in *Mandarin Plaid*, and so on. The partner who does not narrate a given novel is always part of the action, with the proviso that Smith plays a larger part in the Chin novels than the other way around. *Concourse* is particularly one-sided, with Chin in a decidedly minor role.

Rozan's alternating narrative perspective is an ingenious strategy and deserves our admiration: it is a tour de force that not many crime writers would be capable of and significantly expands the possibilities of the series format. But it also deserves our interest. The fact that a single writer creates both a male and a female investigator and has them operate side by side while allowing them separate and distinctive narrative voices offers us a unique possibility to assess the private eye tradition at the end of the twentieth century. It may be objected that no single writer's work can be representative of that tradition, certainly not in a period in which fictional private eyes are doing a booming business. This is obviously true. Still, the fact that *Concourse* won the Shamus Award for Best Private Eye Novel (1996) – making Rozan, after Sue Grafton, only the second woman to win the award – and that *No Colder Place* has won the Anthony (while also being short-listed for the Shamus, just like the recent *Stone Quarry* [1999]) surely suggests that whatever Rozan is doing certainly touches the right chord among crime fiction watchers. What I want to argue is that Rozan very successfully avails herself of what by the mid-1990s have become two distinct PI traditions: the familiar one of the male PI and the more recent one of the female PI. As a result, her work offers an ideal opportunity to see how these traditions are presented in the work of a new writer. Bill Smith and Lydia Chin more or less sum up where the PI is at, some 70-odd years after the role's creation. As we shall see, Smith conforms in many ways to the traditional (male) PI, while Chin's ethnic allegiances – she is a Chinese American PI, who lives in New York's Chinatown – magnify most of the characteristic traits of the contemporary female investigator.

Lydia Chin, whose Chinese name is Chin Ling Wan-ju, is an unlikely investigator. Only five feet one inch and 110 pounds she is, as she herself puts it, not very intimidating. She does, however, have a black belt in karate, and defends herself well in the only fight she gets into in *China Trade*, even if her attackers leave her, aching and with her pants stripped down – the classic macho ploy to humiliate a woman – in the courtyard where they have surprised her. Chin exemplifies the female PI's vulnerability because of her small stature and more generally adolescent appearance ('I look twelve when I'm insecure'; *Trade*, 38).

Because she is still part of her ethnic community – to the point of still living with her mother, who does not speak English, so that conversations take place in Chinese – she also exemplifies the censure and restrictions that female investigators are often subjected to. Her traditional mother disapproves of her profession and so does her older brother Tim, who sees her as a liability: in a world where what one member of a family does has immediate repercussions for all the others, she can, at any given moment, cause him to lose 'face'. '"You're worried I'm going to screw up,"' she tells him, '"and then everyone, not just you, will know what a jerk Tim Chin's little sister is. That's what this is about. Your face, not my ass."' (63) It is, ironically, this same view of the family as a collective rather than as a number of related but otherwise independent individuals that forces her extremely reluctant brother to hire her in the first place when he must find a private investigator, just as for the same reason Lydia can not very well refuse the assignment: 'In Chinatown [refusing to work for one's family] is not that easy. They can't not ask you, and you can't say no.' (20) Although we do not see too much of it in the novel, this view of family ties, which Lydia does not really share but of course cannot ignore since she still lives with her mother, constitutes an added and serious responsibility. Mobilizing her sense of responsibility towards her family in pulling herself together after the attack in the courtyard, she tells herself: 'If you're found like this . . . your mother will never be able to show her face in Chinatown again.' (95)

The traditional subservience to her mother and the family males that is expected of her is an additional burden and magnifies the socio-psychological restrictions that usually add to the female investigator's problems. Lydia's father is dead – we learn in *Mandarin Plaid* that he died when she was 13 – but the patriarchal order has not disappeared with him. As a result Lydia's mother, who in a modest way plays the stock market and has a better track record than her lawyer son, is at pains to hide the fact from him: 'it would embarrass her deeply to outshine her son' (62). The 'natural' order that has decreed that males are inherently superior must be respected, even if at another point it means siding with her son against Lydia when he is blatantly wrong. Because of the traditional mother–daughter relationship Lydia cannot express her anger at what in this and other instances she sees as her mother's injustice: 'Then I would have snapped at her, which would have been undaughterly of me and would have made me feel guilty' (32). Here we would seem to be far removed from the standard white female investigator, who either no longer has a mother – Sue Grafton's Kinsey Millhone, Linda Barnes's Carlotta Carlyle, Nevada Barr's Anna

Pigeon, Karen Kijewski's Kat Colorado, Gloria White's Ronnie Ventana – or else knows how to neutralize her mother's nagging, even if a certain measure of guilt is always incurred in the process, as is the case with Sandra West Prowell's Phoebe Siegel, Barbara Neely's Blanche White, J.J. Jance's Joanna Brady, or Sandra Scoppettone's Lauren Laurano. The difference should not be exaggerated, however. Virtually every female investigator has to cope with unequal treatment and gender-related social pressures. What is more, if we take a closer look at Lydia's mother, we see that much of her behavior is itself the result of social pressure: the traditional unspoken demand that women practice total unselfishness. Lydia sees through the mild form of deviousness to which such self-effacement invariably leads, but shows no awareness of its first cause:

> '... is there anything I should pick up?'
> 'No', [mother] said. 'Nothing I need. Unless you want oranges and water spinach with fish tomorrow.'
> That meant: buy oranges and fish.
>
> (*Mandarin Plaid,* 48)

In *China Trade* these disadvantages are more or less in balance with Lydia's one great asset: her intimate knowledge of Chinatown and its cultural peculiarities, central among them, at least in the novel, the rules that pertain to losing face:

> 'Why did you tell Mr. Gao it was a friend who wanted this favor, and not you?' [Bill] asked.
> 'Oh, Mr. Gao shouldn't be doing this, setting up a meeting between a respectable daughter of a respectable family and a gangster. If anything bad should happen to me .... Mr. Gao would lose face in a big way. This gives him an out: he didn't know it was me. If I hadn't given him an out he would have turned me down.'
> 'But he knew?' .... 'Of course he knew. Everyone always knows. But those are the rules. Everyone knows those too.'
>
> (*China Trade*, 24–5)

In a novel in which virtually everything, from the first killing to the last shootout, has in one way or another to do with saving face – even former lovers must be protected if one does not want to lose face – knowing the rules is of paramount importance. In a world where the application of mere force does not lead anywhere, and in which Smith is completely out of his depth, Lydia can do well in spite of the double handicap of being female and being a female in a traditional Chinese American environment. The novel ends, moreover, with a hint that Lydia will from now on have a little more leeway because she has earned her mother's grudging respect: '"If you listened to your mother more often you would solve many more cases." I picked up a dumpling in my chopsticks. That was practically permission, I thought, as I dipped it in scallion sauce and took a bite. From a Chinese mother that was just about carte blanche.' (254) No wonder that in the very last scene 'the cloudless blue sky seem[s] huge, endless, and full of possibility' (263). And indeed, in *Mandarin Plaid* Lydia's profession is on the surface still 'a daily aggravation' to her mother, but she has come to understand that her mother's incessant criticism hides a fierce pride in her daughter: 'let it never cross anyone's mind that I'm anything but the world's biggest success at it' (*Plaid*, 181).

In spite of its Manhattan locale and its two or three violent scenes, which disqualify it as a cozy mystery, there is something endearing about *China Trade*. We have the prominent presence of Lydia Chin's family, especially her mother; the rather innocent crime – a theft of porcelains – that triggers the events of the novel; the fact that Lydia's best friend is an NYPD policewoman (while in so many PI novels there is no love lost between cops and PIs); Lydia's habit, shared by so many female investigators, of talking to herself by way of encouragement, and so on. By comparison, *Concourse* is definitely urban: the violence is more unpleasant and messier, the tension is uglier, the black street gang that we are introduced to is more hopeless than anything in *Trade*; the traditional unfriendly cop is much nastier than his counterpart in the earlier novel; we have not only violent street crime but also extortion, fraud and real estate manipulation, the latter of which even leads us to the higher reaches of Brooklyn's administrative apparatus. The interweaving of various criminal activities, and more in particular, the entanglement of street crime and politically sensitive white-collar crime, remind us of Paretsky's best novels. We have definitely left the minor leagues. What is more, because the black is so much blacker, the white is whiter, too. The thoroughly nasty and cynical cop reveals his soft spot when the vicious gang-leader dies in his arms, seeking to re-establish the father-son relationship they once had – and the breakup of which has apparently led to his alcoholic cynicism and general nastiness. Smith blackmails a corrupt administrator into creating a job for a former gang member who has reformed his life; he buys an old lady a piano with criminal money found in a dead man's locker; and he even finds a home for two abandoned kittens. In comparison with *China Trade,* both the negatives and the positives are heavily accentuated.

This black-and-white scheme does not mean that Rozan has lost her touch. As in *Trade,* Rozan shows herself to be a master of her craft. *Concourse* is tougher, less concerned with the psychology of crime – the fear of losing face, for instance – and presents familiar situations and themes. This in no way discredits the novel's intricate and intelligent plot line. Rozan may have opted for a formulaic approach, but she turns the formula to brilliant use. This formulaic approach is most obvious in the presentation of her protagonist. In *China Trade* Smith is very visible; we get to know very little about him, however, apart from the fact that he is Lydia's senior by some 15 years and is in love with her. Although his sometimes tiresome banter-cum-sexual innuendo might suggest otherwise, he keeps a respectful distance in the classic Marlowe/Archer tradition. There are other signs that he stands firmly in the classic tough guy tradition: he is a confirmed smoker and is virtually oblivious to weather conditions: 'He'd been driving, as usual, with [his window] down; he'll do that in any weather, unless the rain is actually falling sideways.' (137)

Concourse fully confirms Smith's membership of the tough guy fraternity. We are told, though of course not by Smith himself, that he is a top-notch operator. He is virtually fearless, is good and fast with his fists, has a strongly developed sense of loyalty, and unravels a complicated web of criminal activities. He has the required melancholia and disaffection: 'Suddenly I was bone tired, tired of posturing, tired of parrying, tired of these vicious, ruined children and their brutal world' (*Concourse,* 112) – which will of course not keep him from going on or from saving the lives of people that do not seem worth the effort. Smith is an updated, East Coast version of the classic private eye and Rozan even gets the voice right: 'Maybe I was boring, now that I was shaved and clean. Maybe I was always boring' (127) reminds us of Marlowe's voice, while the 'pink air-freshener that clung desperately to a window waiting for a chance to escape' (126) has the Archer touch. Lydia's description of him in *Mandarin Plaid* clinches the matter:

> He threaded his way through the crowded cafe. I watched him, his familiar, fluid walk, the easy set of his shoulders, the way his eyes covered the room as he moved through it, looking everywhere without seeming to look anywhere in particular. Deep-set eyes in a worn face, a face even I couldn't call handsome. (45)

In both novels the self-confident independence suggested by this description is fully evident, while in the later *No Colder Place* Smith even keeps insisting on his independence from his client, the owner of a large investigative firm who, as it turns out, has farmed out the assignment with an ulterior motive.

As is so often the case with tough guy PIs, there is trouble and tragedy in Smith's past. Regularly picked up by the police for various offenses when he was still in his teens, which at one point has led to a six-month sentence, he joined the Navy to straighten out – acquiring an impressive tattoo during a three-day drunken spree in Singapore – and after college went to work for a security firm. He has been briefly married, losing his only child, a girl, in a car accident when she was nine years old. And there is also the occasion, only obliquely referred to, when in an encounter with a criminal gang the uncle who more or less raised him, an NYPD captain, was killed, while Smith himself got badly wounded, but not before killing one of the criminals. In short, unlike Lydia Chin, Smith has seen it all and been through everything. He knows 'that anger, that volcanic rage that claws a man apart inside unless he finds a way to let it erupt', and knows that such an anger 'searches, in a bottle, in a stranger's unthinking words or a friend's meaningless joke, for an excuse, a trigger, a reason to explode' (*Concourse*, 42). He has survived his daughter's death because of his music – Rozan, adopting the romanticization of the classic PI, makes him an accomplished piano player – but is also familiar with that more traditional defense against emotional pain: the bottle. Like that of the classic PI, Smith's narrative voice never articulates deep feelings. Even when he sees somebody kiss Lydia Chin and sees her respond he simply records the event. Still, Smith's voice, with the openly confessed love for Lydia, is one of the things that distinguishes him from the classic PI and betrays his origin in the 1990s. Although he is given to the self-deprecation that we expect from him, and is typically close-mouthed, he never uses the distinctive PI voice, with its cynical wisecracks, to establish emotional distance and express detachment. Smith is committed to things and people and not uneasy with that commitment. Still, he is the classic loner, a man without family or friends, while Lydia's family is very much in evidence, to the point that she feels smothered by their sometimes self-serving concern.

As the kissing scene suggests, in *Concourse* Lydia is more of a personality than in *China Trade*, a development that we also see in her increased self-assurance in the banter she and Smith exchange:

> 'How come you know about Santa's reindeer?'
> 'It's incumbent upon a member of the model minority to study the social customs, political organization, and religious mythology of the ruling class.' (202)

Still, there is an enormous, gender-based difference between the way Rozan has realized her and the way she has realized Smith. We simply cannot imagine her in the world Smith moves in so confidently in *Concourse* or, for that matter, in *No Colder Place*, where he goes undercover on a building site as a bricklayer – one of his many skills, acquired on the job when he was younger – and where Lydia hovers around as a temporary secretary. (Rozan must, by the way, be congratulated. The scenes in which we see Smith at work are completely convincing and it is refreshing to have detailed descriptions of blue-collar work in a crime novel.) Smith is out of his depth in the Chinatown of *China Trade* and, to a lesser degree, *Mandarin Plaid*, but his ineffectuality is due to cultural differences: he does not speak Chinese and has little knowledge of the culture. Lydia Chin, however, cannot be imagined in the worlds of *Concourse* and *No Colder Place* because those worlds are male.

As the above has already suggested, *Mandarin Plaid* and *No Colder Place* repeat and reaffirm the differences between *China Trade* and *Concourse*. *Mandarin Plaid* centers around the fashion industry – the events of the novel are triggered by the theft of sketches for designs – with a brief excursion to the world of prostitution, while *No Colder Place* follows *Concourse* in its focus on urban corruption. Central to the novel is a scam at a Manhattan building site, but its complex plot line involves race relations – the developer of the site is a black woman – money laundering, organized crime, and so on. Typically, *Mandarin Plaid* ends with a fashion show in which Lydia, substituting for a professional, makes her debut as a model. In *No Colder Place* Smith has the final satisfaction of having laid a neat brick pattern somewhere up one of New York's highrises, but that is after he has just left hospital. Just as in *Concourse*, the case ends with Smith rather badly battered. Lydia has admittedly saved his life – in fact, she does so twice in *No Colder Place* – but it is Smith who, Christlike, again pays the physical price for the restoration of the moral order.

Perhaps in spite of herself, Rozan occasionally draws attention to the gender bias in the rather different roles she assigns to Chin and Smith. Early in *Mandarin Plaid*, after Chin and Smith have botched an assignment, we find the following passage: '"First of all", I said with great dignity as I stood up, "nothing else is going to go wrong. And secondly, I'm Lydia Chin. I can blame anybody I please."' (18) This does not quite take Lydia seriously. Clearly, she takes herself seriously here, but we cannot: the phrases 'with great dignity' and '"I'm Lydia Chin"' undermine that seriousness, making her endearing rather than formidable or even impressive. Smith's voice is never turned against himself and made to carry his creator's somewhat condescending affection.

Rozan is an important and versatile new writer, whose status has been confirmed by the awards won by *Concourse* and *No Colder Place*. Presumably unintentionally those awards have also had the effect of establishing a gendered pecking order in her oeuvre: it is the Smith novels that are singled out for official recognition. Clearly the truly masculine, although no longer macho, private eye who takes on complicated forms of urban corruption still generates widespread admiration while his petite but brave female partner is seen in terms of endearment. Strangely enough Sarah Paretsky's V.I. Warshawski, the only female private eye who gets involved in cases similar to the ones Smith solves in *Concourse* and *No Colder Place* – and who usually ends up in a similarly battered condition – has never won her creator a major American award, Paretsky's honors being limited to a (British) Silver Dagger. Since Paretsky most certainly does not lack writerly skills we are faced with an unpleasant conclusion: while women writers are more than adequately represented among the award winners of the last ten years, the woman who presents the most outspoken feminist investigator and whose novels are the most politicized of all mainstream PI novels has been strangely overlooked. It is difficult to believe that this is merely accidental. Let me immediately add that it is equally hard to believe that Paretsky is the victim of a conscious and widespread conspiracy. But there cannot be much doubt that the fact that Warshawski is a woman who refuses any easy gender role and, therefore, emits confusing gender signals has to do with this curious inattention. The least the Mystery Writers of America can do by way of redressing a historical wrong and of showing that it takes women writers seriously, even if their protagonists are often unreasonably irritating, is to induct Paretsky into its Hall of Fame as a Grand Mistress.

Primary Bibliography

Abella, Alex. *The Killing of the Saints*. New York: Crown, 1991.
Andrews, Sarah. *Mother Nature*. New York: St. Martin's, 1997
Baker, Nikki. *In the Game*. Tallahassee: Naiad, 1991.
— *The Long Goodbyes*. Tallahassee: Naiad, 1993.
Barnes, Linda. *A Trouble of Fools*. London: Coronet, 1993 [1988].
— *Coyote*. London: Coronet, 1992 [1990].
— *Hardware*. London: Coronet, 1995.
— *Cold Case*. London: New English Library, 1995.
Barr, Nevada. *Track of the Cat*. London: Headline, 1994 [1993].
— *A Superior Death*. London: Headline 1995 [1994].
— *Ill Wind*. New York: Avon, 1997 [1995].
— *Firestorm*. New York: Avon, 1997 [1996].
— *Endangered Species*. New York: Avon, 1998 [1997].
Bland, Eleanor Taylor. *Dead Time*. New York: Signet, 1994 [1992].
— *Done Wrong*. New York: St. Martin's, 1995.
Block, Lawrence. *In the Midst of Death*. New York: Avon, 1976.
— *Eight Million Ways to Die*. New York: Avon, 1983.
— *When the Sacred Ginmill Closes*. New York: Avon, 1987.
— *A Dance at the Slaughterhouse*. New York: Avon, 1992.
— *The Devil Knows You're Dead*. New York: Avon, 1993.
— *A Long Line of Dead Men*. New York: Avon, 1994.
— *The Burglar Who Traded Ted Williams*. New York: Onyx, 1994.
— *Hit Man*. New York: Avon, 1998.
— *Tanner On Ice*. New York: Avon, 1998.
— *Everybody Dies*. New York: Morrow, 1998.
Bowen, Peter. *Coyote Wind*. New York: St. Martin's, 1994.
— *Specimen Song*. New York: St. Martin's, 1995.
— *Wolf, No Wolf*. New York: St. Martin's, 1996.
— *Notches*. New York: St. Martin's, 1997.
Buchanan, Edna. *Miami, It's Murder*. New York: Pocket Books, 1996 [1994].
Burke, James Lee. *Dixie City Jam*. New York: Hyperion, 1994.
Carr, Caleb. *The Alienist*. New York: Bantam, 1995 [1994].
— *The Angel of Darkness*. New York: Ballantine, 1998 [1997].
Chandler, Raymond. *The Big Sleep*. Harmondsworth: Penguin, 1948 [1939].
Churchill, Jill. *The Silence of the Hams*. New York: Avon, 1996.
Coben, Harlan. 1995. *Deal Breaker*. New York: Dell, 1995.
— *Drop Shot*. New York: Dell, 1996.
— *Fade Away*. New York: Dell, 1996.
— *Backspin*. New York: Dell, 1997.
— *One False Move*. New York: Dell, 1998.
— *The Final Detail*. New York: Dell, 1999.
Coel, Margaret. *The Eagle Catcher*. New York: Berkley, 1995.
— *The Ghost Walker*. New York: Berkley, 1996.

Connelly, Michael. *The Black Echo*. New York: St. Martin's, 1993 [1992].
— *The Black Ice*. London: Phoenix, 1996 [1993].
— *The Concrete Blonde*. New York: St. Martin's, 1995 [1994].
— *The Last Coyote*. New York: St. Martin's, 1996 [1995].
— *The Poet*. New York: Warner Books, 1997 [1996].
— *Trunk Music*. London: Orion, 1997.
— *Blood Work*. London: Orion, 1998.
— *Angels Flight*. Boston: Little, Brown, 1999.
Cornwell, Patricia. *Postmortem*. New York: Warner, 1992 [1990].
— *Cruel and Unusual*. Boston: Little, Brown, 1993.
— *Cause of Death*. New York: Berkley, 1997 [1996].
Crais, Robert. *The Monkey's Raincoat*. New York: Bantam, 1992 [1987].
— *Stalking the Angel*. New York: Bantam, 1992 [1989].
— *Lullaby Town*. New York: Bantam, 1993 [1992].
— *Free Fall*. New York: Bantam, 1994 [1993].
— *Voodoo River*. New York: Hyperion, 1995.
— *Sunset Express*. New York: Hyperion, 1996.
— *Indigo Slam*. London: Orion, 1998 [1997].
— *L.A. Requiem*. London: Orion, 1999.
Crumley, James. *Bordersnakes*. New York: Warner, 1997 [1996].
D'Amato, Barbara. *KILLER. app*. New York: Forge, 1996.
Dreher, Sarah. *Stoner McTavish*. London: Women's Press, 1996 [1985].
Early, Jack. *A Creative Kind of Killer*. New York: Carroll and Graf, 1995 [1985].
Edwards, Grace F. *If I Should Die*. New York: Bantam, 1998 [1997].
Ellroy, James. *Brown's Requiem*. London: Arrow, 1995 [1981].
— *Clandestine*. London: Arrow, 1996 [1982].
— *Blood on the Moon*. In *L.A. Noir* [1984].
— *Because the Night*. In *L.A. Noir* [1984].
— *Suicide Hill*. In *L.A. Noir* [1986].
— *The Black Dahlia*. London: Arrow, 1993 [1987].
— *The Big Nowhere*. New York: Mysterious Press, 1989 [1988].
— *L.A. Confidential*. New York: Warner, 1997 [1990].
— *White Jazz*. London: Arrow, 1993 [1992].
— *American Tabloid*. London: Arrow, 1995.
— *My Dark Places*. London: Arrow, 1997 [1996].
— *L.A. Noir: The Lloyd Hopkins Trilogy*. London: Arrow, 1997.
— *The Cold Six Thousand*. New York: Knopf, 2001.
Evanovich, Janet. *One for the Money*. London: Penguin, 1995 [1994].
— *Two for the Dough*. London: Penguin, 1996.
— *Three to Get Deadly*. London: Penguin, 1997.
— *Four to Score*. London: Pan, 1999 [1998].
— *High Five*. New York: St. Martin's, 1999.
— *Hot Six*. London: Macmillan – now Palgrave, 2000.
Forrest, Katherine V. *Murder at the Nightwood Bar*. New York: Grafton, 1993 [1987].
— *Liberty Square*. New York: Berkley, 1996.
— *Apparition Alley*. New York: Berkley, 1997.
Friedman, Kinky. *God Bless John Wayne*. London and Boston: Faber and Faber, 1995.

Furutani, Dale. *Death in Little Tokyo*. New York: St. Martin's, 1997 [1996].
— *The Toyotomi Blades*. New York: St. Martin's, 1998 [1997].
— *Death at the Crossroads*. New York: Morrow, 1998.
— *Jade Palace Vendetta*. New York: Morrow, 1999.
George, Elizabeth. *A Great Deliverance*. New York: Bantam, 1989 [1988].
— *Payment in Blood*. New York: Bantam, 1989.
— *A Suitable Vengeance*. New York: Bantam, 1991.
— *For the Sake of Elena*. New York: Bantam, 1992.
— *In the Presence of the Enemy*. New York: Bantam, 1996.
— *Deception on His Mind*. London: Hodder & Stoughton, 1997.
— *In Pursuit of the Proper Sinner*. New York: Bantam, 1999.
Gores, Joe. *32 Cadillacs*. New York: Mysterious Press, 1993 [1992].
Grafton, Sue. *'A' Is for Alibi*. New York: Bantam, 1987 [1982].
— *'B' Is for Burglar*. New York: Holt, Rinehart, and Winston, 1985.
— *'G' Is for Gumshoe*. New York: Holt, 1990.
— *'J' Is for Judgment*. New York: Holt, 1993.
— *'L' Is for Lawless*. London: Pan, 1996 [1995].
— *'M' Is for Malice*. London: Pan, 1997 [1996].
Grant, Linda. *Blind Trust*. New York: Ivy, 1990.
— *A Woman's Place*. New York: Ballantine, 1995 [1994].
Grimes, Martha. *The Man With a Load of Mischief*. New York: Dell, 1985 [1981].
— *The Anodyne Necklace*. Boston: Little, Brown, 1983.
— *I Am Only the Running Footman*. London: O'Mara, 1986.
— *The Five Bells and Bladebone*. New York: Dell, 1988 [1987].
— *The Horse You Came In On*. London: Headline, 1993.
— *Rainbow's End*. London: Headline, 1995.
— *Hotel Paradise*. London: Headline, 1996.
— *The Case Has Altered*. London: Headline, 1997.
— *The Stargazey*. New York: Onyx, 1999 [1998].
Grimes, Terris McMahan. *Somebody Else's Child*. New York: Onyx,1996.
— *Blood Will Tell*. New York: Signet, 1997.
Hackler, Micah S. *The Dark Canyon*. New York: Dell, 1997.
Harris, Thomas. *Red Dragon*. New York: Bantam 1998 [1981].
— *The Silence of the Lambs*. New York: St. Martin's, 1991 [1988].
Heck, Peter J. *Death on the Mississippi*. New York: Berkley, 1995.
— *A Connecticut Yankee in Criminal Court*. New York: Berkley, 1996.
— *The Prince and the Prosecutor*. New York: Berkley, 1997.
Hendricks, Vicki. *Miami Purity*. London: Minerva, 1996 [1995].
Henry, Sue. *Murder on the Iditarod Trail*. New York: Avon, 1993 [1991].
— *Death Takes Passage*. New York: Avon, 1998 [1997].
Hess, Joan. *Mischief in Maggody*. New York: St. Martin's, 1988.
— *O Little Town of Maggody*. New York: Dutton, 1993.
— *Miracles in Maggody*. New York: Dutton, 1995.
Hightower, Lynn S. *Satan's Lambs*. New York: Walker, 1993.
— *Flashpoint*. London: New English Library, 1996 [1995].
— *Eyeshot*. New York: HarperCollins, 1996.
— *No Good Deed*. London: New English Library, 1998.
— *The Debt Collector*. London: New English Library, 2000 [1999].
Hillerman, Tony. *The Blessing Way*. London: Macmillan, 1970.

— *Dance Hall of the Dead*. New York: HarperPaperbacks, 1990 [1973].
— *Skinwalkers*. New York: HarperPaperbacks, 1990 [1986].
— *A Thief of Time*. New York: HarperPaperbacks, 1990 [1988].
— *The First Eagle*. New York and London: HarperCollins, 1998.
Holbrook, Teri. *A Far and Deadly Cry*. New York: Crime Line, 1995.
— *The Grass Widow*. New York: Bantam, 1996.
Jance, J.J. *Desert Heat*. New York: Avon, 1993.
— *Tombstone Courage*. New York: Morrow, 1994.
Kaminsky, Stuart. *Death of a Dissident*. New York: Ivy, 1981.
— *A Cold Red Sunrise*. New York: Ivy, 1988.
— *Hard Currency*. New York: Ivy, 1995.
— *Tarnished Icons*. New York: Ivy, 1997.
Kijewski, Karen. *Katwalk*. London: Headline, 1989.
— *Alley Kat Blues*. London: Headline, 1995.
King, Laurie R. *A Grave Talent*. London: HarperCollins, 1995 [1993].
— *To Play the Fool*. New York: St. Martin's, 1995.
— *With Child*. New York: St. Martin's, 1996.
— *A Letter to Mary*. New York: St. Martin's, 1997.
Lansdale, Joe. *The Two-Bear Mambo*. London: Indigo, 1997 [1995].
Lawrence, Margaret, *Hearts and Bones*. New York: Avon, 1997 [1996].
Lawrence, Martha C. *Murder in Scorpio*. New York: St. Martin's, 1995.
Lehane, Dennis. *A Drink Before the War*. New York: Avon, 1996 [1994].
— *Darkness, Take My Hand*. New York: Avon, 1997 [1996].
— *Sacred*. New York: Avon, 1998 [1997].
— *Gone, Baby, Gone*. New York: Avon, 1999 [1998].
— *Prayers for Rain*. New York: Morrow, 1999.
Leonard, Elmore. *Touch*. New York: Avon, 1988 [1977].
— *Get Shorty*. London: Penguin, 1995 [1990].
— *Maximum Bob*. London: Penguin, 1992 [1991].
— *Rum Punch*. New York: Dell, 1993 [1992].
— *Pronto*. New York: Dell, 1994 [1993].
— *Riding the Rap*. New York: Dell, 1996 [1995].
— *Out of Sight*. London: Penguin, 1997 [1996].
Lescroart, John. *Dead Irish*. London: Headline, 1996 [1989].
— *The Vig*. London: Headline, 1996 [1990].
— *Hard Evidence*. New York: Ivy, 1994 [1993].
— *The 13th Juror*. New York: Island, 1995 [1994].
— *The Mercy Rule*. London: Headline, 1999 [1998].
Margolin, Phillip. *Gone, But Not Forgotten*. New York: Bantam, 1994 [1984].
Maron, Margaret. *Bootlegger's Daughter*. New York: Mysterious Press, 1992.
— *Southern Discomfort*. London: Headline, 1995 [1993].
— *Up Jumps the Devil*. New York: Warner, 1997 [1996].
McCrumb, Sharyn. *If I Ever Return, Pretty Peggy-O*. New York: Scribner's, 1990.
— *The Hangman's Beautiful Daughter*. New York: Scribner's, 1992.
— *She Walks These Hills*. New York: Scribner's, 1994.
McQuillan, Karin. *Deadly Safari*. New York: Ballantine, 1990.
— *The Cheetah Chase*. New York: Ballantine, 1994.
Medawar, Mardi Oakley. *Death at Rainy Mountain*. New York: Berkley, 1998 [1996].

Meyers, Maan. *The Dutchman*. New York: Bantam, 1993 [1992].
— *The Kingsbridge Plot*. New York: Bantam, 1994 [1993].
— *The High Constable*. New York: Bantam, 1995 [1994].
— *The Dutchman's Dilemma*. New York: Bantam, 1996 [1995].
— *The House on Mulberry Street*. New York: Bantam, 1997 [1996].
— *The Lucifer Contract*. New York: Bantam, 1999 [1998].
Monfredo, Miriam Grace. *Seneca Falls Inheritance*. New York: Berkley, 1994 [1992].
— *North Star Conspiracy*. New York: Berkley, 1995 [1993].
— *Blackwater Spirits*. New York: Berkley, 1996 [1995].
— *Through A Gold Eagle*. New York: Berkley, 1997 [1996].
Mosley, Walter. *Devil in a Blue Dress*. London: Pan, 1992 [1990].
— *A Red Death*. New York: Pocket Books, 1992 [1991].
— *White Butterfly*. London: Pan, 1994 [1992].
— *Black Betty*. London: Pan, 1995 [1994].
— *A Little Yellow Dog*. London: Serpent's Tail, 1996.
— *Gone Fishin'*. New York: Pocket Star, 1998 [1997].
Muller, Marcia. *Edwin of the Iron Shoes*. London: Women's Press, 1993 [1977].
— *Games to Keep the Dark Away*. London: Women's Press, 1994 [1984].
— *Wolf in the Shadows*. New York: Warner, 1994.
— *Till the Butchers Cut Him Down*. New York: Warner, 1994.
— *A Wild and Lonely Place*. New York: Warner,1995.
Nava, Michael. *The Hidden Law*. New York: Ballantine, 1994 [1992].
— *The Burning Plain*. New York: Bantam, 1999 [1997].
Neely, Barbara. *Blanche on the Lam*. New York: Penguin, 1993 [1992].
— *Blanche Among the Talented Tenth*. New York and London: Penguin, 1995 [1994].
— *Blanche Cleans Up*. New York: Viking Penguin, 1998.
Paretsky, Sarah. *Indemnity Only*. New York and London: Penguin, 1987 [1982].
— *Deadlock*. New York: Dell, 1992 [1984].
— *Killing Orders*. New York: Morrow, 1985.
— *Burn Marks*. New York: Dell, 1991 [1990].
— *Guardian Angel*. New York and London: Penguin, 1992.
— *Tunnel Vision*. New York: Dell, 1995 [1994].
Parker, Robert B. *The Godwulf Manuscript*. New York: Dell, 1996 [1973].
— *God Save the Child*. New York: Dell, 1994 [1974].
— *The Promised Land*. New York: Dell, 1993 [1976].
— *A Catskill Eagle*. New York: Dell, 1993 [1985].
— *Crimson Joy*. New York: Dell, 1997 [1988].
— *Small Vices*. New York: Berkley, 1998 [1997].
— *Night Passage*. New York: Jove, 1998 [1997].
— *Family Honor*. New York: G.P. Putnam's, 1999.
Parker, T. Jefferson. *The Triggerman's Dance*. London: Headline, 1997 [1996].
Pelecanos, George P. *Shoedog*. New York: St Martins, 1994.
— *A Firing Offense*. London: Serpent's Tail, 1997 [1992].
— *Nick's Trip*. London: Serpent's Tail, 1998 [1993].
— *Down By the River Where the Dead Men Go*. London: Serpent's Tail, 1996 [1995].
— *The Big Blowdown*. New York: St. Martin's, 1999 [1996].

— *King Suckerman*. London: Serpent's Tail, 1998 [1997].
— *The Sweet Forever*. New York: Dell, 1999 [1998].
Pickard, Nancy. *Generous Death*. New York: Pocket Books, 1987 [1984].
— *I.O.U.* New York: Pocket Books, 1992 [1991].
Prowell, Sandra West. *By Evil Means*. New York: Walker, 1993.
— *The Killing of Monday Brown*. New York: Walker, 1994.
— *When Wallflowers Die*. New York: Walker, 1996.
Rowland, Laura Joh. *Shinjū*. New York: HarperPaperbacks, 1996 [1994].
— *Bundori*. New York: HarperPaperbacks, 1997 [1996].
Rozan, S.J. *China Trade*. New York: St. Martin's, 1994.
— *Concourse*. New York: St. Martin's, 1995.
— *Mandarin Plaid*. New York: St. Martin's, 1996.
— *No Colder Place*. New York: St. Martin's, 1997.
— *A Bitter Feast*. New York: St. Martin's, 1998.
— *Stone Quarry*. New York: St. Martin's, 1999.
Saylor, Steven. *Roman Blood*. New York: Ivy, 1992 [1991].
— *Arms of Nemesis*. New York: Ivy, 1993 [1992].
— *Catalina's Riddle*. New York: Ivy, 1994 [1993].
— *The Venus Throw*. New York: St. Martin's, 1996 [1995].
— *A Murder on the Appian Way*. New York: St. Martin's, 1997 [1996].
— *Rubicon*. New York: St. Martin's, 2000 [1999].
— *Last Seen in Massilia*. New York: St. Martin's, 2000.
Scoppettone, Sandra. *Everything You Have Is Mine*. New York: Ballantine, 1991.
— *I'll Be Leaving You Always*. New York: Ballantine, 1993.
Scottoline, Lisa. *Final Appeal*. New York: HarperCollins, 1994.
Skinner, Robert. *Skin Deep, Blood Red*. New York: Kensington, 1998 [1997].
— *Cat-Eyed Trouble*. New York: Kensington, 1999 [1998].
Smith, Julie. *New Orleans Beat*. New York: Ivy, 1994.
Soos, Troy. *Murder at Fenway Park*. New York: Zebra, 1995 [1994].
— *Murder at Ebbets Field*. New York: Kensington, 1996 [1995].
— *Murder at Wrigley Field*. New York: Kensington, 1997 [1996].
— *Hunting a Detroit Tiger*. New York: Kensington, 1998 [1997].
— *The Cincinnati Red Stalkings*. New York: Kensington, 1999 [1998].
Stabenow, Dana. *A Cold-Blooded Business*. New York: Berkley, 1994.
— *Blood Will Tell*. New York: Berkley, 1997 [1996].
Standiford, Les. *Spill*. New York: Harper Prism, 1993 [1991].
Thurlo, Aimée and David. *Blackening Song*. New York: Forge, 1997 [1995].
Uhnak, Dorothy. *The Bait*. New York: Simon and Schuster, 1968.
— *Policewoman: A Young Woman's Initiation into the Realities of Justice*. New York: Simon and Schuster, 1964.
Van Gieson, Judith. *Raptor*. New York: Harper and Row, 1990.
— *The Wolf Path*. New York: HarperCollins, 1992.
— *Parrot Blues*. New York: HarperCollins, 1995.
Ventura, Michael. *The Death of Frank Sinatra*. New York: St. Martin's, 1997 [1996].
Walker, Mary Willis. *Zero at the Bone*. New York: St. Martin's, 1991.
— *The Red Scream*. New York: Bantam, 1995 [1994].
— *Under the Beetle's Cellar*. London: HarperCollins, 1997 [1995].
— *All the Dead Lie Down*. New York: Doubleday, 1998.

Wesley, Valerie Wilson. *When Death Comes Stealing*. New York: Avon, 1995 [1994].
— *No Hiding Place*. New York: Avon, 1998 [1997].
White, Gloria. *Charged With Guilt*. New York: Dell, 1995.
— *Sunset and Santiago*. New York: Dell, 1997.
Wilson, Barabara. *Murder in the Collective*. Seattle: Seal, 1984.
— *The Dog Collar Murders*. London: Virago, 1989.
— *Gaudí Afternoon*. London: Virago, 1991.
— *Trouble in Transylvania*. Seattle: Seal, 1993.
Wilson, John Morgan. *Simple Justice*. New York: Bantam, 1997 [1996].
Wiltz, Chris. *The Killing Circle*. New York: Mysterious Press, 1988 [1981].
Wings, Mary. *She Came Too Late*. London: Women's Press, 1986.
— *She Came by the Book*. London: Women's Press, 1995.
Woods, Stuart. *Heat*. New York: HarperCollins, 1994.

Select Secondary Bibliography

Bailey, Frank Y. *Out of the Woodpile: Black Characters in Crime and Detective Fiction*. New York: Greenwood Press, 1991.

Barbara, A. and Howard G. Zettler, eds. *The Sleuth and the Scholar: Origins, Evolution, and Current Trends in Detective Fiction*. New York: Greenwood, 1988.

Bell, Ian A. and Graham Daldry, *eds. Watching the Detectives: Essays on Crime Fiction*. London: Macmillan, 1990.

Binyon, T.J. *'Murder Will Out': The Detective in Fiction*. Oxford: Oxford University Press, 1990.

Bloom, Clive, ed. *Twentieth-Century Suspense: The Thriller Comes of Age*. Basingstoke and London: Macmillan, 1990.

Booth, Alison, ed. *Famous Last Words: Changes in Gender and Narrative Closure*. Charlottesville and London: University of Virginia Press, 1993.

Budd, Elaine. *13 Mistresses of Murder*. New York: Ungar, 1986.

Carr, Helen, ed. *From My Guy to Sci Fi: Genre and Women's Writing in the Postmodern World*. London: Pandora, 1989.

Cawelti, John. *Adventure, Mystery, and Romance*. Chicago: University of Chicago Press, 1976.

Craig, Patricia and Mary Cadogan. *The Lady Investigates: Women Detectives and Spies in Fiction*. Oxford: Oxford University Press, 1986.

Cranny-Francis, Anne. *Feminist Fiction: Feminist Uses of Generic Fiction*. Cambridge: Polity, 1990.

DeAndrea, William L. *Encyclopedia Mysteriosa: A Comprehensive Guide to the Art of Detection in Print, Film, Radio, and Television*. New York: Macmillan, 1994.

Dove, George N. *The Police Procedural*. Bowling Green: Bowling Green Popular Press, 1982.

Gamman, Lorraine and Margaret Marshment, eds. *The Female Gaze: Women as Viewers of Popular Culture*. London: The Women's Press, 1988.

Geherin, David. *Sons of Sam Spade: The Private-Eye Novel in the 70's*. New York: Ungar, 1980.

Geherin, David. *The American Private Eye: The Image in Fiction*. New York: Ungar, 1985.

Grella, George. 'The Hard-Boiled Detective Novel'. In Winks, *Detective Fiction*, 1980, 103–20.

Hilfer, Tony. *The Crime Novel: A Deviant Genre*. Austin: University of Texas Press, 1990.

Hobby, Elaine and Chris White, eds. *What Lesbians Do in Books*. London: Women's Press, 1991.

Irons, Glenwood, ed. *Feminism in Women's Detective Fiction*. Toronto: University of Toronto Press, 1995.

Klein, Kathleen Gregory. *The Woman Detective: Gender and Genre*, 2nd edn. Urbana and Chicago: University of Illinois Press, 1995.

Knight, Stephen. *Form and Ideology in Crime Fiction*. Bloomington: Indiana University Press, 1980.

— 'Radical Thrillers'. In Bell and Daldry, *Watching the Detectives*, 1990, 172–87.
Longhurst, Derek, ed. *Gender, Genre and Narrative Pleasure*. London: Unwin Hyman, 1989.
Mandel, Ernest. *Delightful Murder: A Social History of the Crime Story*. London: Pluto, 1984.
McCann, Sean. *Gumshoe America: Hard-Boiled Crime Fiction and the Rise and Fall of New Deal Liberalism*. Durham and London: Duke University Press, 2000.
Messent, Peter, ed. *Criminal Proceedings: The Contemporary American Crime Novel*. London and Chicago: Pluto, 1997.
Munt, Sally R. *Murder by the Book?: Feminism and the Crime Novel*. London and New York: Routledge, 1994.
Nichols, Victoria and Susan Thompson. *Silk Stalkings: When Women Write of Murder*. Berkeley: Lizard Books, 1988.
Ousby, Ian. *The Crime and Mystery Book: A Reader's Companion*. London: Thames and Hudson, 1997.
Palmer, Jerry. *Thrillers: Genesis and Structure of a Popular Genre*. London: Edward Arnold, 1978.
— *Potboilers: Methods, Concepts and Case Studies in Popular Fiction*. London and New York: Routledge, 1991.
Palmer, Paulina. 'The Lesbian Feminist Thriller and Detective Novel'. In Hobby and White, *What Lesbians Do in Books* 1991, 9–27.
— 'The Lesbian Thriller: Transgressive Investigations'. In Messern, *Criminal Proceedings*, 1997, 87–110.
Paretsky, Sara. 'Shooting from the Hip and the Lip'. *Books* 6 (1992), 3: 4.
Pederson, Jay P, ed. *St. James Guide to Crime and Mystery Writers*, 4th edn. Detroit: St. James Press, 1996.
Porter, Dennis. *The Pursuit of Crime: Art and Ideology in Detective Fiction*. New Haven and London: Yale University Press, 1981.
Pykett, Lynn. 'Investigating Women: The Female Sleuth After Feminism'. In Bell and Daldry, *Watching the Detectives*, 1990, 48–67.
Reddy, Maureen T. *Sisters in Crime: Feminism and the Crime Novel*. New York: Continuum, 1988.
— 'The Feminist Counter-Tradition in Crime: Cross, Grafton, Paretsky, and Wilson'. In Walker and Frazer, *The Cunning Craft*, 1990, 174–87.
Slide, Anthony. *Gay and Lesbian Characters and Themes in Mystery Novels*. Jefferson, NC: McFarland, 1993.
Soitos, Stephen F. *The Blues Detective: A Study of African American Detective Fiction*. Amherst: University of Massachusetts Press, 1996.
Symons, Julian. *Bloody Murder. From the Detective Story to the Crime Novel: A History*. 3rd rev. edn. London and Basingstoke: Pan, 1994.
Vanacker, Sabine. 'V.I. Warshawski, Kinsey Millhone and Kay Scarpetta: Creating a Feminist Detective Hero'. In Messent, *Criminal Proceedings*, 1997, 62–86.
Walker, Ronald G. and June M. Frazer, eds. *The Cunning Craft*. Macomb: Western Illinois University Press, 1990.
Walton, Priscilla L. and Manina Jones. *Detective Agency: Women Rewriting the Hard-boiled Tradition*. Berkeley, Los Angeles, and London: University of California Press, 1999.
Willett, Ralph. *The Naked City: Urban Crime Fiction in the USA*. Manchester: Manchester University Press, 1996.

Winks, Robin W., ed. *Detective Fiction: A Collection of Critical Essays*. Englewood Cliffs, NJ: Prentice-Hall, 1980.

Woods, Paula L. *Spooks, Spies, and Private Eyes: Black Mystery, Crime, and Suspense Fiction of the 20th Century*. New York: Doubleday, 1995.

Index: *Contemporary American Crime Fiction*

(NB: The names of authors and other real persons are printed in **bold type**; those of detectives and other fictional characters in ordinary type; titles are printed in *italics*.)